AUTOMATIC STAY

MARK SHAIKEN

AUTOMATIC STAY

A 3J MYSTERY

Published in 2022 by

Mark Shaiken and 1609 Press LLC

© 2022 Mark Shaiken

ISBN (print): 978-1-7345571-4-5

ISBN (ebook): 978-1-7345571-5-2

Library of Congress Information: copyright registration no. Txu 0-023-009-66

Cover Design and Interior Layout by designforwriters.com

To Loren, Zac, and Emily. For all the times that bankruptcy got in the way of life and all the times you forgave me.

"Bankruptcy is about financial death and financial rebirth. Bankruptcy is the great American story rewritten. We're a nation of debtors."
– Elizabeth Warren

PROLOGUE

Phillip Dewey recalls Wednesday, October 27, 2023

I SAT AT MY basement conference table, alone, in silence, in the pitch-dark. It is how I like it. It is what I am used to.

I like dark places. I've had several in my life. In the dark, I can think and plan without the annoyance of outside interferences, like people, music, light, colors, sounds. No sensory stimulation. Just my brain neurons and their electrical impulses. My brain is different. So am I.

I needed my quiet time now to gather my thoughts.

I had just returned to my plush, designer-appointed, pastel-colored, tastefully furnished, Hallbrook home in suburban Kansas City from a meeting about Adam and Bey Rapinoe; *the newest banes of my existence*, I thought to myself.

The Rapinoes and their company, BJB LLC, owed my lending company – Veridical Lending LLC – $17 million, the largest loan on VL's books. Ten years ago, in 2013, I made the loan because I felt it was good for business – my business, not theirs. I really did not care whether it was good for them. $17 million was more than I kept lying around, so I knew I would have to borrow some of the capital needed to make the loan to the Rapinoes. That gave me cause to pause.

But I reviewed their extensive financials, actuals and projections, and concluded that their business – a chain of Kansas

City nightclubs and high-end restaurants – was sound. Not that I knew anything about music and food, but that was ok; I am a quick learner. They owned significant real estate, quite valuable, and the nightclubs would generate enough robust cash flow to pay me back.

The Rapinoes stayed on schedule, and after launching their clubs, it was clear to me that they were good at what they did. The nightclubs outperformed expectations, just as Adam and Bey had projected. Both the real estate and the cash flow were my collateral, and it looked like they would pay me back every dime, plus interest at 7%, as planned. Particularly profitable for me. So, I borrowed what I needed: $8 million at 4.5% interest from a bank group in Denver that had lent to me in the past. I used the Rapinoes' monthly payments to pay back my $8 million loan and I pocketed the rest as profit.

They paid me like clockwork, and the clubs really took off. All good.

But as much as I plan for every eventuality, every contingency, I didn't plan for an infernal pandemic that would take down the world economy, shut down all in-person commerce, and, overnight, virtually eliminate all cash flow in the hospitality sector.

I plan for everything, but I did not plan for Wuhan. Did anyone … other than Bill Gates?

The Rapinoes told me yesterday that the effects of the pandemic had finally caught up to their businesses; there would be no further payments on the loan, and they were now meeting with bankruptcy counsel.

I know bankruptcy. They will file, and the bankruptcy automatic stay will stop me in my tracks. I've been there before with people who owe me money. No demands, no payments, no collection, no foreclosures. Automatically. No judge who will listen to me. No lawyer who will take up my cause, and actually win.

Not this time. No way!

I dislike people who do not pay me back. If they file, and I assume they will, I will muster all my energy to take them down. That will be good for business and send the proper message to my other debtors: *You signed my documents. You took my money. You will pay me back.*

Messaging is so important in my business. In any business.

I will fight these Rapinoes until they beg for mercy and wave the surrender flag. I despise everyone who has ever owed me money.

These two *will* pay up.

I *will* get my money back out of the foreclosures of the real estate, out of the revenues, and out of the Rapinoes; one dollar at a time, if need be.

Bankruptcy be damned. Automatic stay be damned. Rapinoes be damned.

I am Phillip Dewey. I will get my money back. Eventually, I always do.

This is my story.

CHAPTER 1

Friday, October 27, 2023

IT WAS ANOTHER FRIDAY night. Josephina Jillian Jones –
3J – switched off the desk light in her corner office high atop
downtown Kansas City, Missouri, and gazed out the 27th floor
windows to the Power and Light District below at the corner
of 13th and Walnut. Another week in the world of bankruptcy
law in the Midwest was drawing to a close. The other attorneys at the esteemed Greene Madison LLP law firm where
she plied her trade had mostly cleared out, and, as on most
Friday evenings, she was one of only a few attorneys left in the
office; a habit she had developed when she had arrived at the
law firm many years ago. Work harder and work longer – rules
she had set for herself as she tried to make her way through
the labyrinthine law firm world as a black woman in what was
then a predominantly white male profession.

Now that she had risen in the firm to be a partner of some
acclaim, and as the firm slowly diversified, she couldn't ditch
her work-harder-and-longer practice. She didn't just need to
be good at her trade – she needed to be better.

As she looked out the windows and her thoughts drifted, the
sun was setting and the P&L lights had begun to illuminate the
outdoor, partially covered area known locally as the Quad. A
premier entertainment destination – an entire city block with

two levels of restaurants, taverns and night spots, a full-concert stage, and huge screens. The Quad's festivities took place beneath metal sculptures of two cowgirls and a cowboy, who overlooked the space and reminded all who visit that Kansas City was in the heart of what used to be the Wild West. Some called Kansas City the easternmost Western city; how fitting that cowboys and cowgirls oversaw the P&L's nightly downtown drinking festivities in the clubs that replaced the dusty, swingin' door, Wild West saloons of days gone by.

3J knew that every Friday, the bars opened their doors and welcomed the P&L patrons who never failed to arrive. The lure of a downtown Kansas City buzz; the appeal of socializing outdoors in the Quad; the cure for a week of the blues; the distraction of another weekend before Monday brought the return to life behind a desk and the grind of the American way to ensure they paid the bills.

3J broke her gaze from the growing revelries twenty-seven stories below and sighed loudly to herself. She grabbed her backpack, made her way to the elevators, and rode down to the basement garage that housed the cars for over two hundred lawyers who called Greene Madison's Kansas City office their second home. She headed for her favorite bar; not in the P&L, but O'Brien's at the corner of Westport Road and Pennsylvania, in the Westport District. It was the place where she and her law partner in crime – Bill Pascale – met almost each Friday to survey the damage sustained, both personal and professional, by another week in the high-stress, high-value practice of corporate bankruptcy law. It was the place where they quietly celebrated another week under their bankruptcy belts.

During the pandemic, 3J and Pascale had eschewed in-person meetings for Zoom cocktail hours. No crowds, no O'Brien's, no face-to-face comradery – and not the same. To support the bar, they had ordered food and drink deliveries for their Zoom sessions. Zoom had got them through the virus but was no substitute for sitting across from each other at the bar. 3J had been unutterably relieved that in the spring of 2023, the post-pandemic era, life had returned to some semblance of normal, not least their traditional in-person Fridays at O'Brien's. *It's the little things we humans crave*, she thought.

She drove down Main Street south to Westport Road, passing Union Station, Crown Center, the National World War One Memorial that stretched like a monolith to the heavens capped with the eternally burning fire at its pinnacle, up the steep hill past the turn-off for Union Cemetery, the burial grounds for the Civil War casualties – both Union and Confederate, who in death found something they could finally agree upon: the location of their eternal resting place.

She passed the building that formerly housed the now-shuttered Grand Emporium, the almost-forgotten home to some of the best blues and Americana music in the Midwest. As she drove, she listened to Jay McShann on her car stereo sing his version of "Ain't Misbehavin'" from his album, *Big Apple Bash*, a duet with Janis Siegel of The Manhattan Transfer – silky smooth, liquid swing jazz; free-flowing, as if Jay was sitting in her living room playing the piano for only her. It was as weekend-ready as any modern era song that McShann had recorded, perfect for the beginning of a mid-October weekend in the Midwest.

She loved Jay McShann, the rotund piano player with a strong connection to Kansas City, where he had led his big band in the 1930s and 1940s with his own version of Kansas City swing as he pounded out the melody on the black and white keys with his right hand, and the Kansas City bluesy bass line with his left.

Like 3J, McShann's connection to the city was simply fate. He had stopped over for a few hours on a bus trip to Omaha and decided to catch a couple of Count Basie sets at the Reno Club. He never made it to Omaha, staying to play gigs in Kansas City and eventually forming his own big band in which he had collaborated with a young Charlie Parker, after Parker had finished a stint with the Ten Chords of Rhythm dance band before moving on to New York City. McShann was à propos for her meeting with her new prospective clients that afternoon: Adam and Bey Rapinoe, husband-and-wife owners of six combination restaurants and nightclubs throughout Kansas City, with more planned throughout the Midwest. She knew of them from articles she had read in *The Kansas City Star* and *The Kansas City Business Journal.* They were well-known figures in the community – real estate developers who had turned their attention and substantial wealth to their efforts to single-handedly bring live jazz back to Kansas City. 3J thought they were brave and adventurous, to marry live music with the promise of fine dining in their aim of recreating the hub of jazz that the city had once been, back in the day.

Kansas City, Missouri. KCMO. The largest city in Missouri. The Paris of the Plains, named for its many boulevards; the City of Fountains, with over two hundred; the Barbecue Capital, for obvious reasons. And one of America's four original jazz capitals: New Orleans, Chicago, New York City, and Kansas City. Certainly, other cities claimed jazz as their own. But from 1920 to 1950, Kansas City had been an epicenter. An epicenter that had faded and was now a distant memory. By 2023, bands led by the bigger-than-life personalities of Benny Moten, Jay McShann, Count Basie, Harlan Leonard, and Andy Kirk were long gone. Gone were the clubs they had played in. Gone was the Kansas City style, known far and wide on the east and west coasts. Like so much of the 1920s, 1930s, and 1940s, gone were the nights filled with swing, and dance, musical innovation, and free-flowing drink, gambling, and sex, and the hope each brought to music lovers throughout the country, leaving behind only the recordings and the memories. *Ahh, the memories and the rich history*, 3J thought. The memories and history her father had taught her to appreciate as she grew up dangerously close to the poverty line in New Orleans.

All gone until the Rapinoes, whose vision was to fill the metropolitan area with Kansas City swing to go along with its deserved reputation for barbecue. The Rapinoes, who placed a bet on Kansas City with their own fortune – a bet that, with a little cajoling, Kansas City could reclaim its place as a musical and entertainment capital. *An ambitious vision.*

3J arrived in Westport, parked her navy blue Prius, and headed into the bar. She clicked her fob and the car lights blinked once to let her know it would be safe and secure and dutifully wait for her return.

She entered the front door of the bar to dim lights and music (not jazz); no thick smoke, not anymore. The jukebox belted out a Dwight Yoakam Bakersfield country tune, "Take Hold of My Hand." *Great song. If it has to be country, Dwight's the way to go,* she thought as she made her way to the back of the bar where Pascale awaited her arrival. Pascale was already working on his first wheat beer, and had ordered her the usual double-shot glass of Irish whiskey, neat. No ice, no water, no need.

The Friday quitting-time tradition of whiskey and wheat beer with Pascale dated back more than a decade. It was their own little week-in-review; a way to take a breath and put another seven days in the record books, and she always looked forward to it.

"How goes it, 3J?" Pascale asked as she sat in the old oak booth.

3J caressed her double-shot glass, admired the caramel-colored nectar about to be transferred from the glass to her lips and smiled broadly. "It went, alright, and now it's over," she said, completing the traditional, nonsubstantive pleasantries that started every Friday routine.

"Anything to report?"

3J smiled as she sipped her whiskey and gathered her thoughts. "New client today, Pascale. Interesting couple. I liked them. A lot. Very much of a what-you-see-is-what-you-get pair of business people. Very sincere in their story of the financial problems in which they find themselves." She paused and added, "Quite a different gut reaction from how I felt after that first meeting with our old client, Quincy Witherman, a few years ago. I wonder how he's doing."

Pascale knew 3J had mixed feelings about Witherman, and that she had visited him in prison several times since he had ended up there after he had pled guilty to the felony of hiding assets during his bankruptcy case. She could curse him and moments later, say she felt sorry for him, and then quickly say, "What the hell did he expect would happen – not disclosing assets. Damn fool!" He encapsulated the dichotomy that some debtors presented. But Pascale didn't want to waste a good Friday night at O'Brien's on Quincy Witherman, so he quickly steered the conversation back to the new clients. "What kind of business?"

"Hospitality. Music night clubs – jazz and fine dining, to be specific. They own clubs throughout the metro. They named them after famous Kansas City clubs from days gone by. Some operate in old historic buildings that they own. Pricey endeavors. Their first clubs opened in 2015 and it sounds like they exceeded all expectations, and then – 2020 and Covid-19. They tried to survive through the pandemic as best as they could, but…"

"Yikes!" Pascale exclaimed. "Not the best business sector to be in during a pandemic, at all."

"You got that right: Covid took its toll. They had to shutter several clubs for an extended period – no cash flow. They tried to survive by offering takeout and delivery, just how O'Brien's got through the pandemic, and they even tried internet music events. That started up the cash again – more of a trickle than a flow – but with no in-person dining, and no music acts out on the road, frankly, it was a complete shitstorm for them. They had stockpiled money for a rainy day, but not for a pandemic monsoon. Adam and Bey Rapinoe. Do you know them?"

"Actually, I've met them at charity fundraisers over the years. Pretty prominent in the community. As I recall, they made their fortunes in commercial real estate before cashing out and pursuing their dream of bringing live jazz back to Kansas City. Very impressive power couple."

"That's them."

Pascale gathered his thoughts before he delivered an all-too-familiar Kansas City history lesson, the type that 3J had heard ever since her arrival at the law firm. "Y'know, back in '81, the Hyatt Regency at Crown Center ran a Friday night tea dance every week. It grew to more than a thousand people who would show up to celebrate the weekend, some of whom would dance to jazz music in the atrium area just like folks danced in the Kansas City of the 1930s and 1940s. People would gather on the skywalks above the atrium to watch the party. But the skywalk structures were suspect. The second-floor skywalk hung from rods connected to the fourth floor skywalk which also hung from rods connected to the roof. A fourth-floor walkway channel box and bolts supported the second – and fourth-floor rods. So, the bolts in the fourth-floor skywalk channel box had to support the weight of both the second – and fourth-floor skywalks. Not how the architects originally designed it." Pascale took a sip of beer and continued. "When the bolts supporting the fourth-floor skywalk failed one July evening, nothing was holding the second-floor skywalk in place so it fell, followed by the fourth-floor one. One after the other, crushing and burying many of the dancers. It was just horrific. Catastrophic. More than a hundred dead. Over two hundred injured. Lawsuits seeking billions of dollars in damages. Some called it the night the music stopped in Kansas City. I think I read that the collapse was the largest non-deliberate structural failure in American history. I could argue the city was never the same after that."

3J raised her eyebrows, pursed her lips, and nodded her head. The collapse had happened long before 3J began working for Pascale, but no one who had been in Kansas City for any length of time – whether before, during, or after that fateful evening in 1981 – escaped the Hyatt collapse story. It was part of the fiber of Kansas City history that many residents wore like a tattered sweater they couldn't just discard.

"And then came the Rapinoes decades later," 3J said. "With a dream to bring back tea dances to KC … this time without the skywalks."

Pascale nodded. "I admire them."

"They gave me a ton of info that I need to sort through and organize. I could use some help on this one."

"Whatever you need," Pascale offered.

3J closed her eyes and rotated her head to relieve the soreness in her neck. She was used to neck pain, caused by high stress, high stakes, high finance, high emotions. The protection bankruptcy afforded came with a price: a price for the debtors, a price for the creditors, and a price for the lawyers in the bankruptcy trenches.

She opened her eyes and refocused. "I just don't know if bankruptcy can save their clubs. Not sure Congress built the Code to fight Covid and help a business get through a complete loss of revenue. Bankruptcy can do a lot of good things for struggling businesses, but it can't manufacture cash. What the clubs need is a payment moratorium while they wait for the patrons to return and the cash to flow again." 3J paused, looked away from Pascale and around the bar, as it filled up to some degree. The post-pandemic world was still adjusting to a return to some measure of normality; the bars had not yet returned to full capacity, and Friday evenings were still not a shoulder-to-shoulder scene in the pandemic's wake. She scanned the room without focusing on anyone or anything. Several patrons gazed back at her; 3J was still striking in her forties, perhaps even more so than in her younger days.

She finally returned her attention to Pascale. "Certainly, folks are ready to get out and feel good. It's been far too long since we've all felt good about much of anything. We can file the bankruptcy cases and, of course, the bankruptcy automatic stay will halt all collection activity on the debts owed for the immediate future. That'll get them the breathing spell they need." She gazed into the viscous liquor as she swirled it in her shot glass and watched the liquid legs form on the inside of the glass. "We can park their company in bankruptcy for a while, but at some point, they're gonna have to show solid, dependable cash flow. I'm just not sure ..." She didn't finish her thought but Pascale let her own the silent moment and said nothing. "Yep. This may be an ugly one in bankruptcy court."

Pascale nodded his agreement. "Well, if it's all beautiful, you can't believe it, as Ernest Hemingway once said."

"Ain't that the truth," 3J agreed. "I'm just thinking that as we come out of this pandemic, we're gonna need our bankruptcy judge to have some of that St. Jude – patron saint of lost causes – attitude to get the Rapinoes through."

"Look, why don't we do this, 3J: let's meet up tomorrow at work, go through what you have and start to put together some options."

"I'd appreciate that. Hey, if it's ok, I think I'll pass on another round. I'm just gonna head home. I'll see you at nine tomorrow. Okay?"

"Sure. You alright?"

"Fine. Just a long week at the bankruptcy version of the O.K. Corral, I'm afraid. Lots of bankruptcy gunfights concluded now, at least for the moment, and I survived just fine. Just tired."

"No worries. I had a couple of things to talk to you about, but they can wait."

"Are you sure?"

"Absolutely. Go home, curl up on the couch, and we can talk tomorrow."

"Thanks, Pascale."

3J rose from the booth and turned to leave. She knew there were any number of eyes on her as she made her way across the bar, but she didn't care. People liked to look, admired what they saw, and while she didn't care if they did, she also didn't mind. Sometimes she smiled at them and made their day, but this time she felt no connection with the onlookers; they remained detailess faces from a surrealist painting. She felt spent and in need of some alone time back at her condo.

As she reached her car, she thought, *I'm lucky to have Pascale to partner with me on this case. I'm going to need the help.*

On her short drive back to her high-rise, modern home downtown, 3J's thoughts drifted to her mentor, friend, and professional confidante. Pascale, now in his late sixties, was a widower, and of late had started to pursue other interests outside of the practice of law. 3J thought that was a good thing. She worried about him: he had been through so much since his wife and child had died in a tragic car accident. Until recently, he had seemed lost and drifting through life.

But then he told her that he was back to playing his guitars as a first step in rediscovering purpose, and joked that some day he would retire from bankruptcy law and start playing guitar on a downtown street corner, with a pork-pie hat turned upside down on the sidewalk. Maybe he'd even get an ear pierced, so he'd look the part. He had said that people would put money in the hat to reward his playing skills, or to encourage him to stop playing. Either way, he said, music money in the hat was music money in the hat, one dollar at a time. He called his Martin D28 acoustic guitar his girlfriend, and his Fender Stratocaster his medicine for when he was feeling blue. He said he had almost named the Strat Eddie, for Eddie Cochran, because it was a cure for his summertime blues, like Cochran's monster hit. But he'd decided against a name in the end, and so it was just "the Strat." For a while after the crash, he'd stopped seeing his girlfriend, the Martin, and hadn't allowed his Strat to help with his blues but now, thankfully, they were both back in his life.

3J parked the car and made her way up to her twentieth-floor, two-bedroom, open floor plan, corner condominium, with its floor-to-ceiling windows and pale yellow, glossy oak hardwood floors. Her windows faced both north, with a view of downtown's compact but beautiful skyline, and the Missouri River beyond, and west across the Kansas River toward Kansas City, Kansas; the "other Kansas City," with its high unemployment, abject poverty, and no skyline, and the beautiful Kansas sunset beyond that never seemed to disappoint. A *Tale of Two Cities* if there ever was one.

The condo was her home in the clouds.

She turned on some Count Basie mellow swinging music from his Kansas City era and uncorked a 2017 bottle of Sleight of Hand Levitation Syrah from Walla Walla, Washington, and the Columbia Valley, her favorite vineyard from her old collegiate stomping grounds. After giving herself a generous pour, 3J flopped down on her couch, kicked off her Sergio Rossi ruby red high heels – a high-heeled homage to the Wizard of Oz – pulled her legs under her, watched the flickering lights of downtown Kansas City, and tried to turn off the random thoughts about the inevitable upcoming Rapinoe Chapter 11 bankruptcy case.

CHAPTER 2

Saturday, October 28, 2023

3J AWOKE ON SATURDAY, brewed a pot of her favorite Earl Grey tea, and hopped into the shower. As she dried herself off, she paused, then dropped her towel to the floor in front of the mirror, and surveyed what she saw. She performed this solemn ritual every so often — not to admire, but to scrutinize and take stock. Five foot seven; a hundred and twelve pounds; hazel eyes; smooth, medium-tone, chocolate-brown skin; high cheekbones; dimples when she smiled; no wrinkles — at least not yet — still athletic, slender, modest curves where curves should be, and no evidence, just yet, of significant gravity intervention. A chin-length bob, with feathery layers at the top and sides for a neat, well-groomed appearance. Very lawyer-like, but it also suited her face well. And not yet graying. *Mother Nature's been kind to me so far. Don't know how long I can expect that to last.*

Now if I only had a regular social scene, or pray tell, a love life, she mused. She knew she needed to work on her social scene, but she went through periods of time during which she believed that a love life might be too much for her to hope for. She was in one of those periods now but thought to herself, as she stood there naked, *Well, a girl can dream.*

Most importantly, she observed no change from the last time she had engaged in the ceremony. Another "no change" box checked, although she wasn't so naïve to believe that could go on forever. Each time, she wondered if she was the only forty-something woman who performed this solemn act; each time she concluded likely not. Each time, she wondered when the time would come when she would have to check "the changes are a-comin'" box, and each time she decided not to allow herself to think about it.

She gazed back into the mirror at those hazel eyes – oh, those hazel eyes. Some people found them compelling. To her, they were a daily reminder that her ancestors were slaves on a Louisiana sugar plantation where the owner's son had forced himself on her great-great-grandmother and implanted his hazel-eye genes for generations to come. A reminder of her roots, handed down to 3J in strands of white slaveowner DNA a century later.

She dressed, finished her tea, and went down to the street to walk from her condo to the Greene Madison office building. She arrived on the 27th floor to find Pascale at his desk and they co-opted a conference room where 3J deposited a stack of papers for them to review, organize, collate, and then discuss. *It'll be a full day*, 3J thought. *They usually are.* Quietly they sat and, with the efficiency borne out of years of living in the bankruptcy world, they began to better understand the Rapinoes' business and the woes caused by Covid.

The Rapinoes had started their business career as real estate developers, mostly acquiring and operating shopping and strip centers throughout the Midwest. They earned a stellar reputation and amassed a respectable fortune. Then, in 2013, they suddenly pivoted. They turned their attention away from the centers, sold off their holdings, paid off their real estate lenders, pocketed the profits, and began to develop a combination fine dining and live music concept in the Kansas City metropolitan area. They were avid jazz fans, and keenly aware of Kansas

City's music history and culture. Their thought: bring the production of regular, live jazz shows back to Kansas City. Their belief: build the clubs and they – the fans and musicians – would come. Their own musical field of dreams. Offer the patrons the best food and drink in the city to enjoy as the music played on. They partnered with two Kansas City celebrity chefs who prepared the unique menus, trained the staff, and opened the restaurants and their hearts to the throngs of Kansas Citians who flocked to see the shows, the legends, the up-and-comers, and dine on the world-class cuisine, all right there in the country's heartland.

It turned out to be a splendid idea whose time had come, and by February 2020, they had plans to expand to St. Louis, Omaha, and Oklahoma City, all Midwest strongholds of jazz in the 1930s and 1940s. Then Covid hit, ravaging the hospitality industry – the restaurant and live music businesses in particular.

"What do you have on the Rapinoes' debt structure, Pascale?" 3J inquired.

"Just finished reviewing the loan docs, and their debts are singularly straightforward," Pascale responded. "A private lending outfit named Veridical Lending LLC financed the six Kansas City establishments; the lender is owned and operated by one Phillip Dewey. I've heard of this guy – I listened to him talk last year on a drive-in radio talk show. He sounded like he'd worked hard to achieve a kind of air of refinement; had a speech pattern like a dial tone, no emotion, no changes in volume. As far as I can tell from some quick internet research this morning, he seems to specialize in loans that the banking world might be reluctant to take on, such as start-up ventures in industries without a lot of reliable collateral to offer. So a restaurant and music business would be a good fit."

3J listened with interest. "Yeah, what would the collateral be in a restaurant? Used tables and chairs, plates and utensils, and kitchen equipment. No real inventory, other than a day or two of fresh food in the fridge. No real receivables. People pay as they go, some in cash, others with credit cards. So maybe whatever VISA might owe the restaurant each evening? Same with the live music operations. Not really any conventional assets to speak of, except maybe the piano that remains on stage for the musicians, and that's probably the only instrument the clubs have; the musicians would bring their own portable instruments and gear."

Pascale smiled and slowly nodded his head. "Agreed."

3J continued, "They own five of the locations and lease the sixth. Two of the five they own, however, are historical properties. That might make them more valuable, but the designation also could be a drag on value because no one can alter the structures without approval from the historical property commission, which has been pretty tough on alteration requests."

"I assume that Veridical's interest rate is above-market?" Pascale asked.

"It is – 7%. But the Rapinoes likely had no options and figured they would move the loan to a more traditional lender when the businesses established themselves. Veridical… odd name."

"It is odd. I did a quick internet search and learned from dictionary.com that 'veridical' means truthful, not illusory; genuine. Interesting choice of a name for a high-interest-rate lending company."

"Hmmm. Noted, and interesting," 3J said. "So, how much do they owe Veridical?"

"From one of the recent loan statements, looks like around $17 million. A little less than $3 million per location."

"How could they possibly have serviced that size debt during the pandemic?" 3J asked with a look of amazement.

"Not sure. My guess, however, is that their personal shopping center fortune is considerably smaller now than it was when they exited the lucrative world of real estate development," Pascale offered.

"I bet that's right," 3J said. "Other creditors?"

"Looks like they have a pretty significant number of unsecured creditors who they owe money to – food vendors, linen companies, cleaning services, security companies, as well as owing money to the staff. Can't tell what's current debt and what's past due. Doesn't look like they owe money to any national jazz artists, but it looks like they owe money to some of the up-and-comer, local performers. Quite the mix."

"Any bank debt?"

"Doesn't look like it, except they look to have maxed out their personal credit cards as well." After returning to the documents again, Pascale asked, "Where do the Rapinoes live?"

"Pretty sure they live in one of the big ones in Mission Hills."

Mission Hills, Kansas: the storied, near-in, suburban enclave on the Kansas side of the KC metro just yards west of State Line Avenue, and just south of Kansas City's famed Country Club Plaza. J.C. Nichols founded the town in 1914 and its name reflected the missions established there in the early to mid-1800s by Methodists, Baptists, and Quakers. Now home to many of Kansas City's rich and famous, it sported numerous mansions and was once ranked third in *Forbes'* most affluent U.S. neighborhood list.

Finally, the duo finished going through all the data provided by the Rapinoes, and leaned back for their post-review discussion and strategy session.

3J led off. "Seems to me I'm in the same place I was last night at O'Brien's. They simply have to produce cash or the Bankruptcy Code won't be of much help in the long run. They told me they would work on projections with their accounting staff and email them to me early next week."

"Same here." Pascale sipped his coffee. "There's one interesting point to note. With no real receivables from the sale of inventory, it's likely that the bankruptcy court will let their company use the cash with little in the way of restrictions. In other words, the cash generated after we file the bankruptcy cases will be theirs to use, even over the objection of Veridical."

3J nodded her agreement as she grabbed her cup to refresh it with fresh tea. "My feeling exactly. I really think the problem here won't be the law. This will be a business performance problem, plain and simple. We'll need a credible, achievable sales pitch for the Judge at the beginning of the cases and then you and I will just have to hope that the business performs."

Pascale nodded his head but added nothing more to the analysis. As 3J left to go to the coffee and tea station, she asked, "You want anything?"

"No thanks," Pascale said distractedly, as he returned to his laptop to see if he could find any information about Phillip Dewey.

When 3J returned to the conference room, she continued, "I asked Adam and Bey to come in for a meeting on Wednesday, assuming they get us the projections sometime on Tuesday. Will that work for you?"

"I'll make it work. No problem."

"Great. Thanks for the help, Pascale. As always, much appreciated. Oh, I almost forgot – what did you want to talk about last night?"

"After you left O'Brien's, I decided that what I'd like to do is to have you over to the house for dinner and we can talk then. I can cook some steaks out and we can catch up. Do you have time tomorrow for dinner?"

Pascale rarely invited 3J to his house, especially after the car accident, so she opened her eyes wide and said, "Sure. This sounds serious. Is everything ok?"

"For certain. I didn't mean to alarm you and I'm not trying to make this into a dramatic event at all. Come over, we can enjoy some food, talk about Mahomes and the Chiefs and drink some wine."

"I'm game, and I'm free tomorrow. You know I love Mahomes, but maybe we can also talk about those first-place Sporting Kansas City Boys in Blue?"

"Also fine, but you know I'm not much of a soccer crazy, so you'll have to lead that discussion," Pascale smiled as he begged off the local, wildly popular Major League Soccer franchise in the city many called the United States' soccer epicenter.

"Well, they're a firm client, but don't let that put you off. Go to a match. Fun evening at Children's Mercy Park. It's much more exciting than the uninformed sports public thinks."

"Perhaps I'll expand my horizons," Pascale conceded.

"See you at five, then?" 3J asked.

"Five it is."

As 3J turned to leave the conference room, she waved her right hand in the air by the side of her head with her pointer finger extended and said over her shoulder, "Remember, I like my steaks from grass-fed cattle, and medium rare."

Pascale yelled back, "Duly noted, counselor! I'll make a run to Bichelmeyer Meats in Strawberry Hill," as he grinned.

INTERLUDE

Tuesday, September 23, 1986

"PHILLIP, COME IN AT once!" Mother bellowed. It was nearing 4 p.m., and eight-year-old Phillip Dewey had been playing alone – as he did most days – near his rusty backyard swing set, left there by a prior occupant of the house where Phillip and Mother lived.

Not *on* the swings. He saw no purpose in swinging back and forth over and over again. He observed other kids in the concrete school yard going back and forth on a seat tethered by rusty chains to a wobbling metal frame, and he simply could not fathom the attraction, nor why all the back and forth elicited such howls of joy. Swings were for the weak-minded, narrow-thinking children of Kansas City, not for him; he saw himself as strong, focused, and purposed. Instead, as he usually did, he crawled around in the wood and rubber chips beneath his own swing set looking for ants or other insects he could capture, so he could study them and eventually pull them apart to watch the parts writhe and then, slowly, stop. He enjoyed that project immensely – it was an exercise in dominion and control. If, in fact, insects experienced pain, he felt comfortable in providing it. After all, he was all about paying it forward – he could absorb and store any pain he suffered, and then redistribute it.

He enjoyed his power over the insects. It was much like the power Mother exercised over him, day in and day out, in which he found no joy.

Eight-year-old Phillip and Mother lived in Kansas City near the intersection of Forty-Fifth Street and Troost Avenue, just east of Rockhill Road and the Country Club Plaza. Troost, originally nothing more than fruit plantations, pastures, and cornfields, had become the eastern edge of Kansas City just before the Depression era, and had been home to millionaires: it had been nicknamed Millionaire Row. Over the decades, as Kansas City sprawled further east, Troost's wealthy white population migrated just west to the Country Club Plaza developments, and the black populations transitioned to Troost from the cattle drive West Bottoms area as it industrialized. Troost, a major north-south thoroughfare, became a racial and economic dividing line.

In Phillip's youth, the stability of the Troost neighborhoods varied from block to block. Phillip and Mother were one of the few white families on his block. Their particular part of Troost was stable enough and served as the home to lower middle-class residents. Nearby, however, Troost and its cross streets had spawned significant elements of crime, drugs, prostitution, and homelessness, and the thoroughfare boasted only abandoned boarded-up stores, businesses, and houses. Troost represented the daily challenge just to survive one more day of ghetto life on the east side of Kansas City; textbook urban blight, American decay in real time.

The block west of Troost where Phillip and Mother lived was a transitional neighborhood of small houses, many without air conditioning, and more still with termites that slowly and meticulously devoured the structures. Low-cost rentals, owned by landlords with no interest in repairs or upkeep, as long as they got their slumlord rent payment reasonably promptly.

People who called Mother anything, called her Mrs. Dewey. The "Mrs." moniker was a misnomer, since she had never married. She was five-foot-two, one-hundred-fifty pounds, with nondescript dark brown hair of shoulder length, brown eyes that always looked dull and blank, and thin eyebrows. Her nose was broad. The hair was not-so-slowly turning gray – thanks to Phillip, she would say – and her eyes sat just above burgeoning bags – also because of Phillip, she believed. Mother didn't know who Phillip's father was and didn't care. All men served one, and only one, purpose in her life – sex. Nothing more. She didn't believe in relationships and she had none.

Mother paid for the rent and the other bare necessities of life with a home-cleaning business in which she tended to the houses of many of the wealthy Kansas Citians just a few blocks away. They didn't pay her well, and she regularly complained that the rich stayed rich by failing to share more of their wealth with working class laborers like her. She drank all too often and much too much. Before Phillip was born, she liked to say that she never drank before 6 p.m. Since Phillip's arrival, she had altered her saying to "never before 1 p.m."

One of her many evening, too-much-to-drink encounters had yielded Phillip. She never knew which encounter it was, and she made no attempt to assign a sex partner to fill in the blanks of Phillip's heritage, so Phillip's birth certificate said "unknown" on the father identity line.

She was angry most of the time. Bitter, annoyed, offended, sullen. She was an angry drunk, an angry sober; an angry single parent, and an angry sexual partner for whomever drew the short straw on whatever day it was. She was an angry house cleaner, grocery shopper, and child disciplinarian. She didn't try to hide her principal guiding emotion – anger – and cared little if that offended anyone with whom she came in contact. If she had any love, a debatable point to say the least, it was lost in all the sea of anger. Phillip felt no love, and so he lacked an appreciation of what love could feel like.

In blunt contrast to the houses she cleaned with great efficiency and skill, her two-bedroom, thousand-square-foot rental house didn't suffer from cleanliness. Grimy didn't begin to describe the squalor: Mother liked to smoke Chesterfields when she drank; cigarette butts littered the house; and the house smelled like stale tar and nicotine. So also did Phillip and his clothes – sour and stagnant. But the house was so tainted by cigarette odors that he couldn't appreciate how he smelled. Despite everything, Mother was all that Phillip had and all that Phillip knew, and soot, and dust, and filth, and malodorous air were all that Phillip had experienced.

Mother was also liberal with corporal punishment. Just enough to keep Phillip in check; just enough to satisfy her anger for a few fleeting moments. Just enough to make Phillip cry from the sting of being struck by the back of a hand, or a wooden clog, but not enough for bruises to show when Phillip went off to school each day. Over the years, she had become an expert in administering pain or, as she called it, imposing discipline. She would drag Phillip to the dark, cobwebbed basement that she liked to call "the dark place." Often, she struck a phone book with one hand while she pressed it with her other hand against Phillip's face, back, or ribs – the phone book delivered the pain while minimizing any obvious bruising. She was an innovator.

To defend himself from her regular onslaught, Phillip retreated into himself and hid in a corner of his brain where light didn't fall and where he could find protection, comfort, safety. His real dark place, as he called it. When Phillip disappeared into the dark place, Joshua appeared. Joshua liked to say he wasn't a Dewey. He said his name was Joshua Parsons. Compared to Phillip, he seemed taller, wider, and stronger. He had a deeper voice and showed more street savvy. His shoulders were squarer. His tone was more menacing. His fists appeared larger. He was simply more physical.

Not that Joshua would ever strike Mother. She was, after all, still Mother to Joshua. But he was better able to process pain than Phillip. And so he did. For a period, neither Joshua nor Phillip knew of each other. When the beatings started, Phillip closed his eyes, retreated to the dark place, and Joshua awoke to absorb the pain. It was as if Phillip went to sleep. When Phillip awoke, he often recalled nothing of the beating and had no idea where his bruises came from. Eventually, Joshua became aware that a weaker version of him lived in the same body – not "Phillip's body," just "*The* Body." It took Phillip much longer to realize that Joshua existed, but eventually he did. Neither Phillip nor Joshua ever sought or received help for their disorder. Once Phillip learned that his stronger companion could protect him from Mother, he often sought the safety of that dark place, feeling confident that when he reached it, someone else would absorb whatever punishment Mother might dole out. At some point, Phillip learned to peek out from his dark place and watch Mother strike Joshua over and over again. He looked and was always horrified and often fearful, but he was careful to stay hidden.

Once Phillip learned of Joshua, he wondered if all kids were like him. He read a little about multiple personalities like Billy Milligan, Eve, and Sybil – a strange disease that he described to Joshua only as "my kind of illness." He wondered if he was just two "alters," or if there were others hidden away in the Body that he had not met. Were other alters in there, he wondered? If they were hidden, were they nice or were they undesirables, doing bad things while both Phillip and Joshua slept?

Before she struck Joshua, Mother would always put her tongue on the roof of her mouth, and, to no one in particular and as if to offer justification for what would shortly follow, she would say, "tssk, tssk, tssk." At night, Phillip would press his face into his pillow and mimic the sound he had heard, but he never knew if Mother directed the sound to Joshua or if it was just the preamble announcing the arriving punishment. Mother felt no obligation to link the punishment to a particular act, and indeed, the punishment was more to relieve Mother of her anger than to adjust Phillip's (or Joshua's) conduct for any action either had taken. Phillip feared the pain, but Joshua never thought too much about it; neither ever understood why they had to incur it. Only later in life did they learn that not all kids suffered like they did.

The pain left them isolated; all they had was each other and, of course, Mother. They trusted no one as a result of the beatings, and therefore, they wanted no friends, and had none.

Phillip went to school. Joshua wasn't studious. He was street smart. That's all he needed. In school, remarkably, Phillip quietly excelled, despite all the odds against any possible positive academic outcome.

And so Phillip, Joshua, and Mother existed, each day and each night, until on Phillip's sixteenth birthday, he arrived home from the inner-city high school he attended to find Mother slumped in her frayed, under-stuffed and cigarette-burned easy chair, silent and still. He shook her and said, "Mother, wake up," assuming she had drunk too much and had nodded off; but she had not. Oh, she indeed had drunk too much, as was her custom, but rather than nodding off, she had "passed on," as Phillip later in life liked to say.

Phillip heard Joshua from deep within say, "Leave her. Good riddance. She got what she had coming." Later in life, Phillip privately wondered if Mother's death was natural, or if Joshua had anything to do with her demise. Phillip kept these thoughts private and didn't share them with Joshua.

Phillip ignored Joshua's plan to leave Mother where she died, and instead called the police because he didn't know what else to do. He figured the police could help him attend to what was left of Mother. And they did. The funeral home cremated Mother, and one social worker or another gave Phillip a small vessel in which he deposited the ashes that were once his angry parent. Somehow, he always felt that when he held the vessel or talked to it, he could still feel her anger pulsating from it.

The vessel was ornate, displaying what he thought were complementary, hand-painted flowers – two blooms. At some point, he learned one was a light blue monkshood, and the other, a vibrant, deep purple petunia. *Beautiful*, he had thought. *A fitting resting place for Mother.* Some years later, on a whim, he researched both flowers only to learn that scholars commonly associated monkshood with hatred and petunia with anger and resentment. He could have changed vessels but decided that the symbolism should remain as a reminder of what Mother was really like in life.

Social services came and shuttled Phillip and Joshua off to a foster home, followed by another and another. They no longer smelled of stale cigarette smoke, they no longer lived in grime, Phillip ceased the dissection of insects, and Joshua largely stayed in his shadows once the beatings ceased. But they still had and wanted no friends. For two years until they turned eighteen, moving from foster home to foster home was just fine because that allowed them the license to not get close to the foster parents and the other kids living in the foster homes. A life that made it impossible to get close to anyone satisfied their needs.

Against all odds, Phillip graduated from high school and headed off to the University of Kansas on a full scholarship where he and Joshua made no friends, had no enemies, partook in no social events, and achieved nothing of note other than graduating with high honors in the economics department. While Joshua came along to college, he avoided studies. It just wasn't his thing.

After college, Phillip received his Master's in Business Administration from St. Louis University, on a full scholarship, in its one-year MBA program. Joshua had completed his role of protecting Phillip from pain when Mother ceased to exist. No more Mother meant no more physical pain, so Joshua retreated, and largely observed Phillip's day-to-day life. Always there – on call – but rarely needed anymore. He surfaced only when Phillip became highly anxious. Occasionally, the two talked, but more and more, they did not. Joshua used the time to relax and restore his strength. It had been a draining experience to expend so much energy absorbing Mother's beatings to protect his weaker companion, Phillip. Now Joshua could kick back, relax, and enjoy the easy life in the shadows of Phillip's daily existence. Joshua was fine with his life of leisure.

After graduating from SLU, Phillip learned banking at large banks, first in St. Louis, then Minneapolis, eventually returning to Kansas City. It was Phillip's decision to return to Kansas City, but he was never quite sure why he ended up back there. Joshua had strenuously opposed the move, but Phillip – the Primary, and firmly in control – ignored Joshua's views. By the time of his return, he had long ago left behind the life Mother had afforded him. He had no feelings towards Kansas City. He didn't think of it as his hometown; it held no place special in his heart. He never said he was happy to be rid of Kansas City, any more than he ever said he was happy to be rid of Mother. He was unemotional about both. Glacial.

Joshua, on the other hand, hated Kansas City, and all the memories that it spawned. The pain, the squalor, and the daily interactions with Mother. He wanted no part of the memories and only referred to it as "that place." The return to Kansas City forced Joshua to work hard to avoid the recollections. He resented Phillip's decision to move back to the City of Fountains.

As Phillip learned the lending trade, he found borrowers an interesting lot. Most repaid what they owed. But some did not. He focused his attention on those who didn't. He fixated on the documents the borrowers signed when they received their loan, documents that clearly stated that the borrowers would repay what they owed, and succinctly set forth when the payments were due and in what amount. *What kind of person,* he wondered, *would sign such documents and fail to follow the terms? What kind of legal system would permit them to avoid payment? What kind of banker would allow someone out of their agreement?*

He excelled at the banks where he trained and worked, swore off personal relationships with any of his co-workers, invested his earnings wisely, and, eventually, left the banking world to form his own private lending company, Veridical Lending LLC. He was especially proud of the name he selected – Veridical – corresponding to two singular facts: that he and Joshua had survived Mother; and that borrowers would repay what Veridical had lent them. He would see to it.

He never liked working for others – his managers' power over him reminded him too much of Mother. It made him anxious, and occasionally fearful. When Phillip was anxious, occasionally he would close his eyes and sleep to allow Joshua to appear and assess, firsthand, the situation to assure Phillip's safety. Phillip would re-open his eyes as Joshua retreated into the shadows again and, often, Phillip had no recollection of Joshua's actions while Phillip slept. Phillip hoped Joshua did nothing that would cause problems when Phillip returned. He didn't think Joshua had, but he didn't know for sure.

In Veridical, Phillip finally had the chance to work for himself. He moved to the Hallbrook development in the middle of Johnson County, described as a "quiet golfer's paradise in suburban Kansas City," with its exclusive club; a development that oozed style, class, wealth, and discretion.

The move to Hallbrook was important to him. While he played no golf and spent little time at the club, nevertheless, with the move, he finally lived among the very people Mother had despised. Of this he was quite aware, and quite proud … for reasons he couldn't quite explain.

The move surprised Joshua, though. He had no use for material things or status, and Hallbrook was nothing but material and status. But he found it innocuous and left it to Phillip to make such decisions about living accommodations and location.

Phillip rarely thought about his upbringing, but sometimes, when he drove from his new house to downtown Kansas City, he made it a point to drive north on Troost. "Roots are overrated," he liked to say, but he also said, "You can't know where you are going, unless you know where you have been." *We humans are all about our contradictions,* he thought.

Whenever Phillip drove on Troost, Joshua took note, peered out, and remembered the pain he had endured for Phillip's benefit. That was his job. That was his calling and purpose. Phillip seemed to remember the Troost days based on the famous expression, "never forget." Joshua, on the other hand, didn't approve of Phillip's trips down memory lane and often believed that Phillip was too naïve. To Joshua, a failing memory was far more preferable than the recollections of Mother on a Troost side street.

Veridical was a success story, and as its only lending officer, Phillip gained a reputation for never raising his voice, yet getting his way from his borrower clients. *They had their place,* he liked to think. *He helped them understand their place.* Just like Mother had tried to help Phillip understand his place.

CHAPTER 3

Sunday, October 29, 2023

As she drove to Pascale's house, 3J's thoughts were focused, not on the Rapinoes and their bankruptcy cases, but on Pascale's mysterious dinner invitation. Not that he had failed to open his house to business associates in the past; just not since a drunk driver had plowed into a car driven by Pascale's wife several years ago, killing both her and their child. Since the accident, understandably, Pascale had retreated into himself. 3J recognized him as a great mentor and rock-solid bankruptcy attorney, and by some healthy dose of providence, neither of those descriptions had changed after the tragedy. But Pascale himself had ... who wouldn't?

It was one of those treasured October days in Kansas City where the temperature hovered in the mid-sixties as the leaves on the trees continued to morph into a rainbow of colors, soon to part with their host and fall to the ground. Pascale's Loose Park neighborhood had one of the best displays of these colors year in and year out. The urban park was a place of frisbee, tennis, picnics, family outings, and contemplation. It was 3J's favorite place in Kansas City to walk and unwind and think, with its proximity to Country Club Plaza, its small lake, wading pool, Civil War markers, and a Japanese tearoom and garden dedicated as a cultural exchange between Kansas

City and its sister city, Kurashiki, Japan. But 3J's favorite was the Laura Conyers Smith Municipal Rose Garden, the best rose garden in America in her view, even better than the New Orleans roses that she remembered from her childhood. The garden always made 3J long for a garden, like her mother's in the Crescent City, to which 3J would tend … someday, just not now. No time.

Promptly at five, 3J arrived at Pascale's stately stone house across from the park. Pascale let her in and they walked together through his home and out French doors to the gray pavestone patio overlooking the tree-lined backyard. They sat and took in the fall afternoon's waning sunlight as Pascale poured them each a glass of French rosé from the Languedoc region; dry, cheery, and bright. 3J noted that he left the bottle – quite a departure from Pascale's usual Kansas wheat beer – within easy reach. *Good idea – I may just need that; something is obviously up.*

Pascale dove right in without small talk, just as 3J raised her glass for her first sip of wine. "You know, when Jess gave birth to Nikki, it was the happiest day of my life. And when Jess and Nikki died that night, I thought that was the saddest day I would ever know. But I was wrong. Every day after that awful night was worse than the day before. You know why? Pretty simple. Because I was still living and breathing and they weren't."

3J was surprised at the abruptness with which Pascale raised the topic. She instantly listened intently, trying not to react other than slowly to nod her head in acknowledgement. This was the beginning of a longer monologue that she realized Pascale had been working on for quite a while. He almost never talked with her, or anyone else for that matter, about the death of the rest of his small family. This was going to be a significant conversation; perhaps there would be tears at some point. She just hoped it wouldn't be at the beginning of whatever Pascale was about to say.

Pascale continued, "When they died, I didn't like to talk about the car crash, so I started to call it the 'night I lost my family.' How odd to describe it that way – as if I misplaced them and couldn't find them. As if they were like a spare mobile phone I knew I put down somewhere, that I'd find eventually if I looked in all the right places. No. Not like the mobile phone at all. I didn't lose them: they're gone, not lost. They ceased to exist, except in my heart. All I had left of them were the memories but I didn't really deal with them either."

Pascale looked off into his treed backyard. Without looking back, he continued, "I used to be an extrovert. I loved being out there. Then, after the accident, I still wanted, needed to be out there. I *should've* been out there. But I wasn't. Quickly, my life became a daily processional – going from Loose Park to downtown KC, to my office, where I sat and mostly consulted with you. Consultations. And then I retraced my steps to Loose Park at the end of each day."

Pascale slowly looked back at 3J.

3J felt the need to say something. "I can't pretend ever to know what you have gone through, Bill, or how you feel. It's nothing short of a miracle that you get up each day and go from home to downtown and back again. But you're not a *consultant*. You're a colleague, a friend, a mentor, and a co-counsel on every case we work together. Equal partners. That's always been our handshake deal."

"Thanks for saying that, 3J. I know I can always count on you, and I hope you also know you can always count on me."

"Absolutely."

"Someone who felt compelled to try to get into my head about the accident told me recently, 'Bill, we live the lives we are meant to live.' Maybe I believed that once upon a time. But I don't any longer. No. We live the lives we live, because that's all there is. No meaning. No grand plan. No one pulling the strings; no strings to pull. Just a deep need to find a way forward without a great deal of help and no manual with directions." Pascale paused and held the glass of rosé wine up to the sunset, watching the rich oranges, pinks, and reds of the sky refract and dance through the pink liquid swirling in the glass. "Shit happens. You know you need to move on, but you can't or you won't, so you don't. But if you're lucky, at some point, you realize it's time – time to move on. I'm lucky, I guess. I realize it's time. That's life. Or at least, that's my version of life."

3J nodded with a look of understanding. So far, she had avoided crying, but she felt certain that whatever would come next would open up the waterworks. *It sounds like he's ready to get on with the rest of his life and that he's finally processed those deaths. Good for him. He deserves a life of fulfillment.*

"Bob Swanson, the firm's managing partner, approached me a month ago, as he does for all the over-sixty crowd. He asked a simple question: 'How long did I think I would stay at the firm?' Over the years, Bob's become good at these types of discussions – prompting the aging lawyers to think about their own succession plan. He's had a lot of us elderly partners to deal with over the years." He smiled as he said, "elderly," and he spoke slowly and deliberately. He was in no rush. He wasn't in court trying to convince a judge. There was a softness to his delivery. "When Bob showed up at my office, I had no good plan in mind. My thinking was day-to-day, month-to-month. So, I told him, 'Bob, I need to think about a suitable answer for you and get back to you.' I have my answer now, but I haven't gotten back to Bob just yet. To start with, I wanted *you* to hear this first."

3J could no longer hide the intensity with which she was listening to each of Pascale's carefully chosen words. She realized he wasn't rambling at all – he was easing her into the topic of his decision. 3J leaned forward in the chair, holding the wineglass with both of her hands resting on her knees, encouraging Pascale to continue, which he did.

"It's time for me to conduct my life on some basis other than the one-foot-in-front-of-the-other plan I've been using the last few years. Some lawyers get to thinking that the ride will never end. But it always does, one way or another. The question is: will it end on your terms or will it end suddenly, with no terms? I've decided I want to do things on my terms."

"Which are ... what, exactly?" 3J prodded slowly.

Pascale smiled. "Many years ago, I had a Texas friend older than me by about ten years. He wanted me to leave the practice of law along with him to operate oil wells in the oil and gas 'bidness' as he liked to call it."

Oh my god, thought 3J. *Here comes another Pascale parable. Well, it's what makes him lovable.*

Pascale continued, "He left his law firm, invested in a small oil and gas exploration company, bought an old, beat-up Chevy pickup truck with 200,000 miles on it, and, every day, he sat on the back of the truck and drank beer as he watched the roughnecks drill what he called 'his wells.' And for every six-pack he drank, his crew found another dry hole. No black gold. No Texas tea. He lost more and more of his hard-earned lawyer money but, he would later report, he had the time of his life. You see, my friend left the practice of law to implement a plan. Turns out, not a brilliant plan at all, but a plan nonetheless.

Instead of going with him, I stayed. At the firm. Doing my bankruptcy thing. No real plan, except to stay the course. But now, I've decided it's time to implement a plan."

"What kind of plan?" 3J asked, as tears started to roll down her cheeks.

"I'm gonna tell the firm that I want to wind down my practice. I won't leave the law firm, cold turkey. But, I want to wind down and transition out quickly. Not over years, over months – probably no more than twelve. It's the natural course of events for me and it's time." Pascale reached for the rosé and refilled both of their glasses. 3J nodded her thanks. He looked down at his lap and, without making eye contact, said, "I know when I tell Bob, he's gonna want me to go into a longer-term wind down, part-time for a few years. I don't like that idea. I think that would encourage an existence of just 'phoning it in' rather than really performing at my peak. That's not for me. I need – no, I *want* – a clean break." He looked back up at 3J and said, "3J, you need to know that you don't need me to succeed. All you need is yourself. You are amazing. Most people can see the people they talk to; you look inside of them. That's your special power and you don't have that power because I'm around or because I taught you the Bankruptcy Code."

Ignoring the compliment, 3J asked, "What will you do?"

"Not sure. For all too long, I've known with precision and certainty what lies ahead for me each day. That's the nature of the law biz, I suppose. You know what to do. You do it. Then you repeat. In my new plan, I don't need to know what comes next and, hell, maybe I don't wanna know. I wanna get up each day and not know what the day, week, month, year will hold for me."

Silence.

Pascale smiled. "I really like playing my guitars. Y'know, they don't call it working my guitars, right?" 3J rolled her eyes but said nothing, and Pascale continued, "The music moments for me are great."

Silence again. Both 3J and Pascale were good with silence. For them, not every moment of the day needed to be filled with sound. Silence is its own sound, its own point, its own moment.

3J shook her head ever so slightly in disbelief; she had things to say. So she broke the silence and asked, "Pascale, you're serious, aren't you?" She felt like she needed further affirmation from him that he had truly made up his mind. She was struggling to picture Pascale in a role other than as an attorney.

"As serious as a large mortgage debt that just came due," he quipped.

"But why? You're healthy and vibrant, and integral to our bankruptcy group. You actually like what you do, or at least you give off that vibe."

"Oh, I like it well enough, but well enough isn't good enough at this point. There are so many things I haven't had a chance to do. Or haven't had the guts to do."

"Like what?"

"Well … I think the time to sit on the back of an old Texas pickup truck has probably passed, but lots of things – well, *anything* but what I'm doing full-time right now and when I reach the end, I want to check out knowing that I had something other than my lawyer boots on at that moment."

3J thought she needed to say something. Anything. But she knew she needed time to process. *This is Pascale's stage tonight,* she thought. *I'm in the audience.*

Pascale smiled at her and raised his eyebrows and tilted his head slightly to invite comment from 3J. None was forthcoming. He could see she was in mostly listening mode, and he was fine with that.

Silence. The sky had turned to a deep, uniform color of bluish black. The silver sliver of the moon lit little of the yard.

But the lights on Pascale's patio had turned on automatically, so the two colleagues – friends – sat in silence, but not in the dark.

After a few minutes, though, 3J felt like it had been at least a full thirty minutes of no talk, Pascale broke the quiet.

"I think it's time for me to come to grips with who I am and who I'm not at this point in my life. Those two change as we get older. Time to figure out what I know and what I don't. Those also change. The practice of law interferes with those determinations sometimes, and has been interfering with them for me since the crash." Pascale gulped his wine, closed his eyes for a few moments and said, "It's all about timing. When to go to law school. When to work your tail off at a law firm. When to make the partnership run. When to go all in as a partner. And, inevitably, when to cycle out and move on."

Another pause as he seemed to construct his next observation. Another Pascale smile. More wine for each of them. *The Languedoc vintners had done good*, 3J thought.

"You asked 'why?' Let me take one more shot at answering. I've spent my life in the law. A country of laws, right? Laws to straighten out crooked messes. Laws to make sense. Laws to adjust conduct. Laws to protect us from one another. Laws to resolve differences. Laws, like the Bankruptcy Code to help people out of problems and catch them when they fall on hard financial times. But there are no laws to solve the mess I got in. I did nothing to get myself into that mess, but there I was, in the mess nonetheless. Law's not helping with that. The only way to help is to move forward and, to some degree, start over."

3J said softly, "I get it, Pascale. I really do, and I'm happy for you. You are in my life, and just know that a life outside of the law ain't gonna change that, my friend."

Pascale smiled. "Like I said, I can always count on you, and you can always count on me." He looked up at the stars that were coming out in the night sky. Silence again. Not an uncomfortable silence, but a restorative hush.

3J broke the silence as she wiped some of the tears from her cheeks. "Hey! What about those steaks you promised? A girl's gotta eat!"

It was usually only a fifteen minute drive from Loose Park to downtown. On 3J's drive home, however, it felt like a several-day-trip in an Old West, horse-drawn covered wagon. Traffic and traffic lights seemed to move in slow motion. All she could do was wonder about the practice of law without Pascale. *Maybe it won't be so bad*, she thought. He wasn't leaving Planet Earth, after all. Just seeking a new life outside work. *Good for him. It's time for him to reclaim a life. At some point, maybe we all need to do that.*

CHAPTER 4

Tuesday, October 31 to Wednesday, November 1, 2023

3J ARRANGED TO MEET with their new clients, the Rapinoes, on Wednesday morning. By early Tuesday afternoon, the clients delivered cash flow projections to 3J and Pascale, and by 4 p.m. on Tuesday, 3J and Pascale sat down with each other to discuss the projections and fashion a plan for the meeting the next morning.

"These projections aren't really as bleak as I thought they might be," 3J said to Pascale, "but the devil is in the assumptions. Assumption number one: patrons continue to return and to do that, they'll have to feel comfortable in close quarters again, as we all hopefully put the memory of the pandemic behind us."

"That's a biggie," Pascale observed. "Tough times to be in the entertainment and hospitality business."

"Number two: the clubs being able to book acts, meaning older, famous jazz musicians are back on the road performing live. Again, something of a Covid issue. The musicians want and need to perform, but they're older and more at risk for their health, and they'll also have to navigate tight quarters and these small, intimate clubs. Not all of them will immediately return to the road to gig in-person concerts."

"Another biggie, I'm afraid," Pascale said, looking very serious, raising his eyebrows high on his forehead.

"And number three: normally, we base the projections on recent years of actual cash flow, but here, 2020 through mid-2022, cash flows were in the toilet because of Covid."

Again, Pascale agreed and responded, "So, they're going to have to lean on older actual cash flow performance, and that may or may not be acceptable to a bankruptcy judge."

3J said, "Exactly. I'd like to say 'it is what it is because what else could it be,' to quote your favorite phrase, but it seems a cop-out in this case."

Pascale paused for a moment. "Well, 'it is what it is' has always been a derivative of 'what you see is what you get,' but here, we're just going to have to drift from the 'what you see' notion to using some smoke and mirrors. We'll have to create the illusion that the projections are reliable and are just what they appear to be, even if they're based on some seriously uncharted territory. It'll be a challenge, but I think we can pull it off – with the right witness."

"I hope so. I really do," 3J responded slowly.

"Say, what else do we know about this guy, Phillip Dewey, and Veridical Lending? Do we know any of the bankruptcy lawyers in town that have tangled with him before? Because I sure haven't, and all I know about the company or him is what I told you the other day – that is, next to nothing."

"I have a friend at Brewer Hopkins, who I called over the weekend. She said he's an odd duck; on the shorter side, dapper to an extreme, partial to bow ties. A bit of a dandy. Middle-aged. She described his speaking style as one where he chooses every word carefully and articulates each word perfectly. Soft-spoken. Little to no inflection. And she said his tone is 'eerie.' When I asked what an eerie voice sounds like, she said it was a nasally sort of whisper, no emotion – just like you heard on the radio show. She said when he talks, it's coupled with ill-timed smiles, and a weird, occasional 'tssk' noise at the back of his mouth before he starts a sentence, as if to announce that important words will follow the tssk."

"So he really is an odd duck, with odd mannerisms?"

3J nodded her head, and then continued, "My friend said that Dewey looks at the entire business of lending and collection as something of a holy war. He tells anyone who'll listen that he always gets his money back, no matter what. She said that when Dewey says that, he sounds like a Vegas gambler who tells you in a soft-spoken voice with all seriousness that he never loses at the craps table. She said Peter Lorre should play Dewey when the movie comes out and we should rename the Dewey character Joel Cairo, like the strange little guy in *Maltese Falcon*."

"Oh, sounds just wonderful," Pascale observed sarcastically.

"She actually called him a complete 'fuck knuckle.'"

"Not familiar with *that* descriptive term."

"Means he struggles to make socially acceptable decisions," 3J explained, shaking her head slowly from side to side.

"So, what next?" Pascale asked.

"I'll go ahead and draft up the usual bankruptcy memo to explain the process to the Rapinoes. Would you have time to prepare to lead the discussion on cash usage and the projections?"

"Sure thing."

3J grabbed her now lukewarm cup of tea and stood to leave the conference room. As she rose, Pascale added, "And thanks for listening last night. Sorry to burden you with my meditations and musings, but it was thoroughly therapeutic for me to talk with someone – well, not just someone, *you* – about all of it."

3J turned, looked pleased, locked eyes with Pascale, and said, "Anytime, any day, anywhere, 24-7."

Pascale nodded a slow affirmation, and they each headed back to their offices.

Early the next morning, Bey and Adam Rapinoe arrived with their outside accountant, Ralph Kane, and met 3J and Pascale in the 27th floor Conference Room B, that 3J called the "War Room." Not fancy, sometimes messy with boxes from other cases strewn around the perimeter, but always comfortable enough.

Both Rapinoes were in their fifties. Adam was five-foot-ten-inches, maybe 180 pounds, athletic, and he sported a navy blue jacket, white button-down shirt, gray pants, polished black leather loafers, and no tie. He had short, straight, salt and pepper hair brushed forward, light brown eyes, and a Roman-esque nose. Bey was a trim five-foot-four-inches, slender, maybe 105 pounds, and wore a similar navy blue jacket, light blue button-down shirt open at the collar, black pants, and flats, dark gray-colored. She had sandy blond hair, cropped short, dark red-painted, professionally manicured fingernails, a short nose, and blue eyes – one of which was slightly crossed, adding a hint of intrigue to her gaze. They could both have passed for bankers in any Hollywood movie. 3J thought to herself, *I guess if you've spent your life dealing with bankers, you start to dress and look like them. Maybe it can't be helped.*

At the first introductory meeting, 3J had learned that the Rapinoes met in college at George Washington University, were an item for three years, and married when they gradu-ated. Both were economics majors and, after college, they had joined Bey's family real estate development business before venturing out on their own. Over the years, they developed, built, operated, and sold shopping centers, and repeated the process for decades before cashing out to pursue the return of live jazz to Kansas City.

3J had not met Ralph Kane before, and she was interested to hear his take on the projections.

She addressed the Rapinoes and Kane. "Thanks for coming in, folks. Here's a memo we give to all of our business debtor clients that explains the bankruptcy process. Read it after this meeting and let either of us know if you have questions."

"Thanks," Adam said. "Unfortunately, we've had experience with some parts of the bankruptcy process as a number of our commercial tenants over the years commenced bankruptcy cases. Just part of being a landlord in the shopping center world."

3J nodded and said, "Let's turn to the problems at hand. We've gone through all the information you sent me and the projections you put together, and we have some questions. Let's start with the jazz club concept. What made you give up a successful and lucrative development business and dive into the deep end of the entertainment and hospitality industry?"

Bey responded, "I'll field that one. There've been many late nights since we made the shift when I thought we were certifiably crazy to have gone down this path. Pure bonkers. We learned over the decades since college that we were good in the development game, very good, and very lucky. Luck helps a lot. But unlike other real estate developers who seem to have passion in their blood, almost an inherent need to keep bringing new projects to market, we didn't feel passionate about it. When we finished a project, cut the ribbon, and stepped back to admire the creation, we just didn't see ourselves in the handiwork. We got into the business because it's what my family did. But, unlike other family members, we always planned to exit the business when we identified what else we wanted to do."

Bey had a smooth, mid-range, silky voice. No accent, like so many born and bred Midwesterners. She was poised in her comments, and spoke in a way that conveyed she was used to speaking, used to people listening, confident in herself, and her manner let the audience know she expected people would believe her. She made eye contact as she spoke and seemed to have the ability to lock eyes and control the other person's field of vision. Her gaze was commanding and even disarming.

Bey paused for a sip of the firm's Filling Station dark-brew coffee from a tan, Greene Madison-branded mug. Adam continued for her. "Yeah, so why? Why indeed? We've been actively involved with the American Jazz Museum over on 18th and Vine for years. Events, board service, fundraising, membership drives, interviews for the press, concerts, curating exhibits. And, in particular, the Kansas City Jazz Academy at the museum, started in 2016, that provides jazz instruction for middle and high school students teaching them improvisation, and offering master classes taught by national and international jazz musicians. You name it; we did it. And still do."

As 3J listened, she observed that there could be no mistaking the Rapinoes' passion.

Bey asked, "Did you know that over 160,000 people visit the museum each year? Maybe they come because they're jazz aficionados. But maybe they come to see Charlie Parker's plastic Grafton alto saxophone because there's nothing more American than Parker and jazz."

Adam cupped his coffee mug with both hands, nodded his head, and continued, "We've been active with Steve Penn's Coda Jazz Fund since its inception in 2002. The project raises money to help cover funeral and burial expenses for the families of deceased Kansas City jazz musicians and vocalists. Musicians come from all over the country to donate their live performances to raise awareness and money.

"As we got more and more involved in these projects and the jazz scene in KC, we wanted to do more – return our city to the hub for jazz that it once was. Hence the idea of trying to bring back the small club and restaurant concept that so pervaded the Kansas City jazz scene in the 1920s, 1930s and 1940s, and even into the 1950s. We named our clubs after the iconic clubs from the 1940s: The Hi Hat, The Hey Hay, The Cherry Blossom, The Boulevard Lounge, The Paseo Club, and The Spinning Wheel."

Adam spoke with a soothing tenor tone, and sounded to Pascale much like Merle Haggard, complete with a bit of the Bakersfield twang by way of Oklahoma. Most importantly for the lawyers in the room, he spoke with authority and presence, commanding attention without being overbearing. As he finished discussing the club venture, Bey took over again and said, "Sounds crazy, but it's important work for us and it's beyond hard work, so it gives us a way to fill our days and keep ourselves out of trouble. We built the clubs and, just as we had hoped, they came, and many of them. We developed quite a loyal following. We were a destination not only for patrons, but the word got out quickly and the musicians lined up for us to book their shows. The clubs received stellar reviews. Everything was better than we could have hoped for. At least until the pandemic. But we're optimistic that the crowds will return as well as the musicians."

Tireless ambassadors for jazz as an art form and for Kansas City's place in jazz history, 3J thought.

Adam added, "At least hopeful they'll come back, even on those days where it's a little harder to find the island of optimism in the sea of bad news, after what we've all gone through worldwide." .

3J found it interesting that the couple passed the lead speaking role back and forth, much like a jazz ensemble using a call and response technique between the musicians – one playing a musical phrase and the other answering, a musical conversation of two instruments speaking to each other while the audience listens in. Everyone on stage gets a chance to take the lead in the spotlight, to the delight of the audience. *Good old gospel and native African music roots*, 3J thought. *The musical version of democratic participation. The Rapinoes shared the spotlight equally with each other. Quite effective. Probably good for the marriage as well!*

Pascale asked, "What about this Dewey guy? How did you hook up with him as your lender?"

Bey responded, "The project wasn't a good fit for traditional bank lenders to take a chance on us. Remember also that we began looking for financing in 2013, just after the end of the 2008 to 2012 financial crisis, and banks were pretty conservative in their lending practices then. We'd never been in the nightclub business before. We had no history and no real business experience in either music concerts or food. We were following by a few decades the collapse of the Hyatt skywalks, which we think tainted the prospect of live music in our city for many years. We had many bank contacts from our years in the shopping center business. Good relationships; we approached all of them. They were respectful, and many liked the project concept. But most weren't interested in banking us and none were willing to go out on the limb with us."

Adam continued, "A friend of a friend told us at a cocktail party that they knew a private lender who was more risk tolerant than the banks. Just that easily, we met with Phillip Dewey. He was, to be sure, a different sort, and his loan pricing was higher than we would've liked, but we figured it was a short-term arrangement and we took his money. We frankly had little contact with him after we signed the loan documents and Bey and I guaranteed the BJB debt, other than the occasional 'how's it going' phone call from him. He wasn't big on site visits and in-person meetings with us, but I'm guessing that in his mind, we were model debtors because we always paid on time. So we made him thrilled, to the extent he *has* the capacity to be thrilled. Have you met him? A truly strange man."

Pascale nodded in understanding then said, "No, we don't know him, but we're learning of his eccentricities." He had been using the time that the others were discussing Dewey to gather the projections he and 3J had reviewed the day before. "Ok, let's talk about the projections. We see them as the cornerstone to a successful bankruptcy case. Walk us through your assumptions."

Bey turned to Ralph Kane and said, "Ralph, can you take this one?"

"Sure thing." Kane was a burly man, six feet tall, with large, weathered hands, graying medium brown hair cut Marine-short, and spoke with a deep-pitched voice. He folded his hands on the conference table and began. "The last two years of Covid have ravaged the industry, and Adam's and Bey's business in particular. So, in my estimation, pulling data from 2020, 2021, and 2022 to construct the prediction of what the next five years will be like isn't a useful exercise. 2023 has begun to turn around, and so what I did was to take data from 2018 and 2019, as well as the first nine months of 2023, to project what the cash flows could look like for the rest of this year and five years into the future. Not necessarily ideal or textbook, but there's no other way to make sense of the numbers as we come out of the pandemic."

Kane paused to see if 3J or Pascale had questions. Hearing none, he continued, "The good news is that while the method may take some liberties with what used to be standard operating procedure in the world of business cash flow projections, there's also no good way to challenge the assumptions. We'll probably be in court on this, right? So my thought is that the only way to 'force' us to use the numbers from the pandemic years in projecting for the years after 2023 would be if the judge determined that 2023 and beyond will be like the pandemic years; rather than coming out of the pandemic, these years will be more of the virus continuing to hurt business. But even the flu pandemic in 1918 didn't last that long, so we'd hope that the judge wouldn't be of a mind to imprint the future years with the financial woes of 2020-2022. The three of us have given this quite a bit of thought and it's our considered view that this is the fairest method to use to project numbers into the future in the current world we live in. And we hope that you can help us sell it to the judge."

3J and Pascale listened carefully to how Kane presented the thesis. This, of course, was the elephant in the room. They liked what they heard, and how Kane presented the projections and defended the method.

Pascale said, "We'll work with you to tighten up how we present this, but it sounds logical and believable. We'll just have to hope that besides us five, the judge will be the sixth believer in the room."

3J added, "You should know that the Bankruptcy Code doesn't require the judge to find that the projections will in fact come true. The standard is a good bit lower. The judge just has to find the plan, based on projections, isn't likely to be followed by liquidation. It's the feasibility requirement. The courts regularly say that the plan isn't a guarantee of success, and the mere potential that the plan might fail isn't grounds to toss it out. The judges are looking for projections that are well-reasoned and credible." 3J stood to stretch her back and continued, "The judges want to avoid approving visionary schemes. No hope-upon-hope testimony that's just wishful thinking."

3J returned to her chair and Bey said, "Good to know. But it seems like a fine line between 'well-reasoned' and 'hope-upon-hope.'"

"To be sure. Largely, it's the judge's reaction to the presentation that carries the day. If the judge gets a whiff of too much conjecture, he tosses the plan and says it's impermissible wishful thinking. If he finds the testimony credible, he says the projections are well-reasoned. If we run a good, dependable ship during the case and before the plan, we'll have a better chance of the judge going with 'well-reasoned' when he gets to the plan."

"Well, using those guidelines, these projections are certainly feasible – at least in my estimation," Kane stated confidently.

"We agree, and we just need to hone the presentation. It'll be the cornerstone for our success in getting a plan approved," 3J assured them.

Pascale asked, "Any reason we should try to meet with Dewey before filing?"

Bey answered, "I'm not sure. What would that accomplish?"

"Not always, but sometimes it's helpful to meet with the lender before a bankruptcy filing to see if there is any common ground that could form the basis of a compromise without necessitating bankruptcy filings," 3J said.

"I don't see that happening here," Adam chimed in. "I don't mean to dump cold water on the negotiation idea, but we met with Dewey and told him we'd have to restructure our payments for a period of time. We didn't get a chance to identify how long or how much, because he shut the conversation down. He can be very offputting, to be honest. He speaks softly, but his eyes light up and seem to flicker with anger. The whole package, especially those eyes, comes across as a bit menacing."

"I think that's the effect he's going for," Bey put in.

"In any case," Adam continued, "we couldn't even finish presenting to him the notion of a restructuring or a compromise. He wasn't interested." Adam paused. "I want to make sure I accurately quote him here: 'You will pay every penny you owe when you owe it. That is what the papers we signed say. That is my unwavering expectation.' Then, I think for emphasis, he lowered his chin, raised his eyebrows, and asked us as he loudly tapped his conference room table twice with his pointer, 'Do I make myself clear?' I took from the confrontation that he'll fight us at every turn and has little interest in a gentlemanly discussion of alternatives to bankruptcy."

Bey added, with disgust at herself, "After that exchange, I did what I should have done way back when, before taking this man's money. I did some deep dive, due diligence. What we witnessed wasn't an act. It's how the man is. He has a well-earned reputation for cutting no deals. It's menacing, the way he looks at you, especially as it's such a stark contrast to his stature and measured tone. He's been through some bankruptcy cases before. I mean, this is America – what lender hasn't? But, believe me, there's no deal he's looking for. There are no loan modifications he's interested in."

Adam jumped in as Bey took a sip of coffee. "We've talked about this a little, and we think we just file the bankruptcy cases and get on with the process. Which brings us to our fundamental question. What should we expect? Because, what we need and want, is some form of scaled-back payment plan, a lower interest rate, and maybe even an initial short moratorium on payments to our friendly private lending service."

3J shook her head knowingly and responded, "We've talked as well and here's what we think we should ask the judge for on day one, and what we think will likely happen. First, let's talk about the collateral. Veridical has a lien on your business furniture and fixtures, receivables and inventory. You have tables, chairs, some art on the walls, some autographs, some food in the fridges, etc. Not much inventory in your business. You have a day or two of money due to you from credit card companies; that's it. You're not like Walmart, where you have a store full of inventory or a manufacturer who makes goods from raw materials. With this in mind, we need you three to figure out what the used furniture and fixtures are worth, as well as your average float owed to you by the credit card companies – that would be your receivables. We're guessing those items won't yield a lot of value."

Bey responded, "We can do that quickly. We know those numbers."

"Good. Then we need to understand the value of the five pieces of real estate owned by your company, BJB LLC, where clubs operate. By the way, what does 'BJB' stand for?"

Adam and Bey smiled, and Adam said, "Bring Jazz Back."

Pascale smiled broadly. "Ahhhh. Of course. Got it."

3J continued, "With that information, we'll have an understanding of what Veridical's collateral is worth on day one of the bankruptcy cases. Our guess is that the collateral package will be worth significantly less than the balance left owing on the loan – do you agree?" As Bey and Adam murmured agreement, 3J went on. "Good. Then we'll need to be able to show that the value of the real estate is stable. Should be, right?"

Bey said definitively, "Right. No issue there."

"Great. Then, turning to the cash, we'll ask the judge to approve a budget for the use of the cash to operate the clubs, and we'll exclude payments to Veridical from the budget – we suggest for the first sixty days. When Mr. Dewey's lawyer objects, we'll argue that since the real estate isn't diminishing in value, no payments are due. And, for a little bankruptcy icing, we'll argue that when new patrons frequent the clubs after we've filed the bankruptcy cases, Veridical has no lien on the cash paid by patrons. So Veridical has no say in how that money's spent."

This last point caught the Rapinoes' attention.

"Can we actually get away with that last argument?" Adam asked with a tone of surprise and hope.

"We think we have a good chance to make that one fly."

"And what of the operations once we file?" Bey asked.

"The bankruptcy filings will result in the imposition of what's called the automatic stay, a cornerstone of the protections afforded to debtors who file for bankruptcy relief. The stay enjoins creditors from taking any steps to collect their pre-bankruptcy debts. It's a powerful tool that gets you a breathing spell from creditors. We'll be relying heavily on it to get you the protection you need from Mr. Dewey and Veridical. You'll be in command of the narrative; something like 'Clubs file to restructure debt and keep live jazz in Kansas City.' In the absence of collection efforts, the businesses should be stable. Bankruptcy and the automatic stay will manage Dewey for a good while."

"And creditors abide by the automatic stay?" Bey asked.

"Unless they have a death wish, they do," 3J responded. "No judge would countenance a creditor ignoring the stay."

"Ok, then," Bey said. "We have some work to do to get you what you want."

3J then explained, "When we get to the Chapter 11 plan process, you can expect to reset the interest rate to something akin to a market rate. So, much lower than 7%. As well, we can restructure the payments over a longer period of time than the remaining term set forth in the loan documents. In other words, we should be able to alter a number of the terms in Dewey's sacred documents."

Bey smiled and shook her head. "Dewey will shit a brick."

Pascale replied, "Yeah, the Bankruptcy Code can do that to some creditors."

"One other thing Dewey told us at the non-meeting we had," Adam recalled. "He said he might run out and get a receiver appointed shortly."

"We're worried about that possibility," Pascale revealed. "We need to get this project in order quickly to file the bankruptcy cases before a state court judge appoints a receiver. A receiver would displace you from running BJB and would wreak havoc on an operation already deeply bruised by Covid. It might also preclude you as the owners from seeking bankruptcy protection for BJB." Pascale paused to let his analysis sink in. "We need to beat Mr. Dewey to the filing finish line here."

3J then asked, "One last topic, please. Give us an overview of who else BJB owes money to."

"We'll get you a complete list as soon as we get back to the office, but the high-level picture is this," Adam explained. "We have a group of vendors we rely on for food, linens, cleaning, ticket sales, and web page operations … all the things you might imagine a restaurant needs to stay in business and serve its patrons. One reason we want a moratorium from Dewey is to make sure we don't fall behind in payments to these vendors, who have worked with us throughout the pandemic. We need them to keep working with us."

Adam looked at Bey and she continued, "At any given time, we owe tens of thousands of dollars or more to our vendors in the aggregate."

3J responded, "Ok, get us the list, with addresses, contacts, debts owed, and amounts past due. We'll start to put the papers together quickly and we'll be ready to quick-file even if we haven't finished all the papers yet." She made eye contact with the threesome sitting across the conference table. "Questions?"

Adam looked at Bey, then back to 3J, and answered, "None, but we know how to find you if we think of any."

CHAPTER 5

Wednesday, November 1 to Thursday, November 2, 2023

AFTER THE RAPINOES AND Ralph Kane departed in the late morning, 3J and Pascale headed back to his office to review what they learned. 3J sat in Pascale's overstuffed club chair after setting aside the papers that were strewn there, kicked off her shoes, tucked her legs under her, and said, "I'm really worried about the receivership issue. If Dewey sought a receiver, and the state court judge decided to first give BJB notice of the request, we'd still have enough time to file the bankruptcy papers before the state court judge heard and ruled on the receiver request. But the mortgage documents say that Veridical can seek a receiver without notice to BJB. If it did, and if the state court judge granted the request, then we'd be in a world of hurt."

"My concerns exactly," Pascale confirmed. "3J, I don't think we have any choice but to implement one of the 'quick-file' cases for BJB and the Rapinoes, and follow that up with the necessary paperwork to complete the filings."

3J grimaced but agreed. "Quick-file cases aren't my favorite. So easy to file, and then chaos as we rush to get the rest of the paperwork completed and on file. Playing catch-up from the very beginning." She paused and then said, "Well, no choice on this one, I'm afraid. I'll get them back in here to sign and we can file tonight electronically. It'll be a bare bones filing, but we'll still get the automatic stay and that'll prevent Veridical from running to state court. It's the only way to end the receivership threat."

3J prepared the minimum required, quick-file, Chapter 11 papers, as well as a motion to permit BJB to use cash for the first two weeks of the bankruptcy case. Her staff prepared several other uncontroversial first day motions to allow BJB to continue to operate in the normal course of business. The Rapinoes had their accounting staff send a list of the twenty largest creditors, with addresses and amounts owing. 3J then contacted the Rapinoes, who came in at six that evening to review and sign the papers.

Later that evening, 3J's and Pascale's staff filed the Chapter 11 papers on behalf of BJB and the Rapinoes and commenced the three Chapter 11 bankruptcy cases. With the filing, the automatic stay came into effect, barring Veridical and all other creditors from taking any steps to collect the debts owed to them. *Protection achieved. No receivership. That levels the playing field*, 3J thought with a sigh of relief. First thing in the morning, she would determine which of the three bankruptcy judges would preside over the cases and contact that judge's chambers to see how quickly she could get a hearing on the cash usage motion.

Quick-file cases were not the controlled, planned, organized filings that most bankruptcy attorneys pined for but rather a filing whose principal purpose was to get the full-stop protection of the automatic stay. Control and organization would follow in due time, after-the-fact. *Never ideal*, 3J thought. But, harkening back to something as Pascale liked to observe, *you can't always control everything, and sometimes you can control nothing.*

The next morning, 3J learned Judge Daniel Robertson would handle the cases, the same judge who had so admirably handled the Quincy Witherman cases several years before, his first large, complex Chapter 11 cases. 3J and Pascale had great admiration and respect for Judge Robertson, and both were grateful that he would handle the BJB and Rapinoe cases. These would be a different breed of cases, to be sure. 3J expected no hidden Swiss assets in the Rapinoes' proceedings, and as peculiar as Phillip Dewey sounded, given his soft-spoken, even-toned mannerisms, she expected no courtroom outbursts from him, unlike the drama Witherman's banker, Stacy Milnes, had displayed. No, on this one 3J envisioned a calm, respectful setting, a return to courtroom normalcy and decorum, as she attempted to sell Judge Robertson on the promise of better times for the jazz club industry. Little did she know.

CHAPTER 6

Phillip Dewey Recalls Thursday, November 2, 2023

I SAT IN MY living area, alone with my thoughts, but not alone. I always had Mother. And I knew Joshua was always around. Joshua did not like that Mother resided with us in our Hallbrook home. He had made it quite clear what he would do with Mother if he was in charge. I always listened, but I was in charge, not Joshua. So, Mother was safe.

I was in the midst of considering whether to reach out to business acquaintances who I knew did business with BJB and the Rapinoes, people I thought I could trust. But can you really trust anyone? People I hoped would be like-minded – but can you really rely on anyone to be like-minded? People I thought I could convince to join me in my repayment journey. People with whom I had nothing in common except BJB and the Rapinoes.

There is simply no accounting for unwise business decisions in these contentious times we live in. Small thinking by small-minded business owners when faced with big issues. The mere thought of collaborating with such creditors made me shudder. If I joined with others, and I was sure others would join with me, I would need to listen to them and hear what was on their minds. No. What a supreme waste of my precious time that would be. Nothing such creditors could say to me would amount to useful information.

No. I would simply have to go it alone and quickly implement my plan of – shall I call it, persuasion – to encourage the Rapinoes to repay me.

As I rose from my couch, I knew Mother *agreed*. I returned to my desk, and I saw an email from Josephina Jillian Jones advising me that BJB and the Rapinoes had just filed their bankruptcy papers. Not a surprise, not after I told them I expected them to adhere to every single word and requirement in my loan documents.

But the filings heightened my need to stay on course. I knew I needed to finalize and implement my plan. And I needed a bankruptcy lawyer. Plenty of those in Kansas City, and points beyond, to choose from. Not quite a dime a dozen, but I have observed that they all struggle to distinguish themselves from one another. Not unlike the lenders of the world. Over the years, I had talked to many bankruptcy lawyers and hired several handfuls of different lawyers for Veridical. My tendency was never to hire the same one again. Lawyers tend to find things out about their clients. I didn't want that, so I exercised my right to change horses with each new bankruptcy race I found myself in. I would just take out my virtual Rolodex and peruse the offerings.

As I considered my lawyer options, I also knew I needed to engage a tech person to implement my plan, leaving no footprints or breadcrumbs to trace back to me. I didn't need to think long – I had just the right chap in mind. A Kansas City businessman. A gent I had met after my MBA program, who also got a master's in business administration from SLU. Someone I've used in the past for mainstream services – contract information systems work for Veridical; and for less traditional campaigns to help debtors see their way clear to pay me.

For a fee, this business compatriot was willing to turn to the internet, at my direction, to assist in behavior modification for certain debtors. He was good at what he did, and that's what I needed.

CHAPTER 7

Thursday, November 2 to Friday, November 3, 2023

JUDGE ROBERTSON'S NEW LAW clerk, Jennifer Cuello, called to let 3J know that the Judge would hear her first day motion requests the following morning at 8:30 a.m. and asked her to make sure that she notified all the principal creditors by email of the hearing. 3J advised Jennifer that the main motion for consideration would be the motion for BJB to use cash under the cash flow budget.

After the phone call, 3J filed the cash motion along with the budget, as well as other standard first day motions to permit the clubs to continue to operate in the ordinary course which her team drafted the night before. She emailed the package of motions to Jennifer with the request that she share them with Judge Robertson, and she emailed them to the principal creditors – including Veridical – with a notice that the hearings to consider the motions would be the next morning at 8:30 a.m.

The Rapinoes and Ralph Kane came to Madison Greene later that morning to prepare for the first day hearings. "Before we get started, can you tell us a little about Judge Robertson?" Bey asked 3J and Pascale as they took their seats around the conference room table.

"Most certainly," 3J replied. "Judge Daniel Robertson has been a bankruptcy judge for about four or five years now. He presided over his first big Chapter 11 bankruptcy cases about three years ago. Those were doozies. He handled the cases well despite felonies galore, hidden assets, crazy bankers, Fifth Amendment issues, people yelling in his courtroom, and people that ended up in jail. Since those were real estate developer cases, you may have read about them? Quincy Witherman?"

"Oh! Yes, indeed we did," Adam responded. "For all of the millions who live in the metropolitan area, Kansas City's still a small town in many regards. We met Witherman a few times at Kansas City events, probably one jazz-related fundraiser or another. He liked jazz. He had a pretty extensive vinyl jazz collection, as I recall. Despite our musical taste intersection, we didn't socialize with him. A slick dude, that one. Distant as well." Adam paused to recollect something about Witherman that he decided not to share. Instead, he asked, "Any more flavor about the Judge?"

Pascale jumped in and said, "Judge Robertson is very good on the bench. He was a medium-sized firm practitioner for many years, very experienced in bankruptcy cases, and has shown patience and skill as a judge. He has a great disposition, and usually seems to make the right decision for the right reason, which is all you can really ask for of a judge. Pretty hard worker. Not at all controversial. I think he was pretty burned out before the circuit court appointed him to the bankruptcy bench. The whole judicial gig seems to have revived and reinvigorated him. Really a pleasure to have a case in front of him."

Adam continued with his interest in the Judge, "Is he considered pro-debtor, pro-creditor, or something else?"

"My feeling is that he's in the 'something else' category, as I think he should be," 3J responded. "He's pro-Bankruptcy Code. He'll protect the debtor for a while because he's supposed to under the law, but if the debtor takes a position it should lose, it *will* lose in the Robertson Court. Sometimes, we've used a golf analogy to describe the good Judge: he plays the ball where it lies. As a bankruptcy lawyer, that's just fine."

"Very helpful. I look forward to meeting the Judge and seeing him in action," Adam said.

With the deep dive into Judge Robertson complete, the four began to prepare for the next day's hearing. 3J recapped what she had touched on two days ago. "Normally, a creditor has a lien on all the cash the debtor's business generates, and, therefore, the Court must approve the use of the cash – called cash collateral under the Bankruptcy Code. As I mentioned before, a music venue and restaurant are different, so I'm going to diverge from the usual request. I'll tell Judge Robertson that technically we don't need his permission to use cash because no one has a lien on it. But in an abundance of caution and to make sure we're transparent in our operations, I'll tell him we seek approval of the budget under which the businesses would operate."

"Understood," Bey said.

Adam nodded his head in agreement. "Will he buy the argument?"

"We think so – it's what the Code says. While restaurants and music venues are different sorts of business animals than stores and manufacturers, restaurants and venues file bankruptcy cases, so we aren't really plowing new ground. We just need the Judge to shift from thinking in terms of inventory and receivables to cash from meals and music. That part shouldn't be a problem. He's handled some restaurant cases in the past." 3J paused after her last comment, alerting the Rapinoes that there may be more to the story.

Bey asked, "So, then, is there a problem I'm hearing in your voice – and if so, what is it?"

3J smiled reassuringly and said, "The only problem we see is the method used to create the budget. After all, the budget is the guess, you know, an educated hunch, of what revenues will be in the future months and while it doesn't address years into the future, it nevertheless is the first time we'll unveil the method to predict future cash. If challenged, that's where Ralph comes in. We'll spend most of this afternoon refining his testimony if we need to call him to the stand. We'll need to tackle that head on, but I feel good about the explanations we've discussed. I can't imagine how Judge Robertson will reject the methodology this early in the case ... but we'll see his reaction tomorrow."

They spent the rest of the day preparing Ralph Kane for court. Ralph was a seasoned accountant who had testified numerous times in the past. As Pascale had observed many times, "Just because you do it a lot don't mean you do it well," but as the afternoon wore on, both 3J and Pascale concluded Kane would be good on the witness stand. He had a way of explaining without lecturing; of convincing without arguing; of offering logic and reason without sounding antagonistic or defensive.

At six, the meeting broke up and 3J and Pascale headed out of the conference room to 3J's meticulous office. Pascale always marveled at the sharp contrast between his style of mid-century messy office decoration – papers everywhere, on the verge of pandemonium, no color coordination – with 3J's professional designer organization, the complimentary pastel colors, papers neatly stacked and filed; the stuff of an office design magazine feature article. The two couldn't be more polar opposites in their approach to the rooms where they spent so much of their time each day of the week.

"Tomorrow's gonna be an early one for us," Pascale noted.

"Indeed."

"Predictions?" Pascale asked, looking for a quick discussion.

"Ya' know, it should be fine," 3J said as she sighed ever so slightly. "I think the Judge will let us operate under the budget and won't let on too much, if at all, what he thinks about the methods used to create the budget. I don't intend to hit the methodology issue at all unless pressed."

"Agreed. Kane'll be ready to testify if need be, but I doubt we'll have to call him. Not at this early stage."

"Have you heard anything from Veridical?" 3J asked as she checked the voicemails on her mobile phone.

"Not a peep," Pascale replied.

"Calm before the storm?" 3J said, more of a statement than a question.

"Always," Pascale agreed. "Every single time. That's why we love this part of the process."

"Or at least, 'loved' – past tense," 3J corrected Pascale, based on their Sunday dinner conversation.

"Fair enough, 3J. Fair enough." He nodded and smiled. "No one said the impending switch of my gears would be easy or smooth sailing. I can see I've got some retraining in my immediate future."

3J then turned to a housekeeping item. "Meet here at 7 a.m.?"

"In my favorite navy blue suit."

"Aren't all of your suits navy blue?"

"Touché." Pascale smiled. "I think we're done for tonight. I'll go down the elevator with you."

"All rise," the courtroom clerk commanded and Judge Robertson, followed by his law clerk, entered the courtroom, stepped up on the elevated bench, and stood momentarily as the clerk announced, "The United States Bankruptcy Court for the

Western District of Missouri is now in session, the Honorable Daniel Robertson presiding. You may be seated."

A wood and metal railing divided the courtroom between the public pews behind and the space in front of the railing reserved for attorneys and their clients, filled by the Judge's bench in the front of the courtroom three steps above the floor, the witness chair, lawyer podium, and two rectangular attorney tables. Jennifer Cuello sat at a built-in table, along with the courtroom deputy, in front of and beneath the Judge's bench to the left of the witness stand. Jennifer was within easy reach to pass notes to and from the Judge during hearings. Assorted creditor representatives populated the courtroom pews. In the front row sat Phillip Dewey, in a dapper, gray houndstooth suit and a vibrant green, red, and brown striped bow tie. Several members of the press sat in the pews, poised to take notes of the hearing. Moments after the courtroom clerk completed her announcement, 3J rose and approached the podium to make her presentation to the Judge.

Both 3J and Pascale wore dark navy blue suits and white shirts. 3J's shirt had modest frills where the buttons were located. Pascale also wore a deep solid burgundy tie, and his favorite Allen Edmonds shiny black wingtip shoes, just like generations of male Greene Madison had worn to court. All conservative, bankruptcy lawyer attire; not the place or time for the Greene Madison team to make a fashion statement – except for 3J's signature high heels; today, a pair of Bing patent crystal-strap pumps, made by Jimmy Choo. Few lawyers could pull off the combination of the conservative suit with the splashy Choo shoes, but 3J made it seem easy.

"If it pleases the Court, Josephina Jones and William Pascale of the Greene Madison law firm representing the Debtors: BJB LLC, Bey Rapinoe, and Adam Rapinoe. The Rapinoes are the owners and principal officers of BJB, and appear here with us today in person," 3J said as she gestured towards the Rapinoes with an open hand, palm up.

"Thank you, Ms. Jones." Then, looking around the courtroom, Judge Robertson inquired, "Who else do we have here today that would like to enter their appearance?"

A tall man in a dark gray suit approached the podium, and in a silky voice reminiscent of Lou Rawls, said, "Alexander Fuentes representing Veridical Lending LLC, the principal secured creditor." Grabbing the sides of the podium, Fuentes said, "Your Honor, if I might, I practice largely in Chicago. I'm not licensed in the Western District of Missouri, and I will be filing a motion later today for permission to practice before you, *pro hac vice*. Pending that, would the Court extend me the courtesy of allowing me to appear here today and represent my client?"

"Absolutely, Mr. Fuentes. Welcome to the Western District."

"Thank you, Your Honor."

Judge Robertson enjoyed out-of-state attorneys from large cities practicing in his Court. He felt it made him a better judge to have big-time practitioners from other venues filing briefs, calling witnesses, and making arguments before him. He liberally extended them the courtesy of appearing in his Court even if they lacked a Missouri or Western District license.

Fuentes nodded to 3J and Pascale as he turned away from the podium and returned to his seat. 3J leaned over to Pascale and whispered, "Do you know him?"

Pascale whispered back, "Negative."

3J returned to the podium and began her presentation. She had a black three-ring notebook she used in each debtor's case she handled. It contained notes, key documents, and, in this case, an outline of her presentation to the Court. As much as possible, she tried not to look at the outline and thereby maintained almost constant eye contact with the Judge. Occasionally,

3J also looked over to Jennifer Cuello to make sure the law clerk appreciated that she was an important part of the Court and that 3J was talking to her as well as to the Judge.

"Judge, you may know something of the Rapinoes from the many articles written about them over the years. They are well-known, successful real estate developers who left their burgeoning real estate business to pursue their passion – Kansas City jazz, and in particular, the jazz scene in our fair city." Judge Robertson nodded his head, showing he was familiar with the Rapinoes. 3J was not sure to what degree, so she continued with her overview. "The Rapinoes' business plan was simple – bring live jazz back to Kansas City to the same degree as it existed in jazz's heyday in the 1930s, 1940s, and the beginning of the 1950s. Your Honor may also recall that during the 1980s, the Crown Center Hyatt promoted a Friday night tea dance to replicate the swing jazz good time dancing culture in KC, until the night the skywalks collapsed. After the collapse, while there was still live jazz in town, it struggled.

"The Rapinoes are established fixtures in Kansas City's music scene. They served for many years on the board of the American Jazz Museum on 18th Street. They give their time and energy to the Coda Fund, set up to assist the families of deceased jazz musicians. Bey and Adam acquired five properties in the city, two of which are designated historical, and leased the sixth. By 2015, they were ready to begin operations, with these six live jazz clubs and fine dining establishments.

"The clubs have been wildly successful – that is, until March 2020, when the pandemic engulfed us and changed all of our lives. Between the lockdown, followed by the era of distancing and masking indoors, the clubs suffered enormously. Even after the vaccines arrived in 2021, the different Covid variants substantially slowed down the clubs' attempts to return to some semblance of normality.

"National jazz acts have been slow to get back on the road as well. Veridical lent BJB approximately $17 million. Veridical charges 7% per annum, so it was a costly lending facility, but the Rapinoes believed it was a bridge loan BJB would use until it established the viability of its club operations, after which it was the Debtors' intent to move the loan to a conventional bank or bank group, at a more modest market rate of interest."

3J paused, and the Judge nodded his understanding of the history. She twirled her pen absentmindedly in her left hand once, and continued, "Unfortunately, the projected time to reach stability of the new operations and shop for a new bank loan was five years after they opened the doors ... or, Your Honor, just as the pandemic hit." 3J paused again for emphasis, and locked eye contact with Judge Robertson. She thought she could see in his eyes empathy toward the Rapinoes for their situation. "Well, as you might imagine, Your Honor, no banks were interested in looking at jazz club and restaurant loans when there were no patrons and no musicians on the road gigging live performances. The Rapinoes used their own wealth to keep current on the Veridical loan for some three years. They have burned down that wealth now, unfortunately. Just prior to these filings, the Rapinoes and Veridical's owner, Phillip Dewey, could not reach a deal on how to address the impact of Covid, and it was therefore necessary to commence these bankruptcy cases to prevent Veridical's pursuit of a receiver." 3J again paused and said, "Does the Court have any questions before I turn to the cash usage motion?"

"I do not, Ms. Jones. Thank you. Does anyone else have anything to say before we turn to the principal motion that brings us here today?"

Fuentes stood and addressed the Court. "May I be heard, Your Honor? I will be brief."

"Of course, Mr. Fuentes. Please, step up."

As Fuentes walked to the podium and 3J yielded her position, Fuentes began talking. "Your Honor, I just want to clarify that Veridical does not necessarily concur with Ms. Jones's eloquent presentation, not at this time. Ms. Jones was merely summing up what I would characterize as the Debtors' view of the world. We will all have time to ferret out what the truth of the business really is, and the *genuine* reasons for filing the bankruptcy cases." As Fuentes spoke, he raised his eyebrows in an attempt to show through body language that Veridical had a different story to present, suggesting there were other underlying reasons for the filings. He continued, "In particular, I want to dispel any implication suggested by Ms. Jones that Veridical took any action to cause these filings. Veridical didn't call the loans. Veridical didn't seek any state court remedies like the appointment of a receiver. Veridical didn't sue BJB and the Rapinoes. All Veridical did was ask the Rapinoes to adhere to the loan documents as they had during the pandemic." Fuentes nodded once and concluded, "Unless the Court has questions, I'll reserve any further comment at this time."

"The Court has no questions, Mr. Fuentes," Judge Robertson said. "I appreciate your comments, and since you have not practiced before me until today, rest assured that I don't take as gospel what Debtors' counsel says to me in my courtroom on the first day. We can all recognize and acknowledge that Ms. Jones' presentation serves to bring me up to speed with her clients' view of the facts leading up to the filings, none of which do I challenge – nor accept as true – today."

Fuentes bowed his head slowly toward the Judge in non-verbal thanks and took his seat. Phillip Dewey leaned forward with interest as Fuentes made his presentation, and upon completion of the presentation and the Judge's comments in response, sat back in the uncomfortable oak pew showing no emotion. Inside, however, he felt Fuentes had made a reasonably good first day impression. His choice of counsel pleased him; it had been the correct decision to look for his counsel outside the Kansas City tight-knit bankruptcy community.

3J returned to the podium and began her presentation on the Cash Usage Motion with an explanation on the complicated and arcane Bankruptcy Code point that there really was little to no cash on which Veridical had a lien because the Bankruptcy Code cut off the lien on the cash paid by the post-bankruptcy patrons who either bought concert tickets or dinner, the Judge nodding in understanding. 3J outlined that the food on-hand, as well as the furniture and equipment, on the filing date were not particularly valuable and that as there was no diminishment in value of the land owned by BJB where five of the six clubs operated, the stable value of the land protected Veridical.

"Your Honor, because the cash generated in the clubs is not Veridical's collateral, we submit that under the Bankruptcy Code, we need not obtain Court permission to use the cash. Nevertheless, we understand that at the beginning of cases like these, credibility and transparency are important. Everyone is going to feel more comfortable with us if we operate pursuant to a budget, which we have attached to the cash usage motion. So what we seek here today is, in effect, a comfort order from the Court that the Debtors may operate pursuant to the budget attached to the motion.

"We have Mr. Ralph Kane here today, available to testify about the budget. He is BJB's long-standing accountant, and worked with the Rapinoes to prepare this budget. I want to make clear, however, that if we are called upon to offer Mr. Kane's testimony, he will not testify about the legal issues I just discussed. He is not an attorney, nor a Bankruptcy Code expert."

"The Court appreciates that, Ms. Jones. As you know, normally on a first day motion like this I don't take testimony. For today's purposes, the budget is the budget, unless someone has real issues with the attached spreadsheet. This is just a preliminary hearing. We'll hear testimony and take evidence, if need be, at a final hearing. I will also refrain today from making a ruling about the lien-on-the-post-bankruptcy-cash issue you outlined. But I will say, mostly for Mr. Fuentes's benefit, that this is not the first Chapter 11 restaurant case I've handled on the bench. Although the clubs and restaurants before me in these cases are much more prominent and high-end than the other restaurant cases over which I've presided, nevertheless all the attorneys here today should understand that I've already ruled on this lien issue in these other restaurant cases and my ruling was just as you outlined, Ms. Jones – the lender has no lien on the post-bankruptcy cash. My law clerk will email to both of you a copy of that ruling after we complete the hearing today. With that comment, let me invite Mr. Fuentes to speak at this point in time."

Fuentes and 3J did the same courtroom dance as before – 3J pirouetted from the podium as Fuentes arrived. They sought and made no eye contact with each other.

"Your Honor, I have no real comments to make at this time. The Debtors want to use cash for fifteen days, pending a final hearing. Mr. Dewey, the owner of Veridical, has reviewed the spreadsheet. He advises me that the expenses are what they are and understands that they need to be paid to keep the doors open in the short term. We will leave for another day the lien issues and whether BJB can, in fact, operate in a way that will keep the doors open in the longer term. I'll review the Court's ruling in these other cases you mentioned. And the budget, as I am sure the Court observed, provides for no payments to Veridical." Fuentes stopped, stood even straighter and gave the appearance that he was about to deliver a stern lecture, and said, "That may be the status quo for a brief period in these cases, but is unsustainable in our estimation."

Judge Robertson noted the sternness in Fuentes's voice and filed it away as something to deal with … just not today. Instead, Judge Robertson said simply, "Thank you, Mr. Fuentes."

Fuentes returned to his seat and Judge Robertson delivered his ruling. "The Court approves the Cash Usage Motion and authorizes the Debtors to operate under the terms of the budget attached for the next fifteen days, or until we have the next hearing, whichever is later. We'll set another hearing, that one evidentiary, and notify the parties of the setting. Mr. Fuentes, if after you read my prior ruling, you wish to take issue with its application to these cases, file a brief seven days before the next hearing, and Ms. Jones, you may file a response three days thereafter. If you file no brief, Mr. Fuentes, I'll consider its absence to be your client's capitulation on the post-bankruptcy lien issue."

After the ruling, 3J presented the remaining perfunctory motions, and the Court authorized BJB to make payroll, pay critical vendors, and deal with utility companies.

Judge Robertson then asked 3J, "Since these were quick-file cases, Ms. Jones, when can you reasonably file the rest of the customary filing papers – all the schedules and statements of affairs in particular?"

"Filing them in the next few days will not be a problem, Your Honor."

"Excellent, thank you. Unless there is anything else, we will be adjourned," Judge Robertson announced. As he and his law clerk rose to leave, 3J and Fuentes simultaneously said, "Nothing further, Your Honor."

CHAPTER 8

Friday, November 3, 2023

UPON RETURNING TO HIS chambers with Jennifer Cuello, the Judge removed and hung his black robe, sat down behind his desk and Jennifer took her place in the club chair in front of his desk.

Judge Robertson leaned back in his chair. "Your first Chapter 11, first day motion hearing, Jennifer. What did you think?"

"All interesting and new to me, of course. Ms. Jones seems very poised."

"She is good at her trade, and a regular here in the courthouse. She knows what she is doing. What did you think of Fuentes?"

"A little stern, but he came across as knowledgeable," Jennifer observed, as she frowned ever so slightly. Jennifer was a recent grad from the University of Kansas School of Law, passing the bar exam a mere month prior, and starting her clerkship just a week before the BJB hearing. She was short – five feet two inches tall – and one hundred twenty pounds; she had long dark hair and dark, piercing eyes with naturally full, long eyelashes, and thick eyebrows. She was a first-generation American, her parents having immigrated to the United States some twenty-five years before from Nicaragua. She had graduated second in her law school class and was articulate, as Judge Robertson expected of someone with her class standing. Most importantly, when the Judge had interviewed her, he'd instantly felt comfortable with her demeanor and her stated work ethic. He had concluded that she would be a great addition to his small team.

"Agreed. Could you please get a little info on him from Google searches? Years out of law school; Martindale Hubbard rating; news articles about him, if any. Bankruptcy experience. You get the idea."

"For certain, Judge. Shouldn't take too long." Jennifer paused. She had a question on her mind, but wasn't sure how to phrase it. After a moment, she ventured forward. "Judge, on the issue of whether Veridical has a lien on the post-bankruptcy cash generated in the businesses, since you've already ruled on that issue, why did you invite Fuentes to submit a brief?"

"Great question. I'm unlikely to change my mind from what I've already ruled, but maybe he knows something I don't. Maybe they handle this issue differently in Chicago and, if so, I'd be curious to know how. Maybe these businesses are somehow distinguishable from my prior restaurant cases. Who knows? I don't mind giving him a chance to ponder and analyze. Like I said, in the end, I'm not likely to change my mind, which means Veridical is going to be out of luck for a while in these cases."

"I see," Jennifer said as she absorbed the Judge's thinking. "Do you need any research on this issue or do you just want to wait until we see what Fuentes comes up with?"

"The latter for now. You have enough on your plate in your first week on the job. There'll be plenty to sink your teeth into in these cases in due course."

"Very well. Thanks," Jennifer said with more than a hint of relief in her voice.

Judge Robertson smiled at her. He remembered the feeling of being overwhelmed during his first several months after he took the bench; private self-doubt as to whether he could be a good judge and perform the duties of a member of the federal judiciary.

He had taken the bench after a long career as a bankruptcy lawyer in Kansas City at a time when he had begun to question his continued practice as a lawyer. At that point, he felt he had moved, once again, into a period of career assessment, a syndrome he believed almost every lawyer went through more than once in their career. Eventually, after considerable soul-searching, he came to look upon the switch from bankruptcy lawyer to bankruptcy judge as a chance to hit his professional life reset button and start anew. He realized the switch could be a huge mistake – he had a good commercial and bankruptcy law practice going, lots of clients, good cases, and decent partners and colleagues at the law firm. He knew he would give most of that up, but he decided to trust his instincts, in what turned out to be a spot-on decision. He fit perfectly into the judiciary, and quickly validated to the other judges in the Western District courthouse that their recommendation, and the circuit court of appeals' selection, were right – uncontroversial, hardworking, practical, patient, and not so far removed as time went on that he forgot how hard it was to practice bankruptcy law and appear regularly in court in front of a bankruptcy judge. The regulars at the courthouse respected and admired him and looked forward to appearing before him. They also enjoyed talking with him when he lingered in the courtroom after a hearing.

Continuing to smile, Judge Robertson said to Jennifer, "Don't worry. In a month or so, you'll be an old hand at your important piece of how this chambers works. Don't rush it. Soak it all in and try to enjoy it. There are very few bankruptcy judicial law clerk positions in the country – only three here in the Western District – and you hold one. Relish it, my friend."

Jennifer smiled and nodded her head in agreement. "Thanks for putting your trust in me, Judge."

"Absolutely," the Judge replied quickly.

Jennifer left to start her search to gather information about Alexander Fuentes, and when she left, Judge Robertson returned to his stack of motions, proposed orders, and briefs to read. *Like traffic on the other side of Metcalf Boulevard at night,* he thought. *The headlights just keep coming, one after the other.* He smiled to himself. *And I love it!*

3J and Pascale walked back to the Greene Madison offices. When they arrived, he followed her into her office where she sat down at her desk and surveyed the many unopened emails displayed on her monitor. Over the years, Pascale had regularly – and wistfully – told her about the days before email and texts and mobile phones. 3J would grimace and ask, "How ever did you practice law?" Pascale would typically reply, "How ever did the human race live from day to day without connectivity?" As 3J surveyed her in-box, however, she thought, *I'd be willing to try a day or two with no connectivity before I completely condemn the days before the internet and mobile phones as ancient history!*

"Have you given any thought to possible restructuring suggestions we could present to the Rapinoes?" Pascale asked.

"Not just yet, but we need to turn our attention to that element pretty quickly," 3J responded. "I mean, despite what Fuentes said in court this morning, we have a lender who wants out and, frankly, we have clients who want a new lender. Keeping these two groups married in their debtor-creditor relationship worries me, a great deal. Maybe we can help the Rapinoes find a take-out lender and offer Dewey passage out …

of course, at something less than a hundred cents on the dollar," 3J said, developing a slow, lengthening smile and raising her eyebrows.

"Discounts are always nice," Pascale confirmed. "Let's get the rest of the papers finalized and filed, see if there is going to be a cash battle, and really start to zero in on the restructuring vs. new loan issue, eh?"

"Agree completely. So far, things have gone more smoothly than I would've expected for quick-file cases. Hopefully, that continues," 3J said as her computer dinged, announcing the arrival of yet another email. She sighed and repeated, "Hopefully."

Sometimes, what we hope for and what we get could not be more disparate. 3J was about to find out that the BJB and Rapinoes cases would not be smooth-as-glass proceedings.

A few hours later, 3J's paralegal emailed 3J and Pascale with information about Alexander Fuentes – the same information that Cuello would find and deliver to Judge Robertson.

The email explained that Fuentes graduated fifth in his class at The Loyola School of Law in Chicago. He grew up in a middle-class, stable household on the south side of Chicago; Puerto Rican descent. On graduating from law school, he took a job first in Chicago's Public Defender's office, and later made the switch to a medium-sized firm in Chicago, turning his focus from criminal to bankruptcy law. *Probably good in court,* 3J thought, *because of his criminal practice.*

He had a rating from the principal attorney rating service in the country – Martindale Hubbell – of "AV," the highest rating given by the service. In her search of the court records on the national search service, PACER, the paralegal found numerous cases in which Fuentes appeared throughout the country. There were no disciplinary proceedings against him, and recently, he had left his firm to open his own shop as a solo practitioner.

Pretty plain vanilla, 3J thought. *I wonder how Fuentes hooked up with this Dewey character and why Dewey went with a Chicago attorney, instead of one in Kansas City?*

CHAPTER 9

Phillip Dewey Recalls Friday, November 3, 2023

AFTER THE FIRST DAY of hearings, I met with my new lawyer in a meeting room at the courthouse to discuss next steps. He was very ... well, lawyer-like. I know these professional creatures are a necessary evil, especially because we all live by a social contract and we therefore live in a society of rules and laws. But in my experience, they can be a significant evil nonetheless. When I deal with these creatures, I always find it hard to not only hear what they say, but truly to listen and comprehend. I keep thinking of one of those novelty coffee mugs that might say, *What a lawyer says – "we will present this and ipso facto, the Court will find and conclude" and what a client hears – "blah blah blah."*

I wanted to listen to Fuentes less than he wanted to listen to himself. After a few minutes, I interrupted him and said, "Alexander, I need to get to a meeting. As we have discussed, let's keep the costs in check, but let's not give in to the Rapinoes if we have a leg to stand on. I don't want to pursue any Hail Mary strategies, but I don't want to leave any valid arguments on the table either. Call me in the morning to discuss further, if that fits with your schedule and your needs."

"Absolutely, Mr. Dewey," Fuentes said and as he completed his short statement, I stood, turned, and left for the drive back to Hallbrook and the beginning of implementing my plan.

As I drove south to my home, I went over the plan in my mind, which I had named "Project Dis," short for disinformation. The project was really quite simple and straightforward; the best plans always are. My internet guru would set up fake accounts on Facebook, Instagram, LinkedIn, Reddit, Twitter, and any other social media platforms he could recommend. He would then use the accounts to begin to first dribble, and then flow, and ultimately cascade, disinformation about the Rapinoes and BJB. The principal purpose of the disinformation would be to sow seeds of doubt with patrons – that they should not reserve concert seats far in advance because BJB was going to fail quite soon and they would lose their advance ticket purchase money. Similarly, he would call into question whether any music acts could book performances into the future because the bookings would have to be canceled when BJB failed. Last, he would begin a campaign of saying that the Rapinoes and BJB don't pay their debts back. This last piece was particularly satisfying to me, as it is exactly how I felt and exactly why I told the Rapinoes that they would follow the terms of the loan documents to the letter.

It was my strong view that I had a right to say whatever I wanted about the Rapinoes. After all, just like Mr. Fuentes said in court, I had not made a demand, sued anyone, or sought the appointment of a receiver.

While Joshua really did not care about the whole affair, he asked me why I would take steps to injure the Rapinoes' business and bruise their reputation – wouldn't that diminish the chances for repayment? Ahhh. Good questions, indeed ... but not well thought through. Sometimes Joshua was superficial in his analysis and binary in his views: good and evil; pain and pleasure; safety and danger. But he was entitled to an answer, and I was happy to provide one. The object of my campaign, I told him, was to convince the Rapinoes to sell my real estate collateral when their business no longer had any cash flow. Proceeds from the real estate sales would then repay me. If they dug in their feet, and refused to sell, then the campaign would simply run its course and hasten the demise of their businesses. Then I would foreclose on the real estate, and get repayment from the sale proceeds that way.

And, of course, they could always choose to repay me from their personal fortune. When I last met with the Rapinoes, I told them clearly that I expected payment in full, and if that meant from their personal fortune, then so be it. Ms. Rapinoe informed me that there was no longer a personal fortune, that in the year since they had submitted financials to Veridical, they had drained virtually all of their wealth to fund the clubs through the pandemic and its aftermath. Perhaps ... and perhaps not. My view has always been that all members of the wealthy sodality keep a hidden trove for rainy days like the pandemic, almost as if it was an admission requirement to join the moneyed cohort. The Rapinoes merely needed to access their own hidden cache; and if, by some happenstance, they had no such hidden reserves, then shame on them, for acting in a manner different from any other member of the wealthy class I had ever met.

My information systems and internet guru, Edmond Richardsen and his small tech company Dark Moons Technology, would run the plan for me. Edmond split his time between servicing his traditional clients and his life on the internet. He sported several tattoos on his forearms, rarely visible because he typically wore starched white long-sleeved shirts. But I have seen them. One was the word "hope," with a semicolon at the end of the word. Edmond informed me some years ago that the semicolon symbolized the importance of believing that he wasn't at an end, but rather a new beginning. Another was what he called a Zen circle – an incomplete circle. He said it represented the universe and inner strength and illumination. The illumination angle was of interest, given that his work for me involved stealth and hiding in the darkness – anything *but* illumination.

We met at an SLU alumni event. He was unremarkable save for his mastery of all things tech. He called me Dewey – and while I rarely liked such methods of familiarity, I didn't object; privately, I even liked it. Edmond was remarkably sophisticated, but had an odd way of communicating which often grated on me, but he did good, discrete work, so I refrained from objecting.

Joshua told me from time to time that he did not trust Edmond. Whenever I met with or talked to Edmond, I could feel Joshua peer out from his resting place with narrowed eyes as he assessed him. I always noted Joshua's views; he had good instincts and was rarely wrong. But sometimes, when it came to business matters, I overruled Joshua. I had to. This was one of those occasions. I was the businessman, not him. I alone had an MBA.

I had engaged Edmond's services from time to time over the years to help with – let's call them, *unusual* – technological endeavors, including one which was similar to what I had in mind for the Rapinoes. He was one of my valued vendors providing necessary services to me from time to time. I paid Edmond in cryptocurrency tokens for the less traditional services he provided to me, which I was certain he deposited in an unreported, Dark Web cryptowallet.

He was due to meet me at my house an hour after I'd left Fuentes, to discuss the plan.

When I arrived home, I had a few minutes to prepare for my guest. I looked over to the decades-old vessel sitting on my neo-modern, stylish mantle and said, "Not to worry, Mother. I have things in hand. An old colleague will be helping me."

Joshua rarely took part in my discussions with Mother. Indeed, he and I talked about it only once. He chastised me for continuing any relationship with her. *She is our mother*, I pointed out. *No longer*, he replied angrily, judgment dripping from his tone. I so wanted the three of us to get along. I knew I would have to continue to work on the complicated three-way affiliation.

I decided to hold my meeting with Edmond in the basement. Promptly at 1 p.m., Edmond presented himself at my front door. We shook hands, and I led him to the basement conference table. Edmond looked a little older and more weathered than the last time we had worked together on a discreet project, such as the one I was about to reveal to him. His dark brown hair was now a little thinner, and a good deal grayer. Overall, life looked to have been hard on poor Edmond. *Oh well*, I thought. I wasn't hiring him for his looks.

Edmond spoke first, in a soft voice. "Good to see you again, Dewey. It'll be a pleasure to work with you, as always, on one of your special assignments. One hundred percent."

I responded, "But, my dear Edmond, you don't even know what the project is."

"Oh, no worries, Dewey. I'm sure it'll be fine and a pleasure." Why did I enjoy the company of this business associate? Perhaps because he was sufficiently subservient. I do so enjoy working with subservient sorts such as this curious individual.

I proceeded to outline for Edmond the parameters of Project Dis. As I spoke, he leaned forward and listened carefully.

He took no notes. He well knew that notes in this facet of his line of work were a potential liability. When I concluded my presentation, I asked, "Any questions?"

"Just two, Dewey. Everything you want is one hundred percent do-able. Not a problem. But ... are you going to write the text for what the posts should say?" Edmond asked slowly, appearing to hope he would not offend me.

No offense taken. "Indeed I will. I would like us to use our usual system of burner phone communication. I will feed you the content in that manner. Is that acceptable?"

"Works for me, Dewey," Edmond said, relieved he would be the tech guy and not the wordsmith. "Second question. I just want to confirm that if anything in this project goes awry, you will hold me harmless from damages, lawsuits, and the like? Just like last time."

I did not mind Edmond seeking to clarify the arrangement. Precision is what we should always strive to achieve.

When Edmond posed his second question, I could hear Joshua utter a low moan, perhaps a warning to me. I ignored Joshua. There was time to appease him later.

"Of course. Most assuredly, Edmond. But please know, I do not expect there will be anything to hold you harmless from. It will all go swimmingly, just like our last project."

"I hope so, but I can't be too careful these days, Dewey."

"I understand, Edmond."

"When do we start?"

"Monday morning, just after midnight," I directed. "Will that afford you sufficient time to set up the accounts you will use?"

"One hundred percent." When he agreed, everything was *one hundred percent*. If he couldn't do something or if he disagreed, he would say *negatory*. Once one understood Edmond's cadence, it was easy enough to follow along.

"Splendid, Edmond," I said. "Your renumeration will be the usual for this type of project, plus 15% more than our last engagement."

"One hundred percent, Dewey, and thank you for your generosity."

"My pleasure. Edmond, this is an important project for me. Please do not let me down, and please remember, burner phones only."

"One hundred percent, Dewey."

"Very well then. Let me get you back to the front door and on your way."

After Edmond departed, I reviewed the particulars of Project Dis once again. All the details. Everything I'd planned. Always good to take it from the top and make sure I missed nothing. It was a solid plan that should reasonably quickly bring the Rapinoes to their senses, if not their knees. *Knees are a good place for borrowers to be*, I thought. I looked over to Mother on the mantle and saw no need to talk to her. I knew she would agree.

CHAPTER 10

Monday, November 6, 2023

JENNIFER CUELLO WAS AN early riser, and her usual routine involved a two-mile run, then coffee in her kitchen and a quick review of her various social media accounts before heading to the courthouse and her law clerk position with Judge Robertson. Since starting her new job, she had begun to follow bankruptcy issues being discussed in social media. Normally, these led to topics dry to anyone other than a budding bankruptcy lawyer. The posts covered the gamut, such as drug companies who marketed opioids and filed for Chapter 11 relief to try to manage the many suits and investigations; how many consumers filed for bankruptcy protection during the pandemic; discussions about the safety net bankruptcy provided; and predictions for a fresh wave of business bankruptcies as the world adjusted to Covid's new status as an endemic, rather than a pandemic. Jennifer found the level of social media discussion and treatment of bankruptcy fascinating, albeit not quite as robust as the strident and divisive political discourse that dominated social media.

Jennifer had a Reddit account, and had found several bankruptcy-related subreddits whose posts she frequently read. Normally, the subreddit posts were plain vanilla. But this morning, as she sat at her small kitchen table in her North

Kansas City apartment, she froze as she read a series of posts, the first of which had dropped just after midnight, all about BJB and the Rapinoes. In increasingly vitriolic language, the posts all challenged the "real" reasons the Rapinoes sought bankruptcy protection. Each suggested, in not-so-subtle terms, that no one should trust the Rapinoes, and that no one – NO ONE – should purchase advance tickets for any jazz shows at any of the clubs because the businesses would soon fail and there would be no refunds of ticket sale proceeds.

"Holy shit!" Jennifer said softly, and quickly poured her remaining coffee down the sink. She grabbed her backpack, raced outside to her 2012 Subaru Impreza, and headed off to the courthouse. The drive across town seemed to take hours, but she eventually arrived, parked her car, and sprinted into the courthouse, flashing her credentials to the marshals to speed through security on the main floor, and grabbed the elevator to ride to the sixth floor. A right turn off the elevator followed by a right down the hall, and she was finally at the door to the chambers. She keyed in the security code to Judge Robertson's chambers and hustled to his office, where she found him at his desk with his oversized coffee mug and the usual piles of papers to review.

She knocked. "Judge, do you have a moment?"

Judge Robertson looked up and found a very flustered, out of breath law clerk peering in from outside his office door. "Absolutely. What's up? You look serious."

Jennifer extracted her laptop from her backpack, set it up on the Judge's large dark mahogany desk, and when she quickly found the subreddit page with the discussion of BJB, she turned the laptop around, saying nothing so Judge Robertson could read the post for himself.

He reached for his reading glasses, squinted at the screen, and asked, "What am I looking at here, Jennifer?"

"This is a subreddit page, normally a community of people interested in the bankruptcy process. Most posts provoke a lively discussion about bankruptcy issues in society that I follow; bankruptcy geeks and dorks, I suppose." She looked at the Judge to make sure she hadn't offended him by her slang, and, reassured, she continued. "Usually, the posts are generic in nature and, frankly, pretty dry. But this morning, I found these posts you're looking at, that appear to have dropped very early this morning. They're all about BJB and the Rapinoes. They're basically a call to BJB patrons to stay away from the clubs."

The Judge read the posts as he listened to Jennifer's explanation. As he finished, he whistled softly and said, "Wow. I don't think I've ever seen anything quite like this before. Parties-in-interest don't usually resort to social media to air their complaints about bankruptcy debtors – although in the modern era, I guess, it's bound to happen and maybe nothing should surprise me. Of all the debtors in the country, though, I wonder why BJB and the Rapinoes?"

The Judge slowly turned the laptop back to Jennifer, leaned back in his chair, clasped his hands behind his head and swiveled his chair around to the windows behind his desk that overlooked the Missouri River and the northlands beyond. After a few minutes, he spun back around to face Jennifer, now sitting, waiting for him to think and speak.

"Can you do a couple of things, Jennifer? First, I assume you have other social media accounts besides Reddit?"

"Yes. I'm mostly a voyeur on social; I read but I don't post, at least not too much. But I follow some topics on Twitter, Facebook, Instagram, and LinkedIn – to different degrees."

"Great. That's what I was hoping for. I don't have any accounts on any of these platforms. Can you please search the platforms for any current posts about BJB and the Rapinoes? Print out what you find, and then let's gather up again and see what we have here."

"Absolutely. Give me an hour or so."

"Thanks."

Jennifer wheeled quickly and headed out the door to her small office to begin her searches. After she left, Judge Robertson set aside the pile of motions, briefs, and proposed orders on his desk and instead directed his thinking to the implications of the subreddit posts. Anyone familiar with the Bankruptcy Code well knew that the filing of a bankruptcy case froze all efforts to collect a debt the debtor owed. At the same time, there were limits to the automatic stay, and opinions from bankruptcy judges – on struggling to balance creditors' actions with the clear automatic stay prohibitions – filled the casebooks. So, for example, the automatic stay did not typically end a criminal prosecution, as long as the intent of the prosecution was not the collection of a debt. And he had recently read a law journal article about the intersection of the First Amendment's protection of free speech and freedom of the press with the automatic stay's prohibitions. At the time, he'd finished the article thinking, *Fascinating. So what am I supposed to do? Look into the creditor's brain and heart and determine magically if their speech was intended to collect a debt – prohibited – or just the exercise of their First Amendment right to speak their mind and air their opinion? Not looking forward to that type of trial.*

He now realized the subreddit posts found by Jennifer might be the beginning of just such an issue in the BJB case. More significantly, he noted to himself that it was an odd series of posts. *Any creditor hoping BJB could pay back its debts should be loath to hurt BJB's business,* he mused. *At least, any sane creditor.*

Within ninety minutes, Jennifer returned to the Judge's office to find him again staring out his windows. She had found similar posts on each of the additional social platforms she searched. In addition, some form of SEO was at play, she thought, because already a Google search for "BJB" listed the malicious posts at the top of the search hits, driving down hits about BJB's business, upcoming concerts, and links to BJB's website. BJB's business, its award-winning food and the many scheduled jazz concerts, were no longer displayed as the most important hits; instead, a Google search quickly "advised" the searcher to be wary of spending any money at a BJB club.

"Is there any way to tell from what you've found, Jennifer, who is behind these posts?"

"Way over my pay grade, I'm afraid, Judge."

"Hmmm. I see."

"But I'm sure you've read all about fake accounts, and the dissemination of disinformation on the internet. The articles I've read focus on foreign nations using these fake accounts to affect American public sentiment, but I'd expect fraudsters could use fake accounts for other purposes."

"But why? A competitor maybe?"

"Could be, but from what I've read about BJB, it's unique in the Kansas City market, and really doesn't have competing jazz clubs to deal with; at least, not at the moment, here in the metro."

"Thanks for all of this, Jennifer. I need to think about this a little more. I wonder if Ms. Jones and Mr. Pascale are aware of this development? Not sure if it's my role to tell them. I need to collect my thoughts and try to figure out the proper role of the judiciary in this kind of matter. In the meantime, can you monitor for additional posts?"

"Will do," and Jennifer returned to her office.

After a few moments of contemplation, Judge Robertson picked up his phone and called one of the other bankruptcy judges in the courthouse, Judge Kenneth Redstone. Judge Redstone had been on the bench about five years longer than Judge Robertson, and the two had struck up an immediate friendship as Judge Robertson took the bench. Their backgrounds, however, could not be more different. Judge Redstone was African American, one of the few black bankruptcy lawyers in Kansas City, who had plied his trade at the largest firm in Kansas City before applying for the bankruptcy judge's position. He grew up in poverty on the east side of Kansas City, attended public schools, graduated *Summa Cum Laude* from Washington University in St. Louis, and then on to Columbia University for his law degree, before returning to Kansas City. His reputation before his judicial appointment was that he was sharper than a Wilkinson sword, opinionated, and respected; he was commanding.

As a judge, his reputation was one of hard work and respect for those practitioners who appeared before him, who he deemed to be hardworking as well. He had disdain for those practitioners who came to his Court unprepared, and he didn't try to hide it.

"Kenneth? Daniel here. I have a problem I'm wrestling with and could use a consult. Any time for a walk and talk over the lunch hour?"

"Daniel! For you? Of course. Today works. Noon?"

"Great, and thanks. Pick you up at noon."

Promptly at noon, Judge Robertson arrived at Judge Redstone's chambers, and the two headed downstairs for their walk together. On this occasion, they headed south toward Ninth Street, and then west past the Kansas City Public Library's main branch, housed in the former First National Bank building, with its easily recognizable one-story garage's community bookshelf theme. Then over to the Cathedral of the Immaculate Conception and its iconic bright gold dome, once the site of the Chouteau Church erected by a French fur trader in 1822; then up a steep incline to Quality Hill, sitting on a two hundred-foot bluff overlooking the West Bottoms below and the Kansas River beyond; what was likely the very spot visited by Lewis and Clark in 1806, on their return from their excursion to the Pacific Ocean, proximate to the American Hereford Association's large fiberglass statue of a bull, and near the streets where the richest and most famous of the Kansas City residents once called home during Quality Hill's zenith. They had made this trek before, and the overlook provided quiet solitude and a place for the two bankruptcy judges to talk in private.

As they walked to the overlook, they caught up on family, the Chiefs, the Royals, Sporting Kansas City, and all other things Kansas City. Once at their destination, they sat, alone, as they looked out over the view. Judge Robertson explained the social media posts, and his dilemma over whether it was his role to inform the relevant parties of these events.

Judge Redstone listened quietly and when his colleague finished, he said, "I am reminded of a little courthouse lore from some years ago: way back when, you may remember hearing that the Justice Department caught Sears in a scheme to violate the automatic stay and the effect of a bankruptcy discharge nationwide. While the Bankruptcy Code may have prevented collection of the debt, nevertheless, Sears would contact the debtor – not debtors' counsel – and work out a 'new arrangement' for payment of a debt the uninformed consumer didn't owe anymore. Sears counted on the unsophistication of the consumer. And it worked for a good long while, until one day, it didn't work anymore."

"I never had a Sears case, but I certainly heard all about it. Pretty bodacious."

Judge Redstone's gaze drifted to the Hereford Bull statue overlooking the West Bottoms. The fibreglass-and-steel bull safeguarded the memory of the slaughter of tens of thousands of cattle driven east across Kansas to Kansas City during the Wild West Days to feed America's insatiable desire to eat beef, all made possible by the construction of Kansas City's Hannibal Bridge in 1869 as the first Missouri River crossing, and the resulting development of Kansas City as a major rail hub.

"Yes, it was. And lucrative. Well, after the Sears story quieted down, one of our predecessor Kansas City bankruptcy judges got wind that something like that might be going on with a large Pennsylvania bank who had done business here in Kansas City. So what did the Judge do? He issued an order, all by himself, directing the bank, its counsel, the trustee, and debtor's counsel, to appear in his Court; he ordered the bank to show cause why he shouldn't hold it in contempt and fine it."

"So he did all of that on his own impetus?"

"Exactly."

"Was that kosher?"

"Well, as I am sure you're learning, kosher is oftentimes in the eye of the judicial beholder."

"Did any of those parties complain about the process?"

"No, and I'm sure none of them had the bad sense to challenge the Judge's order itself. They already had an angry judge on their hands; no reason to poke the beast any more than necessary."

"Kenneth, how do you know all of this?"

"You're looking at the bank's lawyer, Daniel."

"Ahha. So not just courthouse lore. You are Aesop himself in this fable."

"Guilty as charged," Judge Redstone said as he smiled.

The two judges sat in silence while Judge Robertson absorbed the story and tried to sort out how to apply it to his own situation.

Judge Redstone continued, "Our alum judge told me after the fact that he felt justified in taking matters into his own hands because he believed he was protecting the integrity of the bankruptcy system. He hadn't gone out looking for an issue to require him to intervene in an ongoing case, the whole matter just fell into his lap. Yet he also felt that one of his jobs as bankruptcy judge was to ensure that no one felt they had license to gig the system. He said his job was to enforce the bankruptcy rules."

"I see. So, if I go that route, I'd step in and at least advise all the parties of what we've found."

"Affirmative."

"Recommendations?"

"If it was me, I'd invite the major players in the case to a chambers conference and reveal what Jennifer found."

Judge Robertson absentmindedly stroked his chin with his left hand as he nodded his head and said, "Sound advice, as always, Kenneth … Sound advice."

The two rose and headed back to the courthouse, stopping at a favorite coffee shop near the former Folgers Coffee roasting plant on Broadway for a cup of joe and a sandwich, before finishing their walk and talk.

Judge Robertson thought, *When I took the bench, I shrunk down my universe of colleagues from everyone at my firm and in the practice of law with whom I hung around, to just those in the black robes and their law clerks. Thank God for Kenneth!*

Upon arriving back at his chambers, Judge Robertson told Jennifer the Sears story, said he wasn't ready yet to point fingers and threaten to hold people in contempt, but he liked the idea of a chambers conference. He asked her to draft a notice of a chambers conference to inform the parties of the smear campaign, making sure to be specific in the notice of the social media discoveries. Moments after he gave Jennifer the assignment, she returned with new posts – this time, advising live music acts not to book with BJB because the company would shortly fail in bankruptcy. Jennifer added the latest post to the notice.

3J's laptop dinged softly, alerting her to a new electronic filing in the BJB case. She opened the email and clicked on the link to read Judge Robertson's notice. A chambers conference early in a Chapter 11 case was not all that unusual in one of his cases; the content of this notice, however, was like nothing 3J had read before. She quickly got online herself, and was shocked to see the malicious posts. Undoubtedly, this development would be injurious to the business, and would not bode well for the Rapinoes' efforts to bolster the veracity of the projections that would serve as the keystone to a plan confirmation effort.

3J looked up to see a worried Pascale leaning on her door-jamb. Pascale said in a husky whisper, "Motherfucker!"

"Couldn't have said it better. What the hell is this, Bill?"

"This is trouble, with a capital T, right here in River City."

3J did not count herself a fan of Broadway musicals and she ignored the theatrical reference. Instead, she said, "Well, somebody, or bodies, has it in for the Rapinoes, and they're not fooling around. For fuck's sake! This'll be devastating to the business if this catches fire on the internet." She paused and added, "What I'm worried about is that, from my non-tech vantage point, *everything* catches fire on the internet."

"But who?" Pascale asked.

Pointing a left pointer at Pascale, 3J said, "That Dewey guy comes to mind, but no lender would be dumb enough to pull a stunt like this. Violating the automatic stay right out of the box."

"Well, is it a violation? Or just an angry creditor voicing an opinion and warning patrons?"

"How the hell could that be the reason a creditor would post something like this? A public service announcement? No fuckin' way. It's an attempt to collect a debt, plain and simple, by leveraging the Rapinoes with disinformation," 3J said, her ire and volume rising as her choice of descriptive words turned vulgar.

"That's our story, for sure. First, we've got to figure out who's behind this. It's almost as if our perpetrator wanted to get caught quickly. Nothing secret about posting on the internet for all to see."

"Or, whoever is doing this thinks they're too damn smart to get caught," 3J offered.

"We'll figure this out. We just need to get mobilized," Pascale said. "Can't sneak the sunrise past a rooster; and can't sneak the cheese past a rat."

"Who's the rat and who's the rooster?" 3J quipped, feigning disgust at Pascale's comment.

"I'm happy to be the rat on this one," Pascale offered. "We'll sort it all out."

CHAPTER 11

Wednesday, November 8, 2023

TWO DAYS LATER, 3J and Pascale were sitting in Judge Robertson's chambers along with the Rapinoes, Jennifer Cuello, Alexander Fuentes, and assorted creditor representatives. Everyone looked somber, including the Judge. In the two days since the Judge's notice went out, half a dozen new social media posts had been spotted, ratcheting up the stakes, and clearly signaling that the disinformation campaign was not fleeting. The latest round of posts stated that the Rapinoes and BJB didn't pay their debts back. Again, a statement of opinion – or perhaps, from the poster's perspective, a statement of fact, but 3J wondered whether she could show it was an attempt to collect a debt, rather than an exercise of free speech. She wasn't sure how the chambers conference would unfold.

Judge Robertson spoke. "First, thanks to all of you for coming over here on such short notice. Mr. Fuentes, you could have appeared remotely, but I am glad you could hop a plane and get here."

Fuentes nodded once in acknowledgement of the Judge's comments. The Judge continued, "When we discovered these posts initially, I was unclear what my role would be in the absence of a motion pending before me asking me to take action. But on the other hand, I felt it was incumbent on me to bring this to everyone's attention, so that I was not the sole keeper of the kind of information that could alter the course of these bankruptcy cases."

3J listened closely to the Judge explain his thought process, and what appeared to start out as a dilemma for him.

Fuentes took notes on his yellow legal pad without looking up and without making eye contact with anyone present. The Rapinoes looked unexpectedly composed as they listened to Judge Robertson, who continued, "Now I have brought the matter to your attention and I take no position, and will have no further comments, at this time. I just felt it was my duty, as a gatekeeper of the automatic stay and all things bankruptcy, to share this matter with you. I recognize the notice was out of the ordinary, but so are these posts."

The Judge paused and surveyed the scene in his conference room. The facial expressions he saw ran the gamut from poker-faced, to concerned, to no eye contact whatsoever. *Does someone in this room have a client responsible for these posts?*

3J spoke. "We have no questions at this time, Your Honor, and thank you for bringing this to our attention. We are, of course, quite concerned with how these posts will impact our clients' business, and we are most assuredly suspicious about the motivations of whoever is behind the posts. But we have some legwork to do now, before we take any action."

"I understand, counsel," the Judge responded. He looked around the table to see if anyone else wished to be heard. No one spoke, and Fuentes continued to jot on his pad. "Very well then. Thanks again for coming over, everyone, and we can adjourn this conference."

3J and Pascale exited the building, and selected Oak Street to walk south back to the Greene Madison building. Definitely a street that had seen better days, now populated with boarded-up storefronts, and older mid-rise, brick-facade buildings in need of tender loving care, in search of someone to give them that attention. 3J spoke first. "Pascale, I think we'll need to find the poster, sue him or her in Bankruptcy Court to enjoin them permanently from posting, and seek damages for the harm to the BJB business. As we file the suit, we'd also ask for a Temporary Restraining Order to stop the posts immediately."

"Completely agree, but to do that, we'll need to know who's doing it so we'll know who to sue."

3J nodded as she thought about how to find the poster. "I'm not an internet sleuth, but I'm feeling like that's what we need. I don't think the computer folks in our Information Systems department are set up for the kind of tech help we will need."

"No doubt," Pascale agreed. "I don't think we can ask them to help figure this out for us."

"I'm thinking we'll need an investigator, private eye type, to assist us, with a specialty in tech issues."

"Agreed. Any ideas who to hire? This kind of thing rarely arises in the life of a bankruptcy lawyer. I'm of the generation that lacks the required DNA strand to understand much about any tech, let alone social media."

3J said, "I do. I'm thinking of reaching out to a guy in New York City named Moses Aaronson."

"Who's that?"

"After the Witherman case ended, I had a drink with Jacob Steinert, First Commercial's final bankruptcy lawyer in that case."

Recalling the case, Pascale said, "Oh, sure. I remember his role. Poor bastard drew the short straw and had to try to manage his client's crazy special assets officer, Stacy Milnes, when she went off the rails in Robertson's courtroom. I didn't envy him. Solid attorney. Hard assignment, dealing with Stacy."

"Indeed. We were talking, and I wondered out loud how Milnes ever figured out what Witherman was doing." 3J stopped walking, turned to Pascale, and said, "Steinert said she used an old guy in New York – Moses Aaronson – to crack the mystery that was Quincy Witherman and the Swiss assets. Apparently, Aaronson has a team that he works with, including a tech wizard who's in London. Calls it the 'Moses Team.' This tech wizard was the one to get into Michaela Huld's computer and ultimately pieced it all together to bring down Witherman."

"Fascinating."

"I think we should reach out to this guy, Aaronson, and see if he has any interest in working for us. You know, switching teams to work for the good guys now."

"Sounds like a good idea. Let's call him when we get back to the shop," Pascale concurred.

When 3J and Pascale returned to their offices, they each had a voicemail from the Rapinoes. Together, they returned the calls on the speaker phones.

"Thanks for calling back," Adam said. "Look, we tried to appear calm and composed around the Judge's conference room table. And, from our years in the real estate development business, we're certainly no strangers to controversy and contentiousness. People get in our faces from time to time – tenants, creditors, mall patrons, city regulators, even mayors and city council. But when *they're* in your face, you know who they are, you know their beef, and you very well know the options available to handle the situation. This is different. This feels like a nameless, faceless adversary who's pursuing a vendetta, and we don't know who and we don't know why. It's like fighting a ghost and we don't like it at all."

"We hear you," 3J said. "We're putting together a plan to combat this and we'll know more, we hope, by the end of the day."

"That's good to hear," Bey chimed in. "But in the meantime, this new shitstorm is going to be bad for business. Real bad. In other words, it'll accomplish exactly what it was intended to: dramatically impede the prospect for our recovery."

3J assumed that everyone in real estate development knew how to cuss like a sailor when necessary, but Bey had not sworn in front of 3J and Pascale until this moment; her vulgar description of the situation drove home just how concerned the Rapinoes were about the posts. "Look, we share your concern and then some. Let's circle back up at the end of the day and we can report more to you then."

As the call ended, 3J looked at Pascale, frowned, looked concerned, shook her head, and sighed. "Not good, Bill. Not freakin' good at all."

Alexander Fuentes left the courthouse and ordered a ride share car to take him to the airport and the short Southwest Airlines flight back to Chicago. He found himself disturbed by the chambers conference. Not the conference itself; he liked a judge who felt comfortable gathering the parties around a conference room table to discuss relevant case issues. He wished more judges would avail themselves of the chambers conference judicial tool. No, that part was fine. What he found disturbing was the topic. Like Debtors' counsel, he had no idea what the Judge would say, only what the notice had cryptically reported. After receiving the notice and buying a seat on a flight to Kansas City, he'd forwarded the notice to Phillip Dewey and then called him to discuss. Dewey never answered, nor returned the call; not what Fuentes hoped for when starting a relationship with a new client.

Now, having heard the details of what was on Judge Robertson's mind, it concerned Fuentes that Dewey might have something to do with the smears. He had strict rules about clients following the law and refraining from seeking ways to bypass the Bankruptcy Code's requirements. *It better not be Dewey who's behind the posts. I've got no interest in navigating this case with such a client. None at all.*

As Fuentes entered the ride share car, he again checked his emails, voicemails, and texts, hoping to see a communication from Dewey but finding none. So, as his driver navigated north to I-29 and the Kansas City International Airport, Fuentes communicated with Dewey by text, email, and voicemail once again. The message was the same in all forms: "We need to talk IMMEDIATELY about a troubling new development in the Rapinoe bankruptcy cases. I must have a phone call with you first thing in the morning. I will call you at 8:30 a.m. – please take my call. Alexander."

Fuentes realized it was forward of him to dictate that there would be a call, rather than be politic and ask if a call would work. But sometimes politic takes a back seat to necessity, and he really did need to speak with Dewey immediately. To his surprise, when Fuentes arrived at his airport terminal to await the departure of his flight, his phone rang: it was Dewey calling. Fuentes had forty-five minutes before his flight would board, so he walked to a part of the gate area where he could be alone and took the call.

"Alexander Fuentes."

"Mr. Fuentes, Phillip Dewey here. I picked up your messages. Tomorrow doesn't work for me; I can speak now." Dewey believed he was a master in taking control and dictating the course of a conversation – specifically here, the timing. He didn't like attorneys who told him what to do or when to do it and was determined to make that crystal clear to Fuentes.

"Very well. The purpose of my messages is to let you know the latest development in the Rapinoe cases – it's got me on edge and more than a little concerned."

"Well, we certainly don't want you on edge," Dewey replied. In the absence of any inflection or emotion in his voice, Fuentes couldn't tell if Dewey was sincere or sarcastic.

Ignoring what may have been a snarky comment, he explained the revelation of the smear campaign. Dewey said nothing. Breaking the silence, Fuentes said, "The Bankruptcy Code has strict rules about what creditors can and can't do. I don't require much of clients, but I do insist that they must follow the Code's rules. No gigging the system …"

Dewey did not let Fuentes finish his sentence. "Mr. Fuentes, I feel like I should be offended by the question you are obviously leading up to. So go ahead, be bold. Take the initiative; ask me."

Dewey's tactic of going on the offensive caught Fuentes off-guard, and he blurted out, "Well, *are* you posting these smear posts?"

"Absolutely not, sir," he responded emphatically. He paused for emphasis, then continued, "And now I am officially offended. *I* have requirements of my lawyers, Mr. Fuentes. One is not to question my bona fides, as you just did. Another is not to tell me what to do or not do unless I seek your input and advice. In addition, if there is a smear campaign against the Rapinoes brewing, I would expect that our country's robust rules, ensuring freedom of speech to each and every one of its citizens, would protect whomever is behind it."

Fuentes found the reference to the First Amendment too curious for his taste. He thought for a moment before responding. "I will accept your response, Mr. Dewey. You may not agree, but we did need to have this discussion, uncomfortable as it may be. But please know that in my estimation, the First Amendment would not protect a smear campaign from the wrath of a bankruptcy judge charged with maintaining the integrity of the bankruptcy system through enforcement of the automatic stay."

"Again, offended, Mr. Fuentes."

Silence.

Dewey then delivered a not-too-veiled warning. "I am a respected businessperson and, frankly, *no one* talks to me as you have in this conversation. I will have to hope, having gotten this matter off your chest, you will have the good sense and decency to refrain from revisiting the topic – or the tone – again." Silence again. Dewey was pleased with himself and, believing he had Fuentes on the ropes, he continued, "I would hope you will be more careful in the future, lest you suffer the same fate as the Rapinoes. *You*, of course, would have no automatic stay to hide behind." If Fuentes was having the discussion in person, he would have seen Dewey's practiced, trademark smile revealing perfectly white teeth; one of Dewey's borrowers called it a forty-dollar smile, with a million-dollar message of sneering superiority.

The turn of the conversation stunned Fuentes, and he countered, "Isn't that an admission that you are somehow behind the smear? I could certainly take it that way."

"Not at all, sir. Not at all. And I repeat, I am *not*. You can take my words any way you choose to, but you'd be in the wrong if you conclude I have admitted anything. No sir, not at all." Before he continued, Dewey smacked his tongue on the roof of his mouth, then said, "But if some shadow creditor can post against the Rapinoes, it couldn't be terribly hard for a client to post about a former counsel in a way that might negatively impact his precious bankruptcy practice and brand new solo practice."

On the call, Fuentes could only hear Dewey's annoyingly calm and even-toned voice, and that annoying "tssk" sound. If they had been in the same room, however, he would have seen embers in Dewey's eyes, smoldering behind his irises. He decided to end the discussion. "I think we have covered all that we can today, Mr. Dewey. My plane is boarding. We can talk again if need be."

"Good day, sir," and Dewey hung up.

Fuentes turned to return to the gate seating area and sighed audibly to himself. *This is going to be one heck of a representation. I sure know how to pick 'em. And I sure don't believe Phillip Dewey one bit.*

When the phone call ended, Phillip Dewey paced the floor of his home, passing his many knick knacks, pieces of artwork and sculptures, selected by his designer without a great deal of consultation with him. "Whatever you pick out for me will be just fine," he had told the designer. "Just ensure they are expensive and noteworthy." His designer had intended the appointments to make his living quarters comfortable, but today, they served no purpose and he saw none of them as he paced.

The Judge had stumbled on to the postings, and Fuentes was now running with the issue, undoubtedly believing that he was behind them. Phillip had come close to becoming emotional in the call, despite his need to remain soft-spoken. It had been a trying few minutes and he was concerned that even if he fired Fuentes, that might not end the problem.

As he paced, Joshua peered out. He could feel Phillip's tension but, seeing no threats, stayed in the shadows.

Phillip paused his pacing to stare at the urn on the mantle containing Mother, the only piece in the living area not selected by his designer. He just glared at the vessel. He muttered, "Mother, maybe I was always a throwaway, a discard, but I survived and thrived. I learned to value money and I *will* get my money back."

Joshua listened to Phillip begin a conversation with Mother. He raged at Phillip. When he did, Phillip's irises darkened. It was usually Joshua's reaction to something Phillip did or said, or some situation Phillip got himself into that caused Joshua to become angry, and that anger manifested itself in the irises.

Phillip broke off his stare, resumed pacing and thought, *Keep your friends close and your enemies closer.* No, he would not fire Fuentes. He would keep Fuentes where he could keep track of the lawyer – in court, representing Veridical.

CHAPTER 12

Wednesday, November 8, 2023

3J ASKED HER PARALEGAL to find the investigator used by Stacy Milnes to bring down Quincy Witherman several years before. Within an hour, 3J had the phone number for Moses Aaronson and his email address. She debated whether to make an introduction by email, and in the end decided just to phone him. The phone rang twice before Aaronson picked up the phone and said, "Good morning. Moses Aaronson here. How may I be of service?" His voice was gravelly, and he cleared it as he concluded his greeting. 3J imagined him sitting in a Manhattan office, but Moses maintained no office apart from his small apartment in the Flatiron District of New York City. Instead, he sat in a wood and weathered leather chair at his old oak roll-top desk, complete with sun-bleached wooden bins for inbox and outbox papers, as the sun streamed in a large window. His small, faithful rat terrier mix dog, Emily, laid in his lap asleep as she basked in the late morning sun. Her morning ritual. Her white and brown fur was as soft and smooth as silk and Moses absentmindedly petted her as he worked.

"Mr. Aaronson, my name is Josephina Jones; I'm a bankruptcy attorney in Kansas City. You may not know me, but our paths crossed indirectly several years ago …"

Moses interrupted her, "Yes, yes. Indeed. I know *of* you: you were Quincy Witherman's attorney in his bankruptcy case. We may not have met, but our paths certainly crossed in that engagement." In his voice, 3J heard an older man who sounded educated, with a refined New York accent and a deliberate, unhurried way of speaking, in which he carefully enunciated all syllables. She knew from her get-together with Jacob Steinert that those in the know considered Aaronson a private eye's private eye, although he strongly pushed back at any suggestion that he was a traditional investigator. He didn't believe he solved mysteries, and he certainly didn't hide in the shadows with a camera, photographing rich men as they slinked around in sordid affairs outside the purview of their loyal spouses. Rather, Aaronson liked to tell people that his profession was to "shine light on that which is dark." He considered himself an intellectual in the business of investigation and illumination.

"Ahh, yes. Well, good to finally speak with you. You come highly recommended, and I find myself in need of investigatory assistance for my current bankruptcy clients, Bey and Adam Rapinoe, and their company, BJB. All are chapter 11 debtors here in Kansas City."

Moses listened patiently as he stroked Emily's ears absentmindedly. Occasionally, he took notes on an old-school yellow legal pad with his blue 1950s Parker fountain pen.

"What type of investigation, Ms. Jones?"

"Please, call me 3J. Everyone does."

"If it doesn't offend you, at this stage, I prefer Ms. Jones; formality shows my respect for my new clients. What type of investigation, please?"

3J explained the nature of the investigation. "The campaign of misinformation to discredit my clients will undoubtedly have a devastating impact on their business and could signal their financial demise. Unless we can stop this campaign, they may never get to the Chapter 11 plan phase of the case and could end up closing up their jazz clubs for good. Obviously, that would be a terrible outcome for them."

"I see. Do you suspect who is running this campaign?"

"They have lots of creditors and owe a good deal of money; about $17 million to one lender in particular. I can email you a list of all their creditors, with contact information as well as how much they're owed."

"Yes. That will be helpful. Where is the misinformation posted?"

"Pretty much on every social media platform we know of – Facebook, Twitter, Reddit, Instagram, LinkedIn. The posts are reaching many people, telling the public not to frequent the clubs, and musicians not to book gigs, and that the Rapinoes don't pay back their debts. One even called them deadbeats. Childish name-calling, but it has an effect. They're coming at the rate of two a day, and each day, the tone of the posts gets more and more strident."

"I see. Let me do a little digging and then we can speak again. My inclination is to involve a member of the Moses Team, as I call them, who specializes in the digital world – she actually worked extensively on the Witherman matter. There are ways to get to the bottom of these fake accounts that disseminate incorrect information to sway the public sentiment, and my colleague is a master at these kinds of things. She is in London, but in this day and age, one can sleuth in the digital world from anywhere one has an internet connection."

"That would be wonderful, Mr. Aaronson. As I am sure you can hear in my voice, I am extremely concerned, and time is not our ally here at all."

"So I am gathering, Ms. Jones. Message received and understood. Stand by, and I will be back to you in short order."

"Thank you, Mr. Aaronson."

Moses replaced his black, corded phone back on its cradle. It sat just below the raised imprint of the logo of "New York Bell Tel;" a relic, but one which still worked quite well. Moses would not throw away a relic, anymore than he intended to change his own relic methodologies which worked so well for so many decades. *Progress is a wonderful thing, but so is the world of tried and true,* Moses thought. He never resisted progress, as he believed, like Harold Wilson, that the only human institution that rejects progress is the graveyard. *No,* he firmly believed. *Both must exist together and respect each other.* He pondered the new engagement. He would turn to Belita Davies – nicknamed Rome – his tech guru, to provide the digital expertise he knew he would need for this new engagement.

Moses used the rotary dial to input the long international phone number for Belita Davies next. She picked up the phone on the first ring, seeing from caller ID that the call was from Moses. "Good morning to you, Moses," Rome greeted him, "although it's hardly morning here in cloudy London."

"Greetings, and bonjour, my friend," Moses replied.

"Is this a personal or business inquiry?" Rome inquired.

"Why can't it be both?" Moses replied as he chuckled.

"Touché."

"First to business, then we can return to a discussion of how you are doing."

"Very well, sir."

Moses explained the nature of the engagement to Rome, and concluded by saying, "I know there are ways to uncover fake accounts in social media and shut them down. Here, we want to identify who is at the root of the accounts, and deliver that information to the attorneys. I suspect they will then run to the bankruptcy judge to enjoin further use of the disinformation mechanism to attack the debtors. So, my friend, how docs one go about uncovering the source of a disinformation campaign?"

Without pausing to think, Rome asked, "Have you heard of Bellingcat?"

"I have read a bit about it."

"It is an open source investigation outfit using sleuths around the world to do crowd sourcing investigations. There's one in New York that does the same named name *Crowded!*, italicized with an exclamation point."

"*Crowded!?* Hmmm, fascinating. As always, Ms. Davies, I am in awe of the digital world, and the breadth of your knowledge. How quickly can something like this progress to a revelation of what mastermind lurks in the darkness behind the misinformation?"

"Hard to say, Moses. Sometimes, we can get lucky and find a slip-up by the perpetrator, in which case we could have an answer reasonably quickly. In other situations, the investigation could drag on for months, or longer."

"Months, I am afraid, will not make the new client a happy attorney at all." Moses paused as he thought. "Ms. Jones is sending me an information packet shortly and I will forward that to you immediately. With that, I would like you to get started with *Crowded!* and any other crowdsourcing you can put together, and we will see if we in fact can get lucky. I am sure with your stellar guidance, we will give ourselves the best chance."

"Thank you, Moses. Good to work with you again. I'll do my best."

"As I know you will, Ms. Davies. As I know you will."

By the time the call ended, Moses had his information packet from 3J and went to work immediately. He noted the posts lacked sophistication; rather, they were social media-friendly sound-bites. Short messages and to the point: "Don't do business with the Rapinoes" was the general message; "They are bad people, and you will lose more money." He observed that in the latest several posts, whoever was behind them devolved into name-calling by designating the Rapinoes "deadbeats," "moochers," "spongers," and even "parasites," all a change in tone from the initial string of opinion posts. In the name-calling posts, he felt the beginnings of the need for a profile of the perpetrator. "What kind of creditor might resort to name-calling?" he wondered out loud to Emily. She looked up at him with partially shut eyes as if to say, *I have no idea.* Moses smiled at her and decided it was time for their afternoon walk.

He donned his navy blue beret hat, a signature old-school look of his, and a gray, raglan cardigan with weathered suede elbow patches. He put Emily into her harness, and headed down to the street for their stroll toward his beloved Madison Park. It was an unseasonably mild Fall day. As they walked, Emily stayed within inches of his left leg, a habit his tiny companion had adopted all by herself rather than being taught. She came ready to adore him straight from the foster home where he found her, and fully compliant, almost by instinct. Indeed, he quickly learned that she felt most comfortable near him at all times; a common characteristic of rescue dogs, who appear eternally thankful to and united with the person who saved them. Moses regularly mused that if she had been a human, she would be telepathic and easily able to finish all of his sentences and thoughts.

Once they got to the park and found a bench to sit on, Moses organized his thoughts about the new case. *Definitely in need of a profile,* he thought, scanning the extensive creditor list contained in 3J's packet. While it tempted him to eliminate all creditors owed a *de minimus* amount, deciding on that amount would be arbitrary and could inadvertently leave the perpetrator out of the analysis. *No,* he thought, *at least at the outset, better to try to develop a profile of what type of creditor might post on social media like this and then present that profile to Ms. Jones. Let her clients try to narrow the universe based on the suggested personality traits. That method is more scientific than just establishing a random cut-off point.* Moses hoped that with a smaller list of creditor candidates, Rome could focus her crowdsource search and more quickly identify who was behind the smear campaign.

While Moses had some profiling experience in his long career, he also knew just the person to turn to for more significant profile expertise: his long-time friend from the Columbia University psychology department, who was now retired from the world of criminology – Beverly Simons. Beverly was also his occasional "plus one" at society events in the City, although as he got closer to the eighty-year-old marker, he found his interest in attending such events waning. He hoped Beverly would have time and interest to assist him on this project.

When Moses returned to his flat, he called Beverly and was pleasantly surprised that she was available and at the ready. He explained the situation and asked if she could quickly develop a profile merely from four factors: a creditor, concerned about repayment, who had taken to social media to call out the debtors, and whose posts had quickly turned to name-calling.

"Well, Moses, the more data points, the better the profile, but I think I can come up with something for you quickly that may be of use to your clients."

"Beverly, as always, thank you so much. We must find a moment to share an espresso and catch up."

"I would truly look forward to that, Moses."

Later that evening, Moses received an email with an attached memo from Beverly.

Moses, I would look for a creditor with some or all of the following personality characteristics; the more of these characteristics that a potential target has, the more likely they are the bad actor. This exercise will clearly require the debtors to know their creditor base, so I hope they are familiar with the personalities involved – if they're not, I am not sure who would be.

Have them look for someone who is a bully, with tendencies toward repressed anger. Someone who seems to enjoy inflicting pain on others. Someone who is insulting, has a holier-than-thou attitude; maybe someone who has been hurt in the past; who takes a fight to new grounds; childish.

I suspect this person could also possibly be a narcissistic sociopath. An excessive and persistent need for others' admiration and reinforcement characterizes a narcissist. Someone with grandiose opinions of themselves. Someone who believes they are superior. Who has difficulties maintaining relationships. The sociopath element manifests itself in a noticeable lack of regard for the rights of others and a tendency regularly to violate those rights. This person needs praise and deference from others. He or she can be manipulative at times, cunning and self-serving, and won't be concerned about wrecking others' lives.

Smear campaigns, such as the one you are reviewing now, can suggest a narcissistic sociopath. If this person justifies such a diagnosis, he or she will lack remorse; will have no human attachment; will likely be secretive; and will lack empathy.

Hope that helps.

Bev

Moses immediately forwarded the email memo to 3J, with an explanation of Bev's credentials, and his plan. He suggested 3J should share the memo with the Rapinoes and have them quickly identify creditors who might sync up with the profile. Moses also suggested a conference call with the attorneys, the Rapinoes, Rome, and himself, to discuss and identify possibilities.

It was 10:30 p.m. central time when Moses' email arrived on 3J's iPhone. She read it, forwarded it to Pascale, and the two attorneys talked. Late evening connectivity – the life of a bankruptcy attorney. Since the bankruptcy cases were so new, neither 3J nor Pascale had a good feel for the members of the creditor body, but hoped that the Rapinoes were hands-on with their creditors and could identify a small pool who might fit at least part of the profiled characteristics. They agreed 3J would call them first thing in the morning, explain what Aaronson suggested, and try to arrange a conference call for the afternoon, giving Bey and Adam a chance to look at the profiling factors and apply them to the extensive list of creditors.

To 3J, it seemed like a long shot, but she knew it was their only shot at the moment. *Of course, in retrospect,* she thought, *taking down Quincy Witherman probably also seemed like a long shot three years ago, but the old man in New York somehow pulled it off. So who am I to doubt him?*

CHAPTER 13

Thursday, November 9, 2023

FIRST THING IN THE morning, 3J forwarded Aaronson's email to the Rapinoes, and then phoned them to explain fully what was brewing. They listened and Bey then said, as she read the emailed factors, "Well, we don't need to spend a ton of time here – these all describe Dewey to a T. The bastard is a narcissistic sociopath. I just didn't know how to diagnose what I was seeing and hearing from him. Now I do. What a mess. I blame myself for not doing the due diligence about this nutcase years ago, before we booked the loan."

Adam then spoke before 3J could say a word. "Bey, let's not jump to conclusions. Definitely fits Dewey, but I also can think of several others on the creditors' list off the top of my head who could fit many of those factors, and who are less than enthralled with us right now. Let's do what Aaronson and 3J ask: go through the factors for the creditors we know, and try to come up with a list – *besides* Dewey."

Bey said nothing.

"We're shooting for a call at three Central Time, five Eastern Time, which would be around midnight in London," said 3J.

"London?" Adam asked.

"Aaronson's high-tech colleague is in London."

"Alright, we're on it," Adam agreed. "We'll try to email you a list by 2:30 Central. Send us the conference call information and we'll be off and running." This time, after Bey's instantaneous reaction to the revelation that they were looking for a narcissistic sociopath, she and Adam did not trade comments. Bey was silent.

3J reported her call with the Rapinoes to Pascale.

"I'm not surprised at Bey's reaction. She takes the blame for hooking up with Veridical and Dewey, so I'm sure all of this hits a raw nerve for her," Pascale said.

3J pondered the profile. "If we're looking for a narcissistic sociopath in the body of creditors, who is very good at smearing, we have to assume that this creditor knows how to mask themselves on the social media platforms. I sure hope this tech wizard that Aaronson speaks so highly of is up to the task."

"Certainly was up to it in the Witherman cases."

3J looked off into the distance and concurred quietly. "Yes. That she was, indeed."

Approximately twenty minutes before the call, the Rapinoes emailed to 3J and Pascale a short list of five creditors who they believed filled many of the factors outlined by Aaronson's contact, Beverly Simons. The Rapinoes reported that the names on the list were in order from the most factors met to the least of the five who made the list. To no one's surprise, Dewey was number one on the list. Two and five were small vendors who the Rapinoes believed were extremely hard to deal with. Three and four were larger creditors: Belle Chi – security services, and Benny Woodson – landlord. There was a significant gap between the number of factors the Rapinoes believed Dewey met, and those that fit Chi and Woodson.

At 3 p.m., all relevant parties dialed into the conference call: the Rapinoes, Moses, Kane, and Rome, while 3J and Pascale were both in his office on the speaker phone.

Moses spoke first. "Let me introduce all of you to Belita Davies. We gave her the code name 'Rome' for an operation several years ago, and the nickname stuck, so that's what we all call her now. She is in charge of all things tech on my team. Before I turn this over to her to talk with you about next steps, let me suggest that we should focus, to begin with, on the three largest creditors on the list – Dewey, Chi, and Woodson. They have enough debt to warrant the kind of thinking necessary to start a smear campaign, and Ms. and Mr. Rapinoe have attributed enough of the Simons factors to them to warrant investigation. In other words, we should triage right now and have Rome direct her attention and skills to the most likely of the group. Agreed?"

"Fine with us," Adam said. Bey was again silent.

"Ditto from the lawyers," 3J concurred.

"Very well. Rome?"

"Thank you, Moses. Here is an overview of what I propose we do." Rome then posed the same question to the group that she had posed the day before to Moses. "Have any of you heard of Bellingcat?" No one on the call said anything, so Rome continued. "Bellingcat, at its core, is a global corps of sleuths. An investigative collaborative which relies on both paid and volunteer researchers combing through 'open-source' digital data available to anyone with the right searching skills. It occasionally uses what is essentially a black market for data.

A gent named Eliot Higgins founded Bellingcat in 2014. At the time, he was an unemployed blogger and gamer, and now investigators, newspapers, corporations, and even governments covet his work. He has assembled a worldwide team whose work relies almost exclusively on digital data; his team specializes in piecing together a variety of clues that are available online, often the Dark Web. It has been so successful that knockoffs have sprung up, one in particular that does a great job in New York City, named *Crowded!* I would gather some preliminary data, and then use *Crowded!* to help come up with other data. In addition, I have my own network of in-the-know onliners whose information I can easily access. It is my hope that through a comprehensive search of this kind, I will discover other smear campaigns that are similar, or information leading me to operatives who conduct such smear campaigns. If I can tie together the similarities, I may be able to identify who is posting, and if not for their own account, on whose behalf the poster is operating. In this search, I will focus on the three people the Rapinoes identified. Questions?"

3J spoke after absorbing the plan outlined by Rome. "Could you send me some links to get a better handle on the work Bellingcat and *Crowded!* perform?"

"Of course. In fact, Fresh Air's Terry Gross interviewed Bellingcat's founder on NPR several years ago. I can send you a link to the transcript of the interview. It covers lots of ground and it will give you a great overview of Higgins and insight into Bellingcat. It is quite legitimate. As is *Crowded!*"

3J responded, "Thank you, and legitimacy is what I'm getting at. I've had prior familiarity, unfortunately, with a 'commit-a-crime-to-catch-a-criminal' matter – with which I believe you are also familiar – and I want to ensure I don't have two of those types of cases in my lifetime ... at least, not this close in time to each other."

"Understood," Rome said, avoiding a discussion of whether she had actually committed any crimes in her role in the Witherman case. "We will commit no crimes in conducting this research project for you, I assure you."

"Very important to me," 3J said. Thinking it necessary to be specific, she added, "So thank you for agreeing to stay within the bounds of the law."

Pascale then asked, "Can you please speak a little to the Dark Web piece of this?"

"Certainly," Rome said. "The internet is made up of at least two components, often referred to as the Dark Web and the Clearnet. We all know the Clearnet as the place where the sites we visit are located using browsers like Safari, Chrome, and Firefox. The Dark Web, on the other hand, is a part of the internet made up of hidden sites you cannot find through conventional web browsers. To get to the Dark Web, you must rely on browsers and search engines designed specifically to unearth these hidden sites. Sites on the Dark Web use encryption software so their visitors and owners can attempt to remain anonymous and hide their identities and locations.

"It is why the Dark Web is the home to illegal activity. If you tap into the Dark Web, you'll find everything from illegal drug and gun sales, to illicit pornography, and stolen credit card and Social Security numbers. On the other hand, studies also show that over half of the Dark Web consists of legal traffic, just encrypted. There is nothing illegal about surfing the Dark Web and gathering information, as I will be doing. For my purposes, I will be focusing on Reddit-like sites on the Dark Web where sophisticated and stealthy techies can exchange information; forums on various subjects where the posting parties do not wish their thoughts to be public.

"The principal benefits of exchanging information on the Dark Web are its layers of encryption, and conventional search

engines like Google do not index the information, so your
search on Google won't return any Dark Web hits. Clearnet
searches, therefore, are out. I will have to employ a special web
browser to access the Dark Web."

"Firefox, Safari, and Chrome can't search the Dark Web?"
Pascale asked.

"Correct. In order to find and access Dark Web websites, I
will use an app called 'Tor;' Tor stands for 'the onion routing,'
and Dark Web sites distinguish themselves from Clearnet sites
with a 'dot onion' extension. The 'onion' refers to the several
layers of encryption used on the Dark Web, which are peeled
back, layer by layer like an onion, for the creator of a communication to communicate with recipients. I should also mention
that names used by Dark Web sites do not sound at all like
their Clearnet counterparts. For example, DuckDuckGo, a
popular Clearnet search engine, has a Dark Web counterpart
site entitled 3g2upl4pq6kufc4m.onion. As you can tell, the
Dark Web has a unique way of naming websites. Questions?"

No one posed a question, so 3J spoke next and asked, "Rapinoes, what say you?"

"Let's proceed … with haste, please," Adam directed. Bey
said nothing.

"Very well," Moses said. "Rome will begin immediately and
report regularly to Ms. Jones to disseminate to her clients and
team members."

When the call ended, 3J looked at Pascale and asked, "How do
I get myself into shit like this? Dark Web? Onion? Encryption
layers? Tor? My Lord! I hear this stuff and I realize how little
of the modern English language I use."

"The challenge of keeping up is what keeps us young, or at least some of us," Pascale countered.

"Nope. It's what makes us old before our time."

"Well, that too, I suppose," Pascale agreed with a big smile. He continued, wiggling his eyebrows, "One of the many contradictions that is the practice of law."

As 3J gathered her papers to return to her office, Pascale leaned back in his desk chair, put his hands behind his head, and said, "Not all that long ago, there was no such word as disinformation. And just one reality – Planet Earth, where we all lived. Now there are fake news realities, alternative realities, artificial realities, different dimension realities, my reality, your reality, Jane Doe's reality, warped reality, and, if I might observe, a growing number of people and politicians out there with little or no connection to reality. We all used to have to start with the same common indisputable reality. No more. People are losing track of what is really real. Thank you, social freakin' media, if I might editorialize and give away my age in doing so."

"I'm not in your age bracket, but I agree, so … amen to that."

"Y'know, if she finds something on the Dark Web, we're gonna have a helluva time figuring out how to get it into evidence," he observed. "Maybe a live demonstration for Judge Robertson in the courtroom?"

"Maybe," 3J agreed, thinking about the evidentiary issue raised by Pascale. "I'm guessing it'll be the first time the Judge surfs the Dark Web; this'll certainly be *my* first encounter on this particular dark side."

"Yep. Me too," Pascale agreed, shaking his head slightly left and right. "Me too."

"What a mess," 3J said, as she gathered her things to return to her office.

CHAPTER 14

Thursday, November 9, 2023

3J HAD INTENDED TO begin work on the lawsuit and TRO papers as soon as she got back to her office, but she found a message from Bob Swanson, the head of the firm. She liked Bob, though she had little contact with him over the last few years as her practice, her good name in town, and her workload, had grown. The limited contact fit fine with her strategy of getting along in the firm. She found it better for her longevity and sanity to have less contact with management, and simply keep her head down and work on growing her list of clients. *Stay just beneath the firm's radar*, she liked to say.

Bob's message said that he wanted to get together with 3J and talk about Pascale's decision to wind down. She assumed it would be a friendly meeting, where Bob would assure her that the firm fully supported her work and stable of clients, and would do whatever it would take to increase that support. In other words, that the firm loved her and needed her, in the laid-back way that only Bob could pull off. After all, that's why he was the managing partner.

She called Bob back, and the two agreed to meet at O'Brien's that night at 6 p.m. 3J didn't tell Pascale of the scheduled rendezvous, just slipping out of the office at 5:15 to get to O'Brien's a little early. When she got there, it was largely empty, and rather than sit at her usual table and wait, she took a seat at the bar.

The head bartender, Ronnie Steele, made his way over to 3J quickly to take her usual order for an Irish whiskey, neat. Ronnie was a handsome, five-foot eleven-inch, one hundred ninety pounds, middle fifties, light-skinned African American, with a square jaw, a trimmed salt-and-pepper beard, and a head of wavy hair that had not yet thinned. The two did not know each other well. She knew only a little about him – that he and his wife had divorced, and that he had two teenage kids in a joint custody arrangement. Excellent talker; even better listener. *Perfect bartender,* she thought.

Steele knew her as a regular, friendly to the staff, and a patron who tipped the waitresses well. When he brought her the American sipping glass containing the caramel-colored Irish elixir, he slid a dish of the bar's signature hickory house-smoked assorted nuts in front of her and lingered, wiping down the surface next to where 3J sat. As he finished, he asked, "Where's your regular drinkin' buddy tonight?"

"Just me tonight, Ronnie," 3J said smiling, happy to have someone to talk with before the MP's arrival.

"You guys have a quarrel or something? A falling out?"

"Oh no, nothing like that at all. We're good buddies. BFF's. He's my mentor at the firm."

"Good to hear. You guys make a real nice couple," Steele said with a feigned Southern accent, teasing 3J.

She smiled at his attempt at a joke. "No, I'm just here to have a drink with the head of my law firm, and thought I'd have a nerve-calming drink before his arrival."

"Head of the firm," Steele repeated. The meeting impressed him, and he raised his eyebrows to show it. "Sounds ... well, sounds like pretty serious stuff."

3J chuckled. "Hopefully not, to be honest. He's a decent chap and I'm not one of his problem children at the firm. I don't tell him how to run his firm and mostly he doesn't tell me how to be a bankruptcy lawyer. He pays me periodically and the checks clear. So the relationship works pretty well."

"I see. You both stay in your lanes."

"Well, his lane is way bigger than mine, and his car is way faster, but … yes, I suppose so," 3J agreed as she nodded and smiled.

Steele continued to work on cleaning the bar, and 3J silently concluded that was a pretense so he could stay in her proximity and talk to her. It didn't bother her; she preferred not to drink alone.

"Mind if I ask you a personal question?" Steele inquired.

"Can't promise I'll answer it, but I don't offend easily. So sure, what the hey, go for it," 3J replied without hesitating.

"Any Black folks in your firm help run it?"

"No Black folks run the firm … just yet. Not all that many senior partner Black folks at the firm to choose from if they wanted one of us at the top."

"Oh, I hear ya," Steele concurred, more to keep her talking than to delve into the topic himself. "No Black folks in management here either, although the family likes to say I'm running the bar when they feel the need to point out that they're progressive." Another look of sympathy, this time perhaps directed more to himself than 3J. "What about you?"

"What about me?" 3J asked.

"You could help run the firm."

"Not really interested in that, career-wise. I like just being a bankruptcy lawyer. That's plenty for my plate. And I'm more of a mid-level partner right now; not really a senior partner-type just yet. Some day. But not yet," 3J explained, thinking of the hierarchy at Greene Madison.

Steele nodded again. After a little more silence, he smiled and asked, "What's with the old white guy you drink with?"

"I trust him. I'm a friend to him and he's a friend to me. He's a helper, not a hater. He's got my six. Turns out, that seems to help me with my trust issues."

"So, what is it? He grow up in the ghetto?"

"Nope. Western Kansas."

"No shit," Steele exclaimed. "Maybe there's some bit of hope after all."

"What about you, Ronnie?"

"What about me?" Ronnie asked, feigning confusion.

"You gonna own this place some day?"

He smiled and replied slowly, "Well, look at us. Two Black folks gathered here at a public bar, on the very site Daniel Boone's grandson owned a general store where he kept slaves in the basement for months before he sold them; right here in a neighborhood where Confederate white people fought and died in the 1800s trying to keep our kind in slavery workin' in their fields. Here we are, openly talking about white folks and someday running our businesses. If that ain't progress, I don't know what is. Ole Daniel Boone's grandson must be spinning in his grave."

"Ha!" exclaimed 3J. "But seriously, what about you?"

"To be continued, my friend. Come back again, sit at my bar, drink my whiskey, and we can do some of that TBC."

3J smiled at him and said, "Alright, Ronnie. Fair enough. TBC it is," letting him have his way of deferring on his part of the conversation. 3J reached into her purse to pay Ronnie and he put his hand up and said, "This one's on the house, counselor."

"Why, thank you so much!" 3J said with an appreciative smile.

Just then, Bob Swanson entered the bar, surveyed the scene as his eyes adjusted to the reduced light, saw 3J, smiled and waved to her, and made his way to the bar. Steele, seeing that 3J's appointment had arrived, turned away from the bar and toward the bottles of alcohol, and 3J stood and said, "Hey, Bob. The bar's gonna fill up soon as people drift in after another hard day at whatever shop they hang around at. Let's take a booth in the back so we can talk."

As they walked to the booth, Swanson said, "Sounds good. Thanks for making the time to talk."

"Of course," 3J said with a smile. She chuckled to herself, thinking, *What choice do I have when the head of the firm says he wants to talk?*

Swanson was 3J's height, a good one hundred eighty pounds (at least thirty pounds more than he needed on his frame), bald, with bushy, gray eyebrows that could use trimming, and a nose that was larger than his face could handle. Yet his blue eyes always seemed to dance with optimism – the perfect eyes for his job – and, almost to match his eyes, he was a bastion of positivity in every situation that 3J could remember. His main job description: steer the ship through all kinds of troubled waters, and deal with the varied personalities of the lawyers in the firm, many of whose motto must be that no problem they had was too small to bring to Bob's attention. *Not a job she would be good at,* she often thought. *She wouldn't trade her job for his for all the Earl Grey tea in China.* 3J liked him and thought he did an admirable job running the firm, although she knew that not everyone at the firm did and even those that did, didn't like him all the time. In private, some of his harsher critics took issue with his title of Managing Partner, opting instead to call him the Damaging Partner; behind closed doors and always behind his back, of course. The comments were unfair in 3J's view. She never took part in such discussions and avoided the childish name-calling. She knew he had a job to do and the job description necessarily didn't include making everyone happy all the time. The unflattering nickname assigned to Swanson by some partners certainly illustrated yet another reason she would never want to trade jobs with Bob Swanson. She wondered if he knew, or cared, about the nickname and the comments; perhaps not caring about such matters was a significant prerequisite to holding the head-of-firm position.

As they took their seats, Swanson ordered an IPA beer. 3J passed on a refresher for her whiskey, and Swanson said, "Pascale's news took me a little by surprise. I mean, that day of departure comes for everyone at some point. Some leave on their own terms, some never leave and die at their desk, and then there are many variations on those themes. On many levels, I am so glad for him, but I really can't help feeling that it's premature." Swanson paused, taking a drink to let 3J respond.

"I'm happy for him," 3J said, choosing her words carefully. "I don't have an opinion about whether it's premature, Bob. I have faith that Pascale knows the answer as to timing best of anyone, don't you?" She watched for Swanson's reaction.

Swanson took his time replying and when he did, with what seemed to 3J to be genuine concern, he said, "I'm really not sure he does. Coming off such a tragedy, I just don't know if he knows best."

Swanson's comment surprised 3J, and she quickly responded, "Well, if Pascale doesn't know what's best for Pascale, I don't know who would."

He didn't pursue that question but instead surprised 3J again and said, "I'd like to find a way to convince Pascale to stay on with us full time and not move into a fast wind down and then an exit. We need him; we *want* him. He is such an integral part of the culture of Greene Madison. He's good for the firm. He's good for *you*."

3J wasn't expecting him to make a pitch to convince Pascale to stay. The entire notion made her instantly uncomfortable.

She shook her head slowly, and said quietly, but firmly, "Look, Bob. I appreciate that you appreciate Pascale. But his decision is all about himself, and not about me, and really not about the firm either. Am I concerned about my future at the firm without Bill as my colleague and mentor? You bet. Am I ready, however, to go it without him at the firm? I have some self-doubt, but Bill says I'm ready and I trust his judgment. I feel kind of selfish asking and answering those questions, because the focus should be on what's right for Bill, not how it'll affect me." She continued, "Will the firm be fine? Sure. Do I want to help talk him out of the decision?" She sipped her whiskey and she let her question sit like the summer humidity in Kansas City sits in the air, thickening it and making it supremely uncomfortable. She took a slow, deep breath, exhaled, and answered her last question, "I'm sorry if this disappoints you, but I really, really don't."

Swanson listened respectfully and said nothing. He was prepared to let her own how she felt and had no urge to try to talk the two most important bankruptcy lawyers in the firm out of their feelings. One would be hard enough.

3J watched as she could see the wheels in Swanson's head turning. She waited dutifully for him to respond, but when he didn't, she smiled wistfully and said, "Bob, after the accident, Pascale told me this story touching on how he felt. In typical Pascale fashion, it was a little obtuse, but there was a lesson he wanted me to extract. He said, '3J, sometimes I think about the drunk driver. When I do that, I think about how mad at him I feel. Sometimes I think about the loss of my family. When I do that, I think about how unfair it was for me to have my family taken away from me. Sometimes I think about my sadness. My memories of my family have scared me, so I focus on me. Me, me, me.'" 3J watched Swanson's eyes as he followed along. She continued. "He said these were his own 'I Me Mine' moments like the song George Harrison wrote when he complained about the Beatles as they were nearing the end of their demise." Swanson's face was neutral. He was attentive, so she continued. "He told me that once he tried to process what had happened, he forced himself into periods of selfishness – all about him … except that it *wasn't* him. It wasn't how he wanted to be. He needed to find joy again in the memories. Honor their memories. Stop wallowing and start living again. What he's telling us now is that to do that, he's finishing up his career in the short term, and pursuing whatever life offers in the longer term. And it's all about Bill, and not about you or me or the firm." She folded her arms gently on the booth table and said, "I just don't think it's for any of us to try to alter that path. The firm can't be in an 'us, us, us' mode. For my dime, it not only should happen, it has to happen just as Pascale envisions it … for his well-being." 3J paused, watched for a reaction, and seeing none asked softly, with a tone of hope in her question, "Do you see what I'm saying?"

Swanson smiled at 3J, his blue eyes appearing to light up and sparkle, and said, "You are a wise, wise person, Josephina Jones. One of so many reasons I'm grateful that we're partners at the firm." He smiled and nodded in agreement. Silence, and then he added, "I'm glad I reached out to you. You know him best. I'll simply accept his plan and you and I can help him implement in any way that he needs."

"Thank you, Bob." After a few moments, she moved her arms off the tabletop, grabbed the edge of the table with both hands, and stood up to exit. "I'm very grateful that you feel that way."

On the drive back downtown, 3J whispered out loud to herself: "What a fuckin' day." *Bellingcat and Dark Web and Tor and*

smear campaigns and then that chat with Ronnie Steele and his views on running the law firm, and then Bob Swanson and his spin on Pascale. And it's not even 8 p.m. yet. I must be getting old, or at least older. In my younger lawyer days, I could focus on one thing only and I could never have had a day like this.

When Rome finished the call with the new clients, it was well past midnight, London time. But what she learned about the project energized her, and she immediately began to map out how she would conduct her searches on the Dark Web. She felt the sense of urgency in the voices of the attorneys and their clients, and wanted to do everything in her power to get them a result – and quickly.

She opened her laptop and launched the app she created to do automated searches for her on the internet. The app worked fine with the Tor Dark Web browser, and all she needed to do was to establish search parameters. She focused on Dark Web forums that catered to techies and on topics addressing fake social media account creation and disinformation techniques. She expected there would be many such posts in the Dark Web forums, where techies exchanged information out of the watchful eye of Clearnet internet searchers.

In so many respects, the posts railing on the Rapinoes that she read were relatively unsophisticated and reasonably low-tech. Anyone could open a fake account and, with the veil of fake-account-obfuscation, post whatever they wanted. She knew that the use of fake accounts was rampant; she knew Facebook liked to tell anyone who would listen that it was addressing the problem and had taken down well over two billion fake accounts each quarter, a staggering statistic. *Per-*

haps the stat is so large because Facebook makes it so easy to open a fake account in the first place, she thought. Rome also knew from a 2021 news story that if a post was bogus, it got six times the engagement – and engagement was how Facebook made its billions, so Rome was naturally suspicious of Facebook's stats about policing fake accounts. People were simply more inspired by hateful, polarizing content – the things that make them angry. The BJB and Rapinoe posts would make the creditor body angry, and unfortunately would amplify the worst part of human nature.

She envisioned several rounds of searches. Round one of the search process would be broad, to be followed, she hoped, by ever-narrowing searches. For the next two hours, Rome constructed dozens of search parameters to cast a wide net to see what information she would capture. If she could develop a pool of information, she hoped then to turn to *Crowded!* and her own network of contacts to identify who was behind the Rapinoe smear campaign.

Finally, satisfied with what she had constructed, she opened Tor and launched her search app, and hoped to wind down for a few hours while the app worked. She always found it hard to sleep consistently when she was on the job for a Moses project: exhilarating and exhausting at the same time. While her app explored the Dark Web, she laid on her bed, closed her eyes, and tried just to relax. Sleep might be too much to hope for.

CHAPTER 15

FUENTES SAT AT HIS desk and tried to finalize the advice he needed to give Dewey about the use of cash. Dewey seemed satisfied with the budget, and there was little room in it for payments to Veridical in the short term. "No Hail Mary arguments," Dewey had said. *Perhaps the best avenue,* he thought, *was the commencement of payments after forty-five to sixty days.* He next wondered if he should first engage with Dewey, or if it would be better to reach an agreement with BJB's legal team, subject to client approval. The latter method of negotiation was often successful with one huge caveat – he could employ it only when he had a good feel for his client's decision-making process. Here, he had no such feel.

Fuentes also had reviewed Judge Robertson's prior restaurant opinion and a lender's lien on cash generated post-bankruptcy filing, and done some research of his own. On this point, he saw no leg to stand on whatsoever. The Judge was right, and he needed to report that conclusion to his client. So, painful as he was finding it, he needed to have another call with Dewey to discuss both matters.

To his amazement, when he emailed Dewey to explain the issues and try to set up a conference call, Dewey immediately wrote him back and said a call in the morning would fit well into his calendar. *Hard to predict with this one what he'll do.*

The next morning, when Fuentes spoke with Dewey, he floated the idea of an agreed use of cash without a court fight in exchange for payments to Veridical beginning in no more than sixty days. Without hesitation, Dewey said, "That is agreeable to me. Make it so."

Fuentes was expecting push-back and a lecture. Dewey's reaction again surprised him. He even found Dewey's agreement to be commendably businesslike. Fuentes next turned to the matter of Veridical's lien.

Dewey listened to Fuentes quietly and attentively, and said, "Counsel, here is where you earn your hourly rate. I am not a lawyer. If you tell me that Veridical has no lien on the post-bankruptcy cash, my choices are to fire you or to accept your analysis. I don't intend to fire you, so I shall accept your analysis."

Fuentes found the idea of the only alternatives Dewey could see being either to fire him or accept his advice just one more example of how odd and quirky his client was turning out to be. *Clients come in all sizes and shapes, and all states of craziness.* But as Dewey's acceptance of the analysis was what Fuentes wanted to hear, all he could think of to say was, "Thank you, Mr. Dewey."

"Anything else for us to discuss?" Dewey inquired.

"Nothing for the good of the order."

"Very well. Good day," Dewey said, and ended the call.

Dewey thought to himself as he sat back, *The cash order will be irrelevant in the near term. As soon as BJB goes out of business, the cash from the sale of the assets will be all mine.*

Fuentes next reached out to 3J to discuss the trade of future payments for no fight. To create some measure of risk for 3J to consider the trade, Fuentes knew he would have to sell her on the notion that Dewey was quite capable of undertaking a budget battle if the Rapinoes declined the deal. Classic negotiation strategy – craft something significant the other side could lose if they decline to negotiate. Fuentes wrote an email to 3J and asked if she had time to talk. She quickly replied and said that she was at her desk and he could call whenever it was convenient for him.

He dialed her up and she answered straightaway. Fuentes said, "Thanks for taking my call. We haven't worked together in the past, but my research leads me to believe that you'll be an easy lawyer to work with, and I believe you'll find that I am as well."

"Good to hear," 3J said, trying to mask her feeling that Fuentes was trying too hard to set a conciliatory tone before they even got to the reason he was calling.

"I'm reaching out to you on two fronts. First, I've reviewed Judge Robertson's restaurant opinion and done my own research. After discussion with my client, we do not intend to file a brief to challenge the prior ruling that the lien doesn't attach to the post-bankruptcy cash. We can incorporate that ruling in this case in the final cash usage order, if that is an acceptable way to resolve that issue for you."

"Acceptable," 3J said, keeping her comments to a minimum. She had hoped Fuentes would reach that conclusion and that

Dewey wouldn't want to fund a Don Quixote mission of chasing legal windmills on the lien issue. She likewise did not believe that was the principal reason that Fuentes had called her.

"Very well," Fuentes said. "The second – and principal – reason for my call is to discuss the budget and explore the possibility of agreeing for the use of the cash going forward, rather than both of us gearing up to litigate the budget, with the attendant risk to both sides of a loss."

"Reaching a deal that is acceptable to both parties is always preferable. What proposal did you have in mind?"

"A fairly simple and straightforward trade. Veridical is a small-sized lender, as I am sure you know. Mr. Dewey runs a slimmed-down operation. He has authorized me to tell you he is willing to accept the budget as presented with one modification – payments to Veridical must resume in forty-five days."

"Or else what?" 3J inquired and, by doing so, forced Fuentes to lay on the table whatever threat accompanied the offer.

"Or else, we will have to turn our attention to a fight over whether the budget is appropriate, whether BJB should spend less money in the short term while we all try to figure out if and when your clients' little share of the entertainment and hospitality industry comes back online and to what degree. And, of course, whether the real estate truly is maintaining its value as you stated in court. In that fight, we would naturally also press for payments to Veridical. But not in forty-five days – in the present, as I mentioned in court."

So there it was: down to brass tacks. 3J figured Fuentes' cards were as he just played them; before she addressed them, she decided to change the topic slightly. "So, Alexander, what did you make of the chambers conference and the dirty tricks campaign now waged against my clients?"

"Is that relevant to our discussion?"

"Could be. Don't you think the campaign will impact when my clients' 'little share,' to use your words, of the entertainment and hospitality industry comes back online and to what degree? I mean, after all, isn't that the obvious purpose of the campaign? To negatively impact my client's position in the recovery?"

Fuentes responded emphatically, "I am a bankruptcy lawyer and have been for a good number of years. I respect and believe in the automatic stay. In fact, I honor it as a cornerstone of my chosen area of practice. I don't condone the actions of whomever is behind the posts. But, I don't know who is behind the posts and all I think I can do at this point is address the issue in front of you and me – the use of cash and under what terms."

3J sighed. She didn't really expect Fuentes to blurt out and confess, "You're right. You're right. My client is violating the automatic stay!" But at least she put it out there that she and her team were watching. With that, 3J needed to end this discussion and call the Rapinoes and Kane to discuss the proposal. "Let me talk to my clients and we'll be back to you very shortly. Thanks for reaching out. I look forward to working with you on these cases."

"Same," Fuentes said with a hint of goodwill in his tone, and the call ended.

One strong benefit of the proposal was that the Rapinoes would not have to litigate the method used to prepare the budget right at the beginning of the cases. Rather, it would give the Debtors time to show they could meet the budget predictions, and allow the Moses Team time to expose the person behind the smear campaign. *Though the budget won't matter if we can't shut down the posts,* 3J sighed.

When the call with 3J ended, Fuentes sat at his desk and pondered the smear campaign. He had contempt for the hate spewed on social media, and as a result, he didn't even maintain a Facebook or Twitter account. While Dewey didn't *seem* driven to hate, Fuentes still had a nagging feeling about his client. *I told 3J that I don't know who is behind the posts – and I don't know, but I sure have my concerns about my client.*

He enjoyed representing most of his clients, but, while it didn't happen often, in his career over the years Fuentes found it necessary to withdraw from representing a handful of clients, who he had come to believe were not truthful with him or, worse, the court. He was proud that he was principled and demanded honesty from his clients. He knew not all lawyers did, but he also felt it was more than his principles at play. In his experience, he couldn't effectively communicate with clients who lied to him and without effective communication, there could be no effective legal representation.

In the past, the need to withdraw had been based on something more than a suspicion; something more than just a concern. With Dewey, Fuentes felt that the "something more" was just one new revelation away. Fuentes was sure that 3J wasn't sitting around hoping the campaign would run its course. He felt certain that she and her team were on it, and he was sincerely rooting for her to figure out the source of the posts in the near term ... even if that meant a blockbuster revelation implicating his client and forcing his split with Dewey.

3J called the Rapinoes, who patched Ralph Kane into the call, to convey the cash budget offer from Fuentes and his client. She explained the offer and the benefits of cutting a deal. The single downside, she explained, was the payments to Veridical, so that was what they should focus on.

Bey asked, "If we don't agree to pay Veridical, what will likely happen? I mean, how will Judge Robertson likely handle the issue?"

"That's the million dollar question, Bey," 3J began. "As we've discussed, there's going to be a period of time during which we'll be able to get away with no payments to Veridical. But that will make the Judge uncomfortable, and in my experience with him, he'll want the Debtors to start making payments at some point. The question is, at what point? My feeling is that at the outside, we can probably get to ninety days out, but it might only be sixty."

Adam said, "Is the demand for full payment beginning at day forty-five negotiable?"

"In my experience, everything in bankruptcy is negotiable … until it isn't. Fuentes in no way suggested his offer was a take-it-or-leave-it proposal. What kind of counter are you thinking of?"

"I was thinking of a reduced payment to start with, scaling up to something like eighty percent of what we owe each month by the ninetieth day. So, maybe starting on day forty-five, we pay fifty percent of the monthly, on day sixty, we pay two-thirds, and on day ninety, we pay eighty percent. I think the budget refinements we've been working on with Ralph shows we could swing those kind of payments. Bey?"

"I agree with Adam. We *could* swing it, and it would be nice to avoid hair-on-fire litigation at the beginning of the case so we can just focus on the businesses … and surviving the smears. Those two items are more than sufficient to keep us fully occupied."

"I like the scale-up approach. Let me go back to Fuentes with the proposal and see how he reacts."

"Thanks, 3J," Bey and Adam said in unison, and the call ended.

"Alexander, 3J here. Can you talk now?"

"I can. What do you have for me?"

3J laid out the proposal for scaled-up payments, culminating in eighty percent of the regular payment by the ninetieth day. Fuentes listened, and rather than criticizing the offer as something his client would never sign off on, as some lawyers might say in response, he simply said, "Gotta talk with Dewey, and I'll get back to you."

When his call with 3J ended, Fuentes intended to leave Dewey a voicemail, but, again to his surprise, Dewey answered the phone. Fuentes explained the scaled-up payment offer, and Dewey asked, "Is that the only remaining issue?"

"It is."

"Well, my preference, of course, is to receive payments as required under the loan documents. But I suppose there is risk that the Judge will allow the Debtors to avoid making any payments to me for an extended period, correct?"

"Correct," Fuentes advised.

"The proposal will at least afford me enough money to pay my lenders on the portion of the BJB loan I funded with Veridical's own line of credit. So I am staying afloat, so to speak." Dewey gazed over to the vessel on the mantle, and feeling no *anger* from the ashes within, said, "I am fine with the proposal. Let's ink this agreement before they – or I – change our respective minds."

"Understood." Fuentes was quickly learning that the best way for him to communicate with Dewey was to employ a strategy of an economy of words.

"Very well," Dewey said, and the call ended.

Fuentes then called 3J to convey that they had a deal, and they agreed she could undertake the first draft of the agreed order.

When the brief call ended, she sat back in her chair, gazed down at the Power and Light District, and questioned whether, in light of the agreement, Dewey was really behind the posts. It seemed a contradiction for him to try to bring down BJB on the one hand through the posts, while at the same time conceding the use of cash without challenging the budget, on the other hand. A complete contradiction. *But he's supposed to be the 'Lending Devil,'* 3J thought. *So maybe there's a plan here that only Satan and his army of evil demons can know.*

CHAPTER 16

Monday, November 13 to Tuesday, November 14, 2023

ROME ROSE FROM HER bed after several hours of lying on her back, drifting in and out of a light sleep, and checked on her search results. While she often did her World Wide Web work sitting cross-legged on her bed, her lanky frame hunched over as she gazed down at her laptop, this time she moved her operation to her small kitchen table just feet away from the bed for a change of scenery and to give her back some relief. She didn't have many lasting bad habits, but hunching over was one of the big ones. She figured it would catch up with her someday soon, but not that night. She brewed a pot of strong coffee and assessed her search results, a slow process of weeding out irrelevant hits from information of potential interest.

She found a significant number of posts to different Dark Web forums by someone using the handle "noLightpasses31." She started what she guessed would be hours of review of noLight's often asinine posts. NoLight seemed to post about a little of everything, from the latest in spoofing and phishing, to politics, to gaming, to photography, to the latest ways to stay awake: everything she would expect from someone who might be online eighteen-plus hours a day.

But what caught her attention were several posts from noLight that appeared to seek engagements, where for a renumeration to be negotiated, noLight would establish fake social media accounts and conduct low-level disinformation campaigns. A disinformation independent contractor; a social media poster for hire. Again, perhaps not too terribly unusual in the modern era, especially on the Dark Web. What drew her to noLight's posts, however, were several references to past disinformation engagements for people in the lending industry. Rome found that singular fact to be curious. *How many banks run disinformation campaigns?* she wondered. *Can't be that many.* One particular post even read like a job application résumé: "Have conducted successful social campaigns in the past for private lender seeking to sway reluctant/recalcitrant borrowers to pay."

Could it be? She decided to perform a second search of just posts signed by noLightpasses31, and thus eliminate all other information interference. While her laptop performed the new search, Rome realized that if it revealed that noLight was a proper lead to hunt down, linking noLight to a real person on the encrypted Dark Web would be no small task; perhaps beyond her abilities. She hoped that by turning the noLight lead over to *Crowded!* and her own network, the sleuths could develop noLight's digital footprint and find similarities hidden in the internet shadows to provide a name, and if they were lucky, a location.

Rome was a Bryn Mawr College archeology grad, drawn to the assignments she got working for Moses because of her passion for linking old-school, analog methodologies with new high-tech issues. While she drank her coffee and waited for search results, Rome hoped for a little high-tech magic with some help from her network and *Crowded!*, followed by implementing a tried-and-true analog method – in-person contact with, and questioning of, noLight. She wouldn't be the one to question him. She was a wallflower who enjoyed staying out of the spotlight. But she wouldn't mind being a fly on the wall listening to the interrogation.

3J reviewed the crowdsource sleuthing information provided by Rome. All new ground for 3J, having never heard of Bellingcat before the call. She also read the transcript of the Fresh Air interview of Bellingcat's founder. *Interesting*, she thought, *quite a character.* 3J was comfortable with technology, but she was no tech geek, and this experience with crowdsource sleuthing confirmed what she had come to believe – the online world was moving faster than she could keep up. She figured it was even worse for the sixty-somethings, and wondered how Pascale must have felt after the conference call, addressing issues like the Dark Web and Bellingcat. *If I'm confused, it must be dizzying for him.*

She decided to walk by Pascale's office. She peered in from the doorjamb. "Any interest in getting a bite to eat?"

"Always."

The twosome headed to 3J's car and a short trip to Fiorella's Jack Stack Barbecue in the historic Freight House District near Union Station; a rendezvous with 3J's favorite barbecue dish – salmon cooked over hickory, topped with blackberry barbecue sauce, along with six hand-breaded, sweet colossal onion rings. Pascale ordered his usual – chopped brisket and a side of hickory pit beans. Both lawyers were transplants to Kansas City, but like most of the other immigrants to the city, they immediately fell in love with the city's barbecue scene and quickly found their favorite establishment and dish. They shared their love for Jack Stack, and it excited both when the restaurant opened in the Freight House District, so close to downtown.

"Are you comfortable with Rome's presentation about her course of action?" 3J asked Pascale as she savored the sweet, robust hickory smell gently wafting from her salmon.

"Not sure, just yet. We know she was willing to commit a crime or two on behalf of First Commercial Bank a few years ago, and we also know the authorities didn't prosecute her in the States or in Britain. But I sure have no interest commissioning a crime on our account now that she's on *our* team."

"Totally agree," 3J said, then added, "Have some rings," pushing the large stack of onion rings toward Pascale.

As he grabbed two rings from the plate and nodded his head in thanks, he said, "Maybe we should call Aaronson and make the legitimacy of the investigation his problem. After all, it's his associate."

"I like that idea. We can't convey our concern too strongly. He needs to make sure he keeps a rein on this Rome character. I mean, she sounds like she's good at what she does, but so was Al Capone. Y'know what I mean?"

"I'm with you. We can call when we get back to the shop."

The two finished their respective dishes in silence, reaffirming the astonishing effect that hickory smoke can have on the proteins of the world in the skilled hands of a smoke-master.

"Moses? This is 3J and Pascale. Do you have a second to talk?"

"For you both, absolutely. How has your day been so far?"

"We're fine, thanks. Look, we have one overriding concern after the conference call with Rome."

"You wish to discuss in more detail the lawfulness of Rome's methods in this project, I assume?"

3J realized that the gravity of her stated concerns in the conference call had not escaped Moses' attention. "Correct."

"I am not surprised, given your experience with her in the last case and her résumé. Please, proceed," Moses said, clearing the path for 3J and Pascale to state what was on their minds.

"Here's the thing. We don't know Ms. Davies, and we feel it's incumbent upon you to oversee her, and provide us the assurances that all actions she, or her crowdsourcing colleagues, will undertake, will be lawful."

"Understood," Moses stated, awaiting whatever else 3J had to say.

"No hacking. No crimes. Can we agree on that, please?"

Moses sighed almost imperceptibly. In the past, when he turned over a project to Rome, he clarified that if the client wished to use Rome's services, they would directly employ her and he would step out of the middle. He felt he had a greater respect for employing only legal techniques in his line of work than many of his clients had, so he used the device of directly engaging Rome as a way for him to steer clear of any trouble with the law. In this project, however, the arrangement so far was that Moses remained the middle man between the clients and Rome. He wondered if he should try to reset the engagement, with 3J and Pascale dealing directly with Rome, or if he should continue to stay involved – perhaps employing Rome himself? He had given this issue a great deal of thought and had decided to stay involved. Moses looked over to Emily, who was lying on one of the pillows on his bed, chin on her front paws, eyes blinking, staring at him, seemingly unconcerned with his decision. She trusted his judgment on this and all other matters. Occasionally, her eyelids got heavy and she closed her eyes, but each time Moses spoke, she opened them and resumed her steady watch.

"Ms. Jones, I understand your concern. It is completely logical for you to pursue this assurance. Oftentimes, when I introduce a client to Ms. Davies, the client engages her directly and I step away; here, however, I will stay involved. The arrangement will be that you have engaged *me*, and Ms. Davies is one of my operatives. I will ensure Ms. Davies' compliance with applicable laws. I can assure you of that. She is a person of her word and not one to stray from a promise."

3J said, "That's good to hear. We'll just await the next report from Rome, then."

"Have a wonderful rest of your day in America's Heartland, Ms. Jones," Moses said with his usual formality and soothing tone.

When they disconnected, Pascale smiled and shook his head. "What a character that one is. We'll have a more 'wonderful rest of our day here in the Heartland' if we can quickly get to the bottom of these posts and pull the plug on them."

"Yeah, he's a character. But, I guess, he's our character. And we've hitched our bankruptcy covered wagon to his little operation."

Rome's next search turned up similar posts to the ones she had already found by noLight, as well as some older posts. She also did a Clearnet, simple Google search for "noLightpasses31" and, to her surprise, found additional posts and information. Rather than continue to go it alone, she first reached out to her contacts at *Crowded!* and provided the information she had gathered so far, outlining the task at hand and securing a promise that the *Crowded!* sleuths would begin immediately. Rome then reached out to her own network of late night internet geeks, with the same presentation.

Now all she needed to do was to continue her own searching while she waited for these two more robust methods of hunting down noLight to develop.

Rome needed a break before she could start on her searches of the three creditors: Belle Chi, Benny Woodson, and Phillip Dewey. She closed her laptop cover – making sure to attach the charger – left her phone on its charging pad, and decided to stretch and take a walk in the London mist. Walking was the only time she left technology behind. While she worked, she was good for twenty-minute walk breaks before the technology separation anxiety would set in. At some point in her life, she had tried to increase her time apart from the screens, but, despite her best efforts, she always had a hard-stop moment of twenty minutes when she would begin to sweat and tremble imperceptibly and would need to return to work. It was just the way she was wired.

Upon arriving back home, Rome opened her laptop and started with Tor searches of the three creditors on the Dark Web. She found little, if any, information of any use. None seemed to take part in any Dark Web forums. She then turned her efforts to Clearnet Google searches. Here, she found lots of information about each creditor. For Belle Chi, information about her security firm and her personal history; from Rome's perspective, there was nothing that had any relevance to a smear campaign. She found similar plain-vanilla information about Benny Woodson – just another landlord in Kansas City.

The Dewey searches revealed his educational background, and even some papers he had written while in his MBA program. Again, nothing particularly revealing. She found some photographs in the SLU archives of Dewey's classmates. She found few, if any, photographs of the younger Dewey at SLU, and those she found portrayed him alone.

The lack of leads from her searches of the creditors discouraged her. All she could do was continue her own searching and wait for the twenty-first century's crowdsourced sleuthing to perform its magic.

CHAPTER 17

Tuesday, November 14, 2023

JUDGE ROBERTSON USED HIS preferred old-fashioned intercom system to call Jennifer into his office: he leaned out of his door and, directing his voice down the hallway that connected the two, called, "Jennifer, when you have a moment, please."

Jennifer smiled at the retro way he called a meeting, picked up her pad, pen, and a folder containing her First Amendment research, and headed for the Judge's office. Upon arrival, she sat in her appointed chair. The Judge said, "Just checking in to see what you've got so far on the First Amendment vs the automatic stay research. How's it going?"

"Going well. I was just about to start on a memo to you. I found a fascinating case that I think pretty much captures what goes on in this area of the law."

"A memo will be great, but before you start writing, let me know what you've found. I'm all ears."

Expecting to write and send the Judge a memo on the case, she was surprised by the request for an oral briefing. The informality of the Judge's style momentarily flustered her, but she regained her composure. *Not too terribly different from getting called on in law school classes, I suppose, and I managed to survive that experience.* She took a slightly deeper breath than usual, looked down at her notes, and began. "The principal case

I found is *In re Andrus*. It's a 1995 appellate decision in the Northern District of Illinois, which affirmed the Bankruptcy Court's decision. In a nutshell, a debtor named Andrus had borrowed money from his neighbor's company, Stann & Associates. Instead of paying Stann back, Andrus and his wife filed a joint Chapter 7 bankruptcy case. After they received their discharge, Stann posted a sign near Andrus' house that read, in caps, 'ANDRUS, WHERE'S MY MONEY?' The Debtors filed a motion asking the Court to find Stann in contempt; in response, Stann agreed to take the sign down. So at that point, the bankruptcy judge must've thought the problem was over. But then, Stann posted a second sign that read, again in caps, 'ANDRUS WENT BANKRUPT! HE DIDN'T PAY HIS BILLS. HE IS A DEADBEAT! THIS IS A PUBLIC SERVICE ANNOUNCEMENT.'" Jennifer looked up from her notes and saw the Judge's reaction.

He began to laugh, first a chuckle and then almost a guffaw. "Stann was playing with fire, eh?"

Jennifer smiled and said, "I don't know if Stann had a plan or just a bad case of insomnia and came up with his messages while laying awake in bed."

"Maybe just another sleepless creditor unhappy with the way things roll in bankruptcy."

Jennifer continued, "Turns out, Stann had acted badly before he came up with the signs. He had left a harassing and vulgar message on Andrus' answering machine. In the message, he threatened to ruin Andrus' reputation in the community if Andrus didn't pay him back." She paused and then quipped, "Not too bright, leaving a recording." The Judge nodded in agreement. She continued, "He then approached Andrus and his wife as they were getting into their car and repeatedly asked them to repay the debt. But the best, if you can call it that, was what Stann did in the backyard."

"You mean there's more?"

"Oh, yes. Stann outdid himself with his yard antics. Sorry in advance for the language he used, Judge."

"Despite popular belief, I am not a choir boy," the Judge assured her, and smiled.

"Ok," Jennifer said, "from his yard and across the fence to Andrus' yard, Stann shouted at Andrus' wife, no less: 'Who do you think you are? Your husband is a deadbeat. I've told the whole Ukrainian community about you. You're just off the boat. You think that attorney of yours is going to protect you? Your attorney knows nothing. Get yourself a better attorney. No Court is going to protect you. You get that deadbeat husband of yours. I want my money. I want Andrus. I want my money.' The next day, the same yard, but this time it was Andrus, and Stann yelled, 'You're a deadbeat. I want my money. Let's go. I'll beat it out of you. Let's go get over it. I'm going to beat the shit out of you. And if you win, Andrus, because you're such a faggot you're not going to win but if you win, I'll drop the $20,000.' What was interesting was that Stann admitted all of this in testimony. Kind of proud of his backyard outbursts. His lawyer must have been cringing."

"No accounting for some folks' disdain of the rule of law, I am afraid," the Judge concurred, shaking his head slowly in disbelief. "The lawyer probably advised against testifying, but sounds like Stann would have no part of a muzzle. He had something that he needed to say, I guess. I feel sorry for the lawyer. Tough gig, representing Stann."

Jennifer was nearing the end of her research and said, "Stann certainly was passionate ... and demonstratively foolish. Both Courts had no problem finding him in contempt. They both batted away Stann's suggestion that his right of free speech trumped the Bankruptcy Code's prohibition of any attempt to collect a debt during the Bankruptcy case because of the automatic stay, and after the case because of the discharge. The two – the stay and the discharge – really operate the same way."

"Correct," Judge Robertson agreed. "They do; they both bar creditors' actions."

Jennifer continued, "The Courts both said that even though there was a communicative element to Stann's comments, that didn't mean it's protected speech. Both said free speech doesn't give a creditor the right to violate the Bankruptcy Code."

"I certainly agree with that sentiment."

Jennifer paused while she went through her notes, and then observed, "Judge, I should point out that I found another case, *Stonegate Security Services*, also out of the Northern District of Illinois, and there, the Court permitted a creditor to park a car outside the Debtor's business with signage on the front, side and rear of the car with messages that read: 'Stonegate Auto Alarms does not pay supplier;' and 'Crime does not pay, Stonegate Auto Alarms the same way.' The *Stonegate* judge saw no danger that the signs would frustrate the Debtor's reorganization."

"Hmmm. Well, that's interesting. It shows how these kinds of matters can turn on the specific facts, as well as that judge's sense of the effect the communication has on the Debtor. Very helpful. Great work, Jennifer. Finish your memo, and then we can get you some other things to work on." As she nodded in agreement, he said, "My guess here is that this smear campaign is going to hurt BJB. We're coming out of a pandemic – I'm sure times have been really rough on the clubs over the last couple of years because of Covid. Ms. Jones and her team are going to have to find who is behind the smears, and when she does, my guess is that we're going to have a humdinger of an evidentiary hearing. But first she's going to have to find the perpetrator; then we'll just have to see where the evidence takes us."

Jennifer listened carefully to his thought process. The meeting ended and as she returned to her office down the hall, she felt relieved that her first briefing had gone well, and allowed herself a pat on the back. *This is kind of cool. I have a front-row seat into the Judge's thought process, and he said I was very helpful. I can totally do this job!*

When Jennifer left the Judge's office, he thought to himself, *She's going to be just fine in her new role.* He wondered, however, if the Rapinoes would fare quite as well in the face of the onslaught of the posted "public service" announcements trashing them and their company over and over again. He assumed loyal followers would ignore the posts; he also assumed that many patrons would not even see the posts. But they were out there — very public, very accessible, and, he expected, very damaging. *Very troubling.*

CHAPTER 18

Wednesday, November 15, 2023

ROME RECEIVED HER FIRST communication from her own private network of informed techies within twelve hours of putting out her request for assistance and information. The communication was from a techie she knew as Albert, also an archeology major at a small liberal arts school, whom she'd met at a virtual archeology conference after graduation.

She came to know Albert well, although the two had never met in person, only online. After graduating from college, Rome was able to marry her love of the low-tech archeology degree with her love of the internet and all things high-tech. while remaining a wallflower, and not particularly an in-person social creature. While she sometimes liked human interplay, she certainly didn't seek it out. Many of her own network of techies shared that trait. All very comfortable in front of a screen in a dark room with empty energy drink cans strewn around, but not as comfortable with face-to-face interactions.

Rome was a legend amongst her network. Word of her man-in-the-middle attack on the Witherman financial advisor's computer and the resulting location of Witherman's hidden Swiss assets made its way around her network like electricity through a copper wire. So when she put out her latest information request, and stressed that time was of the essence, she expected several private network sleuths would jump right on the project.

She was right.

The information she now reviewed was penetrating and alarming. Albert had focused on noLight to see if he could match the complete handle "noLightpasses31" with a real name somewhere on the internet. Her colleague advised her that he decided to focus on Clearnet searches, on the theory that when noLight posted on the Dark Web, he or she was in character, totally stealth, and potentially less likely to slip up and connect a name with a handle. Her colleague searched the handle on the usual Clearnet sites – Facebook, LinkedIn, Twitter, and Reddit, and each search yielded nothing. After many unproductive Google searches, her colleague took a break and surfed to Flickr to look at some photos posted from all over the world while he regrouped before developing new searches. Flickr was arguably the largest online photo management and sharing website in the world with over a half a billion creative commons photos posted, and growing. He particularly enjoyed looking at landscape images from places he never dreamed of visiting and found them soothing and reinvigorating. As he looked, he realized he hadn't specifically searched *specialized* websites – like Flickr – for the "noLight" handle. On a whim, he decided to search "noLightpasses31" but, failing to catch his typos, accidentally transposed "31" into "13" and changed the tense of "passes" to "passed." He hit the enter key without catching his mistake and immediately discovered a Flickr account with that handle: noLightpassed13. He surfed straight to the account owner's page to see what information he could glean. While the owner didn't list his name, he did offer the following information:

I am an amateur photographer, and have been making images since I was 12. I never switched to digital. I am a film purist creating images with my treasured Minolta camera. While I have lived all over the U.S., I now live in the greater Kansas City area. While I like to take pictures of most anything – landscapes, nature, people – of late, I have begun to make macro images of the inner and outer workings of cameras, new and vintage. This includes sensors, shutters, lenses, old flash bulbs, and the like. I hope you enjoy my posts.

Albert instantly noted two pieces of information from the description: *this* noLight was in Kansas City somewhere; and he seemed to like to take pictures of one specific form of technology, cameras. Not a great deal to go on, but the information energized Albert. He popped open a can of Blueberry Red Bull, instantly forgot that he hadn't finished his break, and began a fresh round of searches for this new handle – noLightpassed13. The new searches yielded much more than he'd expected. First, on the Dark Web, he found posts from noLightpassed13 that seemed quite similar to the posts from noLightpasses31 – similar vernacular; similar topics, similar points of view. But his Clearnet search was more revealing. On a SubReddit group discussing social media's role in monitoring, policing, and banning misinformation, he found noLightpassed13 activity. Lots of it. This noLight had opinions and was happy to express them – all of them. Over and over. This noLight seemed to get into heated discussions with others in the SubReddit group. Rather than read all the many discussion strings, Albert downloaded them to his laptop and immediately forwarded them to Rome. The two then messaged each other so that Albert could bring Rome up to speed on what he had found.

Rome distilled Albert's process, and the discovery of the second, similar handle, and forwarded that to her *Crowded!* contact. Suddenly, the pace of matters had sped up. Rome then read the many posts by noLightpassed13 with laser-focused interest.

CHAPTER 19

I USED MY BURNER phone to contact Edmond Richardsen. I could feel more scrutiny on Project Dis than in prior similar operations, and a certain amount of pressure building. I felt it best to receive an update on the methodologies Edmond had employed to post. Just how stealthy was the operation? Joshua was never one to say, "I told you so," but I could clearly sense his growing discomfort with the entire situation as it was unfolding.

Edmond and I agreed to a rendezvous in Swope Park where we could talk with virtual anonymity. It was my favorite meeting place in Kansas City to conduct the kind of business Edmond and I were working on. At over 1800 acres of parkland, it was easily the largest park in Kansas City, with plenty of wooded hiking trails, perfect for staying off the radar. We met near the Swinging Bridge, a suspension bridge that crossed the Blue River as it meandered through the park about a mile-and-a-half east of the main entrance. The bridge was proximate to a particular trail I enjoyed; once on the trail, I knew we could be alone.

"Edmond, thank you for meeting with me on such short notice. Now that our little operation is in full swing, I wanted to pose two questions for you. First, have you run into any snags as you implement your part of our undertaking?"

"No snags at all, Dewey. Everything is smooth sailing. One hundred percent. You give me the content and it goes up on the web within the hour. No edits. Just like you write it."

"That is good news, Edmond. Very good news indeed." We wandered along a trail thick with oaks and maple trees whose leaves were in full color display. Fallen yellow and red leaves lined the trail. I was not particularly a nature lover, and certainly not at all a connoisseur of leaves, but I did enjoy the peacefulness that the fallen leaves offered in their silent trip from tree to trail.

I continued, "Edmond, my second question is perhaps a bit more complicated. I wonder this: if someone with your level of technological skills wanted to figure out who was behind the posts, how would they go about doing so."

"Hmmm. That *is* more complicated," Edmond said. I could tell the question had taken him by surprise. He collected his thoughts for just a moment, and then continued, choosing his words more carefully than was usually his custom. "I know you want maximum stealth. I get that. But nothing is undetectable in the 2023 online world. We can employ methods to make it hard to figure out who is posting, but if it's written and posted, and somebody who's looking is good at it, there's most definitely risk that, eventually, that person might trace it."

While I appreciated the answer he gave, it did not answer the question I asked – always an annoyance to me – so I said, "How so? How would someone go about tracing it?"

"If I were tracing, I'd develop searches for the Dark Web to find similar style posts – similar style campaigns, other posts by the poster, and try to tie them back."

"So, other posts you may have made over the years."

"Correct."

"Are there such things, Edmond?" I looked straight ahead while I talked. No need to make eye contact with Edmond. If

I became upset and my eyes began to darken, he might shut down. I wanted him to keep talking.

"One hundred percent, Dewey." Back to his normal way of addressing me.

"For instance …?"

"Well, remember, we had a similar project a few years ago. The Debtor wasn't in bankruptcy, but he owed you money and wouldn't pay."

"Did you use the same handle?"

"Negatory."

"Any other ways?" I asked, trying to mask my concern.

"I post on some Dark Web forums."

"Under your own name?"

I could feel Joshua tensing up and coming out of his dark repose as he assessed the veracity of the answers Edmond gave me. The answers concerned Joshua as well as me.

"Negatory. I have a couple of handles I use. Same handles I've used for many years."

"Hmmm. I see," I said. "Shouldn't you use a new handle for our current project?"

"Nah, Dewey. Not necessary. My handles are fine. Handles aren't like a password that they tell you to change every so often."

I absorbed what Edmond just said; I sagged my shoulders, because what was done was done; exhaled loudly to show I was unhappy; smacked my tongue on the roof of my mouth, and then continued, "If they found you, how would they tie a post of yours to me?"

"Now, that'd be even harder, Dewey. You and me, we've done a similar operation before, of course. They could find our prior campaign, I suppose, and try to link those to other folks who borrowed from you. That'd be one way. Or, they could try to get me to tell them about you …" Edmond's voice trailed off as he finished his sentence and he paused as he thought about his statement and added, "Yeah, hundred percent. That's how they could do it."

Joshua growled, but only I could hear him.

"Now I *am* concerned, Edmond."

"Negatory. You've got nothing to be concerned about. You pay me. I don't talk."

"I see, Edmond."

"You were a rock on the prior projects. No concerns at all. Why all the concern on this one, Dewey?"

"My dear Edmond, the last project we worked on did not involve a bankruptcy case with a team of Greene Madison bankruptcy lawyers scrutinizing everything. I ... No. *We* need to be careful about everything."

"You're the risk expert, Dewey. But for my dime, we have protections in place, we're taking all precautions, and while nothing is a hundred percent secret on the internet, hundred percent we'll be fine."

Edmond was correct. I was the risk expert, not him. It was not at all comforting that he thought all would be fine, "hundred percent." It wasn't his place to comfort me. However – yes, there was clearly more risk in this project than in prior engagements with Edmond, but I continued to feel that the risk was necessary when balanced against the reward of a large payback.

We had reached a clearing near the small parking lot where we had each parked our cars, and our clandestine meeting drew to a close. I bade Edmond goodbye, got into my car, and headed on 63rd Street to Wornall Road, and then south to 103rd Street and eventually Hallbrook. I had time in the car to think. *Perhaps the best plan is another week of posts and then ... radio silence as I slide back into the shadows and wait for the smear inoculation to take effect, and for BJB to expire,* I thought. *No reason to overdo things. While sometimes moderation is for cowards, here, too much of a good thing can be too dangerous. Just one more week.*

Joshua listened to my thoughts, as he often did. Once I returned to my car, Joshua returned to his little place. But he didn't sleep. He let me know he sensed danger, and he was none too happy at all. He let me know he didn't trust Edmond. The more Joshua worried about the situation, the more chance he would insist on taking control. I needed to keep control of the situation to ensure I continued as the Primary, guiding the ship. I certainly didn't want to go to sleep and let Joshua take over. Then I might remember nothing that transpired while he was in control.

I preferred when Joshua allowed me to guide the ship. Here, I needed Joshua to remain calm.

CHAPTER 20

Wednesday, November 15, 2023

As Richardsen returned to his car, he pondered Dewey's questions. He'd noted that Dewey had never made eye contact, which he deemed a good thing. *Those eyes give me the creeps,* he thought. *Never liked them, since I first met him years ago.* He opened the car door and sat behind the steering wheel with his forearms on the wheel and his forehead near it for several minutes. He had been honest with Dewey but, perhaps, not completely. True, he had two handles he liked to use. But Dewey hadn't pressed him for the handles, and he hadn't offered them, so he hadn't disclosed how similar they were. Moreover, his answer, that he used a different handle for Project Dis, was correct but again, he had omitted the similarity of the two handles. Had he expounded on the details, Edmond expected Dewey would have done more than just appear unhappy.

For years, before he'd taken on side projects for Dewey and others, Richardsen had operated with only one handle. At some point, he added a new handle to his online persona. But like similar passwords that people create so they don't forget, Richardsen did the same with the additional handle. *If someone wants to find me, they will. I take measures to protect my identity, but I'm not some covert operator from a rogue nation, changing American public sentiment with disinformation. And even those covert operators get caught and shut down,* he thought.

He started his engine and drove back to his home in the Armour Hills neighborhood. He parked on the street and went down to his small, damp basement, where he had his home computer array set up, and awaited the next round of posts from Dewey.

Richardsen had no problem playing the role of subservient vendor as long as Dewey paid him, and Dewey always paid him – and paid him well. The money was the only reason Richardsen did the side gigs. He wasn't one of the moneyed MBAs. He always needed more.

His thoughts turned again to whether he would ever reveal that Dewey was behind the smear posts. *I don't* <u>*think*</u> *I'd ever talk,* he thought. *But I'm not taking the fall for Dewey ... or anyone else, for that matter. If they come knocking, I won't spend too much time with my hands tied up behind my back under a hot white light before I spill and give them Dewey's contact information. His risk, not mine. Hundred percent.*

CHAPTER 21

Thursday, November 16 to Friday, November 17, 2023

3J SAT AT HER desk drafting the cash agreement to deliver to Fuentes. The sun had set; the office was empty; and the only sounds on her end of the floor were her fingers striking the keys, and the muted sounds of the cleaning crew performing their daily tasks of dusting and tidying. The vacuuming would start shortly, and she would have to close her office door so she could focus.

This was her routine, her regular way of dealing with the cleaning crew. It made her wonder if her office furniture was dustier than the furniture and the carpeting in her colleagues' offices who already left for the day. She was a neat freak, so while she didn't vacuum at work, she kept several dusters in her office and sometimes she dusted as she thought. *And people think the life of a lawyer is glamorous. Ha!* She wondered if the big city lawyers in New York dusted their own offices.

She still wasn't sure why Phillip Dewey would allow his attorney to agree to the use of cash so readily. But he apparently had, and she was of the "strike-while-the-iron-is-hot" mindset, so she wrote the agreement, and when she had finished it an hour later, she emailed the draft to Pascale for any edits and input he could offer, as she had done on so many documents over the years they worked together.

After hitting the "send" button, she closed down her computer and opened her office door to find the cleaning crew still hard at work. She waved to them, thanked one of them for her hard work, and went down the elevator the twenty-seven floors to the street level. This night, she would leave her car parked in the Greene Madison garage and just walk home.

Just as she got to the lobby, her phone rang.

"3J, Adam and Bey here. We wanted to report to you on the effects the posts are having on our business," Bey Rapinoe said, with obvious concern in her voice.

"I was hoping, perhaps irrationally, that the report would be better than I hear in your voice, Bey."

"Yes, well, here it is in cold hard facts. Patron attendance down 28%; two acts we had booked, canceled; and four acts we normally book said 'no.' Total effect on business? Kane is still working the numbers but revenues are off somewhere around 30% of projections."

"I know the wait for information from Aaronson's team is tough, but we're all hopeful that we'll have a report in the next day or two and then we'll be in a position to act on it quickly."

"We know that you have little to no control over the situation. And neither do we. But it's hard to fight a shadow," Adam said. He paused and then continued, "We're still able to prop up the clubs with our personal savings for a little while longer, but soon we'll have to make some untenable decisions. Such as, do we dip into our kids' college funds, or do we let the clubs slide down the slippery slope into oblivion, and take our dream with it?"

3J grimaced at the suggestion that either the college fund or the slide would happen, but she knew Adam was trying his level best to be wide-eyed and coldly rational. It's what made him such a forceful businessman.

"We aren't there yet. But I really do understand the problem."

Bey said, "There's more. The agreement to pay Veridical will be in jeopardy if we can't turn this around, and quickly. We just won't have the cash sufficient to pay the lender."

"I understand. But the payments are off a ways and lots can, and I hope will, happen before then. Let's talk tomorrow. I'd say let's sleep on it, but I'm sure sleep is not something that comes easily right now – for me too," 3J said, aligning her own feelings about the posts and their effect with the Rapinoes.

The call ended the same way it began – uneasiness all around the horn. 3J then traversed the lobby quickly, saying "good-night" to Samuel, the nighttime security guard who sat behind a desk in the mostly dark lobby, with the blue light of his computer screen dancing across his face. She wondered what it was like to work the graveyard shift as a security guard in a high-rise office building in downtown Kansas City – or any city, for that matter. She knew Samuel had a wife and a couple of kids, and as 3J pushed open the lobby door and entered Walnut Street, she thought, *What a hard way to put a roof over the family's head and food on the table.* She admired Samuel more than most of the lawyers she had met over the years. *Not enough of _them_ think about the Samuels of the world,* she thought, before correcting her thinking. *Not enough of _us_ think about the Samuels of the world and do something to make their lives better. Yes,* she thought, *that's correct. _I'm_ one of those lawyers, and no better.*

It was 9:30 p.m. when 3J's black shoes hit the Walnut Street pavement. Stylish, simple, elegant Christian Louboutin pointed toe pumps, which accented her shapely calves, still an item years after college.

She made her way south on Walnut Street to the second high-rise building in her life – her favorite of the two – and up twenty floors to her condo. She knew – and worried, sometimes – that living so close to where she worked meant her personal universe had limits – much of her life was in the handful of square blocks between work and home. Her Walnut Street existence. She had decided to buy a practical Prius a year ago to expand her territory, and when she took it out for a spin, she was in love with the mileage it got and her small part in helping the climate.

3J opened her front door to the splendor of the downtown skyline as it filled her windows, like a natural portrait of urban America hung in her condo for her to admire each night. She kicked off her shoes, wiggled and stretched her toes as they were freed from the confines of designer footwear that 3J subjected them to each working day, made her way to her fridge, found a portion of a day-old chef's salad, poured a glass of Walla Walla's Charles and Charles Cabernet Sauvignon, turned on Miles Davis' 1956 bop masterpiece, *Relaxin' with the Miles Davis Quintet*, and, as Miles and Coltrane traded solos, she attempted to make her thoughts drift to anything besides work. But not even the late, great Miles, could impose a state of relaxation on 3J at this point. All she could do was try to force her brain to think of something else besides the current bankruptcy cases.

As 3J got lost in the skyline – just as Miles sustained a note with vibrato on his fabled trumpet – and tried to leave the long day behind, she wondered about the Greene Madison of old. *Did those partners regularly work until 9:30 p.m., or did they manage to secure a life outside of the law firm for themselves?* she wondered, and sighed. *Well, those old guys certainly didn't get texts and emails into the late evening and they didn't have social media to contend with.*

Just as she considered the practice of law without texts and emails, her phone dinged and she looked, of course, despite a significant part of her brain silently screaming, *Don't look tonight!!* But she did, because that's what she knew she was supposed to do; that's what lawyers did in the modern era.

There, on the phone, was a text from Rome. 3J looked at her watch. It was now 10:30 central time, and she calculated that it must be wake-up time tomorrow in London. The text was simply: "Can we talk?" 3J assumed one missing word: "Now." She wrote back one word: "Sure" and hit send, and then thought her answer was incomplete so she jotted a second text: "Please call me, if you can now, on this number." She saw the three ellipses on her phone signifying that another text might be on the way from Rome, but none came. Instead, moments later, 3J's phone rang.

"Ms. Jones, I know it is late there and I really am sorry to invade your evening and personal wind-down time."

3J chuckled and said, "No worries. Not sure how much personal wind-down time I get or expect these days. Just part of the lawyer gig."

Rome accepted without comment what she took to be 3J's permission to have the conversation even at a late hour.

3J continued, "So, whatcha got, Rome?"

Rome quickly outlined the level of searches being conducted by both her and her cohort of sleuths. Then Rome explained the handles the cohort had discovered – both noLights. "Ms. Jones, sometimes these searches are wild goose chases through unlit branches of the Dark Web that, frankly, are time-consuming and yield little except more search terms. But the similar duplicate handles caught our attention. We were first drawn to the 'noLightpasses31' handle as some of his or her posts on the Dark Web forums we focused on seemed similar in tone and nature to the present smear campaign we are trying to address. Then, by the providence of a late night typo committed by one of the cohort, we discovered a similar handle – noLightpassed13. For ease, I'll refer to the second handle as NLP13 if that's ok. You can appreciate the similarity. Almost *too* similar." 3J listened with interest as she took notes. So far, while the path to finding noLightpassed13 was interesting, she wasn't sure she could yet appreciate where it would lead. Rome continued, "My colleague Albert, stationed in Indiana, is the cohort member to figure this out. He searched some specialized websites on the Clearnet to see if NLP13 was active. Turns out, NLP13 is. Very. Apparently, NLP13 is a film photo buff with a pretty active account on Flickr. Are you familiar with Flickr?"

"Just a little. One of my college friends got married just before the pandemic and she posted the wedding photos on Flickr so all her friends could enjoy the wedding if they couldn't attend. Flickr's a photo sharing site, I take it?"

"Yes. Possibly the largest in the world." Rome took a sip of her steaming green tea and returned to her report. "On Flickr, the account holder may write a paragraph describing themselves, and NLP13 did. I'll email you that description when we finish this call, along with other information that I will touch on. Bottom line, NLP13 lives somewhere in the Kansas City Metropolitan area, and has a love – perhaps a fascination – for photographing technical things, such as the inner workings of cameras. In addition, and this seems very telling, my cohort has located many posts on the Clearnet by NLP13 – apparently he or she uses one of these two handles extensively when online. These posts caught our eye because they passionately defend NLP13's right to post false information – disinformation, if you will – as a matter of the First Amendment right to free speech, and in the posts, NLP13 ardently defends the notion that none of the social media platforms should monitor and police the poster of disinformation." 3J sat straight up on her couch when she heard this last piece of information and whistled softly into the phone in surprise. In response to the whistle, Rome said, "Exactly. We think it's much too much of a coincidence that someone who lives in Kansas City and therefore would be proximate to a Kansas City creditor is a champion of disinformation on the internet's major social media platforms – Facebook, LinkedIn, Twitter, and Reddit."

"How do you link NLP13 with the human behind the posts?" 3J inquired.

"How indeed, Ms. Jones. These next steps will be more difficult, but that is where the art and science of crowdsource sleuthing comes in. Perhaps we can find someone who has – let's call it, argued with NLP13 online who will have some insight into who exactly NLP13 is. Or perhaps we can find an archive of past posts where NLP13 was less careful. This will take a bit of luck, but as the discovery of NLP13 illustrates, luck can play a significant role in this type of investigation."

3J certainly understood the power of luck. "Next steps, if we find out who NLP13 is?" she inquired.

"Yes – excellent question. I've talked with Moses, and it is our current thinking that if we find out the name behind the handle, we can then pursue a dual path, with your team and ours attempting to find an address. At that point, we have a choice. First, we could establish a more traditional covert surveillance operation and see what we learn." Rome paused to allow 3J to chime in with questions or comments.

"You mean, we'd follow this person and see what we learn, if anything?"

"Correct. This path could be time-consuming. And we might learn nothing. One never knows."

"Who'd tail them?" 3J asked, thinking that Greene Madison had no capacity to surveil themselves, but someone at the firm probably could recommend a local investigator to do so.

"Either your team could identify someone with whom they are comfortable, or failing that, Moses advises he has some operatives in the Midwest that he could call upon for the surveillance."

"And what is option two?" 3J asked.

"Option two is to confront this person."

"You mean get in his or her face?" 3J inquired, a little taken aback that the confrontation might involve the Greene Madison lawyers.

"While that *is* a possibility, the main aim of the confrontation would be to scare them into doing something quickly that would, hopefully, reveal if someone *else* is really behind the posts. So the confrontation might be from someone who is … shall we say, scarier? A bit more forceful without using force; a bit more forward than a typical surveillance expert."

3J paused as she absorbed Rome's descriptions and slowly said only, "I see."

"Moses asked me to convey to you that if we select option two, then we should talk as soon as we can – tomorrow U.S. time would be great – and decide if the person to confront the owner of the NLP13 handle is someone you would supply, or us."

"Anything else?" 3J asked, already out of breath as she listened to the report unfold.

"Just one more item on my list, Ms. Jones. Again, based on discussions with Moses, we feel that your team and the Rapinoes should make the selection of option one or two, and we are ready and able to implement what needs to be done at our end, no matter which choice you go for. But, we would be remiss if we did not offer at least some opinion reflecting our views. Succinctly, we think option two is the better choice, taking into account the need to bring this to a conclusion as quickly as possible."

"Good to know, Rome. We'll consider the recommendation, which I appreciate. Anything else?"

"Not at this time, Ms. Jones."

"Rome, this is really outstanding work that you and your team have done in such a short time frame. We're grateful."

"Our pleasure," Rome said. "I know Moses values this new business relationship with your team a great deal and we are both hopeful that we can assist you and the Rapinoes to bring down whomever is behind the noxious posts."

The two ended the call with pleasantries. 3J saw her phone was about to run out of battery, so she plugged in a charger and immediately called Pascale. She knew he would be up. Pascale answered on the first ring, and 3J brought him up to speed.

"Simultaneously gripping and distressing news, 3J. They certainly have moved rapidly. Next steps?"

"Need to get all this info to the Rapinoes, pronto. I'll do that tonight with as detailed an email as I can muster at this point. We need to get them on the phone first thing in the a.m. Then we need to talk with Moses and Rome. We'll need to see if their cohort of sleuths has turned anything else up over our evening hours, and if we select option two, we'll need some muscle. I think I'd describe it as sophisticated, intelligent, muscle. Not sure who that'd be. You?" 3J asked Pascale, hoping his electronic Rolodex would contain the name of such a person.

"Need to give the 'who' question some thought. It's been quite a long time since I had a bankruptcy where undercover, and surveillance – and the possible need for muscle – were the themes of the case."

"Understood. I don't think I've ever had one like this before, Pascale," 3J admitted.

"Alright. Well, lots to do. You get to that email and leave it to me to find some candidates to implement option two. I just want to be careful that we don't select some overzealous police wannabe who goes in with a tire iron and not only scares the shit out of NLP13, but commits a misguided assault and battery on our account. That wouldn't be good for the continuation of our coveted law licenses, I'm afraid."

"Oh, I hear that loud and clear," 3J concurred. "Those nightmare scenario thoughts have not escaped me."

They ended the call with each appreciating that they would have little personal time that night for the good of the clients and the cases.

The next morning, on his way into the office, Pascale stopped at the workplace of a potential candidate to carry out option two. He knew an ex-law enforcement gentleman quite well and thought an unannounced stop at his establishment would be in order. The best candidate for the job was an ex-cop, and if the ex-cop he had in mind had no interest in the engagement, he might know one that would.

Pascale pulled up near the establishment and parked his nondescript, brown aging Toyota Camry a few doors down from the front door. He wasn't a car person and had never been interested in driving anything flashy or fancy. He had from time to time thought how interesting it would be to buy a Tesla, but he viewed a new electric car acquisition as something to bring up in the future at one of the microeconomic budget meetings that he had once in a while as he shaved and stared back at himself in the bathroom mirror.

He grabbed the handle on the weathered white door, but it was locked. There was no bell. Pascale was left-handed, but going all the way back to his little league days, he had always preserved his left hand for baseball usage, so he thumped on the door with his right fist and hoped someone inside would let him in. After a few seconds, the door opened, and that someone stepped aside and smiled at him.

"Ronnie, how the hell are you?" Pascale asked Ronnie Steele,

O'Brien's bartender. Pascale and Ronnie had struck up a friendship many years ago. Both had played collegiate baseball at Kansas State, Ronnie fifteen years after Pascale. They first met at an Alumni vs. Varsity fundraiser softball game when Steele was a junior roaming the left side of the K-State infield as the team's captain and shortstop. Steele was a criminal justice major and after college he enrolled in the Kansas City Police Academy before going on to a life in the vice squad, catching bad guys. He chose law enforcement over any attempt to play minor league baseball, often laughing, "All field and no hit – damn curve balls. So no chance in pro ball."

The two stayed in touch. After Steele had retired from the force and become the head bartender at O'Brien's, the two saw each other once a week or so when Pascale arrived for the traditional Friday wind-down beer. On those occasions, they had little opportunity to talk because the bar, and therefore Steele, were busy. After the accident, however, Pascale and Steele saw more of each other, sharing a Sunday beer and the beloved Royals baseball games. Both had been lifetime Royals fans, spanning the seasons from the glory days of the George Brett era, to the extended dismal years, to the world champion era of 2015 and their participation in the sea of three hundred thousand Kansas Citians at Union Station, all celebrating shoulder to shoulder in Royals blue.

Pascale followed Steele to the bar, sat on one of the bar stools, and Steele poured each of them a black coffee in the off-white, ceramic O'Brien's-branded coffee mugs that the bar had used for so many years. As Steele sipped his black coffee, and Pascale mixed in some cream to his, stirring absentmindedly, Pascale explained the situation. Steele listened carefully.

When Pascale finished, he said, "So whadya think, Ronnie? You're ex-vice. Should be right up your alley, and a good fit for your former skill set?"

Steele ignored the question, and, taking Pascale off-guard, instead asked, "You work with that 3J lady, correct?"

"She and I are colleagues at the law firm, and co-counsel on this case. So, correct."

"Would I be working for you, for her, or for both of you?"

Pascale didn't understand Steele's focus on 3J, so he said, "To be determined; but my expectation is that it would be for both of us. Is that a problem?"

"Just the opposite. I would enjoy that," Steele revealed. He paused and then asked, "Does she know you're here presenting this opportunity to me?"

"Not yet. I haven't had a chance to tell her, but we talked last night, and I'm tasked with finding the right person for this gig; it's an unusual one for a bankruptcy case."

"I see," Steele said, as he considered how 3J might react. "Well, since leaving vice, I've done a commendable job of not missing it, and staying far away from the investigation game. I think I'm better for it and I like the bar. But it sounds interesting and not particularly taxing, so … I'm good working for you and her if she's good with working with me."

"Well, if you say 'Yes,' we'll find out in short order about her piece of the equation." He watched Steele look off into the distance in the empty bar. "Sure there isn't something else to tell me before I talk with 3J?" Pascale prodded.

"Not really. Don't really know her all that well. Usually, she drinks with you off in the distance at that table over there that's damn near in the next county. She rarely drinks at the bar. Just wondering, I suppose. Always nice to know that I'm signing on to a club that wants me as a member, I guess."

"Ok. I think I get it," Pascale said, thinking to himself that he really didn't get it. "I'll call you right after I talk with 3J. Best number to use?"

"My mobile. You have it, but here it is again," Steele said as he wrote the number on the back of an O'Brien's napkin. He handed Pascale the napkin and, smiling, said, "My business card, sir." The two shook hands, and Pascale headed out the door to his Camry. As he exited, he yelled over his shoulder, "Stay outa trouble, Ronnie!"

"That would mean I shouldn't be hanging out with you!"

When Pascale returned to the office, he settled in and then walked down the hallway to 3J's office. At the doorjamb, he said, "I think I've got just the person for option two, 3J."

"Progress! Excellent," she said, pleased.

Pascale entered and took a seat. "Good progress, ma'am." He told 3J about Steele, and their history. She tried not to look too surprised by the revelation that Steele and Pascale were buddies going way back but wondered why neither had mentioned it before. "Not sure I ever knew Ronnie Steele was a cop, or a K-State wildcat, or a shortstop – or a friend of yours, for that matter. But it's all good; and if you think he's the man for the job, I do too."

"He is. Then I think we just need to await the miracle connection of the noLight handle to a real live human and we can turn Ronnie loose to do his thing – or at least, his former thing," Pascale observed.

"Ronnie? Pascale here. I've talked with 3J, and you're hired."

"Sounds good. Happy to try to help. Hope I haven't lost my chops."

"Oh, you'll be fine. Once an investigator type, always an investigator type."

Steele chuckled softly into his phone. "You say that. But we'll just have to wait and see."

Pascale then remembered he hadn't told Steele about his recent life-changing decision. "Say, I forgot to tell you something this morning. I've decided to hang up my wingtips and leave the law life."

"No shit!" Steele exclaimed. "Must've been a hard decision. Not sure if that's cause for celebration or if I should join you in mourning the loss of the career."

"I think you well know it's a little of both."

"Yeah, I remember when I decided to leave the force. There were happy moments and bittersweet moments, sometimes both at the same time. An emotionally confusing exit." Steele paused. "And the firm? Ok with your decision?"

"They'll be fine. They'll have to be. People come and go and the firm continues on. Like the river that has to flow. Always."

"Well … good for you. Let's meet up for a beer and have this discussion in person. Not really a mobile phone topic."

"Agreed. When we get together, I'll need some pointers on how to deal with the issue of what comes next."

"Happy to. And you could always mop the bar here with me. Or work the stockroom."

"I'm not saying 'no' to any idea right now, my friend."

They both said nothing for a moment, and then changing the subject back to the engagement, Steele said, "Send me over whatever info you have so far, and let me absorb what we know. Then tell me as soon as you have at least a name on our dirty trickster."

"Will do. Thanks for being willing to help out on this one. The Rapinoes are good folks and I really hope we can help them out of this mess."

"Don't know them personally, but love their clubs."

"Be safe, Ronnie."

"Always, my man. Always. You too, Pascale."

CHAPTER 22

I SAT AT MY kitchen table reading the *Kansas City Star* and thought, *Just a few more days remaining in my BJB plan. Then I shall suspend the posts and sit back and assess the effect on the business. After that, I think it will be time to sit down with them and have a heart-to-heart discussion about repayment of the entire debt from the closure of the business and the sale of the real estate. Of course, they will resist, but what choice will they have? The damage from Project Dis will be irreparable by that time.*

I felt good about my plan.

I turned to face Mother's vessel and said out loud, "What's that, Mother?" I paused for a *response*, and then said, "No, I do not intend physically to hurt the Rapinoes. That was your singular peculiarity. Your raison d'être. Not mine. That matter is between you and Joshua. I am not a violent person. I have always risen above such frailties, such imperfections."

As I said it, I knew I was boasting. I didn't rise above Mother's violence. I hid away in my dark place. As I talked with Mother, Joshua sat up and took note. I could feel his uncomfortableness. I could sense him tensing.

"What's that, Mother?" I paused while she *communicated*. "No, Mother. No. Yours were not petty offenses in the least. They were not designed to discipline Joshua or me. We needed no discipline. We had done nothing wrong. Mother, you're *speaking* nonsense." I again paused for a *response*, and then said, "No, my decision to be cerebral instead of physical with my borrowers does not make me weak. Not one iota. I am strong. Strong of mind. There is strength in my resolve. You well know that."

Joshua let me know he did not consider me to be strong. Not of mind or otherwise. He was not critical, just pragmatic. Nevertheless, I felt I was now arguing with two people at the same time.

I looked away from the vessel to end my *exchange* with Mother. There was strength in my survival of all that she had brought upon us, and she knew that as well. But I felt compelled to turn back to it one more time. I *heard* nothing further from Mother, nor did I feel anything emanating from her resting place. *Silence.* Blissful silence.

I so enjoyed our *discussions* and, more so, I so relished the *silence* that followed. I rarely convinced Mother of the propriety of my plans. She never *admitted* that I have convinced her of anything. But, despite her *silence*, this time I felt I had prevailed in convincing her I was right; that my plan was just; and, most importantly, that it was the best path to payment. On the need for payment, I knew Mother *agreed*.

Now I needed to get Joshua on board as well.

I looked at my calendar to check my schedule for the day. I had already sent Edmond the next few days of posts. So remaining for me were the usual borrowers, borrowers, borrowers. Meetings with potentials; phone calls to existings; prophylactic reminders to the historically dilatory; and thankfully, no engagement with any who had become past due in derogation of their loan documents ... except the Rapinoes. But, I thought, *My campaign will change that shortly.*

CHAPTER 23

Saturday, November 18 to Monday, November 20, 2023

SATURDAY MORNING IN THE legal biz. Indistinguishable from the weekdays. 3J and Pascale often thought that the words weekday and weekend should be banned: they afforded a meaningless distinction for lawyers.

3J arrived at work, still on edge. She had no idea what a reasonable expectation should be for the turnaround of the crowdsource sleuthing part of the endeavor. Indeed, she found the notion so foreign that it made her anxious to even contemplate that the fate of the Rapinoes and BJB was largely in the hands of people she didn't know, located in places throughout the world she had never been, reviewing online information she would never understand. *In other words,* she thought, *completely and utterly with no control over the outcome of the project. Maybe this is what is meant by surrendering yourself to a higher power.* But she wasn't a true believer in a higher power, and she found it hard to imagine that the higher power consisted of geeks and wonks throughout the world, reading not the Five Books of Moses but posts on Reddit and whatever its Dark Web counterpart might be.

No lawyer likes to sit around and wait for an event to occur that is so completely out of their control. As 3J well knew, she was a control freak, like so many of her colleagues, and it was almost physically painful for her to sit and wait for a break-through from the "cohorts" as Rome liked to call them – a breakthrough that might never come.

She kicked off her sneakers, walked to her office door, closed it, returned to her chair, and put her feet up on her desk. Tolstoy said, "Everything comes in time to him who knows how to wait." 3J wondered if that was at all true and if that could ever apply to lawyers. She remembered Woodrow Wilson's spin on that observation: "All things come to him who waits – provided he knows what he is waiting for." *Yes*, she thought. *Wilson's spin was much more accurate. I have no idea what the crowdsource sleuthing will reveal, so I'm clueless as to what exactly I'm waiting for.*

A loud double knock on her door interrupted her thoughts, taking her by surprise and causing her to sit up at attention. She rose to open her door, opting not to put her shoes back on. *A visitor will be nice*, she thought. *It's not like I'm doing or thinking anything that qualifies as productive.* Pascale stood on the threshold with two steaming beverages – his coffee and a cup of Earl Grey tea for 3J.

"Thank you, kind sir. And, before you ask, the answer is 'No.' I've heard nothing from Rome."

"Oh, I figured as much."

3J forced a smile. As if to confirm her stress levels – from Rome's radio silence – she said, "I sure as hell hope Rome isn't off drinking a latte at some swanky London establishment while I sit here and wonder if BJB is going down, or if we can save it."

Pascale smiled back his easy Western Kansas, always-on-call, smile, and said, "I have a good feeling about this one. Don't know why, and I wasn't bit by a radioactive spider, but my sixth sense is that good news will be forthcoming. Once we get it …"

3J interrupted him. "*Once?* Not *if?*"

"Correct, *once* we get it, are we ready to go with filing something? And if not, what can I do to help?"

"I've drafted the lawsuit, used information from the Rapinoes to set out the damages suffered, and I've drafted the motion for a TRO. I described the posts on an Exhibit A to the motion. Exhibit A has grown from a couple of entries to a couple of pages of entries by now, as the posts just keep coming. And I've drafted a request for emergency relief, which I expect Judge Robertson will grant us summarily."

Pascale nodded his head in agreement. He then handed 3J a copy of *In re Andrus*, the same case Jennifer Cuello and Judge Robertson had discussed in chambers. "Have you seen this one?"

"Yep. Found it yesterday on *Westlaw*. We win hands down under that case. No protected speech for the posts; violation of the policy behind the automatic stay. Clear, improper attempts to pressure the Rapinoes; and my guess is a not-so-veiled-attempt to control the Debtors' property and collect."

"Ok. Good. I can do a little more poking around in *Westlaw* to see if there's more out there, but on the free speech question, the truth seems to be that very few creditors are crazy enough to hang signs, let alone post smears." Another strained smile from 3J. "3J, try to remember that the Rapinoes owe the money, not you. Try to keep some degree of separation, or the waiting will eat you up."

"I hear ya'," she said, nodding her head slowly. "Easier said than done, as you well know, but I do hear you."

"Good." He rose to leave. "Don't get up. I'll close the door behind me."

Rome's head rose from her pillow as her laptop dinged. She stretched, assumed a cross-legged position on her bed, and saw an email from her *Crowded!* contact. She gazed at her computer screen as she read the email.

> Rome, my friend, please see the attached report. I think we got him (it's a him), and there are some initial hints about who the compatriot might be. Will keep up the search while you read and assimilate. We'll next try to cross-reference creditors from prior case discussed in attached with BJB case. Never know. Good luck with the dossier m'love."

Rome opened the attachment, which explained sources and methods used, and identified one person – Edmond Richardsen – as the likely source of the posts. Rome found it fascinating how *Crowded!*'s cohorts had attacked the puzzle. Several clues and pieces of information swirled together like disparate ingredients that meld to make a world class stew – here, of data. First, *Crowded!* located archives of another disinformation campaign from several years ago that targeted a different debtor, again calling into question whether the Debtor could survive, advising all comers against doing business with the Debtor, and devolving into name calling, just like the campaign against BJB. Remaining true to a chronological analysis, *Crowded!* then found posts by noLightpassed13 and noLightPasses31 touting the result obtained for the "client."

Crowded! then tried to come up with a way to put a name with the noLight handles. What the sleuths discovered was that a younger version of both noLights was not as secretive and discrete as the older, wiser self. With some deep dives into Clearnet archives, *Crowded!* learned that the younger noLight hung out and posted on the Clearnet and the Dark Web. On the Clearnet, noLight, sometimes signed off as "ER," sometimes as "E," and sometimes as one or the other noLight handles. From the review, *Crowded!* could link noLight to someone named "ER," because the posts signing off as ER came from the same account as the posts signing off using a noLight handle.

The final key was that the cohort located a single post discussing freedom of speech and no policing of posts on the internet from the same account that the noLights used, but on this one, the post sign-off was, "Proudly able to say what I like, from right here in KC Heartland, Edmond Richardsen."

Crowded! had also located the handle in an archive of the Flickr photography account, as it existed five years ago. Back then, in the account owner's description, he mentioned his name, Edmond Richardsen, and likewise wrote he was in Kansas City. This was before Richardsen had sanitized the descriptive paragraph to reflect just the account owner's name as NLP13, as the current iteration stated.

Thus, *Crowded!* concluded that both of the noLights were Edmond Richardsen and he was in Kansas City... somewhere.

Rome absorbed what she read. She realized it wasn't quite complete, but there was indeed a smoking gun, and it appeared there was the potential that gunshot residue was on the hands of one Edmond Richardsen – a.k.a. noLight. *Was he still in Kansas City,* she wondered, *and if so, where?* She stared at the information and thought, *Such a common name.* She blinked several times to return to the task at hand and emailed 3J, cc'd to Moses:

> Ms. Jones. Received an information dump from *Crowded!* just now. Lots to digest. See attached. Bottom line, it points to a bloke named Edmond Richardsen from somewhere in Kansas City. Still working on whether Richardsen is a loner or working for or with someone. Review and then call. Faithfully, Rome.

Rome hit the send key and as soon as she did, she received a supplemental email from *Crowded!* that read:

> Quick follow-up. Just after I sent the prior communication, I received a bit more information on Edmond Richardsen of Kansas City, formerly of St. Louis. This Mr. Edmond Richardsen is pretty highly educated, holding an MBA, is a techie, and a bit dramatic at times. We conclude this from an unusual article in the St. Louis University alumni magazine from twenty years ago. They were interviewing MBA candidates at the school and asked one student – Edmond Richardsen – if he had specific plans of how to use his MBA degree. The answer, odd for a business schooler, was this: 'I hope to find a career using the internet. Something high-tech. Something where there is *no light* unless I choose to let the light in.' Might be a bit of a stretch, but the convergence of the name, the Midwest, and the use of the phrase 'no light' seems too large of a coincidence to ignore. Will hold on further SLU research pending your analysis and direction. Best.

Rome flipped back through her notes and remembered that Phillip Dewey had also gone to SLU, where he got his MBA. She noted that Dewey and Richardsen did not attend SLU at the same time, Dewey graduating seven years before Richardsen attended. *Was it a coincidence or a connection between the two?* she wondered. She remembered something her favorite archeology professor at Bryn Mawr liked to tell her: "Belita, more often than not, there are no coincidences; just hidden connections waiting to be revealed in the light of day ... by us employing good archeological sleuthing."

Rome did not believe in coincidences. She immediately forwarded this latest piece of information to 3J, again cc'd to Moses, with a cover email: "Ms. Jones, supplemental info. Self-explanatory."

Minutes after she hit the send button for the second email, her mobile phone rang and it was Moses.

"Good Saturday evening in London, my dear colleague, and good work to this point. I trust the Fall season is treating you well?"

"Thank you, Moses. Cold, rainy, and overcast here this afternoon. The sun was out for ten minutes and the weatherman called it partly sunny. A very London tradition. Hope springs eternal in Britain," she lamented.

"Indeed, it does on your side of the ocean. Here, full sun all day in the Empire City, and they called it *mostly* sunny. I suppose here, the weather business is skeptical of good news, perhaps like New Yorkers are skeptical of so many things," Moses observed. He took a sip of his deep dark, rich Pu Erh tea and turned to the engagement at hand. "Information is coming in. It is enlightening."

"I take it you have reviewed *Crowded!*'s findings so far."

"I have. Very interesting. It was the second email that caused me to pick up the phone and dial you across the mighty Atlantic. I am curious." Moses allowed the fact that he was curious to set in. "I wonder if we can get your network or *Crowded!* to develop some additional data points about the apparent SLU connection. For example, did this gentleman, Edmond Richardsen, graduate from SLU? If so, when? Was he a good student? Was he a loner or was he a social butterfly? Did he stay in St. Louis? Can we find a Richardsen classmate to talk to? I am sure you will come up with additional queries along these lines. In other words, information that I might share with my criminologist to develop a more formal profile. And can we find any path crossings between Mr. Richardsen and Mr. Dewey?"

"I will turn our attention to those details immediately," Rome responded, energized that the investigation may be onto something important.

"Thank you, Rome. By the way, are you planning to be in New York anytime soon?" Before the pandemic, Rome would make several trips a year to the City to visit friends from her Bryn Mawr days who had settled ninety miles north of Philadelphia in New York after graduation. She didn't miss Bryn Mawr; she'd graduated, and it had served its purpose and led her to the professional life she now lived and so enjoyed, but she missed the handful of close friends she made while in college.

"I have not traveled since the lockdowns of 2020 began. Now that we are told that there is no longer a pandemic, just an endemic like the 1918 flu, I must start to reclaim some of my life. I think that starts with resuming travel. I feel the time is upon me to head to Heathrow and cross the pond to JFK. I just need to figure out when."

"Splendid. I am hopeful you will find time in your schedule for me when you are here."

"Always. For you *and* Emily. Absolutely. Please have a cup of your famous tea ready for me. And we will reserve a bench in Madison Park, I hope?"

"Most certainly. I will look forward to it. Keep me apprised on both the trip and the SLU research. Maybe we shall get lucky on this one. Lucky beats good oftentimes, and to reach a quick result here, we will need healthy doses of both."

"Au revoir, Moses."

3J looked over to her computer screen moments after the ding announcing receipt of a new email. Most of the emails she received that day had not garnered her attention. She found herself in a continuing unfocused state, feeling helpless in the BJB and Rapinoe cases. Waiting patiently was not her strongest quality. She knew it, and while she tried to compartmentalize the posts in a closed room in her consciousness so she could focus on other things, the posts just refused all efforts temporarily to file them away.

The email that caused her computer to ding, however, brought 3J instantly into focus. It was from Rome. And before 3J could put her feet back on the floor and open the email, her computer dinged with a second message.

She went through the two emails and their attachments at a dizzying pace. *Edmond Richardsen,* she thought. *Who are you and why are you after the Rapinoes?* 3J forwarded the two emails and attachments to the Rapinoes, copying Pascale, with a brief cover email: "Edmond Richardsen! Do you know him? Read this and then let's hop on a conference call. 3J."

Within moments, Pascale showed up at her doorjamb and in he walked. No knock and no waiting to see if 3J was busy. "Who is this guy?"

"No idea, Bill," 3J said, shaking her head left and right.

"I checked. The Rapinoes didn't list him as a creditor or a contact person for any of the creditors in either the BJB or the Rapinoes cases."

3J pursed her lips, raised her eyebrows and said, "He's got to be working for someone else, don't you think?"

"Gotta be." Pascale folded his arms across his chest and said sternly, "We need to get this info to Steele and get him out on the streets to find this guy and at least take him offline and try to limit the damage to whatever has happened to this point."

"Yes, please. What's the best way to get this to him?"

"Print out and drive it over to the bar. I can do that."

3J thought a moment and said, "No. That's ok. I'll drive it over to him as soon as we finish with the Rapinoes. I'm curious to know how he'll go about finding this Richardsen guy."

"As you wish," Pascale said, silently wondering if there was any more to 3J's desire to deliver the information to Steele personally. *Maybe she'll express annoyance that he hadn't told her of his connection to me*, Pascale thought. *Oh well, Ronnie's a big boy. He'll handle it.*

3J and Pascale hopped on a conference call with the Rapinoes minutes later. No, Bey told them, they had no idea at all who Edmond Richardsen was. Adam expressed concern that the name was fairly common and that would make it harder to find the correct Richardsen in the large Kansas City metropolitan area. 3J agreed but said, "But it's our first breakthrough, and as soon as we leave this call, I'm going over to our investigator, and get him out into the metro to find this scumbag and shut him down."

"How will he do that?" Adam asked hesitantly.

"He just will," 3J said emphatically.

Pascale then jumped in and said, "We're still working the 'who is Mr. Edmond Richardsen working for' angle as it seems preposterous to believe that someone you don't know and you don't owe money to is working this dirty tricks campaign just for yucks and grins. Makes no sense, unless he's the front man for someone you do know and who has it in for you."

"We agree completely," Bey said. "As we told 3J last night, we really are running out of time because for us, time is money, and we're running out of excess cash to prop up the clubs while we figure this out."

"As fast as we can, and as hard as we can go, we *will* find this guy," 3J said decidedly.

As soon as the phone call ended, 3J grabbed her bag and a printout of the two emails and attachments, and ran for the elevator and the ride down to the garage. She sped out onto Walnut Street, heading south, past Crown Center, wound around to Main Street and the World War I Memorial, up the hill and, as fast as she dared go, west onto Westport Road and O'Brien's. It was Saturday lunchtime, and the bar had its usual weekend crowd of regulars. At first, she didn't see Steele, but then she saw him carrying a box of liquor from the back room to the bar. She went up to the bar and breathlessly said, "Ronnie, can we talk? We have information for you on the dirty trickster."

"Sure," Ronnie said. Then turned to one of his staff and said, "Frank – man the bar for me, would ya' please? I need to go in the stockroom where it's quiet so I can talk to Ms. Jones, here."

"Sure thing, Ronnie. No need to hurry back. I got it."

3J followed Ronnie to the stockroom, where Ronnie and his crew had stacked cases of non-perishables. In the corner, there was an old, worn desk and two chairs, one behind the desk and one in front. Ronnie sat down and as he stretched his hand out to receive the papers 3J brought, said, "Whata we got, 3J?"

"You'll see all the details in the package, which is a hundred percent of what we know, unfiltered. The bad guy's name is Edmond Richardsen. He lives somewhere in the Kansas City Metro. He's a photography buff of sorts, with a Flickr account. It looks like it's not his first disinformation rodeo. He's not a creditor. He isn't the contact person for any creditor. He's not someone the Rapinoes know." She paused as Ronnie read the emails and then started on the attachments. He looked up, and she continued, "What we don't know: who he's working for? Where he lives? And why he's doing this?"

Ronnie said, "The goal, then, is to find the correct Edmond Richardsen, and make contact?"

"Correct."

"Contact by you, me, both, or some other configuration?"

She hadn't gotten that far in her thinking But she didn't spend long thinking it through. "You 'n' me."

"Works for me. That part will be a little tricky – I don't have a badge anymore. But I'm sure we'll be persuasive in other ways and we'll encourage our Mr. Richardsen to speak with us."

3J wasn't sure what "encourage" meant, but her mind was racing, so she set aside any concerns she had about Ronnie's definition. She figured she could revisit that in due course. "While you're trying to find him, I'll be back at the office, ready to file papers in the bankruptcy cases, and I'm hopeful the Judge will give us a restraining order against Richardsen for him to cease and desist. If he posts again after the Judge issues the order, he'll be in contempt, and with any luck, the Judge will have a U.S. Marshal go out and retrieve Mr. Edmond Richardsen for federal processing, an orange jumpsuit, and three federal meals a day for a while." Each time 3J said the name Richardsen, she said it with a disdainful sneer.

"Yeah. Those Fed Marsh' boys and girls don't mess around." Ronnie paused. "I've got personal time off here and as soon as the lunch hour ends, I'm outta here and on the job." He looked down at the papers again. "So, one thing that just jumped out at me. The spelling of the first and last names here. Are we certain about the spellings?"

"I believe so. What's your thought?"

"'Edmond' with an 'o' as opposed to 'Edmund' with a 'u.' Richardsen with an 'e' instead of Richardson with an 'o.' Maybe we get lucky and there aren't too many Edmonds with an 'o' and Richardsens with an 'e' running around these parts. Just seems like the 'o' and the 'e' are potentially unusual spellings that, with luck, will work to our advantage."

3J hadn't thought of that as she raced through the information. It made sense to her. *Something else to hope for,* she thought to herself.

"Alright, 3J. Thanks for driving this over. I'll report to you and Pascale by close of business today. May not have much, but you never know."

"Thanks, and thanks from Pascale as well."

Ronnie smiled at her and said, "So you're not gonna get in my grill for failing to mention that Pascale and I go way back?"

"Nope," 3J said in staccato fashion.

"Well, just so the record is complete, Pascale and I go way back."

"So I've gathered. The other night when we were talking, you asked me about drinking with the 'old white guy.' Why didn't you just tell me you were good friends with that old white guy?"

"Then you wouldn't have told me how you really felt about Pascale, and I was curious. Turns out, you guys are BFFs and we guys are BFFs, so all's good in BFF-land."

3J smiled. "I think the proper phrase, to quote you, is: TBC."

"Yes, now we have two topics on hold for a later discussion. Don't look now, but you might have to give up drinking in a booth and instead start drinking at the bar all the time."

"I'll take that under advisement."

Ronnie gave 3J his mobile number and his email address. They shook hands, 3J left the bar, and as the lunch hour ended, Steele discarded his white bar apron and headed to his car.

On her drive back to the office, 3J called her paralegal, Anna Martinez, at her home; apologizing for the weekend intrusion, she asked Anna if she could figure out how many Edmond Richardsens with an 'o' and an 'e' lived in the Kansas City area. Back when everyone had a landline, the research would be easy – open the White Pages phone book, go to the "Rs," find the Richardsen listings, and see how many were Edmond with an 'o'. In the modern era, however, it wasn't quite that simple, since so many people eschewed a telephone landline in favor of using just their mobile phone for all calls. But there were services to which the firm subscribed and, for a small fee, Martinez could run a similar search.

When she arrived back, 3J's paralegal phoned. "Success?" 3J asked.

"In a manner of speaking," Martinez replied. "Here's what I found. Spelling Edmond with an 'o' combined with Richardsen with an 'e' reduces the pool down to only six in the metro. I did a little more digging on our service and learned that of the six, three are pretty elderly. That leaves three. One or more of them also may be elderly; I couldn't tell. I've made an assumption, which may be rash. But I've assumed that the posts are probably not appearing at the hands of an elderly person."

3J smiled at Anna's assumption. She observed, "Well, three's not too bad at all."

"And I have last known addresses for the three."

"Yes! Excellent."

"I've emailed the three along with their addresses to you."

"Thanks, Anna. You have no idea how important and helpful this is."

"No worries, boss. Help is my middle name." Just before the call ended, Anna said, "Almost forgot. I took a stab at searching the Missouri and Kansas secretary of states websites to see if there are any Edmond Richardsen listings. I got lucky. There's one. It comes up under Dark Moons Technology LLC, and he's listed as the incorporator. It's a Missouri LLC but does business in Kansas as well. It doesn't list a home address but I'll email that record to you."

"That's super!" 3J exclaimed.

As the call ended, 3J opened the paralegal's email and digested the addresses attached to the three Edmond Richardsens. One lived along Ward Parkway in one of the mansions that lined the winding artery. Perhaps irrationally, her intuition told her that no one living in one of those mansions would be behind the posts. But she quickly corrected her thinking: too stereotypical of her to eliminate anyone based on living in a mansion. One lived in Romanelli Gardens, the upper-middle-class neighborhood to the east of Ward Parkway where Judge Robertson lived. The third lived in Armour Hills, the more modest neighborhood to the east of Ward Parkway and Romanelli.

3J texted Steele the information discovered by Anna. She also emailed the information to Rome, Moses, Pascale, and the Rapinoes. Maybe with addresses, someone in the group would have an *ah-ha* moment and remember Edmond Richardsen.

Steele read 3J's text describing the three Edmond Richardsens with interest. He made a mental note to drive by all three residences to check them out.

Monday morning, Steele first drove past the Ward Parkway address – a large stone structure surrounded by a black iron fence and gate, with an expansive lawn and trees galore that were in full Fall color regalia. A crew of five men worked beneath the trees blowing the leaves into an enormous pile for removal as the Fall season was in full swing. Steele sighed.

Wonder what it'd be like to live in one of these Ward Parkway abodes, even for just a day. He then drove about a mile south on Ward Parkway, past Meyer Circle and its iconic fountain to a 1920s Tudor on a side street in Romanelli Gardens. Still a nice-sized home, but it seemed like a one-bedroom efficiency sized structure compared to the Ward Parkway mansion.

Nothing of note to glean from either house.

Steele then headed to 63rd Street and turned south on Main Street into Armour Hills. As he drove, he thought, *Ahhh, the doldrums of investigation. It's all coming back to me. Or maybe, it never left. Not like on television at all. Lots and lots of dead ends and no nuggets of helpful information to harvest.* He quickly found the East 69th Street house a few doors in from Main Street; a small brick, stone and wood Tudor from the 1920s that was one of over a thousand homes that made up the modest, middle-class neighborhood. A concrete walkway leading up to a front stoop and a dark wood door protected by a storm door divided the small front lawn. The well-kept lawn surrounded a mature dogwood tree on one side and a Bradford pear tree on the other. A neat and trim lawn and garden in front of a neat and trim house in a neat and trim middle-class neighborhood. Steele wondered if all the neat and trim was because of the owner, or a landscaping crew. While the crew was common on Ward Parkway, he had his doubts that very many Armour Hills residents farmed out the yard work. He decided that the neat and trim look was due to the occupant, who he extrapolated was likely organized, methodical, and precise; the human version of neat and trim.

He made a note of the license plate for the car – a cherry red, late model Ford Focus – parked in front of the house. As he did, the side door to the house opened, and a man exited with two backpacks, one black and one navy blue, each slung on a shoulder. He carefully placed the packs on the seat of the passenger side of the vehicle, and headed south toward

Gregory Street where it quickly pulled into a strip center. The man parked, exited the car with the blue backpack, and entered a storefront door beneath the sign: Dark Moons Technology. Steele kept his distance and observed.

The man was in the storefront for forty-five minutes. He then exited, got into the car, and drove south to an office building. It appeared to Steele that the man might be making the rounds; perhaps of Dark Moons' clients.

The man repeated this pattern for several hours as Steele followed him. After what turned out likely to be the last client call, the man drove back to 63rd Street and then east for several miles to Swope Park. Still keeping his distance, Steele saw the Ford park in an otherwise empty lot in the park, and the man delayed exiting the car while he appeared to remove something from the black backpack. Eventually, the man exited the car and in his hand he held a black and silver camera with a medium length lens. Steele had his own camera with him, equipped with a 300mm telephoto lens, and took pictures of the man exiting the car. The man hurried into the woods and returned after about twenty minutes. He retraced his journey, drove directly back to the Armour Hills house, and entered the house by the side door.

Steele would later learn that Richardsen could afford a bigger and more lavish lifestyle, but he didn't want either. Richardsen would admit that he was happy with his neighborhood, proximate to his business, and the neighbors. The neighborhood allowed him to keep not just a low profile but, significantly, a *no*-profile existence. While he had nothing to hide, even that was nobody's business.

Steele's quick review of the file left him with the feeling that there was something he'd seen in the information that was related to what he just observed. He opened the file and found the reference to the Flickr photography account. *A connection,* he thought. Then he remembered the secretary of state search that linked an Edmond Richardsen to Dark Moons Technology. Another strong connection.

With these connections, and since he couldn't be in three places at once, he decided that the Armour Hills Richardsen was likely his man, and should be the focus of his attention.

Steele sat in his car several houses away from the man's house and pondered his next move. Having developed snippets of information about Richardsen – photography, and his connection to Dark Moons Technology – he decided he needed to be at a desk online for some quick research on Dark Moons, so he headed back to his apartment. As he made the fifteen-minute drive, he wondered what it would be like to confront the man he'd just finished tailing. He decided that he might need more information before recommending to 3J that it was time.

He would not have to wait too much longer.

Rome was back to sitting on her bed cross-legged and hunching over her laptop screen – this time, reading her latest email from *Crowded!*. Hours before, she passed on Moses' questions about Richardsen.

Now she hunched, sipped tea, and waited. The tea was good; oh, but that hunching. She rationalized that too much body health and well-being was not good for her mental health. She was still young enough to feel that way.

While she waited, she thought about other ways to identify the noLights. She wondered if noLight complemented his many posts with an online gaming persona. Could she be as lucky as searching some of the more well-known online gaming sites for a gamer using a form of the handle? Rome used to game online; she became addicted, and her already prodigious screen time usage passed the danger phase quickly, moving into the unhealthy zone. She tried to moderate her usage but quickly learned that it was an all-or-nothing situation. With the difficulty of a smoker trying to kick the habit without an over-the-counter patch to rely on, she had gone cold turkey over a few days and had never gamed since.

Since this was a work project, however, she decided it was safe to navigate to her former favorite gaming site and see if noLight had a presence. She quickly discovered the noLight-passed13 handle among the active gamers. Thinking about how to exploit this revelation, she decided to try to engage noLight in an online game that night, using the accompanying game chat feature to see if she could coax him into clicking on a link that would reveal his IP address; in other words, an online gaming phish. With luck, it might also give her an avenue to exploit noLight's browser and gather further information.

Then she remembered Moses' admonition that for this client, Rome needed to steer clear of anything that could be construed as criminal activity. She well knew that phishing was a form of wire fraud, a crime under United States federal law as well as under many state statutes.

Reluctantly, she shelved her gaming gambit for the time being until she could consult with Moses. She was confident he would admonish her against a phish to gain noLight's IP address and access noLight's browser, despite the ease with which she believed she could carry out the exploitation – as long as noLight clicked on the chat link. She could not, therefore, say with absolute certainty that the idea would be successful.

At the very least, however, she wanted Moses and the clients to know she was still thinking of other ways to capture information about noLight. A moment later, she thought, *On second thought, I think I'll keep this idea to myself. If I tell them, they'll only conclude that I'm a bit of a loose cannon … and I do not want to have to defend such an unfair accusation.*

Forty-five minutes passed. An email from *Crowded!* delivering answers to Moses' questions brought her back to the ongoing pieces of the investigation. According to this information, Richardsen had graduated from SLU, a loner and a talented student. He had stayed in St. Louis briefly before moving to Kansas City to pursue tech-related positions, although not in a position of management, until he eventually formed Dark Moons Technology LLC. Rome passed the information along to Moses.

In another hour, another *Crowded!* email arrived. This one contained the beginnings of the connection Rome was looking for.

Crowded!'s sleuths found two pieces of information linking Dewey and Richardsen. The first, an older article from a relatively small weekly newspaper in Kansas City announcing the establishment of Veridical Lending LLC, and showing a picture of Phillip Dewey at a gathering shaking hands with Edmond Richardsen.

The second, Rome found more telling. It was an archived Veridical web page showing that for what appeared to be a brief period, Veridical had employed an information systems expert named Edmond Richardsen.

She forwarded the new information to 3J and Moses. They had made the connection. It was hot-wired and live. But she still wanted more – she wanted to see the connection run directly from Richardsen and his tech business to Veridical and what she believed were its illicit debt collection efforts.

She worried about how long she might have to wait for that direct connection.

Back at his apartment, Steele grabbed a cup of coffee in an O'Brien's mug he kept forgetting to bring back to the bar, sat at his well-worn kitchen table, and began his search of Dark Moons. He found the web page quickly and clicked to navigate to the "About Us" page. There, he learned Edmond Richardsen had formed Dark Moons in 2002. Richardsen touted the company as providing contract "information systems consultation" and help for small- and medium-sized businesses for whom it made little sense to have a full-time tech person on staff. At the bottom of the page, he found a list of representative clients.

Halfway down, Steele found that Veridical was Dark Moons' client.

Steele read this information in Mission, Kansas, at the same time that Rome read it in London; they both forwarded the information by email to 3J.

He next downloaded the digital images from his camera's memory card to his computer. He found one photo of Richardsen in particular that he blew up as much as he could. There, he could see the camera Richardsen used was an old Minolta SRT 101, a film camera from back in the day. Steele again turned to the dossier on Richardsen to re-read the Flickr description. *I'm right!* he thought. *The Flickr iteration of noLight uses film, not digital, and a Minolta!*

Steele grabbed his mug, sipped his cooling coffee, sat back in his chair and took stock of what he knew. This Armour Hills Richardsen was a film photographer, owned and worked at an information systems company, went to SLU some years after Dewey, was a loner, and did contract work for Veridical. Many points of intersection; some possible coincidences, but not all. He felt Richardsen was likely the one posting, and it seemed obvious he was doing so for his business connection – Phillip Dewey. But it was still not enough to show what was going on *beyond a reasonable doubt*: the criminal law standard of proof he knew like the back of his hand from his decades on the police force.

It was time to call 3J and Pascale and read them in. He hoped they could reach consensus on next steps.

"3J? Ronnie Steele here. Sorry, I didn't ping you first to see if you could talk. Can you?"

"I can. Let me patch Pascale in. Hold on."

A couple of staccato clicks later, 3J said, "Pascale, do I have you?"

"You do."

"Ronnie, you still there?"

"Roger that."

"Great. We're all ears. Tell us what you've got."

Ronnie described in detail what he'd learned. 3J and Pascale listened without interrupting. They didn't need to seek any clarification. Ronnie was thorough, detailed, organized, and his oral report was precise; clear as a bell. The obvious product of years on the police force. He concluded by saying, "I don't see any doubt that the one posting is this particular Richardsen, and that he's doing it for Dewey and Veridical. But I don't know that all of this circumstantial stuff is proof beyond a reasonable doubt."

3J jumped in. "We don't need to prove things in bankruptcy beyond a reasonable doubt; just by a preponderance of the evidence. Meaning we just have to show the facts as we describe them are more likely than not true."

Pascale joined in. "In other words, greater than a fifty-fifty chance that what you're saying is correct."

3J said, "Everything you've told us syncs up exactly with what *Crowded!* and Rome have discovered. Little pieces of information to fill in what we didn't know – and when we piece the bits of information together, it starts to make a strong connection."

"But is what we have going to be enough?" Pascale asked no one in particular.

"I think it is," 3J said. "There are really two pieces to this and while we have looked at them as one, I think we should decouple to support how we spin it to Judge Robertson."

"The floor is yours, counselor," Pascale said.

"Thank you counselor," 3J joked, feeling suddenly much more confident of their case based on all the information Rome and Steele had fed her. "We just go after Richardsen at this point and scare him. We circle back to Mr. Dewey a little later. Maybe we get lucky and Richardsen gives up Dewey." She paused, then went on to elaborate. "I think we know – not just believe, we *know* – that Edmond Richardsen is behind the posts: *Crowded!* nicely tied Edmond Richardsen to both noLight handles. We know that noLight's in Kansas City. We know there are three possible Edmond Richardsens in Kansas City, but I think we now know that it's the Armour Hills Edmond Richardsen that we're after. How? Pretty convincing circumstantial evidence. We need an Edmond that's a film photographer – we have one. We need a techie – we have one. We need someone with a connection to a creditor – we have one, and the largest creditor at that. That's the cake. Once we say we know that the Armour Hills Richardsen is our man, the frosting is all of his online posts about the first amendment, the role of social media platforms, and his prior disinformation work."

"Certainly sounds much more likely than not to me," Steele offered.

"I agree it's pretty damning," Pascale said as he thought through the evidence as 3J presented it. He rubbed his chin.

"Yeah, it just might fly." After some more chin rubbing, he added, "It might also be helpful if Ronnie could go back to square one for the Ward Parkway and Romanelli Gardens Richardsens, and somehow show that neither's in the tech business."

"No problem, I can get you something about that," Steele said.

"We'd need all of this in an affidavit – or perhaps several affidavits, correct?" Pascale asked.

"Exactly," 3J said, feeling invigorated by how the facts had come together. "Right now, it sounds to me like probably three will suffice. One from Ronnie, one from Rome, and the last from one of the Rapinoes describing the effect on BJB's business," 3J offered, thinking through the mechanics of getting a TRO from Judge Robertson even as she was speaking.

"I'm around to sign whatever you need. Just let me know where and when," Ronnie said. "One other thing. Thinking back to option two, which 3J laid out for me at the bar: when do we confront Mr. Richardsen?"

"That's a real good question," Pascale said slowly as he tried to weigh the options. "3J?"

"Not terribly sure right now. My knee-jerk reaction is that we file the papers, wait to see if we get the TRO, and if we do, we have Ronnie personally serve the restraining order on Mr. Richardsen, maybe tomorrow. That'll be the moment of confrontation. With the TRO in hand, that seems like it would provide maximum pop, if drama is what we're looking for. Is *that* what we're looking for, Ronnie?"

"Oh, I think so. I surely do. Not exactly shock and awe, but my guess is we take this guy by surprise and if he's working for Dewey, we'll find out soon enough. I'd say he's confident in his views when he's online but we show up at his actual door, and he'll be scared as hell. Probably not much of a people person, is my guess. Guys like him probably get from confused to scared to panicked real fast."

"Ok, then. Let's report to the Rapinoes and get the papers finalized. Then we can coordinate the filing with meeting Mr. Richardsen," 3J said.

"And this meeting – no violence. No cross-exam. Just amp up the guy's blood pressure a few dozen ticks and then we exit," Steele responded and the call ended.

Pascale hung up his phone, rose from his desk, and headed around the corner to 3J's office.

"I have two other questions, 3J," Pascale announced as he entered 3J's office. 3J raised her eyebrows to signify she was all ears. "In the TRO, are we asking the Court just to restrain Richardsen from posting any further? Or are we also asking the Court to require Richardsen to take down all the posts?"

"Really good point. Best of all worlds, it would be both. We have to show irreparable harm to get the Judge to enter the TRO, and without the second piece, the posts remain live on the internet for all to see. As long as they're live, BJB will continue to suffer significant harm."

"I agree," Pascale said. "I think we have to go for both."

3J asked, "And the second item you're concerned about?"

"Here's the thing. We're sure that Richardsen and Dark Moons are not creditors of the Rapinoes or BJB. Traditionally, the automatic stay prohibits creditors from taking action. In the *Andrus* case we've both read, the one with the crazy signage, the voicemails, and the abusive screaming across the backyard fence – that guy was a creditor."

3J frowned. The lack of a creditor here could be a problem in obtaining the TRO. Perhaps a fatal problem. "Yeah, this has me very concerned as well," she agreed. "Not sure what the fix is. We either wait until we have more on Veridical and Dewey – but waiting is not good for the clients at this point – or we go forward and hope that this creditor deficiency won't impair our ability to get the TRO."

"It is more than a technical glitch, indeed. So, I went back to the Bankruptcy Code and did some research. Here's what I've discovered. The Code doesn't expressly say that the stay bars actions by a *creditor*. It says it bars action by an 'entity.' And in the way the Code defines things, an 'entity' includes a person – in this case, a human. Edmond Richardsen."

3J had her well-worn Bankruptcy Code book out, and she was madly flipping through its almost five hundred pages as she followed along with Pascale's analysis. "Ok, I see that," she said.

"Next, to paraphrase, the Code bars any human from taking steps to 'exercise control over property of the estate;' here, the cash flow of the BJB business, and its goodwill." Pascale paused while 3J read the specific provision to which he referred. She looked up, raised her eyebrows, and nodded that she was following his analysis. He continued, "So, this particular part of the Code allows a bankruptcy judge to stop *anyone* from exercising control, not just a *creditor*. I think we need to thread this needle carefully as we cast our net around Richardsen, but I think we also need to address this issue transparently."

"I completely agree." 3J paused. "I think, with your analysis in mind, we should modify slightly the plan to go after Richardsen alone. We'll try to get the TRO against him, but we can also lay out the connections with Veridical and Dewey so the Judge has some ammo to support the TRO if he feels there still has to be a creditor connection."

They both paused to take a breath. It had been an animated and fast-paced conversation to this point and they needed a moment now to re-focus.

3J spoke first. "Fuentes is going to see our filings pop up in his email box, delivered by the Court's electronic court filing system."

"Absolutely. No way around that."

"I guess we assume Fuentes tells Dewey and Dewey informs Richardsen."

"Yep. No way around that either, 3J."

"That will certainly diminish the shock and awe a bit."

"Maybe; but I still think it'll be pretty shocking, and with any luck, we'll get the TRO and there won't be a great deal of time between the order and our delivery of it to Richardsen."

Silence as they both were deep in thought.

3J spoke next. "Should we alert the Judge's chambers that this TRO request is heading his way?"

"Normally I'd say yes, and normally, we'd call his law clerk. But she's brand new and I don't know her at all, and now that I think about it, I don't even know her name. My suggestion is to file it first and then call her and let her know we just did."

"That's the plan, then. We've got work to do to get this on file yet today."

Both of their heart rates had increased somewhat as the afternoon events were coming together. 3J had learned to manage that part of the job as rush filings and tense moments in bankruptcy cases were not unusual. She expected an even greater elevated heart rate as she and Ronnie approached Richardsen's front door after the Judge granted the TRO, and she wasn't so sure how she would manage that. She had never gone out to confront someone like Richardsen in person, and she wasn't sure what to expect.

3J called the Rapinoes and brought them up to speed on events and information. They listened intently, and at the conclusion of 3J's presentation, Bey said, "I'm feeling some cause for optimism." She paused. "I *am*." She paused again before continuing, "Some hope … Let's hope my feelings are not for naught."

"Call us when you've filed for the TRO, 3J. And please be careful at Richardsen's place," Adam said.

"I will," 3J said, responding to Adam's first request, and quietly ignoring his admonition to be careful. She was well aware there was a danger factor in the confrontation, but it needed to be done.

As the lawyers in Kansas City began a mad dash to finish and file the lawsuit and the TRO papers before Judge Robertson left the courthouse for the evening, the last email from *Crowded!* hit Rome's inbox in London. One of the crowdsourcing sleuths had come up with the idea to cross-check the creditors of a non-bankruptcy debtor who had suffered through a smear campaign against BJB's and the Rapinoe's creditors. In the pending bankruptcy cases, the creditor list was a matter of public record. But in the prior smear campaign, because the debtor had filed no bankruptcy case, there was no public list of creditors the sleuths could access. Then one sleuth realized that lenders must file their mortgages in the public real estate records. On a flier, she determined the county where the prior debtor lived, and searched the county real estate records to see if the debtor owned real estate, and if so, was it encumbered? The idea was a winner. She discovered that the prior debtor had granted a sizable mortgage to Veridical Lending to secure a substantial loan.

The sleuth passed the information along, with a note that said, "While I can't tell you that Veridical is the only creditor overlap between both smear campaigns, I can tell you it was a significant creditor for the prior debtor, and obviously the biggest creditor in the BJB bankruptcy case." Rome soon was reading about the additional connection. She forwarded the new piece of information to 3J and Moses immediately. Rome leaned back against the wall against which her bed sat. She closed her eyes, and for the first time in days, drifted off into a deep sleep.

3J read the latest nugget in Rome's email, and whistled softly to herself. Another connection. Another piece of information that couldn't possibly be a coincidence. She forwarded it to Pascale and then the two talked. They decided not to alter the plan. Stage one would remain the same – just go after Richardsen for a TRO, but pepper the filing with references to Veridical and Dewey, including all the latest information from the crowdsourcing sleuths.

They could circle back to Veridical and Phillip Dewey after they had the TRO in place. Maybe they'd need depositions of Dewey and Richardsen, or maybe Richardsen would decide that he'd implicate Dewey in an interview. Either way, to make the mission completely successful, 3J believed they needed one or the other of the dirty tricksters to utter the coveted words, that Richardsen posted on behalf of Veridical and Dewey. She knew it would be no easy lift.

CHAPTER 24

JUST BEFORE 5 P.M., the Greene Madison team filed the lawsuit against the Armour Hills Richardsen, the TRO request, a request to take immediate discovery, and a legal brief in support describing the relevant law, along with three affidavits electronically signed and transmitted – one from Steele, one from Bey Rapinoe, and one from Rome. They also submitted a form of order proposing to grant all the relief requested. The papers cited the *Andrus* case, and skillfully laid out everything they knew, and if they didn't know a fact with certainty, they described it as more likely than not and explained why.

They requested far-reaching relief – a restraining order, damages, a permanent injunction, and a citation holding Richardsen in contempt of Court for wilfully violating the automatic stay. In the papers, they advised Judge Robertson of the posts on forums and social media, both on the Dark Web and the Clearnet. They described the posts, setting forth their content, location on the internet, and date, and painted a grim picture of damaging messages, negative in both tone and substance, ratcheting up over just a brief time period and having an immediate harmful effect on the Rapinoes' business.

The papers traced the purpose of the automatic stay and asserted that the posts violated the stay because they were an attempt to control the Debtors' property – the goodwill of the business and the resulting hit to cash flow.

For relief, the papers asked Judge Robertson to direct Richardsen to cease all further posts about the Debtors and their business immediately, to take down all previous posts about the Debtors, to preserve all computer hardware and software used to implement the posts, to permit immediate discovery of Richardsen and Dewey, and, as a throw-in, to allow the Greene Madison team to make a mirror image of all of Richardsen's computer equipment used in the smear campaign, including all computer cookies, browsing history, and emails.

3J and Pascale were unsure what procedure Judge Robertson would employ. He might hold a hearing, likely without testimony; call for a chambers conference; or have a phone call. They also didn't know who would represent Richardsen at any hearing, conference, or call. Ideally, Judge Robertson would issue the TRO with no hearing at all – *ex parte*, as the Bankruptcy Rules permitted him to do – to maintain the status quo.

All the duo could do now was await whatever came next from the courthouse.

Judge Robertson was filling his weathered, dark brown leather briefcase with papers to review at home after dinner. He and his briefcase had been through bankruptcy trench wars for many years before he took the bench, and he couldn't imagine carrying papers in any other bag just because he was now a judge. His wife needled him that a federal judge should carry a less weathered bag, but he responded that he and the bag needed each other, and that it sent the right message – blue collar, hard-working judge, still in the bankruptcy trenches.

While he didn't feel compelled to engage in post-dinner review of court materials since taking the bench – he no longer had clients or opposing counsel or bosses who demanded such post-dinner activities – nevertheless he had developed the habit of working after dinner while in the private practice of law, and old habits die hard. When the family would complain about him working at home, he would ask, "How can you not? When the case is blowing and going, it's the most important thing outside of the family you have going on at the time." Eventually, they capitulated, or at least didn't complain, and his wife was now used to the practice and expected that he would disappear after dinner to his study for an hour or two.

He stood at his desk deciding which of the piles of papers that hid the desktop he should select to review at home, when his administrative assistant, Jill, knocked on his door and handed him a printout of the numerous pages just filed by the Greene Madison bankruptcy lawyers.

"Ahhh," the Judge said. "Look at the weight of that pile of papers. New filings, I take it?"

"Yes, Judge."

As the Judge remained standing, he flipped though the pages and his face changed from resignation that Greene Madison had just selected his evening reading list for him, to concern over the seriousness of what he was reading. "Jill, is Jennifer still here? If so, can you please go get her and have her come in?"

"Absolutely, Judge."

"And do you have a printout of these filings for her as well?"

"I do, Judge."

"Great. Please have her come in here, pronto. Thank you."

Within moments, Jennifer arrived at his office with the filings and her pad.

"Looks like the Greene Madison bankruptcy fan is now on and all kinds of things are hitting it," he quipped. "I hate to do this, but are you able to stay later tonight with me here to go through this and come up with our plan of action?"

Jennifer noted the democratic way he'd described the task at hand. *He said "our plan of action,"* she thought to herself.

"Absolutely, Judge. I skimmed the brief quickly just to get a sense, and it looks like Ms. Jones and her team found the *Andrus* case as well."

"I see. Well, that's good since we already know about it. I suggest you read over the brief and then the request for the TRO in the motion. As you read, here's what you should keep in mind: the TRO is just what its name implies: a *temporary* order *restraining* someone from taking actions, although it can also direct someone to do something. My guess is that this request will ask for both."

Jennifer took copious notes as the Judge spoke and didn't look up from her yellow eight-by-eleven inches, standard-issue Federal judiciary pad.

He continued, trying to resist the urge to speak faster. "Whatever is alleged in the papers as a fact has to be supported by documents and a sworn affidavit. We have both here; it looks like there are three affidavits. As we read the affidavits and the documents, to grant a TRO, we have to accept the supported facts as alleged, unless they are truly beyond the pale and have no support. Ultimately, we will have to believe what the Debtors show us for evidence is more likely than not true. And we have to believe that without the TRO, the Debtors will suffer irreparable harm, that the harm to the creditor is not significant, and that the entry of a TRO serves public good. That last factor is easy when at issue is a violation of the automatic stay. The stay is for the public good.

"Then, the TRO is good for fourteen days, and before it expires, we'll need to have a hearing on a preliminary injunction and decide if we will continue the relief granted in the

TRO." He paused again for her to catch up with her note-taking. When she finished writing, he said, "I think that's all we need for the moment to figure this out and decide what to do. Ok? Questions, Jennifer?"

"None yet, Judge. I'm sure I'll have them as I go through all of this."

"Ok. Good. Let's reconnoiter in about ninety minutes and see where we are."

Jennifer nodded her head in agreement, stood, wheeled to face the door, and walked apace back to her office.

The Judge chuckled. She looked both overwhelmed and intensely serious, and the matters raised in the TRO papers were certainly extremely serious. *Trial by fire for my new clerk*, he thought. He was confident she was up to the task, though, and was interested to see what she thought about the filing and the relief requested; he would find out the answer to both shortly.

He picked up his desk phone and called home. When his wife answered, he said, "Looks like I'm gonna be late tonight, honey. Maybe pretty late. Sorry, kiddo."

"Oh, not to worry, Daniel. I thought we'd just grab a burger for dinner at the bar in Brookside. I can nosh on leftovers instead. What'll you do for sustenance?"

"Not exactly sure. I'll figure out something. Not to worry. See you in a few. Love ya."

"Right back at you, honey."

After the filing, 3J decided to alter her habit of staying at her desk for several more hours and instead walked to one of her favorite downtown institutions – the Belfry, on Grand and 16th, just where downtown gradually seemed to fade away and

morph into the beginning of the Crossroads District, immediately south of the Power and Light District. Celebrity chef
Celina Tio, of Iron Chef fame and a James Beard Foundation
awardwinner for best Midwestern Chef, owned the establishment. It was mostly a small bar, with tables for meals – in 3J's
mind, these meals were the Belfry's hidden gem. The Belfry's
gourmet comfort food was the best in the city – that night,
as she walked over, she had kale salad, decadent mac and
cheese, and bread pudding on her mind. She decided she would
have to forgo her usual drink, a glass or two of Celina's secret
homemade bourbon stashed behind the bar for regulars like
3J. Celina and 3J had met several years ago when 3J began to
frequent the establishment, and when the bar wasn't busy, the
ever-social Celina was easy to talk to about most any topic. 3J
always wanted to talk about food – she kept meaning to book
a private cooking lesson.

As she arrived and took a seat at the bar, the evening crowd
had not yet arrived. The bartender – she knew him only as
Doug – took her dinner order. Celina came out of the kitchen,
surveyed 3J, and said with an all-knowing smile, "You look
like you got wrung out to dry today big time, my friend." She
went back into the kitchen and brought out her famous home
made pretzels, an homage to her youth in Philadelphia, along
with crispy polenta, and set the plate down in front of 3J;
something for them to nibble on while they talked. She then
reached under the bar for two glasses and one bottle of the
private Bourbon stash.

It was the only whiskey besides Irish whiskey that 3J drank,
and it was well worth it to have this kind of variety at her
disposal. But she reluctantly said, "I'm gonna have to pass
tonight, Celina. I'm on call, so to speak."

"Ahh. I see. One of those nights. Well, it'll be here for you
when your on-call duty ends," Celina said as she bent down

to put the bottle back in its secret resting place. As she stood back up, she inquired, "So, what's going on with you?"

"Yeah, no big deal. The beast was fightin' pretty hard today. Takes it out of you to fight back. So I'm here tonight while I wait for the Judge to rule. I need some carb-driven comfort food to recharge my batteries."

The two talked and when the food arrived, Celina faded back into the kitchen area to allow 3J to enjoy the fare. As she ate, she wondered how Judge Robertson would handle the TRO request. She was sure the answer would be forthcoming, but she had no idea how long the wait would be or whether the Judge would rule tonight. So all she could do was savor the bread pudding – best in the world, in 3J's estimation – and wait to see how the evening progressed. *Boy, I could have really used that bourbon.*

Alexander Fuentes left work earlier than normal to meet a prospective banking client for dinner. It was an important meeting for him. If he could land the client, it would mean a significant flow of bankruptcy work, which his new solo practice could sorely use. Before he left his firm to set up his own practice, he couldn't imagine anything harder than establishing a practice and landing paying clients. Now he was living the dream, and he knew first-hand it was damn hard.

He wanted to direct all of his attention to the dinner conversation and, as a result, turned off his mobile phone. With the phone off, he wouldn't accidentally glance at his emails and texts while talking with the client. While everyone did it at a meal, and while he wouldn't mean any disrespect by doing so, glancing at his phone would send the subliminal message to the prospective that Fuentes' attention wasn't completely on the matters at hand – the attempt to woo someone for new business. He wanted the prospective client to know that he was interested in the bank and to do so, he had to block out all distractions.

Drinks and dinner and more drinks went from 6:30 p.m. to 9 p.m., when they bade each other goodbye.

On his walk back to his office and his car, Fuentes thought that the evening could have gone no better and, while he was patting himself on the back for such a promising marketing effort, he forgot to turn his phone back on.

He entered his garage, opened his car door, got in, and started it up. He headed toward the out ramp and onto the streets of Chicago for the short drive back to his townhome in Lincoln Park. Just as he exited the garage and slid into the nighttime Chicago traffic, he remembered to power up his phone. He turned it on, and to be safe, didn't glance at his emails or texts until he arrived at his townhome, entered, and locked the door behind him.

By then, it was 9:40 p.m. He saw several ECF filings. He grabbed his laptop, thought momentarily about heading upstairs to bed and reading the filings in the morning, paused, sighed, and instead sat down at his dining room table to read the Greene Madison filings. *These are serious allegations,* he thought. He vowed to come up with a next-morning strategy to respond. He assumed he had until the next morning, because it was unfathomable that Judge Robertson would address the papers that night. Before closing his laptop, he wrote Phillip Dewey, attached the filings, and said they needed to talk.

Phillip sat on his pristine couch facing his ash-free, unused fireplace, Mother's vessel above on the mantle. He was in no mood for any *communications* with her tonight. He felt good about the plan to take down the Rapinoes and their beloved BJB. He was not a music lover and cared not one bit if the music again died in Kansas City. Not one bit. Not his problem. He was a money man, not a music man.

Feeling particularly happy with his decisions to date, and the course of the posts and the effect they seemed to have, he sipped his French brandy from his brandy snifter, and decided he would turn in early.

Phillip did not offer Joshua any brandy. Joshua was not a drinker.

He went upstairs to his bedroom and took a double dose of Zolpidem – Ambien generic sleeping pills. Dreams were his enemy and sleep never came easy. He didn't want to remember his dreams in the morning; he didn't want any clues from his dreams of how his brain sorted out his life, especially his child-hood. Zolpidem allowed him to sleep. The double dose allowed him to do it without the dreams, or at least without remembering them. Just like when Joshua took charge. Joshua didn't like it when Phillip took the Zolpidem. He preferred to be at the ready at all times to fend off any danger. The sleeping pills made it almost impossible for Joshua to remain vigilant. But there was nothing Joshua could do about the situation. Phillip was still in charge.

Phillip got into his bed and quickly dropped into a deep sleep. He didn't see Fuentes' email. Just before turning his lights off, he set his phone alarm to wake him at 6:15 a.m., muted the sound, and rested it in his charger, as he had done hundreds of nights before.

As they promised each other, ninety minutes later, Judge Rob-ertson and Jennifer sat in his office to discuss the TRO request.

"Jennifer, what do you think? What are your impressions?"

In her office, as she read the papers, she worried about how to answer this very question. Was she ready to offer her opinion? She was so fresh out of law school. Maybe she would form an opinion based on her lack of knowledge of a key issue or a key provision of the law. She had convinced herself that if she answered the question, she would simply be wrong, and she didn't want to be wrong so early into her clerkship. So, rather than answer, she said, "I'm really not sure, Judge."

He smiled at her, came around from behind his desk and sat in the easy chair next to her. Softly and compassionately, he said, "Jennifer. I understand that you're nervous. But you're not here just to research and write me memos. A judge is all alone, except for his or her law clerk. I want the law clerks who work for me, even the brand-new ones, to participate fully right from the start. That includes telling me what you think. I don't bark and I don't bite, certainly not back here in chambers. But when you tell me what you think of a filing, or a legal issue, or a fact presented, it helps me collect and organize my thoughts. There are two of us tackling a problem, not just one. And this give-and-take process makes me a better judge. You'll say something I hadn't thought of. You'll point something out in the papers that I missed when I read them. You'll highlight something that a witness said, or the way they said it, that will prompt me to decide if I believe the witness and if the lawyers proved the fact appropriately. In this process, I'll be wrong from time to time and so will you. That's part of both of our jobs. To be wrong, recognize what we did or thought that was wrong, and adjust before it's too late so that we get it right."

She sat quietly as he spoke to her. She knew everything he said was wise. He wasn't judgmental. It wasn't advice. It was simply the way it was and the way it should be. She took a deep breath, exhaled, and said, "What if I say something and I'm wrong, because I'm inexperienced?"

"What if you are? So what? It's still my job to decide. Just like old Independence, Missouri Harry Truman said, the buck stops you know where," as he looked over to his desk and then back to Jennifer with a smile. He continued, "That you might ultimately say something I reject really isn't relevant. You say things, make observations, and they lead me to consider things I might not otherwise have considered. It broadens my thinking. The more I can consider, the more likely my decision will be the correct one. So if it helps you, think of this part of your job description as helping the Judge get it right, rather than a job description that reads, 'you have to be right.' You don't."

Jennifer smiled at the Judge. She knew he certainly didn't have to go to these lengths to comfort her, especially at this hour. She took another deep breath and exhaled again, and said, "Ok. Impressions. Some things the Debtors know; some things they suspect and offer a pretty good mountain of circumstantial evidence that points to the truth of what they suspect. I went back to the Debtors' schedules and statement of affairs filed a couple of weeks ago, and this guy, Edmond Richardsen, isn't a creditor, and he's not listed as the contact for any creditor." She paused, and she had the Judge's attention. "That got me thinking. Is the automatic stay addressed to only things creditors do, or does it cover others, like this Richardsen character? I think it covers Richardsen, just as the Debtors argue in their legal authorities brief. Is that correct?"

"It is in my mind. It might be a much easier lift to grant a TRO based on things an actual creditor did. But we don't have that here, at least not yet. The things they allege Richardsen did really need to stop immediately or these Debtors' business won't survive. That creditor connection, however, is indeed circumstantial, as you correctly observed, but there are a whole lot of connections, and I am not one to believe in the sanctity of coincidences. The lack of a creditor doesn't make it fatal to the requests, in my mind, just a heavier lift. Do you think they made the lift?"

"I do, Judge. The statute not only bars a creditor. It bars entities, and entities include all humans, not just creditors. It looks to me like Congress intended to be quite broad in the prohibition."

"Agreed. Good analysis."

Jennifer added, feeling much more comfortable about the process than she expected to be, "They aren't actually asking for any relief against Veridical or Dewey in the papers ... at least, not just yet. They offer the circumstantial evidence about both to offer an explanation why a non-creditor would go to the lengths that Richardsen has to so adversely impact the Debtors."

"Exactly," he said, not only to bolster Jennifer's confidence, but because he completely agreed with her analysis. "Here's what I'm thinking. I feel like they made their case for irreparable harm. There is no harm to the poster to stop posting; *Andrus* got it right – free speech gives way to the Bankruptcy Code in this case. And I want to take a practical approach here. I will grant the TRO for fourteen days and give them the relief they have requested."

"All of it?"

"You bet. All of it. As a practical matter, we'll then see if the posts cease immediately. If they do, then he's the one, and he's going to be in a world of hurt in this Court for what he's been doing. I expect that Ms. Jones and Mr. Pascale will get both Richardsen and this Dewey character on the record, under oath, in depositions, which will either confirm the veracity of the circumstantial evidence pointing to Veridical and Dewey, or they'll have to go back to the drawing board, if there is some other explanation floated that is more likely." He nodded his head in thought, paused, and rubbed his temples as the night was wearing on and they still had hours of work in front of them. "I just wonder why a creditor would hire Richardsen to bring down the Debtors. Doesn't make much sense to me." He rubbed his eyes and continued, "Alright. Back to the task at hand. I know they filed a suggested form of the order they'd like entered, but I don't think it says enough, so we'll need to write this up ourselves. Let's split up the parts of the order between the two of us and then meld them together. Ok with that?"

"Absolutely," Jennifer said as enthusiastically as she could muster.

"Wonderful. Let's make it so."

It was 9:30 p.m.

They used the submitted form of order for the outline of the order they would craft, and over the next ninety minutes they wrote the Judge's opinion explaining the reasons he was granting the TRO.

It was now 11:15 p.m. The two had put the finishing touches on the Judge's decision and order and Jennifer filed it. In the restraining order itself, the Judge granted all the requested relief. When they finished, Robertson asked Jennifer to call 3J and leave a voicemail that he was granting the request and entering a restraining order, and that 3J would be able to pick up a certified copy of the restraining order in the morning from the clerk's office and have it served on Mr. Richardsen.

But when Jennifer dialed 3J, rather than a connection to a voicemail, she heard, "Josephina Jones here."

"Oh. Ms. Jones, I didn't expect you to be there so late. This is Jennifer Cuello, Judge Robertson's law clerk." Jennifer then delivered the message the Judge instructed her to give.

3J said, "Ms. Cuello, thanks very much. And please thank the Judge as well, for staying so late into the evening and for handling this so quickly. I know it's very late and you both have definitely burned the midnight bankruptcy candle tonight. I am wondering, however … if I came by in ten minutes, would you be willing to hand me the papers at the front door of the courthouse so I can have them served bright and early tomorrow morning?"

"I'm certainly willing to meet you by the courthouse lobby door, but I need to check with Judge Robertson first. Please hold."

A few minutes later, Jennifer came back on the line. "Judge says, fine." She added that a clerk had stayed late to catch up on work and could certify the order now. It would be ready in fifteen minutes and she agreed to pass the papers to 3J at the front door.

3J threw on her running shoes, and ran seven blocks to the courthouse. Within fifteen minutes of Jennifer's phone call, and not yet midnight, 3J had in her possession the certified copy of the restraining order and what she hoped was the beginning of the recovery for BJB and the Rapinoes.

Fuentes sat at his dining room table as his bedtime approached. He was bone-tired. *Long day at the shop,* he thought. *Then again, most days are long days at the shop.* Feeling the tension rise from his toes, up through his legs, and up his spine to his hairline, he absentmindedly rubbed his fingers through his hair, perhaps in an unconscious and futile effort to exorcise the tension from his body into the air above his head.

He emailed the paperwork to Dewey with a short cover email that read, "Calling in a minute. Standby." It was after 10 p.m. Dewey didn't answer the phone call. Fuentes instead had to leave a voicemail; it was all he could do.

He stepped away from his laptop and moved to his living room table. *Shouldn't have had that extra glass of wine after dinner.* As he mindlessly watched reruns on late night television, his mind drifted to what array of strategies to present to Dewey in the morning. Around 11 p.m., one of the NCIS franchise reruns had some of his attention when his laptop dinged, signifying receipt of a new email. *Maybe that's Dewey.* He slowly lifted himself off of his couch and returned to his laptop, which was still powered on, dutifully waiting in the dining room to service his needs.

The email was another ECF filing; this time, from the Court. It surprised him that events at the Western District of Missouri courthouse were moving so quickly and playing out so late in evening. *How rare for a bankruptcy judge to enter an order after 10 p.m.*, he thought. But there it was – an 11:15 p.m. Judge Robertson restraining order. Given how fast the Judge had granted the temporary relief, Fuentes guessed that its scope would be all-encompassing. A quick read confirmed his guess. He forward the order to Dewey and, in the cover email, begged him to call.

Fuentes returned to the restraining order. Of note, Fuentes saw that the order restrained and directed only one "Edmond Richardsen." *Who the hell is Edmond Richardsen?* The Court's restraining order appeared to take pains to avoid any reference to Fuentes' actual client, Veridical. Not a single reference, despite the significant amount of circumstantial evidence presented by Jones and Pascale in the TRO request, linking both Veridical and Dewey to Richardsen.

Fuentes sat back in his chair and tried to stretch his neck by moving it from side to side. He'd already asked Dewey point-blank about his involvement, if any, with the smear campaign. He knew Dewey was on his high horse, and full of hubris in his denial, and he privately had his doubts about Dewey's veracity. But they were only doubts: he *knew* nothing, and as counsel for Veridical, Fuentes felt he was on solid ground to this point. Now, though, as he read about the connections between Richardsen and Dewey, the contents of the posts, and the restraining order – which, for now, addressed itself only to Richardsen – he was having a hard time imaging the next conversation he needed to have with Dewey.

And he wasn't looking forward to it.

Fuentes was frustrated that Dewey had not returned his call or responded to his emails. If he was in Kansas City, he would have driven to his residence and pounded on the front door until Dewey appeared. But he couldn't do that from his Lincoln Park, Chicago home. *Perhaps that's a blessing. No telling what Dewey would say and how he'd react to such an in-person encounter in the middle of the night.* He rubbed his eyes vigorously, realizing how tired he was. *Tomorrow is going to be a shitstorm of a day. This mess is just beginning.*

It was approaching midnight, but with Court order in hand, 3J returned to the office and made two calls. The first was to the firm's director of litigation support, Rene Alvarez-Thompson. 3J felt bad about it, but she didn't feel she had a choice. She often marvelled at how the firm's staff could remain so calm working for lawyers and responding to what could be unreasonable requests at unreasonable times of the day and night for work to be done on unreasonable timelines. 3J's request for computer hard-drive mirroring help checked all three unreasonable boxes. But, true to her nature, Alvarez-Thompson not only said her group could mirror the drive, but volunteered to do it herself with 3J first thing in the morning.

She then placed a conference call to Pascale, the Rapinoes, and Ronnie Steele. When everyone was on the line, 3J said breathlessly, "Folks: we got it! The Judge entered the restraining order!"

After a brief discussion and repeated "thank you's" from the Rapinoes, 3J and Steele agreed that she and Alvarez-Thompson would meet Steele at O'Brien's at 7:30 a.m. the next day and from there head to Richardsen's house to serve the restraining order, mirror the hard drives, and confront Richardsen. Adam again admonished 3J, and this time Steele as well, to be careful. Steele responded, for 3J and himself, "Copy that," before the call ended.

With that, 3J headed home. The skyline that she so enjoyed each night would not grab her attention tonight. She had no strength left to admire man's vertical steel and glass; the jazz that helped her wind down would not play tonight. She needed to collapse into her bed. As she headed for home she idly thought, *Even money whether I change out of these clothes or just kick off the shoes and do the college flop onto the bed.* As the elevator stopped on the twentieth floor of her building, she dragged her weary bones into her condo. *After midnight flop it is.* But just before she flopped, her phone buzzed: Pascale.

"Yeah, Bill. What's up?"

Bill had concerns for 3J's safety, and had already called Steele to discuss the matter. Steele had assured him he would have matters under control. This call was Pascale's last chance to make a point. He made no effort to hide the concern in his voice, and offered no Wild West parable. He came right to the point: "Nelson Mandela said there's 'no one more dangerous than someone who has been humiliated – even if rightly.' Don't know if this guy Richardsen will feel humiliated that we've caught him." Pascale paused before delivering his heartfelt admonition. "3J, I'm on safe ground to think that Richardsen could be dangerous. Stay well behind Ronnie and let him do his thing. He knows what he's doing. So let him do it. You shouldn't engage. That's Ronnie's job. Trust that and call me immediately when the affair ends."

"To quote Ronnie, 'Copy that.' Thanks, Pascale, for having my six … and … g'night. I can't keep my eyes open any longer and your call delayed my college flop into my bed, my friend."

The call ended, and 3J collapsed into her bed for what she hoped would be a restful handful of hours of sleep. Instead, the sleep was restless. In those moments when she drifted into a partial state of awakeness, she thought, *Oh well. Par for the course.*

CHAPTER 25

Tuesday, November 21, 2023

6:15 A.M.

PHILLIP AWOKE FROM HIS lights-out, no-dreams, black-ether, substance-induced sleep. He was groggy, as he often was the morning after he used medical science to assist in his sleep needs. He sat on the edge of his bed and looked at his phone.

The fog lifted the instant he saw the emails.

He immediately ran for the laptop that he'd left on his glass-and-steel coffee table in his living room, to better be able to read the filings sent to him by Fuentes the night before. As he read first the lawsuit, then the TRO request papers, and then the Court's order, he muttered over and over with increasing volume and concern, "Shit, shit shit, shit."

The turn of events alarmed Joshua, and he considered surfacing. Phillip was not ready to yield.

Phillip wanted his first phone call to be to Fuentes, but he opted instead to use his burner phone to call Richardsen. A groggy Edmond Richardsen slowly answered the call. "Hello?"

"Edmond. We have a problem. Last night, the Rapinoes' lawyers filed a request for a Temporary Restraining Order against you and the Judge granted it just before midnight. Someone must be on their way over to your house to serve you with the papers and to take an image of your hard drive. You need to pack and leave. Straight away. Go ... somewhere."

"Just against me?"

"Yes, Edmond. Just you. That's why you need to leave."

"Look Dewey, negatory. That's nuts. I'm not going anywhere. I have a business to run."

"It is unfortunate that we must have this conversation under such unpleasant circumstances, my good Edmond. But please, pause a moment to think this through. Be rational. Gather yourself. I can help you organize your thoughts."

Silence.

"Edmond, I see no alternative for you but to make yourself scarce while we figure out this sudden, unexpected turn of events."

"Again, Dewey, negatory, Not gonna happen. I don't know why you're so worried. You assured me that freedom of speech would trump any provisions of the Bankruptcy process."

"I believe that with all my heart, Edmond. I do." Dewey then lowered the burner phone from his ear, and looked at the urn on the mantle, and said to it, "What's that, Mother? Can't you see I am busy managing a bit of a situation? I do not need your *assistance*. I do not need your *opinions*." Then he tilted his head back, closed his eyes, and abruptly yelled, "Silence!" No further *communications* came from the urn. Joshua had surfaced momentarily to end Mother's commentary. He then returned to his shadows and Phillip returned his attention to the burner phone and Richardsen.

Before he could say anything, however, Richardsen asked, "Dewey, who the hell are you talking to, and yelling at?"

In a strident voice, Phillip responded quickly, "No one."

"Well, it sure didn't sound like no one. It sounded like someone. It sounds like you're yelling at your mother. Is she there with you? I thought you told me she passed years ago."

Phillip had no time to talk to Richardsen about Mother and had no interest in trying to explain his continuing relationship with her. Instead, he barked into the burner phone, "If you will not leave your home, what exactly is your plan, my good Edmond?"

"I'll read the Judge's order and do whatever it says I have to do. I'm not taking on a federal judge. That's the definition of lunacy. Then, I'll find a lawyer. A lawyer who *you* will pay for, 'my good Dewey.' And, one hundred percent, I'll do whatever the lawyer says to do."

Phillip smacked his tongue on the roof of his mouth and said with a tone of incredulity, "And that is it?"

"Hundred percent: that's it, Dewey."

"As I explained, the order restrains you alone, Edmond. You will, of course, abide by our agreement to keep my name out of this, correct?"

"Dewey, I've already told you what I am going to do. I don't have time or interest in continuing to clarify my course of action for you."

Phillip listened to him impatiently. *Foolish person. How does he expect to protect his interests – and mine – if he doesn't take a proactive approach?* "That is most unfortunate news. And, if I might add, a supremely misguided decision on your part."

Richardsen began to respond, "Now wait a—"

But just as Richardsen was beginning to lose his temper, Phillip hung up. *This is not helpful to me and it is not furthering my cause. If Edmond wishes to have an audience to listen to him, he can seek a stage somewhere to perform on open-mic night.*

Phillip next called Fuentes. Caller ID informed Fuentes who was calling, and it took more resolve than he expected to answer the call, rather than let it roll to voicemail.

"Mr. Fuentes, I have read the papers filed by Debtors' counsel. Rubbish ... All of it is rubbish. And, based on those papers, the Court proceeded to enjoin one Edmond Richardsen. So we have a perpetrator, don't we?"

"Mr. Dewey, I am sure you saw the many references in the TRO request to you and Veridical. The Debtors allege lots of connections with Richardsen. Too many. They seem solid. They've done their homework."

"As I said, sir ... all rubbish."

"It doesn't read that way at all. What they alleged may indeed stink like rotting garbage, but the odor is emanating from the smear campaign, not from the impropriety of the allegations in the papers."

"Mr. Fuentes, we have already covered the topic of your tone and your accusations ..."

But before Phillip could finish, this time Fuentes interrupted and said forcefully, "Yes, we did, Mr. Dewey. This time, however, the tone you are hearing and the accusations you are reading are all from the information gathered on behalf of the Debtors ... and it's *damning*. So you need not repeat to me this morning what you previously said. I heard you the first time, sir, and you appear to have far greater problems right now than my tone and my concerns with your conduct and veracity. Do we understand each other?"

Phillip said nothing. He was losing his ability to manage his emotions. He was struggling to restrain his comments. He could feel Joshua stirring, concerned for Phillip's safety, angling to protect Phillip.

Fuentes continued on offense. "What I need to know, alleged fact by alleged fact, is simple: what is true, and what is not."

Phillip again said nothing.

"Let's start simple. Does Richardsen do information systems work for Veridical?"

"He does from time to time. He does good work for a fair price," Phillip said slowly and guardedly, with distrust in his voice.

"Do you personally know him?"

"I do," Phillip said, again slowly. "Of course I do. I hire him for Veridical."

These were all questions that Joshua could not answer. He stayed in observation mode for the present, listening to the questions and Phillip's answers.

Phillip's portion of the mind was racing. He cut off the question-and-answer session and said, "Mr. Fuentes. I have a guest here – my mother. I am going to have to cut this discussion off until a little later. I will call you to further discuss. Have a good morning." And before Fuentes could protest, Phillip terminated the call.

He looked over at the urn and said, "Mother, matters have taken an unfortunate turn. I will take under advisement any *suggestions* you may have."

Phillip felt no energy from the urn and heard nothing from Mother.

Mother's silence pleased Joshua. His command for silence had worked, at least for the moment.

3J picked up Alvarez-Thompson, and the two drove to O'Brien's. There, they added Steele to their car pool and headed south to Armour Hills and Richardsen's house. It was a short and silent ten-minute drive. Once at the house, Steele exited the car first, told 3J and Alvarez-Thompson to remain in the car, walked to the front stoop, and knocked on the front door. It was 7:40 a.m.

From inside the house, Steele heard a muffled voice ask, "Who's there?"

"Ronnie Steele. I work for Bey and Adam Rapinoe in their bankruptcy cases." Steele had given some thought about how to explain who he was. He wasn't a cop any longer. He wasn't a private investigator, either. He didn't think explaining that he was a bartender would be of much use, so he'd decided to just explain who he worked for. "I have some papers I have to deliver to you."

"Just leave them there on the front steps."

"Yeah, I'm sorry, but I can't do that, Mr. Richardsen. I have to hand them to you."

"Sorry to hear that. I don't open my door for strangers."

"Mr. Richardsen: Bankruptcy Judge Robertson issued a restraining order against you last night. I have the order here and need to hand it to you. He has ordered that you must immediately cease and desist any further posts about BJB LLC and the Rapinoes. Do you understand?"

"I really don't, sir. BJB? The Rapinoes? Bankruptcy? I'm afraid I'm not following you."

"Perhaps that's because we are trying to speak to each other through your solid wood door. That's not ideal, now is it?"

Alvarez-Thompson sat in the back car seat, with the door open and her feet resting on the curb. But, ignoring Steele's admonition, 3J exited the car and walked closer to Steele so she could hear the discussion. From her new vantage point, she could listen to Steele's side of the conversation but she couldn't hear Richardsen, so she walked even closer to the front door. As she got closer, she shouted, "Mr. Richardsen, this is Josephina Jones speaking. I am the bankruptcy lawyer for BJB and the Rapinoes. Do you understand me?"

Silence.

3J continued, "A federal judge has ordered you to do something and to refrain from doing other things. You need to have the order. That's the law. We're required to hand it to you. If you don't open your door and let us do that, I am confident that the next thing that will happen is the Judge will send several large U.S. Marshals to your front door, and they may decide to bring you back to the courthouse. They certainly will *not* talk to you through your door. We should all want to avoid that type of scene, eh? So kindly open the door and take the papers."

Steele and 3J heard a deadbolt turn and a chain lock released. Slowly, the front door opened and there stood Edmond Richardsen in a tattered brown bathrobe, unshaven, with an outstretched, extended arm, palm up, inviting Steele to hand him the papers. Steele slipped his steel-toed right boot in the doorjamb to prevent Richardsen from closing the door and said, "Mr. Richardsen, here are the papers, sir." Steele transferred the papers from his hand to Richardsen's and as he did, Richardsen accepted the papers with a palpable look of pain on his face.

Richardsen looked down at the size 12 shoe in his doorjamb, and back up at Steele, then over to 3J, and then back to Steele.

"Look, Mr. Richardsen, we know you're working for Phillip Dewey. We know you're the one posting on social media at Dewey's direction. We know you're noLightpassing31 and noLightpassed13." Steele paused so Richardsen could absorb what he was saying. Richardsen blinked twice, but didn't twitch or remove his gaze from Steele's eyes. "Mr. Richardsen – why? Why're you doing this? BJB doesn't owe you any money. The Rapinoes don't even know you and I'm betting you don't know them. You're hurting folks you've never even met. I don't understand; why do Dewey's bidding?"

"Who says I'm working for Dewey? I mean, I know the guy. He's a little creepy. But who says that means I'm working for him?"

"So, what're you saying? You're posting just for yucks and grins, and not because Dewey is paying you to do so?" Steele asked, disdainful of Richardsen's answer.

"I'm not saying anything."

"Well, silence and obfuscation are not conditions that will last long for you," 3J chimed in.

Richardsen shrugged slightly, looked down at the ground and back up to make eye contact with Steele, frowned on half of his mouth, and said nothing. Then he floated the Dewey mantra: "But I *do* have the right in this country of ours to say whatever I want, wherever I choose to say it."

3J glared at him. She would not let his free speech comment go, and wanted to give him a preview of the ire that he could expect in the deposition. She squinted her right eye and sternly corrected him. "Actually, you don't. Read the order in the papers Mr. Steele just handed to you. It explains just how wrong you and this Dewey person are."

Silence. Richardsen didn't like making eye contact with 3J. *That little shit, Dewey. If this is how the deposition is going to go, things will not go well for him.*

Steele said, "Our tech person is here with some equipment to mirror your hard drives, and the papers order you to stop posting about the Debtors and to take down the posts you've already made."

Richardsen looked up at Steele and contemplated what he should do and say. He told Dewey he would follow the order, but he didn't want someone just walking around his home. "I am going to close my door now, read the order, and then I'll come back to the front door and we can all decide what the next steps should be."

Richardsen's manner exacerbated 3J's irritation, and she said, "There's nothing for you to decide. Judges make decisions, not you and me. This judge made his decision last night and there's no choice here – just follow what the order says, or you'll be in contempt of Court and big guys from the Marshal's office will fit you for a jumpsuit and take you away to jail for disobeying the order. Am I getting through to you?"

With a slight quaver in his voice from nerves, Richardsen said, enunciating each word precisely, "One hundred percent. As I said, I'll read the order in my living room behind me. Then I'll be back with you shortly," Richardsen said and began to close the door as Steele withdrew his foot from the doorjamb.

Ten minutes later, the door opened slowly and Richardsen stepped aside to allow Alvarez-Thompson to enter with her equipment to clone the hard drives. Richardsen now had on blue jeans and a worn tan short-sleeve shirt, and had placed two laptops on his living room coffee table. 3J and Steele entered first, followed by Alvarez-Thompson. 3J asked, "Are these two machines the only computers you have?"

"These are the computers I used to post on the internet, pertinent to the Court's order."

"No other computers here?" 3J asked, not believing Richardsen.

"These are the only computers I've used to post."

While the back and forth continued between Richardsen and 3J, Alvarez-Thompson silently set up her equipment and quickly made mirror images of the two hard drives.

3J asked to see the other computers that she believed a tech person like Richardsen must have. Richardsen responded, "Negatory, Ms. Jones. That order isn't a search warrant and you're not the police. You don't have my permission to roam around my house."

Richardsen had obviously composed himself somewhat, as he took ten minutes to read the order.

"Are you going to comply with Judge Robertson's order and immediately take down the posts and stop any further posting?" 3J asked.

"I've read the Judge's order and I understand what he's ordered me to do."

"But are you going to comply?" 3J pressed.

"Again, you're not the police and the order doesn't require me to talk with you." Looking over at Alvarez-Thompson, Richardsen asked, "Ma'am – have you completed your task?"

Alvarez-Thompson nodded her head affirmatively.

"Good. Then please," he said, extending his arm and hand to point the way to his front door. "All three of you, leave my house and my property."

As the three exited Edmond Richardsen's house, they heard his heavy dark door slam shut and a deadbolt engage.

Once in the car, 3J turned to Steele, animated, and said, "What a shit stew this whole thing turned out to be. I'm standing outside a white man's home in a white neighborhood raising my voice at 8 a.m. in Kansas City. The whole thing makes me very unsettled. Two black folks and a Latina in a mostly white neighborhood at the crack of dawn, speaking loudly to a white guy within. I don't like it. We must be out of our minds. We need to go, now."

As 3J pressed the pedal and coaxed the car forward at a higher speed than was Armour Hills-neighborhood-appropriate, Steele said, "Well, luckily, nothing bad happened on that front," not exactly soothing 3J's frazzled nerves.

"Yeah, but it could've. We were lucky," 3J corrected him. "It's not a good plan to plan on being lucky. Not one bit."

There was silence in the Prius as they left Armour Hills, and turned north on Brookside Boulevard toward the return first to O'Brien's and then to downtown.

"What next?" Steele asked.

"We get Mr. Edmond Richardsen in for a deposition and hope he gives up Dewey and Veridical," 3J outlined mechanically. "And we depose Dewey as well."

More silence as 3J drove.

Steele broke the silence again and asked, "Why would a guy like Richardsen do what he did on behalf of a guy he describes as creepy?"

"I assume money, but that's what we're gonna have to find out. Do you want to attend the deposition, Ronnie?"

"Wouldn't mind sitting in."

To Alvarez-Thompson, 3J asked, "Rene, thanks so much for all the help, and sorry to drag you into this."

"Not at all a problem, 3J. I kind of found the whole thing fascinating, if not a bit disturbing."

"Well, there are better and safer ways to be fascinated by the practice of law," 3J pointed out. Changing the subject, she asked, "How long before we can start perusing the hard drive contents?"

"We'll need to run the hard drives through our document management software. Probably, given the volume of material that I'm seeing, count on that being an eighteen-hour process. The software will index all the documents so you can construct robust searches. But that takes time. Once we've loaded all the data into our platform and we're done, you can log on to the software, and construct all the searches you would like to your heart's content."

"So, basically tomorrow, later in the day?"

"That's a fair estimate."

"What about his browsing history?"

"Similar process and timeline," Alvarez-Thompson explained. "Electronic discovery is a game-changer, but parts of the process are still slower than we'd like. So while we index, the wheels of justice move slow."

3J pulled up in front of O'Brien's to drop Steele off. He exited the car and then leaned back in through the open window and said, "Thanks for the thrills. Let me know what else you need from me."

3J smiled. "Nothing thrilling about this case so far."

"Oh. I'm not so sure about that. You were pretty thrilled last night at around midnight when you got your order."

3J closed her eyes briefly and nodded her agreement. Midnight last night suddenly seemed like eons ago. Alvarez-Thompson got into the passenger side front seat, buckled up, and they sped away back to their office.

Once back at the office, 3J found Pascale and gave him the update on what transpired.

"Testy. Hmmm. Just what I was worried about," Pascale observed.

"Ronnie called it thrilling. Rene called it fascinating. I called it a shit stew."

"As always, the lawyer's spin is, without a doubt, the more accurate one."

"In retrospect, it didn't go down the way I envisioned and it may not've been the wisest thing to do."

Pascale nodded in agreement.

Both let the topic of the confrontation close. Hearing no further observations about the service of the papers, 3J said, "Say, what about using Ronnie to tail Dewey now?"

"Don't see why not. I can ask him to do that for us," Pascale said.

"No need. I'm going to swing by O'Brien's to thank him for his work to date and get his bill to pay. I'll just ask him to follow Dewey for a while."

"As you wish," Pascale said, smiling with just a hint of an all-knowing look.

"What?" 3J stated innocently.

"Oh, nothing," Pascale said, with just a hint of judgment in his voice.

Judge Robertson stood by the office coffee machine waiting for the pot to finish brewing. He knew it would probably not be the only pot of the day. *The coffee producers of the world count on nights like last night to make their quarterly budget estimates*, he thought to himself.

Jennifer and Jill Walton arrived at the door to chambers at the same time and entered the waiting area together.

"Hardly feels like we went home," the Judge said to Jennifer. Walton asked, "What time did you guys leave last night?"

"Midnight," he and Jennifer said simultaneously.

Walton whistled softly. "Oh, wow. You guys must be wiped."

He smiled and said, "Keep that pot hot and full today." He turned toward his office. "Jennifer, can you bring a pad and come on in, please? A couple of things to go over with you as the day gets started."

Cuello grabbed a yellow pad and followed the Judge into his office. She was smiling.

"Do I detect a bit of a lift in your step this morning?" the Judge asked her.

"Judge, when you're 5'2" tall, you don't really noticeably lift when you walk," she said, kidding him.

"Well, I thought I detected something when you came in the office this morning."

"Perhaps you're right," Jennifer said, smiling. "Maybe just a bounce."

The two then went over what was likely to happen next in the TRO process, and the Judge assigned her the task of digging further into any cases similar to *Andrus.*

Cuello returned to her small office, grabbed her research file and logged on to her computer so she could start the research Judge Robertson requested. She was tired, but she was still energized by the previous evening's tasks. As the computer booted up, she thought, *Maybe not a lift, but this law clerk job is definitely going to work out.*

CHAPTER 26

Phillip Dewey Recalls Tuesday, November 21, 2023

I PHONED EDMOND, AND he took my call. "May I please have a status update, my dear Edmond?"

"Why, certainly, Dewey. One hundred percent." Edmond's voice was dripping with sarcasm. "Well, let's see. Three folks showed up at my fuckin' front door and they banged on it at the crack of dawn. They came, and now they've gone. That's what happened, Dewey. Right here at the front door of my house. For all my neighbors to see, god-fuckin'-dammit!" he said, raising his voice.

I ignored his emotional response. "That is it, Edmond? *That* is the level of detail in your report?"

"Let's see. More detail? Hmmm. Well, like I said, they knocked loudly, I opened the door, they put a large foot in my doorjamb so I couldn't close the door, they handed me the Judge's fuckin' order, they took a mirror image of the laptops that I used for the posts, and then they asked a bunch of questions about you."

"Vulgarity, Edmond. Please. Restrain yourself. Who were they, Edmond?"

"The computer person was a Latina lady, I think from the law firm where Jones works. The second was Jones. The third was a big black guy in civilian clothes who came off like he's ex-cop."

"Hmmm. I see. What did you tell them?"

"That I wasn't under arrest. That they couldn't come into my house and look around. That I would read the papers and hire a lawyer. Just like I told you I would say."

"Excellent. Well said, Edmond. What did you say about me?"

"Nothing."

"Are you certain?"

"Do we need to do this, Edmond? This has me all stressed-out and I'm repeating myself. I don't want to do a rehash with you. I didn't say anything to them; I didn't need to." Edmond sounded fed up with me. I certainly realized I can have that effect on people. I am what I am; some things cannot be changed. So be it.

I found Edmond's teaser surprising, so I asked, "What do you mean, 'you didn't need to'?"

"Didn't talk about you, Dewey. Didn't need to – because they talked about you. A lot."

"I see." I tried to organize my thoughts. I must have still had some of the sleeping medicine in my bloodstream because it was proving a laborious task for me. "What did they ask?"

"Mostly why I posted for you."

"And you said nothing."

"One hundred percent."

Joshua let me know how little he believed what he was hearing from Edmond, and how little he trusted him, stirring as his concern increased. All I could do at the moment was hope upon hope that Joshua would concede control to me. After all, I was the Primary in the Body.

I thought for a moment. "And you're still committed to staying in Kansas City, rather than making yourself scarce?"

"Again, I would just be repeating myself, Dewey. No rehash."

Edmond had become more and more forward in the manner that he addressed me. I wanted to say something to put him in his place, but, sadly, I still needed him on my team. I said, "We will continue to stay in touch using this burner. Agreed?"

"Agreed."

Silence.

Then, Edmond asked, "Dewey, what's your plan? That Jones lady sprinkled your name all over the papers I read like a cook sprinkles a healthy dose of salt on a twelve-ounce Kansas City Strip Steak." I said nothing. Edmond continued, "Are you there? Just a matter of time, don't you think?"

Again, sadly, I feared that Edmond might have had a point. "Edmond, I have a plan for these types of situations. I will simply have to implement it."

"And your mother, Dewey?"

I never discuss Mother with anyone. "My mother? What about her?"

"You sounded like you were yelling at her the other day when we talked. Is she part of your plan?"

"Absolutely not. Edmond, we will talk again, good sir," and I ended the call before Edmond could continue his inquiries about Mother.

Many years ago, under an alias, I had purchased a small farm home about forty miles west of Topeka in a little town – Paxico, Kansas. Near the Kansas Flint Hills. Charming, but quite unmemorable if you are not farming the land. Yes, as I reflected on my call with Edmond, I readily concluded that the time had come for me to move my operation to my Paxico residence.

I am not a survivalist, but one might have looked at the Paxico establishment and believed that I set it up to await the end of the world – all the provisions I could use without the need to venture far for months. In truth, I acquired the home for those moments when I do not wish to be bothered by Mother. Right now, I was in that same state of mind.

The provisions serviced only one. Mother would not be making the trip with me. She so did not like to travel at her advanced age. Unfortunately I could not prevent Joshua from coming with me to Paxico. Where the Body went, he went.

It concerned me that I was thinking only in the moment, and not long term. Not planning, but reacting. I needed time to think; alone – or at least my modified definition of alone.

I packed and as I left my Hallbrook home, I felt energy from Mother's resting place, and said, "No, Mother, you will not be coming with me on this trip."

I waited for a *response*, and of course, one was forthcoming. She was never one to shy away from *providing* her opinion.

"No, Mother. There is no place for you on this trip and you know you do not travel well."

I felt that Mother was not *happy*.

"Mother, you are in no position to threaten me with physical harm. You – we – have moved beyond that. Remember?"

Mother *wished* to continue the useless dialogue, and I needed to get on the road. I drew the blinds on the main floor, *heard* her ask for nothing while I would be gone and wished her a good night. I exited the door leading from the kitchen to the garage, locked it behind me, put my luggage in the car, and drove away. I knew Mother would be fine without me. She always was. As am I without her.

CHAPTER 27

Tuesday, November 21 to Friday, November 24, 2023

THAT EVENING, 3J AND Pascale sat in the conference room planning their next steps. As far as they could tell, the posts had abruptly stopped just as 3J and Steele had completed delivery of the restraining order to Richardsen. "Next step should be to depose Richardsen and this Dewey character," 3J proposed.

"Affirmative, from my vantage point," Pascale said.

"I think first up should be Richardsen. I don't know Dewey, but human nature would suggest that he won't give up anything until someone flips on him. So Richardsen is the man to flip."

Pascale offered, "I can get those papers written and out to set it up for us."

"That would be a great help."

As they talked, Alvarez-Thompson popped her head in the door and said, "Indexing complete, folks. We were way ahead of schedule. You can now log on and search away. Let me know if you need help with the searches or any other part of the project."

"Thanks so much, Rene. You're a lifesaver, as always," 3J said.

Looking somber, Pascale said, "What say we both spend

some time surfing to see what Mr. Richardsen's hard drive might reveal to us?"

"Agreed," 3J said. "The Searchers, you and me," she added, rising to return to her own office for what she expected would be an hours-long enterprise.

Once back at her desk, as she logged onto the firm's litigation management software, she sighed. *People think the practice of law is all glamour and high drama court appearances. Mostly, it's slow-moving, mundane tasks such as searching a document dump for a needle that might not even be in the haystack.* A night of searching was not at the top of her list of professional things she looked forward to doing. But it was an inevitable necessity.

After several hours of searching, 3J concluded there were no conventional emails between Dewey and Richardsen. While she could determine that Richardsen was in fact the source of the many posts, she found nothing to suggest that Dewey instructed him to post, nor that Dewey drafted the posts for him. She concluded there could be only two possible reasons. First: Dewey was not involved. She instantly rejected that possibility. Second: the two were careful in how they communicated – *maybe by burner phones?* Or, perhaps, old-fashioned meetings on a remote park bench in which Dewey delivered written folders to Richardsen, who executed whatever the papers in the folder directed him to do and then destroyed the folder. Kind of old-school, *Mission Impossible*, spy movie, covert operations. *Maybe*, she thought dubiously, her gut telling her it was a burner phone operation. From all she had learned about Dewey, he didn't seem like the type of guy who relished repeat in-person contact, even if on a bench in a secluded area of a park. *No*, she thought, harkening back to the criminologist's profile Moses had delivered, *Dewey has to be more of an above-the-law, and too-smart-for-the-law-to-apply-to-him kind of guy, rather than a spy.*

From the profile, she was looking for someone who was holier-than-thou; with repressed anger; with a lack of regard for the rights of others and a tendency regularly to violate those rights; cunning and self-serving, and with no concern for wrecking others' lives.

Just like Bey had said early on – Phillip Dewey all the way. But where were the communications?

She rose to stretch and walked around to Pascale's office. The white LED lights of the office contrasted with the pitch black sky outside. He had finished the Richardsen deposition notice and had started on his own search terms to apply to the database of documents. He, like 3J, quickly discovered that Richardsen was indeed the owner of both noLight handles, that Richardsen was the poster, and that Richardsen's company, Dark Moons, did periodic contract work for Veridical, updating systems, maintaining tech security, and repairing outages. It appeared Richardsen performed much of that work remotely.

"So, what do we have here?" Pascale asked.

"Well, between what you found and what I found, there's no question Richardsen is our guy, but I don't think we are an inch closer to linking Dewey to him and the posts," 3J said dejectedly, her shoulders sagging as she spoke.

"We'll get Richardsen in here under oath, and maybe he'll break. He's looking at some serious contempt issues here, and I can't believe that he would sacrifice himself for a guy like Dewey," Pascale said with a hint of an upbeat tone to try to help 3J out of her doldrums.

"Agreed. That's got to be the play. When are you setting the depo?"

"Seven days out," Pascale advised.

"You looked at my calendar?"

"I did indeed. We're both free."

"Excellent. You want me to take the depo?" 3J asked.

"I want you to do whatever you are comfortable with," Pascale said.

"I'll take it. I'll plan on bringing my best 'under-the-hot-light' interrogation techniques. I might go home and watch some old reruns of *Dragnet*, with Sergeant Friday and his sidekick grilling the bad guy in a Chesterfield-smoky small room."

"Ahhh. *Dragnet*. No smoking in here, but I'll reserve one of our tiny conference rooms. Easier for you to be right in his face."

3J smiled at that prospect. "I'll let the Rapinoes know. You think both of them should attend?"

"I kinda do. This guy should know the human side of his little operation. He should see his victims. Hopefully, that will soften him a little, or at least crack the exterior and make him realize Dewey isn't worth protecting."

"Sounds right," 3J agreed. "In the interim, I'll take one more shot at Moses and Rome and see if their networks can come up with any more of a connection between Dewey and Richardsen. Nothing would make me happier than shoving a smoking gun document in front of him and demanding the truth based on the document," she concluded, her voice rising matching the rise in her blood pressure as she thought about the prospect of nailing Richardsen and having him give up Dewey under the stress of the deposition process. "Oh, one more thing, Bill. Let's direct Richardsen and Dewey to bring any phones they used to communicate with each other, including any burner phones, to the depositions."

"You mean the burner phones we don't know they have?"

"Exactly. It's an assumption. But a good one, I think."

"Agreed. Done," Pascale said.

3J rose and left Pascale's office and headed back to her desk to close it up for the night. She'd contact Moses and Rome in the morning and then continue the search of the hard drive records. It was likely that the search would yield nothing more for her, and she needed that breakthrough linkage from a different source.

Early the next morning, Pascale decided to have the deposition notice hand-delivered to Richardsen at his home by a process server Pascale had used for years, and who was creative. "Hey, Anthony Rosini. Bill Pascale here. Long time no talk."

"How the hell are you, Bill?" Rosini asked, glad to hear Pascale's voice.

"Can't complain. I'd like to, of course, but I just can't."

"I know the feeling, my friend. What's up?"

"Say, I need some help to serve a guy with deposition papers." Pascale then explained how Richardsen had reacted to Steele and 3J.

"Don't think it'll be a problem, Bill. With folks like this, I'll just use a costume and some subterfuge."

"What do you have in mind, Anthony?"

"Oh, I'm thinking I'll just dust off my Amazon Prime delivery man costume, which should still fit, and show up at his door with a Prime package – I save prime boxes for just this type of gig – and whether in person or through the door, I'll tell him I need a signature. Easy peasy. Who can resist an Amazon box these days?"

Pascale knew that Anthony Rosini was the best process server in Kansas City. A former Jackson County Sheriff's Department deputy sheriff, he had left public service to set up his own process server firm, and lately had expanded his business to include finding accused criminals who skipped out on their bail terms. Some finders used the threat of force to find their targets. Rosini was all cerebral.

"So, the costume thing works pretty well, does it?" Pascale asked, a little surprised, but fascinated, by the method.

"Oh yeah. I've been a UPS man, an FTD florist delivering roses to a wife who resisted service, a grocery boy, a Latter Day Saints missionary … you name it, I've tried it. Got an entire closet of costumes and get-ups. Got an entire brain full of ideas. Never been a ghost, but, no lie, I'm waiting for a Halloween opportunity, and I'm gonna try a little trick or treat service of process."

"Anthony, my man, you are having way too much fun," Pascale observed as he chuckled his way through Rosini's explanation of his methods.

"Y'know, whatever floats the boat. Get the papers over to me with the details of where our friend is and leave the rest to me. I'll serve him Friday if that works."

Ronnie Steele went to Hallbrook to pay an up-close-and-personal visit to Phillip Dewey. As he walked up the front walkway, he noticed Dewey had completely drawn all the blinds on the first floor. He saw no light behind the blinds. He rang the doorbell. No answer, and no movement heard inside. He rapped on the door. Same result. He walked the perimeter of the house and saw no evidence of life inside. He walked past the attached garage and noticed no window treatments, so he gazed in and observed no vehicle inside the garage.

Steele went to Veridical's small office and asked the receptionist to call Mr. Dewey out of his office to meet with him. The receptionist readily told him that Dewey was not present and hadn't been for the past several days. He asked where he might find Dewey, and to his surprise, rather than grill him on who he was and why he wanted to talk with her boss, she simply said she honestly had no idea where the guy was, but if Steele found him, could he please ask Dewey to call her pronto.

Steele reported to 3J and Pascale that Dewey was in the wind, but he didn't know where. 3J added "possible Dewey whereabouts" to the supplemental sleuthing assignments for Rome, Moses and their *Crowded!* network.

3J and Pascale arranged for a conference call with Moses and Rome later that afternoon. At precisely 6 p.m. Eastern Time, 1 a.m. London Time, and 5 p.m. Central Time, all four connected and began their call. 3J updated them on the current status before saying, "We still have two problems. The same old one – tying Dewey to Richardsen more directly, and in particular on the posts against our clients – and now a new one: Dewey is in the wind. He's vanished. He seems to have left his house dark and moved his base of operations someplace else. We need to know where so we can serve him with a deposition notice."

Moses and Rome listened silently. Moses sat at his roll-top desk, as Emily stretched on the floor at his feet. When 3J finished, he said, "I see. A bit of a missing persons investigation has now surfaced."

"Exactly, Moses," 3J agreed. "But missing because he *chooses* to be missing."

"May I assume that Mr. Dewey likely has decided to go someplace familiar to him and comfortable and, shall I say, wait this out?"

"That's a good assumption and the one we're leaning towards," 3J agreed.

"Very well, then. We will examine relevant online data and see what we can see. Stand by. We will report back to you shortly."

3J and Pascale thanked them and the conference call ended.

After the conference call, Moses called Rome to discuss options.

Moses said, "We can attack this on two fronts. First, from real estate records. What else does Mr. Dewey own besides his Kansas City house in a two-state region – I'd say Kansas and Missouri? We can get that pretty easily from county records. Second, assuming he does own something, just not in his own name, we should search 'Veridical' as well, and also try to identify other names he might use as a front to own real estate."

"Agreed, Moses," Rome concurred.

"I have some contacts in the Midwest who can quickly answer the question of what else Dewey and Veridical own, but what about the issue of alias ownership?"

"That is always a bit trickier, Moses. Like we did for Richardsen, we would have to delve into Dewey deeper than before. Perhaps find other names or companies he owns that would provide him a different name under which he would own real estate; at the same time, this alias name would have to be comfortable for him. It is my belief people tend to select alter egos that have something to do with their past. I have some ideas of how we might identify such names to associate with Mr. Dewey."

"Excellent. Let's make it so, my dear Rome."

After their call, Rome reached out to her *Crowded!* contact and outlined the new tasks. She prioritized the alter ego question. To get *Crowded!*'s sleuths started, and thinking, she suggested possible alter ego research avenues: name of Dewey's high school; street where he grew up; birth certificate information; year of birth; mother's and father's names; something to do with lending. All things that would be familiar to Dewey and presumably with which he would be comfortable.

She then made sure her computer was charging, closed the lid, and drifted into a restless sleep. She hoped for a few hours before she would join the search for Dewey. She wished for a more normal sleep hygiene, but thought to herself, *This catnap sleep protocol seemed to work for Thomas Edison. Hope it's fine for me as well.*

After the call, Moses reached out to his Midwest operative and explained the task. He then put Emily's harness on and headed down to the intersection of Broadway and Fifth Avenue for their evening walk. There was a little less hustle and bustle than he had expected, as they made their way to his favorite French restaurant, a café with a seating capacity of twenty small tables and takeout service for a pre-Thanksgiving feast: coq au vin, with a bottle of his favorite Red Rhône – a "Rhône Ranger," as he liked to call it.

"Bonsoir, Monsieur Moses," the maître d' said.

"Bonsoir, Monsieur," Moses replied, executing a perfect Parisan accent.

"The usual tonight, sir?"

"Oui. Merci," Moses responded. "Emily and I will stroll for a bit and be back to retrieve the dinner and wine bottle, Henri."

"Très bien, Monsieur Moses. Merci bien."

Moses and Emily exited the restaurant and began their walk around the neighborhood. Though the sun had disappeared, the lights of Manhattan's Flatiron District provided more than sufficient illumination and the rapidly approaching evening was hardly noticeable. The City that never sleeps. Moses thought about his new clients, the Greene Madison lawyers; like so many of his engagements, he was thoroughly enjoying the work. He chuckled to himself. *Why retire when I am enjoying what I do and enjoying my life? Why indeed!*

Emily also appeared to enjoy her time on the streets of Manhattan, but explored no smell the street offered if it took her more than two feet from Moses. "At his side" was her strict canine mantra.

In due course, they returned to Chez Provence, retrieved Moses' smartly wrapped dinner and wine in a Chez Provence brown shopping bag, and joined the many New Yorkers carrying a bag advertising one establishment or another, as they headed back to Moses' flat. It was vintage New York City to be seen with a shopping bag; it had been since the early 1900s. As he swung the bag gently in his right hand, holding onto Emily's leash in his left, he idly thought about New York City shopping bags. Shoppers, commuters, picketers, and now homeless people, all had The Bag.

When they returned to the flat, Emily attended to her newly-filled dinner bowl while Moses decanted the wine and set out

his dinner on his white, square-shaped, French ceramic din-
nerware. Before he could reheat his dinner, however, Emily
finished hers and, as was the custom, began to flick her head up
and back with her nose in the air, and then back down quickly
to attract Moses' attention, commanding him to look in her
bowl and see she had finished dinner. Silently each evening
she gyrated as if to exclaim, "Look, I've finished! Where's
my dessert?" In response, Moses always said, "Let's look at
your bowl," and he did under Emily's watchful eye. When he
said, "You did! You finished!" Emily became ecstatic because
she knew she had earned her evening dessert – a turkey jerky
square. She never tired of the ceremony, and neither did Moses.
Oh, the life of an Emily dog.

While Emily worked on the jerky square, Moses gently
reheated his dish, and his first bite revealed the splendor of
French cooking. As he ate, he gazed at his laptop to find an
email from his Midwest operative. Through an online search
of real estate records, the operative could quickly determine
that the only real estate owned in Phillip Dewey's name was
his house in Hallbrook in Kansas City. And Veridical owned
no real estate at all.

That leaves the investigation up to Ms. Davies, he thought. He had
every confidence that if there was something to find, Rome
would find it.

Rome awoke to the ding of her email. It was *Crowded!* They
catalogued their information in bullet points:

- Year of birth: 1973
- Mother: Agnes Mildred Dewey

- Father: no information found
- Street where he grew up: 45th Street near Troost
- High School: Lincoln College Prep
- Undergraduate degree: University of Kansas
- MBA: St. Louis University
- Company: Veridical
- Political affiliation: Independent
- Social media presence: none
- Personal web page: none.

Rome then reached out to Moses and asked him to have the operative check real estate records and see if any company whose name contained one or more of the following words owned land in Kansas or Missouri: Agnes, Mildred, Lincoln, KU, or SLU. While she hoped the operative could perform such a search, she was unsure of which search engine he would use and to what degree he could customize the search parameters. She therefore also wrote *Crowded!* again and asked for the sleuths to search Kansas and Missouri real estate records for land ownership using any combinations of the same names.

In short order, *Crowded!* and the operative both emailed with the same additional information. They located a Missouri company named 45Mildred LLC, formed eight years ago and still in good standing and active. *Crowded!* also discovered that the LLC owned land in Paxico, Kansas, due west of Kansas City and just a mile north of I-70. A tiny farm town. *A perfect place for someone like Phillip Dewey to hide out*, Rome thought. *No one knew him, and no one knew he was there.*

Rome quickly drafted a written report of the findings, including a description of Paxico, and emailed them to 3J and Moses.

It was 8 a.m. in London and midnight in Kansas City, and 3J had gone to bed for the evening.

3J awoke at 5:00 a.m. on Thanksgiving, earlier than usual, focused her eyes, retrieved her *Kansas City Star* from her front door, and read her emails. She quickly came to Rome's email and said out loud as the electric kettle began to boil her water, "Paxico, Kansas? Seriously? Shit. This just gets more and more bizarre." She had driven between Topeka and Kansas City many times and remembered passing a Paxico exit – exit 333 – but she had no cause to get off the highway and knew the town just as a sign on the interstate that she had sped past over and over again.

It was too early for 3J to call Pascale, especially on a holiday, so she brewed her tea, and waited for the clock to strike seven before calling him. *Just 'cause I can't sleep doesn't give me license to deprive him of sleep,* she thought, as she considered waking him and opted against it.

But as the clock struck six, 3J decided that she had waited long enough, and it was time for Pascale to get up. She called his mobile, and the phone rang four times before a sleepy Pascale answered. Sounding bleary-eyed, he said, "3J," followed by a long sigh. "What's up? What the hell time is it?"

"Time to get up. It's a new day, sunshine."

Pascale said nothing. 3J continued, "What's up is that we have a lead on where our friend Dewey may be."

"Ok; I'm up, I'm up," Pascale said slowly, trying to convince himself that he really was. "Where is he?"

"I'm guessing – Paxico. Paxico, Kansas."

"Where the hell is that?"

"West of here. Maybe eighty-five miles or so."

"*What* the hell is Paxico, Kansas?"

"Small farming town. Used to be the crown jewel of Wabaunsee County, occupied by the Potawatomi Indian tribe before relocation; seen better days. Used to have German Americans and African Americans living and working and farming together. If you can believe it, used to have the blues playing on Friday night. Now it has some remaining farms, some historical buildings, and pretty much nothing more."

Pascale yawned, still struggling to awaken fully, and asked, "And of all the places he could run to, why do we think Dewey's there?"

3J explained the results of Rome's sleuthing and *Crowded!*'s discoveries. Pascale was instantly alert and intrigued.

"So, if he's there, what's our next move?" he asked.

"Someone needs to deliver the deposition papers to Dewey. Could be Ronnie or a process server," she observed. She paused and rubbed her forehead. "I think we send the process server out to hand Dewey the deposition papers and the demand to bring the burner phone and documents with him to the deposition, just like Richardsen's deposition papers said. And, with any luck, hopefully Dewey shits in his pants."

"So service and Dewey shits? That about the size of it?" Pascale asked, feigning disagreement with the plan.

Concerned with Pascale's reaction, 3J said slowly, "Well … yes."

Pascale let the moment linger and then said happily, "Works for me."

"Will do." 3J paused and then ventured, "Pascale, were you playing with my head just now?"

"Who me? Never. Look, we won't find the process server

on Thanksgiving, 3J. Take the day off. You need it. We can reconnoiter on Friday." Pascale disconnected with a big smile on his face.

"Paxico, Kansas, eh?" Anthony Rosini said to both 3J and Pascale, who had phoned Rosini from the 27B conference room as soon as they both arrived at the office Friday morning. "A little off my usual beaten path. For that matter, a little off *everyone's* beaten path. But sure, I can serve papers in Paxico for you."

"You should know that this guy Dewey is a very different sort," 3J warned Rosini.

"How so?"

3J told Rosini everything she had heard about Dewey and he listened with interest. She shared with him the profile of a narcissistic sociopath, and that caught the attention and interest of the former sheriff.

"Well, I *am* in a sometimes high-risk kind of business. You might imagine that not everyone who gets served with legal papers finds they agree with them, and for some, it brings out the worst. They blame the process server. A version of 'don't kill the messenger' always flits across my mind when that happens. No one has yet," Rosini said, only partially kidding. "Are you saying that this Dewey guy is dangerous?"

"I can't say that, Anthony," 3J said in a reassuring tone. "But I want to make sure you go into this eyes wide open."

"Always, and I'm always careful."

Silence then as Rosini thought about options for service of the papers. He continued, "Well, as I think about this, I may dust off the old meter reader gambit for this one."

"And what's that maneuver, Anthony?" Pascale asked.

"Goes something like this. I show up in a white van, unmarked, with a power and utility jumpsuit on and tell the homeowner that I've tried to read the outside meter but there's a problem and could they let me into their basement just for a minute so I can check some lines. As soon as they open the door, I hand them your papers, return to the van, and drive off. It doesn't always work in the city – big city folks are more trained to suspect anyone they don't know who wants to enter their home. But out in the boons people are usually more trusting. Hell, some of them don't even lock their door."

3J wasn't familiar with all the different methods Rosini used to serve papers. His proposed ploy surprised her and, leaning closer to the speakerphone, she blurted out, "And that kind of thing works?"

"Quite well, actually. You'd be amazed. Pretense is a significant tool of the process server trade."

"Well, I'm sure this guy locks his door," 3J offered.

"Understood. I'll swing by your place for the papers and the info you have on this Dewey guy's whereabouts. Then I'll serve Richardsen and drive over to Paxico freakin' Kansas and serve Dewey, and let you know how it goes."

"As always, Anthony, thanks for all your help," Pascale said as they ended the call.

3J shook her head in amazement. "Bill, where do you find these helpers?"

Pascale smiled and said, "My contacts app is chock-full of people like this. Characters who're great at what they do and make my life easier."

"Before you go, I'm gonna need a download of your contacts and some description of who does what."

"Can do," Pascale said as he continued to smile. "Will you tell the Rapinoes about these developments or wait for the service of the papers?"

"I think – wait. Let's see how this plays out this morning. In the meantime, I have to get cracking on my deposition outline and figure out how to coerce our first witness into giving up our second."

"Short of reaching across the table at the deposition and grabbing him by the necktie, I'm sure you'll be your usual persuasive."

"I hope so. I don't know how hard a nut he's gonna be to crack."

"They can all crack. You just have to figure out where to apply the pressure for the shell to break. I'm sure this one'll crack as well," Pascale offered his assurances.

Dressed in clothing replicating the uniform of Amazon delivery personnel, Rosini rang Richardsen's door bell, and advised that he needed a signature. When the door opened, Rosini handed the confused Richardsen a small Amazon Prime box. As he turned to leave, Richardsen called out, "Hey, what do I need to sign?"

Rosini responded over his shoulder, "In the box, my friend. You've been served."

Mission accomplished, Rosini thought. *I do have too much fun!*

Richardsen closed his front door, box under arm. A second visitor to his house because of Dewey. Things were spinning out of control for him. He knew what was inside, but he opened the carefully taped box just the same to confirm.

Now Edmond Richardsen sat in his living room, looking at, but not reading, the papers the faux Amazon delivery man had served on him. He was none-too-happy with much of anything at the moment. He had allowed himself to get dragged into the world of Phillip Dewey – a world where Dewey used people for his profit and then discarded them, while Dewey lurked in the shadows. He had allowed himself to believe that Dewey was a man of his word and would hold Richardsen blameless if push came to shove. This especially bothered Richardsen, because he well knew Dewey would never live up to his promise; at least, not that one.

He found this particularly ironic because of Dewey's obsession with people following the written word of loan documents – period, end of discussion. He had allowed himself to do something that he knew was wrong in exchange for the significant renumeration paid to him by Dewey. He had debts to pay; he could have made money the slow and steady way, or taken a significant lump sum from Dewey to clear out many debts in one fell swoop. Money ruled. But it frustrated him that because of it, he had allowed himself to get dragged into Dewey's world.

And the crossroads at which he now found himself troubled him; a crossroads for which he felt he had no one to blame but himself. He knew Dewey would do what Dewey does. Always had and always would. But, as he breathed slowly and steadily on his couch, he closed his eyes and resigned himself to the conclusion that he had walked himself right into this problem and he needed to figure out a way to walk himself right out.

He opened the fake Amazon Prime box and found the folded up papers within. He opened and read them. *Shit*, he thought. *They want me to bring the burner phone and any additional documents. That phone is gonna make this even messier. How do they even know about the burner?*

He needed a lawyer and, per the papers, he would have to testify under oath. Dewey expected him to lie. After all, that was the post-deal discussion they'd had at Swope Park and Richardsen, foolishly, had led Dewey to believe that he wouldn't talk. Now he had finally come to his senses; he knew he had to bring the burner phone, talk on the record, and do a tell-all under oath.

Old Dewey is gonna be major pissed. And I no longer care one iota.

Richardsen picked up the burner phone and called Phillip.

"Good afternoon, Edmond," Phillip announced.

"Look, let's you and me cut the crap and cut to the chase. I just got served by Greene Madison for a deposition at their offices next week. They want me to bring this burner phone with me to the deposition, and they want other documents as well."

"Well, you simply cannot do that, Edmond."

"Well, Dewey, I simply will have to."

Silence.

"Dewey, I don't know where you are, but you need to come out of hiding and take over this problem. Y'know, hold me harmless as we agreed."

"I am working on a plan."

"A plan for you, I assume."

"No, my dear Edmond. A plan for *us*."

"Can't wait to hear this one."

"Mr. Richardsen, I sense a touch of derision in your tone. At least allow me the courtesy of presenting the plan to you before you decide to criticize it."

"If you've got a plan, now's the time to disclose it. My lawyer is undoubtedly going to tell me I'm already in an irreversible contempt situation for violating the automatic stay. He's gonna tell me, Dewey, that the automatic stay trumps freedom of speech. Repeat – the posts lose to the stay. In other words, he's gonna tell me you're full of shit and I'm a damn fool for letting you suck me into this. Do you hear me? I'm *not* going to add to my list of problems, lying under fuckin' oath for you!"

Phillip sighed deeply and as he let the air out of his lungs, he said in a consoling manner, "Message received my good friend. Stay calm. Take a breath. Await my call."

Click. Phillip ended the call.

As Edmond Richardsen folded up his phone, he made his decision. *My only way out of this mess is the same way I got into the mess – Phillip Dewey. He's never gonna hold me harmless. He got me into this, and giving him up is gonna get me out of this.*

Richardsen placed the burner phone on his coffee table next to the Amazon box and returned to the task of finding a bankruptcy lawyer to assist him.

CHAPTER 28

Phillip Dewey Recalls Friday, November 24, 2023

MY CALL WITH EDMOND was disquieting. He was cracking. I knew I would need to calm his concerns in the usual fashion: more money. But I decided in the meantime that it was time to talk to Mr. Fuentes again. I had my plan. Under the cloak of attorney-client privilege, I knew the time had arrived to work out the details with him to protect me from whatever the Greene Madison lawyers had in mind.

Joshua wanted to talk.

"Yes, Joshua. I know; I am weak. I know we have entered a new phase in Project Dis – a period of danger. Please, allow me to think." I needed silence to direct my attention to solving my brewing problems.

I phoned Mr. Fuentes – not my usual protocol for dealing with him. My feeling was that he should call me, leave a message, and I would get back to him when I had time and interest; always keep the lawyers back-pedaling and on their heels. But this time was different, and worthy of an exception to the protocol.

So I dialed Mr. Fuentes' Chicago exchange, and had to leave a voicemail. I was none-too-happy. I expected him to be at my beck and call.

Within fifteen minutes, Mr. Fuentes called me back.

"Good day, Alexander," I said, smacking my tongue in my mouth. "I would like to discuss the Rapinoe and BJB cases. There have been some, errrr, developments."

"I have a meeting in about thirty minutes. Is that enough time for our discussion?" Fuentes asked.

I was again none-too-happy. I cared not a bit about his other appointments and obligations.

"I guess it will have to be, Alexander, won't it?" I replied without letting on that his conduct was irritating.

"Go ahead then, Mr. Dewey."

"It seems that the Debtors will require Mr. Richardsen to give a deposition next week and will ask him if he has a business relationship with me."

"Seems logical, but you said you didn't know him, so you should have nothing to worry about."

I was not sure if Mr. Fuentes was sincere or if he was attempting to goad me.

"Well, it turns out that we do know each other."

"Right; you told me the last time we talked that Richardsen did work for Veridical as a contract tech guy – but that was all."

I did not need Mr. Fuentes to remind of our prior conversation. My mental faculties are significantly above-average and I certainly remembered the last time he and I talked and the substance of our discussion.

"Yes, well, there is more. Mr. Richardsen has performed some … special projects for me in the past."

"Such as …?" Fuentes asked slowly, not trying to hide his concern that he was about to hear the proverbial shoe start to drop.

"Such as, some years ago, Mr. Richardsen used the Dark Web and certain social media outlets to help convince a certain borrower to resume required payments to Veridical under the loan documents."

Fuentes said nothing to me. The silence lasted several seconds, and then he said, "Was this borrower in bankruptcy?"

"Heavens, no," I said to him.

"Very well," Fuentes said and I could hear the breath leaving his mouth as he uttered the words. It clearly relieved him. "Is that all you wanted to tell me, Mr. Dewey?"

"No, it is not." I stopped there as I continued to gather my thoughts. "More recently, Mr. Richardsen reprised his performance for me with the Rapinoes and BJB." *There*, I thought. *I said it.* "A perfectly legitimate exercise of his and my right of free speech, granted to us in this great country we love."

Fuentes responded instantly and angrily. "Look, Phillip. We aren't going to do this particular dance again."

He called me Phillip. I took note. He was emotional and angry. At me. I was, again, none-too-pleased. *Gather yourself, Alexander,* I thought. "Mr. Fuentes, this is a complicated situation."

"No, it is not, Phillip. You caused the 'situation,' as you call it. People like you overstate the complexity of situations they create. Always."

He obviously had no idea how the addition of Mother and Joshua could complicate matters and render his overly simplistic view of the situation meaningless. I am a multi. I am different.

I continued, "Well, I beg to differ with you, sir. I had something that needed to be said, and it was – across the internet. The how it was said and where it was said are irrel—"

"For the last time, you can't use speech to put a bankruptcy debtor out of business. It doesn't work that way. I've given you my view of this. I will add to that view now for your continued edification. You can't post on the internet to bring down a bankruptcy debtor, so you can then foreclose and get paid back out of the ashes that once were a viable business. You just can't do that. And, I should add, I don't represent people and companies that think they can."

He was on the offense. I needed to regain control of the conversation, so I said, "I am not firing you, my dear Mr. Fuentes. I still require your services."

"You're right," he barked at me, "you're not firing me. *I'm* firing *you* as a client. I will be filing a motion to withdraw as counsel to Veridical as soon as my day clears up."

"You are what?" I asked with more emotion in my voice than I typically allow people to hear.

"I'm done. I'm out. Representation over. Find another attorney to service your needs."

Silence.

"I need to leave now for court. I trust you have no further questions," he said, and before I could ask anything further, he pressed "end call" and our conversation ended.

Except – it was not the end. He was wrong. I was right. The first amendment allowed me to say what I wished to say, and I did. And it worked. The Rapinoes agreed to resume making payments under the cash motion. As my mind raced, I *heard* Mother clear her throat and *say*, "Ahem," to me.

This was not possible. I left Mother back in Kansas City on the mantle in her flowery vessel in the dark. It was simply not possible that she was here in Paxico with me, let alone that she expected to *communicate* with me. Once she cleared her throat, I could no longer focus on the Rapinoes or Mr. Fuentes. I wanted to scream. But that would not happen. I would not allow it. If Mother was somehow with me in Paxico, I resolved I would not give her the satisfaction of watching me raise my voice. *Always, always in control,* I told myself. *I am the Primary,* I reminded myself.

And as I tried to gather myself, the doorbell rang.

CHAPTER 29

Friday, November 24, 2023

Rosini found the Paxico home easily. He chuckled to himself that it wasn't hard in a town of less than two hundred and fifty to find an address. It only surprised him that the home was within the few blocks that comprised the tiny town, and not outside the main drag in a more remote setting. Paxico had some charm to it, but there was growing evidence of a town in decline, even demise. The house was clapboard, painted yellow at some distant time in the past, and now in need of a paint job. It had a small wooden porch, once painted gray and now peeling, and, of all things, a welcome mat at the foot of the front door – weathered, worn, and grungy, but welcoming nonetheless.

In his beige, nondescript jumpsuit, with a metal clipboard in hand, he first went through the pretense of locating the outside electricity meter, hovered there for a moment, then made his way to the welcome mat and rang the doorbell.

A voice from within asked, "Who is there?" *Low pitched and* slightly *threatening*, Rosini noted to himself. *Doesn't exactly sound like the guy 3J described.*

"Sir, this is Anthony Jones, from the electric company. I just tried to read your meter, just routine. But there may be a problem with it, and I don't want a false reading that could cause a larger than appropriate utility bill for you. Would you mind letting me in so I can take a quick look at the basement wires that connect to the meter, please? Won't take but a minute."

"Do you have some identification you could hold up to the peephole?" Joshua demanded. Phillip had retreated. Joshua sensed danger and was now in charge.

Rosini always came prepared. He opened a brown leather bifold identification holder, and held his fake ID up to the peephole.

Moments later, he heard a latch unlocking a deadbolt, and the front door creaked opened. There, inside, was Phillip Dewey, matching exactly the photographs 3J had supplied to Rosini. He had dressed smartly in a navy blue cardigan, a white button-down shirt, charcoal gray slacks, and a brown and red bow tie. *Very dapper,* observed Rosini. *Very businesslike.* Given the haste with which Phillip had planned the escape, and how he appeared to have a country house for just such an eventuality, it surprised Rosini that he had made no effort to alter his appearance or wear a disguise.

But while he looked like Phillip Dewey, he seemed out of place in the clothing he wore and his voice was far from soft and emotionless. *This* Phillip Dewey sounded aggressive, his voice deeper, and he seemed bigger than 3J and Pascale had described.

Rosini removed the flat, eight by eleven inch envelope from the clipboard, and said in an even-toned, soft voice, "Thank you, Mr. Dewey. Here: this is for you," smiling as he handed Joshua the package.

Joshua became more aggressive, and asked loudly, "What is this? How do you know my name?"

Rosini responded with an ominous joke he had once heard a utility company employee use, "Why, Mr. Dewey. We're the electricity company. We know what you had for breakfast," nodding his head as Dewey slowly took the envelope.

"I don't understand," Joshua said, continuing to be confused. He then turned away from Rosini to look into the house, and said tersely, "Mother, be quiet. I have a visitor at the front door."

As Joshua turned back around to face his porch, Rosini had already departed and was back in the van. Joshua quickly walked out of the house and across the small porch, marched over the wet, fallen leaves covering the small lawn, and approached the van. He looked at Rosini and held his arms out from his side, hands facing upward, eyebrows raised, with a look demanding further explanation.

Rosini continued to smile, and said, "It's all in the papers, Mr. Dewey. You've been served."

Back in his cramped country living room, Joshua opened the envelope and read the papers. Deposition. Demand for production of documents and the burner phone. He didn't understand the papers. As he tried to gather his thoughts, he *heard* Mother. "No. I do not talk to you, old lady." Joshua knew he needed Phillip. These were legal matters. Joshua did not handle legal matters. He slipped back into the shadows and allowed Phillip to re-awaken. Phillip looked down at his hands and saw the legal papers, but had no recollection of Rosini or receipt of the papers. As he read the papers, he saw that the Greene Madison lawyers were commanding him to turn over the burner phone. He heard Mother, and responded, "Not at all. I have no intention of giving them the burner phone. They are fishing, Mother. They have no proof of the phone's existence."

As he sat on the couch, he put his elbows on his knees, bent his face forward, and cupped his face in his hands. He rubbed his eyes. He felt tired. Sore. "Mother. Please. Allow me to think."

Silence.

"What's that? No, Mother. Thinking is *not* what got me into this situation. All I need to do is to contact Edmond and ensure we are both on the same page. If neither of us strays, we will be fine."

Silence.

"No, Mother. I do not wish to discuss this matter further with you. Please silence yourself and allow me the peace I deserve."

Joshua listened as Mother continued to *speak*. He agreed with Phillip. Mother needed to silence herself ... or someone would have to silence her once and for all.

Alexander Fuentes prepared his motion seeking permission from Judge Robertson to withdraw from the BJB and Rapinoes bankruptcy cases. He decided to call 3J as a courtesy and let her know the filing was coming.

"3J, Alexander Fuentes here."

"Good afternoon."

"I am calling to advise you that shortly, I will be filing a motion to withdraw as counsel for Veridical."

"Hmmm, I see. May I ask why?" 3J asked, reasonably certain that Fuentes would tell her as little as possible.

"Ms. Jones. I think you know I can't read you into all the goings on. I need to be careful not to reveal client confidences," Fuentes said with authority but a tone of guardedness.

"I understand. Then, other than a 'heads up,' are there any other topics you wish to cover?"

"Yes. I'd like to represent in my papers that you consent to the withdrawal."

"Ahhh. Well, I don't have any objection, but I also don't think it's my place to weigh in. Your problem's going to be with the Judge, not me."

"How so?" Fuentes asked.

"Well, in these parts, the judges are reluctant to allow counsel to withdraw when the client is a company. I'm sure it's similar in Chicago. Companies may not appear in court except through an attorney. If Judge Robertson lets you out, that will silence Veridical without a new lawyer at the helm. I'm sure the Judge will tell you to find Veridical a replacement lawyer before he'll sign your order."

"Yes, it's similar here, but not all the judges here abide by the letter of the rule."

"Well, they do here, I'm afraid. What does Mr. Dewey say about this?"

"He's been informed."

"Has he found replacement counsel for Veridical?"

"If he has, he hasn't told me."

"Since we're talking, Alexander, were you intending to represent Mr. Dewey at his deposition?" 3J probed.

"Mr. Dewey didn't engage me to represent him personally. My engagement letter is very specific. If he wishes counsel at his deposition, he'll need to hire one specifically to represent him."

"Understood. Well, it's never fun when a representation doesn't work out and counsel and client need to go their separate ways. But it happens. Good luck with the process. Like I said, I won't object, but I can assure you that the Judge won't ask me for my thoughts on this one. This'll just be you and Judge Robertson hashing it out."

The call ended, and Fuentes leaned back in his chair and realized that he would have to make one more call to Dewey to tell him to find other counsel for Veridical and for himself at the deposition. He certainly didn't relish the additional call.

CHAPTER 30

AFTER EXPLAINING HIS SITUATION to several bankruptcy lawyers, Richardsen found himself without counsel. Each lawyer he talked with declined the opportunity to represent him. Each told him they were familiar with the case and said they had concerns about the nature of the representation. Richardsen took that to mean that either they didn't want to go up against 3J, or they believed he had violated the automatic stay, would be in deep trouble at the hearing, and had no interest in sharing in the Judge's ire. Or all of the above.

Somewhere, he thought he read that everyone was entitled to a lawyer, and when he said that to one of the declining lawyers, the response was, "That's only in criminal law. Not true in bankruptcy."

Finally, Richardsen talked with James Toomey. Toomey had been a litigator for fifteen years at Greene Madison before leaving to set up his own firm. While he had handled several bankruptcy matters in his career, no one considered him proficient in this area of law, even though on his website, he described it as one of his areas of expertise.

Richardsen explained the situation to Toomey, who listened carefully as he took notes. Toomey said he would be happy to take on the matter, conditional upon receiving a retainer of $25,000 wired to his trust account. Richardsen agreed, expecting Dewey would fund the retainer.

He called Dewey on the burner phone and demanded that Dewey fund the retainer. Dewey responded, "I will wire the funds yet today. Edmond, how would you feel if we share Mr. Toomey as our lawyer?"

"Dewey, you have a lawyer already, don't you?"

"Well, Alexander Fuentes would like to withdraw from handling this matter for Veridical, and says he never agreed to represent me personally. Hence my question."

Richardsen thought for a moment, and said, "If Toomey is ok with it, and if you're paying for all of his fees, then it's fine with me."

"Edmond, thank you for the courtesy," Dewey said.

Dewey called Toomey, who readily agreed to represent Dewey, Veridical and Richardsen in the bankruptcy cases and in the lawsuit for a $75,000 retainer. Toomey advised he would hold the retainer as security for payment of current bills.

He wasn't new to the lawyer game of devising ways to assure payment for services rendered. While he didn't always ask for a retainer to be held as security, from the little he could find out about Dewey he knew he needed this type of arrangement to assure payment. *Richardsen appeared near broke, and Dewey has baggage.* Without pause, Dewey agreed, and arranged for the wire. Later that afternoon, Toomey filed a notice in the bankruptcy cases that he was now representing all three parties, and Fuentes filed his withdrawal notice.

Pascale saw the notices hit his inbox, and said aloud to himself, "Hmmm. Now this all gets interesting."

He walked around the hall to 3J's office. He peeked in as she huddled over her laptop, preparing her outline for next week's depositions. He sat down and waited for her to look up before asking, "Do you know Jim Toomey?"

"I sort of know who he is, but I've never met him. Why?"

"He just entered his appearance to represent Richardsen, Dewey, and Veridical."

"I see," she said, nodding her head in understanding. "That should make it smooth sailing for Fuentes to leave this case."

"For sure, but there are a few things you'll need to know about Toomey."

3J pushed her chair back from her desk and gave Pascale her full attention. "Like what?"

"Toomey would tell you that he left Greene Madison years ago to set up his own firm."

"And …?"

"And, we fired him. Told him to leave. Perp-walked out the door with a small box of his belongings."

"Oh. I see. Or I guess I don't. Why?"

"He had done some pretty sketchy things that caught up to him."

"Such as …?"

"Well, he likes fancy cars, and he had a client that was a car dealer, and instead of billing the client for work performed, he traded his legal services for a new sports car."

3J raised her eyebrows as high as they could go and said, "So the firm never received payment for the work Toomey did while a partner here?"

"Correct. The firm never got paid and he got a fast set of wheels for free."

"And he got caught, and perp-walked out."

"Correct. Rumor was that the car-for-services trade was just the tip of the iceberg. At this point, Bob Swanson is probably the only person here who knows all the particulars of everything Toomey did. But for a while, the rumors flew like a confused flock of birds down the hallways of Greene Madison."

"What about his lawyering skills?" 3J asked, trying to determine more information about her new adversary.

"Let's just say that many have questioned his ethics. It's like his moral gyroscope doesn't spin the way a lawyer's should."

"I see. What does he know about bankruptcy?"

"Precious little, in my estimation. He's good around a jury, but the judges are on to him, and don't seem to think much of him in the courtroom."

"How about in a deposition?" 3J asked, squinting her eyes as if the answer would be an unpleasant and blinding lightning bolt of a revelation. She was right.

"Judges have sanctioned him in the past for violating the rules of depositions in these parts. He openly coaches witnesses. Sometimes he improperly uses signals during the deposition, and makes ridiculous objections to throw off the lawyer taking the deposition. He interrupts and pontificates."

3J rolled her eyes. "My Lord. What a fuckin' case. I guess I ought to make sure that Judge Robertson is around and available if we need to get him on the phone to resolve any disputes that arise during the depositions. I guess I also ought to video-tape this so there's a precise record of brother Toomey's antics."

"Absolutely. Yes, on all counts."

They both sat there shaking their heads slightly in disbelief.

"I guess all I can do at this point is power forward, finish my outline, and prepare for the coming battle."

"It's the only way, but I thought you should know all the dirty laundry in the basket."

3J shook her head again in disbelief and ended the discussion with a drawn-out all-purpose observation: "Yep." There was really nothing more she could say.

Later in the day, Jennifer Cuello completed her supplemental research for Judge Robertson. She found several additional cases similar to *Andrus*, concluding her memo to the Judge: "Virtually all the cases I found reject the notion that the First Amendment rights somehow provide cover to parties who violate the automatic stay."

Judge Robertson read her memo and the cases she identified, and felt comfortable with his initial gut reaction to the posts: they *had* likely violated the automatic stay. He awaited the evidentiary hearing to see just how much the Greene Madison team could tie the posts to an intent to take control of BJB's property, as alleged in the TRO papers.

As he reviewed the memo and considered how things would play out in court, he noted that James Toomey entered his appearance on behalf of all three potential stay violators – Richardsen, Dewey, and Veridical. He immediately rubbed the temples of his forehead vigorously as he closed his eyes for a moment, perhaps hoping that when he re-opened them, the Toomey issue would have disappeared. But, a few moments later, when he looked at his computer screen again, Toomey's filing was still there.

Before taking the bench, the Judge had several run-ins with Toomey; all unpleasant, all memorable, and all resulting in significant losses for both Toomey's clients and Toomey himself. He knew Toomey counted himself as a litigator first, and the Judge was unimpressed with his command of the Bankruptcy Code. In that respect, he would not be the only lawyer to grace his courtroom who lacked bankruptcy expertise; perhaps surprisingly, bankruptcy expertise was not a prerequisite to an attorney representing a client in bankruptcy court.

Besides his lack of command of bankruptcy law, Judge Robertson was certain that Toomey would bring to his courtroom a high degree of contentiousness, and a lack of respect for the other lawyers in the case, as well as a lack of respect – perhaps even disdain – for the judiciary; an odd characteristic for a litigator who regularly appeared before judges in the courtroom setting.

The local judges, state and federal, were well-aware of Toomey's methods and, privately, they didn't hold him in high regard.

The Judge rose from his chair, stretched, put his hands in his pockets, and walked to his large floor-to-ceiling windows to gaze out at the Missouri River – "Big Muddy," the longest river in North America – thinking about Toomey's involvement and how it might affect the injunction process.

He always found that the river provided a sense of inevitability. When cases seemed unpredictable, and the need to decide issues quickly weighed on his mind, the river seemed to help him ground himself and focus on his deliberations so he could make the correct decision. *Well, Big Muddy, not sure even you'll be able to help control Brother Toomey. The only thing inevitable about his style of courtroom demeanor is his unpredictability.* He shook his head slightly as he turned from the windows and made his way to the entry area of his chambers. He smiled silently at his assistant, poured a cup of coffee in his favorite white and blue Kansas City Royals mug, and sighed long and loud. His assistant looked up at him, smiled, raised her eyebrows, and returned to her computer screen.

Sometimes, sighs in chambers by the coffee pot were the calling card of a bankruptcy judge. Sometimes, when this judge sighed, all he needed was a friendly smile in return.

CHAPTER 31

I DID NOT BELIEVE in a higher power. How could I? If there was one, then my childhood would have been markedly different. And if there was a higher power, "I" would not mean "we." And this would be my body, not *the* Body. I would be me instead of the Primary. No. I was the highest power I had and I was the only power I needed. I trusted Joshua to protect me, but I believed in myself. In my complicated existence, what other choice did I have?

I gathered myself and called Edmond on the burner. It was time to offer up the plan to him. He answered after the first ring.

"Good day, Edmond," I began.

"What do ya want, Dewey?"

"I assume you received deposition papers. I did, as well." Richardsen said nothing. "This will be a brief call, Edmond. I intend to show up at the deposition without the burner phone and then deny there is one. You should do the same. If we just hold the line, it will all be fine."

"How so, Dewey? They know I posted."

"You are not a creditor, Edmond."

"When they were at my house, they said that doesn't matter."

"Of course they did. What else could they say?"

"Look, Dewey, I want again to confirm that you will hold me harmless from anything that happens in this lawsuit. You say you will, but then your plan, if I can call it that, is to let me go down alone for the posts."

"It will be worth your while. Your fee for performing per the plan I have outlined will be an additional $200,000 in crypto deposited into your wallet."

There it was. My tried-and-true offering for Edmond. The resolution for his worldly problems.

Edmond paused. I could almost hear him count the money in his mind like a pirate would count a chest full of gold doubloons. Slowly and deliberately he then said, "That's a princely sum, Dewey. Princely." He paused and then continued, "I need to think."

Richardsen then disconnected before I could say another word.

Edmond needed money. I knew that money was always the answer. That was why I enjoyed the lending business so much. That was how I knew Edmond would agree to my plan.

I felt Mother again. "No, Mother, it will work," I said. "Richardsen always opts for the money." I could feel her *disdain* for my plan. I ignored it. Just as I had learned to do so effectively before she ended up in the vessel.

I was in control. The Primary. Exactly how I needed to be. Of course, in my discourse with Edmond this time I neither raised my voice nor vocalized any emotions. That would be counter to my upbringing and the person I strive to be. But I am quite certain that my eyes took on their usual threatening appearance. I cannot control my eyes, nor the darkening effect of the blood that rushes to them when I am told news that disagrees with me and awakens Joshua. Joshua – always at the ready. I am always under control. At times, however, I am afraid my eyes have a mind of their own.

As I thought about my eyes, I realized there was nothing more from Mother. She rarely weighed in on my dealings with lawyers. Blessfully silent again. Alone with my thoughts, I considered, *We are a loner. We have little need or use for other people. Edmond is a necessary evil. Eventually dispensible, but at the moment, necessary. Soon, we will move on from Mr. Richardsen. Soon we hope to move on from Mother as well. She serves no purpose. Soon enough.*

Joshua agreed.

CHAPTER 32

Thursday, November 30, 2023

THE DEPOSITION PARTICIPANTS FILLED the small Greene Madison conference room to capacity. Around the conference table, going counterclockwise, sat 3J, Pascale, Bey and Adam Rapinoe, and Ronnie Steele. The Rapinoes looked somber, concerned. The lawyers looked businesslike, Pascale in his medium gray houndstooth suit, and 3J in her charcoal pin-striped pants suit and her gray Manolo Blahnik metallic pumps; very expensive, very 3J. Steele wore a blue blazer and looked like he was ready for anything.

Next came the court reporter at the head of the table, testing her stenography machine and confirming that her videographer across the room standing next to the video machine was ready to proceed. On the side of the table across from the Rapinoes' team sat Phillip Dewey, James Toomey, and the first deponent, Edmond Richardsen, sitting directly across from 3J in front of a microphone trained near his mouth.

Richardsen wore one of his few dress shirts, white and pressed; no tie, tan slacks that could also double for tan jeans, and a well-worn navy blue blazer with tarnished brass buttons, one missing on his left sleeve. He'd shaved earlier in the morning for the deposition, but missed several spots on his chin, where a mixture of gray, brown, and white stubble protruded.

He was nervous, and didn't – or couldn't – hide it. He was unaccustomed to legal proceedings, and it was obvious. In his blazer pocket, he'd stashed the burner phone before leaving his house to drive downtown. To this moment, he still didn't know if he would execute Dewey's plan to lie. He needed the money – badly – but he was anxious about the prospect of lying to protect Dewey.

Dewey's face looked drawn, and he had the beginnings of puffy black rings under his eyes. He looked decidedly tired, a condition brought on by the last several days of increasing stress and the resulting lack of consistent sleep.

Behind Dewey was a small corner table he used to lay his navy blue fedora and his neatly folded beige trench coat.

Both Toomey and Dewey wore bow ties, Toomey's a dark brown one with yellow polka dots, and Dewey's his signature medium brown striped. Both wore gray suits. Despite his fatigue, Dewey looked composed. Toomey looked commanding. Both were dapper, stylish, and more than a little chichi.

3J and Pascale had set the stage. It was time.

3J looked up from her notes and asked, "Are we ready to start?"

Toomey responded with a smile. Not a lawyer's smile but one more fitting for a contract hit man just before pulling the trigger to take out a target at point blank range. "The floor is yours, counselor."

As the proceeding began, Phillip sat, confident. Joshua listened in, ready to take over and do whatever it might take to protect Phillip. Joshua had been to some court proceedings with Phillip over the years, mostly related to the lending company and borrowers who wouldn't do whatever it was that Phillip wanted them to do. Joshua viewed the proceedings as largely boring. He decided in short order that a nap might be the way to go.

The court reporter administered the oath to Richardsen, and for the first fifteen minutes, 3J asked background questions of Richardsen – name, address, age, place of employment, education and work history, and what he had done to prepare for the deposition. Richardsen sat with his hands folded on the conference room table near the microphone and made no eye contact. He fixed his eyes on the mesh end of the microphone, to which he leaned closer with each answer he gave. His answers to the introductory background questions sounded rehearsed. He was composed.

Next, 3J looked carefully at Richardsen, and said, "Mr. Richardsen, would you please hand me the burner phone you brought with you today?" Her delivery was a practiced directive – firm but not authoritarian; conversational, but not matter-of-fact. She simply delivered the demand with the expectation that he had the burner phone with him and he would comply.

Richardsen looked up at her, then looked over to Dewey, then Toomey, then back to 3J. He looked confused. *Surely he must have expected the question*, Pascale thought. Richardsen said nothing, and for an extended moment, did nothing.

"Did you understand me, Mr. Richardsen?"

"One hundred percent."

Toomey watched Richardsen closely, but wasn't sure what Richardsen would do. While Toomey had read all about the alleged burner phones in the TRO papers, he never asked either client if they existed. *Don't ask, don't tell*, was his practice in this case, and he was unaware of Dewey's plan to lie and deny. "Counselor, your statement assumes there *is* a burner phone. It makes an improper assumption and has confused my client," Toomey said, signaling to Richardsen that it was a trick statement and he should respond and just say "no."

"Mr. Toomey, your client doesn't need your help in answering questions. Refrain yourself, sir," 3J admonished him. Then she ignored Toomey. She had decided the best way to deal with any interruptions was to ignore them until they became disruptive. The Rapinoes were no novices in litigation, having gotten entangled in more than one lawsuit during their years in real estate development. They looked at each other knowingly as the initial lawyer unpleasantries unfolded.

Toomey then said, "I'm sure this is unsettling to you, Mr. Richardsen. Do you need a moment to collect yourself?"

Another improper signal to Richardsen.

Before Toomey could say anything further, however, Richardsen said, "Negatory. I don't need a break."

3J said, "Then we need you to respond so we can proceed forward."

He looked from his hands to his lap, and mumbled, "I don't have a burner."

The court reporter had not expected the witness would answer so softly, and interrupted, "Sir, you will have to speak up, please. Repeat what you just said."

The court reporter's directive surprised Richardsen, but he collected himself and, this time, said too loudly, "I don't have a burner."

"You don't?" 3J said, raising her eyebrows in disbelief, giving him an opportunity to re-think his answer.

"Negatory. No burner," he said with a quaver, almost a trill, in his voice.

"I see," 3J said, with a hint of judgment in her voice.

Dewey smiled broadly, looking directly at the Rapinoes. They stared back at him. Bey even smiled, but her eyes were pure cold steel daggers. Her smile didn't disarm Dewey. Things appeared to be proceeding according to Phillip's plan, and Joshua relaxed.

3J handed Richardsen several sheets of paper, one after the other, each marked with a sequential number. Each sheet contained a date and one post. For each, she asked him, "Can you identify this exhibit, Mr. Richardsen?" For each, he answered, "No. Never seen it before." For each she asked, "Do you recognize the words on the page?" For each he answered, "Negatory."

Each time he gave the answer, Dewey directed a simpering smile at the Rapinoes. Steele saw the smile and the mind game that Dewey was attempting to play with the Rapinoes. He thought, *I'd love to pop this little shit in the nose and see him smile through that experience.* When Phillip smiled, Joshua believed things were under control.

"Mr. Richardsen, do you use any handles when you participate in forums on the internet?"

Richardsen blinked and looked distant, unfocused. "Negatory."

"So you have no familiarity with the handle noLightpasses31?"

"None."

"And you have no familiarity with the handle noLightpassed13?"

"None."

"I see. Hmmm. Mr. Richardsen, do the Rapinoes owe you any money?"

"Negatory."

"Does BJB?"

"Negatory."

"Before today, had you ever met the Rapinoes?"

"Negatory."

3J then looked down at her notes.

Toomey broke in again and exclaimed with a boorish tone, "Counselor, we are taking a break now. This man obviously knows nothing about the fabricated statements in the TRO papers and you are wasting our time. You are wasting *my* time." 3J was about to object and tell Toomey that it was too soon for a break. But he continued authoritatively, and with an air of pomposity, "Ms. Jones, you can keep talking, but we won't be here to answer your questions for the next fifteen minutes."

Then, in unison, Toomey and Dewey rose and began to exit the conference room. Richardsen didn't move. Dewey said loudly, as if summoning a dog, "Edmond. Come." Richardsen didn't move, and Dewey said even louder, "Now!" In response, Richardsen rose silently and followed them out. Moments later, Toomey came back into the conference room and said, "We require a room where we can talk in private."

Pascale lead them to a small meeting room where they could talk. Pascale then continued to the restroom and on his way back, he could hear muffled loud, and angry, talking from behind the door of the room where Dewey, Richardsen and Toomey were located. *One happy family*, he thought.

Pascale returned to the deposition conference room, and along with 3J awaited the trio's return. The Rapinoes and Steele lingered in the hallway to talk; the court reporter and the videographer were stretching in the adjacent conference room, leaving just Pascale and 3J in the deposition room.

"Not getting very far here, Pascale. Not at all. No cracks that I can see in the Richardsen veneer." She leaned down absentmindedly to scratch her ankle.

"Not so sure about that, 3J. To me, he looks more than just nervous. He looks bothered by the answers he's giving. Maybe he's having one of those internal struggles between right and wrong, good and evil. Maybe like he knows he's lying and a little voice in his head is telling him to man up and tell the truth."

"Maybe," 3J said slowly, as she simultaneously tilted her head slightly to the left, raised her eyebrows, and frowned. "Not sure I quite see that." She sighed and finished, "I just can't tell."

"Just keep at it and we'll see what happens when they come back in. We don't know. Maybe he comes back and does the right thing."

Eighteen minutes after they left, Richardsen and Toomey returned. Dewey did not.

3J looked at Toomey and asked, "Are we waiting for Mr. Dewey to return, or are we proceeding?"

Toomey looked dismissively at 3J and said as he raised his left hand and spread his fingers for emphasis, "Your witness is here, counselor. It's your deposition. I suggest you proceed."

3J smiled at Toomey to let him know that nothing he could say would bother her.

"Alright then, Mr. Richardsen. You heard the man. Back on the record, and you are still under oath. Before you left for your break, I asked you about internet handles you might use. Do you remember the questions?"

"One hundred percent."

"Now that you've had a chance to refresh and collect yourself during the break, let me ask you this: do you ever post on the internet?"

"Occasionally."

"Do you ever post about freedom of speech?"

"I can't recall."

"Do you ever post that we should not require social media companies to police the posts of their account holders?"

"I may have. Not sure."

Each time Richardsen equivocated about his recollection, his voice quavered more and more. He looked to be glistening with a thin layer of sweat on his brow. Above his lips, there were small sweat beads forming. He started to look like someone who wasn't good at lying. There was no need to study his face for micro-expressions that were giveaways to the lies he was advancing. His face was one giant macro-expression signaling each untruth he was about to utter. His facial muscles twitched. His eyelids blinked as he spoke. His right eyebrow rose as he finished each answer. His previously clasped hands were now fidgeting and had begun to tremble. They knocked against the microphone stand several times, sending the videographer scrambling to remove his headphones as the sound of hands against the stand must have been uncomfortably loud. After the third collision of hands against stand, the videographer said, "Mr. Richardsen, I'm going to have to ask you to be careful around the microphone so the video transcript isn't full of loud banging noises."

Richardsen looked at the videographer as if surprised that there were other people in the room. His eyes were wide – deer-in-the-headlights wide. He neither agreed nor disagreed with the videographer's request.

3J decided to remind him again about his oath to tell the truth. "You remember as you answer these questions, Mr. Richardsen, that you are under oath and you swore to tell the truth?"

"Counsel," Toomey boomed, "the witness and I don't need a law school lecture from you about the oath and the truth." He delivered a practiced glare at 3J. "So do us all a favor and move on. Please."

She smiled back at Toomey and then fixed her gaze back on Richardsen. As Toomey bellowed, Richardsen tried to stretch his neck to relieve tension. It didn't work.

"Do you need me to repeat the question?" 3J asked the witness again, ignoring Toomey.

"Negatory. I know what you asked. And I know about the oath," he said so softly that the court reporter had to lean closer to him again to hear his answer.

In the hallway, Phillip completed his silent conversation with Joshua. Both concluded that they were in a splendid position. Phillip then moved to the conference room door to re-enter.

Inside the conference room, 3J probed, "Well, then. Is everything you've told me so far the truth?"

As she asked the question, the door to the conference room opened and Phillip Dewey made his entry with a beaming smile on his face. The first part of the deposition had pleased Dewey. At the last break, when Toomey stepped out of their room, he made sure that Richardsen knew just how important it was to continue with the plan. And, when Richardsen faltered in response, Dewey raised his voice and yelled at Richardsen to just "do as I say," and Richardsen appeared to be resigned to continue lying. Exactly what Dewey needed and expected. Phillip had finished the break believing that the danger had passed and that Richardsen would continue to toe the line. So as he re-entered the conference room, he thought arrogantly to himself, *We are aligned! They have nothing if we stay the course.*

Ronnie Steele watched Dewey closely. He had seen men like this before: above it all, and especially above the law. Smarter than everyone, and especially everyone in the room. Believing themselves to be in maximum control of all situations, especially control of subordinates. The smug smile said it all. As Dewey re-entered, a now full-out panic-stricken Richardsen looked at him, looked at Toomey, looked at Dewey again and began to speak to 3J while retaining his gaze on Dewey. It all happened so fast that Dewey had no time to adjust his smile, which remained frozen on his face as Richardsen spoke.

"I can't do this," Richardsen whispered. The court reporter leaned closer. The videographer adjusted the audio recording levels.

3J looked up from her notes, tilted her head to the right, raised her eyebrows, then lowered them, and asked, "Can't do what, Mr. Richardsen?"

"What I'm doing."

"You have to be here, Mr. Richardsen, and you have to testify."

"No. Not that. I can't answer the questions the way I am."

"What way is that, Mr. Richardsen?"

Together, the Rapinoes slowly leaned forward so their heads hovered above the table, their hands gripping the table edge. Steele continued to watch Dewey. Toomey looked down at his pad, trying to convey that he was unconcerned. In reality, he wasn't sure what was going on.

Richardsen looked down, and then again looked over to Dewey, who made no eye contact with him and whose smile slowly faded. At that moment, Richardsen felt completely alone.

As he sat there, Richardsen could not forget that Dewey yelled at him during the break repeatedly, demanding compliance with the plan. Each time he'd yelled, Richardsen first cowered, and then shut him out completely as the only defense mechanism he could muster to protect himself from the onslaught. In the small meeting room, he'd tried to walk away from Dewey, but Dewey followed him around, continuing to berate him.

Unbeknownst to Richardsen, as Phillip yelled, Joshua watched carefully, waiting at the ready in case matters continued to escalate and Richardsen became physically aggressive, but the moment passed as Richardsen had to return to the deposition conference room.

Now, back on the record, with a court reporter taking down all of his words, a microphone capturing all the nuances of his answers, and a video documenting all of his body language, Richardsen's mind raced as he tried to steel himself for more questions. *It's just like I thought when I was holding the fake Amazon Prime box in my living room: why am I helping Dewey?*

Richardsen then repeated in a whisper, "I can't do this."

Slowly, he unclasped his hands, reached into his blazer's fraying pocket, took a deep breath, removed the burner phone, and placed it on the conference room table gently, halfway between 3J and himself.

3J's face revealed nothing of her thoughts. *Maintain your poker face. Don't reach for the phone. Let it sit there. Let them look at it and take it in. Let them stew.* Rather than look at Richardsen, she looked over at Dewey. For a brief moment, his composure abandoned him and his eyes appeared to be dark and smoldering as if a fire burned behind his irises, until Dewey's eyes closed. Anger, she suspected. Shock, she assumed. She didn't know enough to recognize Joshua as the cause for the change in the irises. She then looked at Pascale and, almost imperceptibly, he nodded. It was a nod of "gotcha!"

Steele and the Rapinoes saw his nod and understood it.

A short moment of silence as the phone sat silently in the middle of the table. There for all to see.

3J looked at the phone, then ignored it, allowing it to remain untouched on the table like a dead body laying in state as visitors filed by to pay last respects, compelled to study the body silently as they passed. Instead of addressing the phone, 3J went back to the paper exhibits Richardsen previously denied recognizing and said in an understanding, soft tone, "Mr. Richardsen, I'd like to go back to the exhibits again. And, just so your lawyer has a reason to interrupt me again, I remind you that you are under oath."

Toomey's eyes got wide as he listened to 3J's sarcastic remark, and his fury, whether real or an act, was apparent. He was about to bellow again, his face getting redder by the moment. But as he opened his mouth, no words came out. Instead, as he remained silent, 3J calmly went through the paper exhibits again, one by one, and again asked Richardsen if he recognized them.

This time, for every exhibit, he said, "It's a copy of a post I made." He also corroborated the date of the posts.

With each answer, he looked at the phone. He didn't look at Dewey. He didn't look at the Rapinoes. He didn't look at 3J. Just at the phone.

"Can you tell us why you made those posts, Mr. Richardsen?"

"It's my job," he said, reverting again to looking anywhere but at 3J's eyes. This time, he gazed at the burner phone, remaining in the middle of the table.

"And what was the nature of that job, sir?" 3J asked.

"I was hired to post on the internet."

"Who hired you?"

"Phillip Dewey."

Phillip's face showed no emotion. Again, however, his eyes began to smolder. He closed his eyes. Joshua.

"Why did he hire you?"

"You'd need to ask him."

"We will. I want your take on it."

"BJB owed him money."

"What did the posts have to do with that?"

"Not sure. You'd have to ask him."

"What were the posts supposed to accomplish?"

"Not sure. You'd have to ask him."

"Who wrote the text for the posts?"

"He did."

"He, meaning Mr. Dewey?"

"Correct."

"How did you receive the words to post?"

Richardsen pointed to the burner phone and said, "Texts."

3J said to the court reporter, "Let the record reflect that Mr. Richardsen pointed to the burner phone he brought with him today as he said the word, 'texts.' Are the texts still on the burner phone?"

"One hundred percent."

"Could you show me them, please?"

Richardsen powered up the phone, got the list of texts to display on the phone, and turned the display toward 3J so she could see them.

"Let the record reflect that Mr. Richardsen is holding the phone for me and showing me the texts with the language corresponding to those in the posts. Are all the texts on the burner phone from Phillip Dewey?"

"One hundred percent."

"Is there a call log on the phone as well?"

"Correct."

"Can you show me that as well?"

Richardsen got the call log list to display on the phone, and once again showed it to 3J, who again noted it aloud for the court reporter.

"All the received calls are from the same number. Is that correct?"

"Correct."

"All the made calls are to that same number as well. Is that correct?"

"Correct."

"Is that the same number that sent you the texts, and to which you sent texts?"

"Correct."

Phillip sat with his arms across his chest and his eyes closed. He appeared to be listening deep in thought, when in fact Joshua had taken control and was paying no attention to Richardsen's testimony. In his dark place, Phillip listened and fumed at Richardsen.

"Whose number is that, Mr. Richardsen?" 3J asked.

"Phillip Dewey's. The other phone is his burner phone. When this started, he gave me this burner phone I brought with me here today and instructed me to communicate with him only using that."

Richardsen answered each question quickly and breathlessly. His demeanor was that of a man who just wanted to get the deposition process over with as quickly as possible. No longer any resistance and no longer any hesitation in answering questions. All the facial ticks had disappeared. As he answered the questions, Toomey continued to look bored. Lawyers learned to look calm when a case is blowing up around them. Pascale was certain it was an act and that inside, his stomach was churning. Dewey re-opened his eyes. Phillip. He no longer had a smile on his face. Instead, he seemed not to blink for extended periods of time and his lips had separated slightly, giving the impression of shock. Several more times, he closed his eyes and appeared to be in a different dimension. Joshua.

"I see," 3J said, pausing to allow Richardsen to catch his breath. "Have you done something like this for Mr. Dewey in the past?"

"Correct."

3J then probed the prior engagement in which Richardsen made posts for Dewey and asked, "What resulted from the prior posts, Mr. Richardsen?"

"I believe his borrower paid him off."

"You believe that because …?"

"Dewey told me."

"Mr. Richardsen, why did you agree to take on this job to post against the Rapinoes and BJB?"

"Money. I needed money. I always need money. Dewey has too much and I have too little of it. He's a have-lots. I'm a have-lots-less. He lives in Hallbrook. I live in Armour Hills." He paused and for the first time in several minutes, he looked up and made eye contact with 3J. His eyes were blank. "Not my finest hour, I suppose. Money, or the lack of it, makes you do strange things."

3J's eyes widened, and she thought, *Amen to that.* She had come from a life in New Orleans of so little and despite her success as an attorney, she had never forgotten how the lack of money affects people.

He paused and looked down at his lap and then back up. "I just really needed the money."

She continued, "Were you promised money if you testified in a certain way here today?"

"What do you mean?"

"Were you promised money if you said here today that you didn't know about the burner phone and the posts?"

"Yes."

"Who promised you the money?"

"Dewey."

"A lot?"

"I thought so."

"How much?"

"Two hundred grand in crypto."

"In writing?"

"Negatory."

Joshua, now in charge, stared at Richardsen as his eyes tried to burn a hole in his body as if he was a superhero from the planet Krypton.

"And the handles, noLightpasses31 and noLightpassed13?"

"That's me."

"And the posts about freedom of speech and social media policing?"

"Also me."

"Mr. Richardsen, why do this to people you don't even know?" 3J asked, pointing with her right hand to the Rapinoes without breaking eye contact with Richardsen.

Richardsen looked down at his clenched hands. His knuckles were white from the force with which his hands grasped each other. He twisted his hands back and forth and, without looking up, he said, "Like I said. Money. Always money."

3J resisted smiling, and instead looked down at her notes and said to Toomey, "We'll be taking a brief break now,

Mr. Toomey. You three can use the same room as before to confab."

This time, without saying a word, Toomey rose, his shoulders not quite as square as they had been only ten minutes ago, turned, adjusted his bowtie, and headed stiffly to the door. Richardsen rose to follow him out. This time, Joshua didn't move. He didn't blink. He didn't twitch. He looked almost catatonic. Frozen momentarily in time. Powerless and speechless. Conditioned to absorb physical pain, but unfamiliar in a world where words and facts were the weapons to administer pain. Powerless, he closed his eyes for several seconds. When his eyes opened, Phillip looked at the Rapinoes and simply said, "Loan documents, people. Loan documents are elegant. That is why we have them, my dear friends." He had not heard all of Richardsen's answers while he went to the dark place, but he heard enough to know the legal worm had turned on him.

He rose, still bent over the conference room table, placed his hands on the table, pushed as if to launch himself in the correct direction, achieved an erect position, adjusted his suit jacket and bow tie, turned, and slowly exited the room.

3J looked at the Rapinoes, Steele, and Pascale, smiled, and said simply, "Bathroom break folks."

"What in God's green earth was that all about, you diminutive, non-intellectual, sad-sap excuse for a member of the human race?" Phillip hissed at Richardsen when they arrived in the meeting room. By now, he lost all control over his demeanor, and was in full castigation mode.

Silence from Richardsen.

"All was going fine. I'm gone for moments only, and when I return, you are in the midst of a panic attack meltdown, and then you lose it," Dewey continued, sounding more like a talking snake than a human.

Joshua listened attentively as Phillip raged, an emotion normally held in check when Phillip guided the ship. He was proud of Phillip even if he didn't understand the full import of the events that had just unfolded.

"Negatory, Dewey. I'm not lying for you. And I'm not taking your fuckin' money. I'm not your boy-toy anymore." Pause. Then Richardsen hissed back at Dewey, "And you told me your mother had died years ago. You're a sick fuck. What the hell is wrong with you?"

A question that would engender a much longer discussion, Phillip and Joshua thought. Rather than respond, Dewey turned his ire to Toomey and said, "And you. What the hell are you doing in there? I am paying you handsomely so that something like this can't happen."

Toomey said nothing and looked away from Dewey, who stayed silent.

Eyes wide open and glaring at Dewey, Richardsen decided to respond, and said derisively, "You of the superior intellect. You'll figure it out. As you said to me, you always do, right?"

Richardsen's decision to speak without a question on the floor surprised Dewey, but before he could answer, Richardsen announced, "I'm going downstairs for a smoke. I'll be back to finish up this fiasco shortly."

Richardsen hadn't smoked in years, but on the way to the deposition that morning, he had stopped at a convenience store to buy a pack of his old favorites – unfiltered Pall Malls in a red package. He was angry at himself for succumbing to the cigarette crutch he thought he had licked so many years ago. But on the other hand, he'd known this day would undoubtedly be like no other he had been through, and he'd felt he needed the crutch.

Once on the street, he first reached in the pocket where the burner phone had been. That pocket still felt warm to the touch, even though he had powered off the phone – as if the phone was nuclear and left a residual heat signature in the pocket. The Pall Mall pack was in the other pocket, along with a pack of matches. He removed the cellophane wrapper, extracted a cigarette, and lit it. His first drag was a deep inhale that he held in his lungs for several moments. Just like the old days when he was a two-pack-a-dayer. He exhaled, looked at the cigarette dangling between his pointer and middle finger, said aloud to himself in disgust, "Oh … shit," lingering on the word "shit" and shaking his head back and forth before he dropped the cigarette to the ground and crushed it out with his shoe. He tossed the rest of the Pall Mall pack in a garbage receptacle in the building's lobby, took a deep breath, and headed back up on the elevator to finish his deposition.

When he got back to the floor, he peeked in the meeting room. Dewey was peering out the window with his back to Toomey, and said, "We will just shift our focus, James. So what if there were posts? There was no damage. BJB was going out of business, anyway." Dewey had regained his composure.

He heard Toomey say too quickly, "That could work."

"I'm going back in fellas," Richardsen said, interrupting their train of thought.

When the Rapinoes' team all returned to the conference room, 3J gathered her notes and asked if anyone had any questions or comments. No one said anything. The moment seemed to speak for itself, and the tension in the air seemed to linger during the break. Pascale wanted to commend 3J for her work, but he would hold off on lawyer's talk until after the depositions ended and everyone left.

Ten minutes passed, and the trio failed to return. Pascale went to the small meeting room, knocked on the door, and Toomey answered.

"Hi Bill," he said with a level of familiarity that suggested they were still colleagues and partners at Greene Madison.

Ignoring the greeting, and without intending to be gruff, Pascale simply said, "We need to get going again, folks. Are you ready?"

"Just a few minutes more, please. I think Edmond is downstairs finishing a cigarette and should be back momentarily," Toomey said.

Wow. Toomey said please. Things must really be bad in that room. "I'll report to 3J that you'll be in shortly." He turned to return to the conference room.

Toomey called after him, "We should grab coffee sometime."

"Hmmm. Ok. Sometime," Pascale said without looking back.

The remainder of the Richardsen deposition was uneventful, and 3J wrapped it up quickly. She was eager to turn her attention to Phillip Dewey. Upon completion of his testimony, Richardsen left, telling Toomey he had a business to run, and he had no interest in hearing whatever Dewey might say. Richardsen made his comments in front of Dewey and the entire Rapinoe team. He seemed to be quickly growing into the role of a *former* member of Dewey's team and becoming more comfortable in letting the world know how he felt.

When everyone returned from the break, Dewey sat in the chair opposite 3J, and, as 3J liked to call it, Round Two began.

"Mr. Dewey, thank you for coming here today."

Phillip was trying to muster his air of complete composure and control. It was proving elusive. Phillip hoped Joshua would appear and protect him. Joshua listened, but had no intention of taking charge. Business, finance, plans, money, loans, testimony. Those were all Phillip's to handle. No direct physical pain involved in them. No need for Joshua's protection.

Following a smack of his tongue in his mouth, he responded, "Ms. Jones. I do not know that I had much of a choice, now did I?"

"Well, thank you nonetheless. I want to remind you at the outset that you are under oath and obliged to tell the truth."

"Thank you for clarifying that for me, Ms. Jones." Tongue smack. "Let me comment, however, on that topic. Is my testimony going to be truthful? I believe it will be. But I wish to point out that the world we live in is full of so many truths and alleged truths and partial truths and disagreements about what is true. Our world is one of different information realities. My dear counselor, in 2023, the notion of truth is not black and white, no disrespect intended. Truth, my dear Ms. Jones, is now comprised of infinite shades of gray."

3J looked up from her notes, surprised by Dewey's philosophical opening comments and more than a little incensed by his patronizing "my dear Ms. Jones." Going completely off-script, she said, "And yet, sir, a court of law is *not* a political arena or a social media outlet. The law still holds that the distinction between truth and falsehoods is indeed black and white." She smiled at Dewey and continued, "Of course, no disrespect intended. So if you say it here today under oath, those of us on this side of the table, and the Judge at the trial, are going to hold you to it; and, I might add, to the perjury consequences if it turns out not to be precisely black and white, correct. I trust you understand me?" Toomey was about to weigh in, but Dewey nodded his understanding and said nothing, so his lawyer decided he would let the matter rest. "Mr. Dewey, you have to answer audibly so the court reporter can record your answers. Nods are not a proper response in a deposition."

Dewey looked directly into the camera and said, "I nodded, indicating that I understood what Ms. Jones said. I don't necessarily agree with her, but I understand."

Pascale watched the fireworks unfold and thought, *Geez. Good thing we have the video. It'll go into the "Greatest Hits" folder for sure.*

3J asked Dewey about the posts. Without denying that Richardsen made the posts on his behalf, Dewey brushed them off and said, after another tongue smack, "The posts are not that significant. I do not believe my conduct has violated the *sacred* automatic stay. I am well-trained in matters of freedom of speech." He paused to smile, and then finished his thought, "And, of course, I would never break any law. I am a law-abiding citizen and upstanding private businessman. I am a lender."

"So, if I understand your testimony, you do not think the posts are that big a deal. Is that correct?"

"That is correct, my dear counselor. BJB would have eventually gone out of business even if Mr. Richardsen had made no posts. So I fail to see how they caused any damage. Your clients suffered no harm from them. Indeed, one could make a strong case that these posts actually helped the Rapinoes and BJB because it hastened the inevitable demise of the company, cutting the losses they would have incurred by a slower death." He paused, smiled again, smacked his tongue, and clarified, "Business death, of course."

3J stared at Dewey. *This tongue smacking is bizarre and annoying. Does he not hear it?* She asked, "So you are saying, 'no harm, no foul?'"

"Counselor, I am saying exactly what I said with the exact words that I used," Dewey said harshly, in a reprimanding tone. "I reject your attempt to put words into my mouth or to summarize what I said with your words. The words I have carefully selected to explain my position are precisely what I am saying. And they are the *only* words that express my position."

"I see, sir." 3J opened her eyes wider and said, "Your exact and precise words will work just fine."

Toomey turned his head to meet 3J's eyes and said, "Counselor, please limit the discourse with my client. You are here to ask questions. I am directing you to limit yourself to questions."

Directing me? 3J thought. *Thank God this guy is no longer at Greene Madison.* She ignored him and returned to Dewey.

"Mr. Dewey, you said that in your estimation, BJB would have gone out of business even if there were no posts."

"Correct."

"What is the support for that view?"

Tongue smack. "My support is the pandemic we have all lived through. It is Covid-19. I have violated no laws."

"Is it your view that because the posts merely hastened the inevitable demise of BJB, the posts were permissible notwithstanding the bankruptcy automatic stay?"

Toomey slammed his hands on the table and boomed, "This man isn't a lawyer. You can't ask him for his legal opinion."

"Counsel, I am not. He brought it up. He said he violated no laws. I want to understand his thinking."

"I don't really care what you want. If you go there, we go there," he said loudly, pointing to the door. "If you continue with this line, we are done and out of here."

3J looked back to the witness, ignored Toomey's threat, smiled, and said, "You may answer the question, please."

Toomey again interrupted and said, "No, he may not, counsel. We are done and we are leaving."

3J said, "Well, you really should linger, because I'm calling chambers and we can let Judge Robertson decide if you and the witness are free to go or if you both must stay."

"You have no idea if the Judge is even in. Idle threat, counselor."

3J countered, "Actually, James, before you got involved in the case, the Judge let Mr. Fuentes and myself know he would be in today, and invited us to call chambers if we ran into any problems. I guess Mr. Fuentes failed to let you know that." 3J flashed Toomey a less than one second smile.

As 3J explained the situation, Toomey froze in the middle of standing up, and 3J used the conference room speaker phone to dial chambers. She had placed the Judge's chambers phone number into the speaker phone's speed dial memory, so with only the press of a button, she was talking to the Judge's administrative assistant. She explained the situation and after a brief moment on hold, Judge Robertson came on the line. He asked both sides to explain their position and asked the court reporter to read the relevant portions of the transcript.

"Ok. I think I appreciate the situation. Mr. Toomey, I am led to understand by Ms. Jones that you were on your way out the door when she phoned me. Is that correct?"

"Yes, Your Honor. She insists on continuing with the improper line of inquiry."

Ignoring Toomey's argument, the Judge said, "So I assume you stood up to go?"

"Correct, Your Honor."

"And you are still standing?"

"I am, Your Honor."

"Very well. Thanks to both of you for your presentations. This is my ruling," the Judge responded with a firm, even tone. "Mr. Toomey, I suggest you seat yourself as well as your client. We're going to finish the deposition without further interruptions and with no need for Ms. Jones to call me again. This is a deposition. Ms. Jones may probe the reasons behind the witness's beliefs. Your client broached the topic of 'no harm and therefore no foul.' That's my characterization of the testimony, not his exact words. Your client said he violated no laws. The point being – your client brought up the automatic stay himself. Since he raised the 'no foul' issue – the violation of the automatic stay being the 'foul' – the question was proper and the answer should be forthcoming. We understand he's not a lawyer, but he should explain his views completely." Judge Robertson paused to allow his ruling to sink in. "Mr. Toomey, I trust you understand my oral ruling, but do you require a written order from me to that effect before you sit so the deposition can resume?"

Toomey cleared his throat and said, "Not necessary, Judge."

"Very well. Good day all," the Judge replied, and terminated the call.

Everyone in the room stood while the conference with the Judge was ongoing. Now they each returned to their chairs, Toomey and Dewey the last to sit down. 3J cleared her throat and asked, "The question is: is it your view that because the posts merely hastened the 'inevitable' demise of BJB, the posts were permissible notwithstanding the bankruptcy automatic stay?"

"Correct. I believe the principle I am educating you on is that there was no harm and without harm, there is no remedy." Dewey paused to again smile at 3J. Each time he smiled, he seemed to communicate that he believed he won the skirmish. He then added, after another tongue smack, "That, and free speech. Surely the First Amendment means something in this country, even in a bankruptcy case, eh?"

3J decided to change the topic. While bantering with Dewey was entertaining, she had gotten what she needed from him and decided to move on before he walked back his view. Changing the topic, she asked, "Mr. Dewey, do you have the burner phone discussed by Mr. Richardsen with you here today?"

"I do not."

"The subpoena commanded you to bring it here today. Why didn't you?"

"My dear Ms. Jones, in my haste to arrive in time to witness Mr. Richardsen's magnificent, award-winning, command performance, I must have placed it on my countertop and forgot it as I left my home in Paxico for the eighty-five mile drive to your beautiful offices." Dewey's sarcasm was thick, intentional, and unmistakable.

Ignoring his tone, 3J asked, "Do you contest anything Mr. Richardsen said today under oath about the burner phones?"

"I do not."

"Did you, in fact, use a burner phone to communicate with Mr. Richardsen about the posts?"

"I did."

"You phoned him and texted him using the burner phone?"

"I did."

"Did you direct Mr. Richardsen to use only a burner phone when communicating with you?"

"I did."

"Did you communicate with Mr. Richardsen about the posts in a manner other than the burner phone?"

"I did."

"What additional manner?"

"We met in person."

"Where?"

"My house, and later, at Swope Park."

3J looked down at her notes and Dewey asked, "May I please have a short restroom break?"

In the hallway, Dewey and 3J passed each other. Dewey leered at her and said, "Do we have much more of this pointless inquiry today, Ms. Jones? I have meetings and a business I must attend to."

"Please, sir, you should talk to your lawyer about those matters. I may not speak with you directly since you have counsel."

Angered that 3J would not answer his question, Dewey walked away from her and as he did, he mumbled loudly, "I am not surprised that your kind is acting this way." He intended that 3J could hear his comment. She did.

In five minutes, everyone regathered around the table. 3J asked, "Mr. Dewey, in the hallway, when I told you I could not speak directly with you because you had counsel, you said 'I am not surprised that *your kind* is acting this way.' Do you remember saying that to me?"

As 3J posed the question, Steele sat straight up in his chair. Pascale leaned forward to be as close as he could across the table, and ignoring 3J and Steele, said, "You said what?" loudly through clenched teeth, his mouth a half-frown of disdain and disgust. 3J looked over at both of them and made a gesture with her right hand, palm down, signaling them to stay seated and calm.

She looked back at Dewey and repeated her question, "Do you remember saying that to me?"

Tongue smack. "I do," Dewey answered unapologetically.

"Just which *kind* were you referring to? That I'm a lawyer, that I'm a woman, that I'm opposing counsel, that I'm Black, or something else?"

"I suppose, choosing from your list, a little bit of each of those categories." Dewey again smiled. Tongue smack. "You are undeniably each of those. And I assume you will not claim that my expressed views also violate the automatic stay."

Toomey leaned over to whisper something to Dewey, who whispered something back. Toomey shook his head imperceptibly and then he squared himself, looked at 3J and said, "I

apologize that this has occurred, counsel. I have talked just now
with Mr. Dewey. There will be no further issues on this front."

3J smiled at Toomey. Then she smiled at Dewey. They might
have thought she was thanking each of them for their attempt
at civility. She was not. It was a smile to disarm; a smile to assert
dignity; a smile to seize power from the opposition.

Calm. Composed. Knowing. In control. Dignified. And well
aware that the world continued to give license to scum like
Dewey to speak their mind and share their racist views, with
the expectation of impunity. Neither Pascale nor the Rapinoes
fully understood the meaning of the smile. Steele got it.

The deposition wrapped up in the next forty-five minutes.
There were no further incidents. Dewey retrieved his trench
coat and Fedora, and he and Toomey exited together.

The Rapinoe team remained to discuss next steps. 3J spoke
first. "The most important thing we need to do is get Kane on
the damages project. He'll need to take the projections and
support them to show what the business would have been but
for the posts. Then he'll need to create a second spreadsheet
and quantify the things that have actually happened that you
told us about on the phone, Bey – loss of act bookings; loss of
customer business. The delta between the projections and the
actuals are the damages. Can he do that?"

"On it. Not a problem. I think we have all of that already in
spreadsheet form and can get it to you in the morning."

"Excellent. Questions, thoughts, comments, about today's
goings on?" 3J asked.

"I don't understand how you didn't rise up out of your chair
and pop that little shit in the nose," Adam said.

Bey added, confused and angry, "He fuckin' deserved much
more than a smile from you, 3J."

"I think it was more important to get him on the record.
Nothing I haven't heard before. I'll be fine. I try not to let the

Deweys of the world bother me. I don't always succeed but …
it's a goal. Dewey's on the record now, including his little racist,
mysogynistic sidebar. I'm confident that when the Judge hears
it, he'll use it against Dewey."

Steele understood, and said nothing as he shook his head
slightly. They shook hands, Steele and the Rapinoes exited
together, and Pascale and 3J returned to his office after stopping
by the coffee room to pick up a cup of tea.

They sat and 3J spoke first. "I should have added to my list
of potential 'kinds' to which I belong the category that I'm
the Black female bankruptcy lawyer that's gonna kick Dewey's
sorry ass in court. He should be glad that the ass-kicking will
occur *only* in court."

Pascale didn't laugh or smile.

Silence.

"What an incredible little shit," Pascale said, breaking the silence.

More silence.

"Bill, the Deweys of the world exist. Always have. Sometimes
they go into their hole, and sometimes they surface. Today,
he bubbled up. Empowered, for reasons only he would know,
compelled by who knows what to share his views on the record.
When people like him feel comfortable enough to tell you
what's really on their mind, it's living proof that whiteness can
be a helluva performance enhancing drug sometimes."

She paused for a sip of tea. "We're still looking for a fix to
that problem, I'm afraid. But, in here I have a job to do, and
today, I did my job. Powered through Dewey's bullshit and
did my job. He hates Black folks. He hates women. He hates
borrowers. He hates debtors' counsel. I'm sure he now hates
Richardsen. He hates me. When it comes to Dewey, I couldn't
care less. I'll sleep fine tonight." She paused. Uncharacteristi-
cally, Pascale said nothing. Finally, 3J said, "We'll get goddamn
Dewey … in court. *That* will be my payback."

Pascale nodded.

After a few moments, they turned to the damages issue. The phone rang. Pascale took the call, and he put the call on speakerphone. The Rapinoes were inviting them for dinner, drinks and music at 7 p.m at their Hey Hay Club. They said Ronnie Steele accepted their offer as well. A chance to think about something other than Dewey and Richardsen and Toomey – at least for a little while before the team was back at it in the morning.

Pascale looked at 3J, who signaled she was willing, and Pascale said they'd be there.

When they hung up, Pascale smiled and ribbed 3J. "Ok if Ronnie's there too?"

3J rolled her eyes and, teasing, said, "You shut up."

CHAPTER 33

I RETURNED TO MY Hallbrook home. I raised the blinds, poured a glass of brandy, and sat on my favorite couch to recall the events of the day. My day had not at all gone as expected. Edmond had everything under control, and then, before my eyes, he disintegrated. "Two hundred K," I told him in the meeting room just before the meltdown. "Two hundred K, you damn fool!" I yelled at him. "Two hundred K," I repeated, shaking my head in disbelief. He looked away from me during the break and said that for the first time in a long time, he just wanted to do the right thing. The right thing? What does that even mean? He told me he would tell the truth. Did he equate the truth with the right thing? Imbecile. I would have nothing of it. I talked Edmond out of his right thing idea. At least, I thought I had. He agreed he would keep to the plan. At least, he said he would.

I could feel Joshua watching me as I gave Edmond his tongue-lashing. I could tell Joshua was surprised but also proud of me.

But railing on Edmond did not work, and now I realize that dear Edmond had never intended to do what needed to be done. Once again, I am surrounded by mediocrity and inferiority. Who knows how Edmond's mind works? I, for one, will never understand.

I had a mentor at the first bank where I worked who warned me about borrowers who did not repay loans; those who insisted they would not. For those, admittedly a small group, my mentor would say, "Lie with dogs and you get fleas." I might now say the same about dear Edmond.

And the Rapinoes – sitting there staring at me the whole time. Hours of them staring. Did they think that would somehow annoy me? Ha! Not a chance.

And Mr. Steele. The quiet one. He certainly spent his time studying Edmond and then me. I am an open book. I wonder what he learned from his studies?

And my lawyer, Mr. Toomey. I am not sure he is of the quality of my erstwhile lawyer, Mr. Fuentes. But he is all I have now, and I will have to make do. I have given him the plan. There are no damages. Even Mr. Toomey should be able to run with that simple plan.

And Mr. William Pascale. Sitting there with his yellow pad, taking notes with his black Mont Blanc pen. How lawyer-like to have a Mont Blanc pen. What possible notes could he take? Did he write in the margin that Richardsen had won the battle until he had not?

And Ms. Jones. Josephina Jones. I must commend her for her disarming smile in the face of extreme adversity. I am sure she believes her people have learned to survive people like me. Perhaps they have.

I sipped my brandy.

"What's that, Mother? What about me?"

I frowned.

"That was not a kind *comment*, Mother. I do not need your *view* of how I performed. How could you even try to rate my performance? You were here the whole time."

Mother *continued.*

"No, I did not become emotional. I had, and still have, things well in hand."

Mother *disagreed.*

"I have had enough!" I yelled at her. "Silence." This was certainly not the first time that she was critical. *But it could be her last,* I heard Joshua say. Joshua wanted to talk with me. At that moment, however, I had no interest in a discussion with him.

But Joshua could be insistent, and I sat on my couch, my eyes closed. Several moments later, they re-opened. Joshua usually knows what I am up to, but sometimes I do not remember events that transpire when Joshua comes to the surface and takes control. This time, I remembered. I was aware. I watched carefully from the dark place.

Joshua rose and with the brandy snifter still in the Body's right hand, he went to the mantle, grabbed the vessel where Mother resided, and threw it against the pastel-colored living room wall. Of course, it shattered into hundreds of pieces. And, of course, in doing so, Joshua distributed Mother all over the floor. He said it was long past the time to rid our lives of Mother, once and for all. Pardoned from a lifetime of serving in Mother's prison. He retrieved the vacuum and cleared the floor of the vessel and Mother. In an instant, the vacuum sucked her violently into the dirt chamber. Did that disorient her even a little? I imagine so.

Before she could gather herself, he emptied the vacuum chamber into a green plastic garbage bag, went to my car, placed the bag on the front seat, and drove us to a deserted strip mall several miles away. Mother tried to *talk* during the drive, but we both ignored her. I believe she *knew* things had changed. I believe she *knew* her time had come. Once at the strip mall, he drove around back and did not hesitate. He knew he would do what needed to be done. That was his role. He accepted it willingly. He tossed the green bag into a rusting, dirty brown dumpster sitting behind the empty shops. We said nothing to her. No goodbyes. I felt an emotion, however, that I had not experienced before. As the green bag descended into the dumpster, I felt a profound emptiness – a loss of a part of my life. My past – discarded. But … perhaps, for the best. Good riddance. Remembrances and recollections are highly over-rated. *The future is all I now care about.* We did not linger. We returned home.

Problem solved.

We had no further use for her. We have had no further use for her for many, many years. No. That's inaccurate. We have *never* had any use for her … nor she for us.

CHAPTER 34

As 3J DROVE TO dinner at The Hey Hay Club, she thought about how bone-weary she felt. It hadn't been her first contentious, confrontational deposition. Not by a long shot. *Sometimes that atmosphere is just par for the course and part of the job,* she thought. But in her experience in managing such situations, those types of depositions always required the expenditure of a substantial amount of additional energy directed to staying on message, and resisting any attempts by the witnesses and opposing counsel to bait her. *Pascale taught me well,* she thought.

The Hey Hay Club was on the corner of Main and 63rd Streets, in a low-rise shopping district called simply "Brookside" by the locals. The district was a popular destination bounded by Wornall Road to the west, Main Street to the east, 62nd Terrace to the north, and Meyer Boulevard to the south, surrounded by residential neighborhoods and comprising one – and two-story brick façade buildings. Quaint, almost all local shops; partially tree-lined and complete with strategically placed benches for locals to window-shop and linger with a perfectly pulled Roasterie espresso coffee or a Foo's Fabulous Custard cup. Built beginning in 1919 to serve the burgeoning Kansas City automobile set, it met the shopping needs of a city that had begun to push south based on the popularity of the internal combustion engine. It had served that purpose well through the decades.

3J arrived and found everyone else seated at a table near the small stage. An ensemble of musicians were awaiting the set. She made her way to the table.

"Hi folks," 3J announced as she took the last seat at the table, in between Adam and Bey Rapinoe.

Adam snapped his fingers and a waiter came by promptly to take 3J's drink order – a double Irish whiskey, neat.

3J said to Adam and Bey, "Thanks for the invite. Much appreciated."

"Our pleasure," Adam replied. "We hope you'll like the set tonight. A little history about The Hey Hay. We named it after the club of the same name owned by Morris Milton at the corner of 4th and Cherry near downtown. The Hey Hay of old brandished a hand-penned sign during Prohibition that offered twenty-five cent whiskey shots and marijuana joints. Milton's thinking – since both were illegal, why not? Just whiskey these days and it's not twenty-five cents a shot. Also, the set tonight will be a tad less bawdy than old Morris' favorite singer, Julia Lee. In 1941, the Kansas City liquor control department closed Morris down for a month and then banned her from the club altogether because she sang suggestive songs – 'The Fuller Brush Man' and 'Handy Man' and 'Two Old Maids.' Tonight, folks, it's just straight Bop."

"So, ok to sell pot and whiskey during Prohibition, but promiscuous songs were out," Steele said with a big smile.

"That was Kansas City and that's about the gist of it," Bey agreed. "Crazy … but our crazy."

Everyone at the table laughed. Talk quickly turned to the depositions and everyone commended 3J for her composure. The lawyers assessed how the testimony would play out in court next week, and shared their thoughts on the only real emerging issue – the damages, and the notion that without damage there is no remedy.

Pascale spoke first. "When the issue is the violation of the automatic stay, the Court may award punitive damages if the violation is wilful. This one sure seems pretty wilful. Not sure what the Court will do here when the violation is *more* than wilful – when Dewey talks, it comes across as gleeful."

"He's his own worst enemy. Thank God for that!" Adam remarked.

"Do you think he even realizes how he sounds?" Bey asked.

"Assholes like him have no self-awareness," Steele offered in his typical to-the-point fashion. "When they get going, they have no filter. They say what's on their mind and dare the rest of us to say nothing."

3J listened to the conversation as she sipped her whiskey. She was even more tired than she initially realized and was happy for the others to carry the conversation. All she really wanted was a good meal and some solid bop jazz tunes. She'd been to the club before, so she knew both were in ready supply at The Hey Hay.

They ordered food and as they waited, the band members gravitated from the bar at the side of the club to the steps up to the stage.

The combo's leader was a flugelhorn player and tucked the horn in the crook of his left arm, like a running back carrying a football. Just before the band took the stage, Adam said, "My favorite flugelhorn jazz man of all time was Clark Terry. I remember a set he did at one of our Coda concert events some years ago. He had aged and needed help to get on stage. He sat in a bar chair as he played for his entire set. In between numbers he smiled one of those ear-to-ear Clark Terry smiles and said, 'Folks, the Golden Years suck!' His body was failing him, but he could still blow the horn. Something to behold for sure. English was his second language; music was his first."

"Other than Coda, did you ever book him for your clubs?" Steele asked.

"No," Adam replied, his sing-song tone conveying just how much he wished that the answer could be *yes*. "Now that would've been something. Us getting the great Clark Terry in here to play, just like he did with the Count Basie and Duke Ellington big bands back in the day. No, Clark passed in 2015 just before we opened the clubs for business. We never even had a chance to ask him."

The band kicked off the set with their rendition of a Clark Terry staple, "In Orbit," from the 1958 album of the same name. One of Terry's signature happy jazz tunes – just what 3J needed. *Nothing like Clark Terry when I need a pick-me-up.* The quintet moved straight into another happy signature Clark Terry tune, "La Riva Gauche," from his 1960 album *Color Changes*, and with that song, they set the mood for the evening. The flugelhorn player was excellent, coaxing a haunting tone from the instrument often mistaken for an oddly-shaped trumpet. As 3J listened, she felt revived. Not her second wind, which had come and gone several days ago; she figured it was more like her fourth or fifth wind by this point.

She must have smiled unconsciously, because Pascale reached behind Bey, tapped 3J on the shoulder, and whispered, "It's good to see you smile, my friend. Y'know, an uncomplicated smile amid a complicated case."

3J mouthed the word "thanks," and raised her eyebrows in acknowledgment of Pascale's concern. *Sometimes, a smile is just a smile,* she thought.

CHAPTER 35

Friday, December 1 to Monday, December 4, 2023

Ralph Kane's draft damage analysis hit 3J's and Pascale's email inboxes the next morning, impressing both of them with its level of detail and precision. The analysis concluded that in the absence of the smear campaign, the clubs would have shown profits for the next five years in the aggregate order of $10-12 million. The analysis then took the loss of business in the period since the campaign had begun, extrapolated that over the first year, and projected the next four years, concluding that the hit to profitability was a significant decline in net revenues. Thus, Kane demonstrated a total loss in the range of $7 to $8.4 million. Finally, he worked the numbers to reflect that through hard work and some luck, BJB could avoid a portion of the projected damages, concluding that the damages could be in the order of $5 million, net.

3J looked over the numbers and tried to poke holes in the analysis. She couldn't and concluded that the spreadsheets were solid, so she moved on to consider what appropriate punitive damages the Court might award if the Judge was as offended by Dewey as she hoped he would be. She concluded it was fair for her to ask for punitive damages in the order of $1.25 million, or about 25% of the actual damages.

Using Kane's methodology, he avoided calculating the effect of the pandemic on the profitability of the clubs. Rather, as he had done in the budget, he took the revenues for the pre-pandemic period and projected a return to the pre-pandemic levels starting in 2023.

She printed out the spreadsheets and walked around the hall to Pascale's office, where she found him with his nose close to his computer screen perusing the Kane spreadsheet. "Whatdaya think, Bill?" she asked him as she sat facing his desk.

"Solid. Really solid work here."

"Let's say the Judge goes with Kane's damage analysis, and also awards punis of $1.25 million to teach Dewey a lesson. Total award of $6.25 million." She paused to make sure Pascale was following the numbers so far. He nodded his understanding, so she continued, "If that was an offset against the total Veridical debt, then it means BJB would only owe $10.75 million. I'm thinking at that level, the Rapinoes might get lucky and find some other lender to pay Veridical the reduced amount and send Dewey packing."

"I don't know," Pascale said with a concerned look. "It's gonna be rough going to find a lender who'll provide financing in the hospitality industry right now, regardless of the total debt. But then again, the Rapinoes have an extensive Rolodex and maybe they can find one to take out Veridical."

They both sat silently as they pondered the task. Suddenly, Pascale had an idea, rubbed his forehead, and smiled.

3J said, "What?"

Pascale said, "Or … what about this? No new lender. In the plan, BJB restructures the remaining debt owed to Veridical, lowers the interest rate to market – maybe 4.5%, extends the amortization to twenty-five years because in the end it's basically a real estate loan, and lowers the payments dramatically in the process. Veridical and Dewey will continue to be a problem, but if we get the permanent injunction, we can use that to keep Veridical and its crazy owner in line. If he steps out of line, the Judge'll smack him, and after a few of those, maybe he conforms."

3J smiled broadly. "I like that. I like it a lot. That very well may be the ticket to punch in this case. Would sure be fun and personally rewarding to watch Dewey when he reads that in the plan and the final order." As she continued to contemplate the many positive facets of keeping Veridical as the lender, she smiled and cracked, "Sometimes this lawyer gig can be just too much fun!"

Monday morning, Phillip Dewey arrived at James Toomey's office. On the agenda: preparation for the preliminary injunction hearing. The receptionist led him into a conference room, and moments later, Toomey arrived. After a handshake, they sat. Toomey said, "With the depositions behind us, we need to talk about the upcoming injunction hearing." Dewey said nothing. He had no pad or pen to take notes. "How did you think your deposition went?"

"Mr. Toomey, I told the truth. I said what I needed to say. I feel good about the testimony."

"I see. Well, I think we're going to need to focus exclusively on the issue of damages, as you testified."

Dewey nodded his head in agreement.

Toomey asked, "Can you create a spreadsheet projecting how BJB would *not* have survived Covid-19, consistent with your testimony?"

"It should not be a problem. My preliminary analysis is that the demise was going to occur anyway in the next twelve months."

"Excellent. Can you get me the spreadsheet in the next forty-eight hours?"

"I can and I will, sir."

"Great. Once I have the spreadsheet, we can spend a little time massaging your testimony for court."

"Do you really think I need to practice, Mr. Toomey?" Dewey wanted to spend as little time as possible with Toomey.

Toomey paused before addressing Dewey's question. He was quickly gathering more information about his client's personality and knew he needed to navigate carefully around a potential minefield when telling him that he was much too opinionated and rough around the edges to offer credible testimony. "Mr. Dewey – we use testimony to tell your story. It's like a good rib-eye: if you cook it right, it doesn't need embellishments. You should have a compelling story to tell. Unfortunately, the story as *you* tell it is littered with distracting embellishments – the potential violation of the automatic stay; your views on the First Amendment; your racial, gender, and professional criticisms about Ms. Jones. All of these – I'll call them side issues – detract from the story. We need to practice keeping you on message, and that message is solely the damages."

Dewey listened, feigning obedience. In response, he said, "Very well. I will adjust my calendar. I am at your disposal, Mr. Toomey. I shall prepare the damages spreadsheet and then we can practice."

"Excellent," Toomey said, smiling. He gently slapped the conference room table, stood, shook Dewey's hand, and the two went their separate ways.

In the car ride back, Dewey had time to think about the "distractions" that Toomey had listed. *Thanks to Joshua, with Mother no longer around I can focus all of my energy and attention on this lawsuit.* He duly noted Toomey's concerns about the "distractions," but he disagreed with his lawyer's analysis. In

Dewey's estimation, presentation of just the damages spreadsheet would be like grilling Toomey's metaphorical steak with no spices. His testimony would need some of the spice for the testimony to be delectable.

3J had arranged for a conference call with Moses and Rome to download to them the results of their work.

"Moses? Rome? 3J and Pascale here. I wanted to call and thank you for all the guidance and great work."

"We immensely appreciate your kind words," Moses responded.

"We've completed the depositions and were able to use all the information your teams gathered to prove that Phillip Dewey was behind the smear campaign posts. No small feat," 3J informed them.

"Wonderful news," Moses said, happy to accept the gratitude. "Your gratitude makes what we do all the more worthwhile."

As Moses talked, Emily laid on her side in her small, taco bed, that folded up around her like a taco shell enveloping its filling. As she laid in the bed looking out to Moses, she stretched her legs and spread her graceful toes, moaning slightly. Moses looked over to her and smiled. *That's my Emily,* he thought to himself. *The sweet miss.*

Rome asked, "Now that we have completed the investigation, can you perhaps elaborate a little about both Richardsen and Dewey? What were they like?"

"Sure. Richardsen is a guy who needs money. Not a complicated personality, but he seemed willing to do Dewey's bidding in exchange for payment. He started off lying in the deposition, but then his dormant conscience must have awakened, and he sold Dewey out. Not sure how Judge Robertson will deal with Richardsen in the injunction hearing," 3J explained. "Dewey, on the other hand, is an odd, complicated fellow. Very much like the profile you secured for us. He believes he's smarter than anyone else in the room. Doesn't much like Black folks. Doesn't much like borrowers. Doesn't much like women. And I predict he won't much like Judge Robertson. He has no concern for the pain he caused. Everything about him is a couple of ticks off-kilter: your profiler's textbook narcissistic sociopath. It's our hope that Judge Robertson will discount or completely ignore whatever Dewey has to say at the next hearing. His insatiable need to be right, even when he's so terribly wrong, will take him down."

The call finished and 3J looked at Pascale and said, "Now for the mad dash to the injunction hearing. I'll amend the injunction request to add Veridical and Dewey as defendants. And, you figure Dewey will have his own no-damages analysis, right?"

"I do. Like you said, hopefully it's viewed as self-serving and not taken seriously in light of all the other things about Dewey that are so wrong, including his wilful violation of the automatic stay. No bankruptcy judge is going to countenance a violation of the most important part of the beginning of any bankruptcy case."

They both sat and contemplated the upcoming hearing only a week away.

"Dewey's damage analysis will undoubtedly project that BJB's business would continue to slide," 3J mused aloud. "Kane's damage analysis projects that, but for the smears, it had already begun to rebound. Kane bases his analysis on something that had actually begun to happen. Dewey will base his completely on conjecture and will ignore the rebound."

"Exactly," Pascale agreed. "The rebound, because it's just begun, provides an awfully tiny sample size, but Dewey's analysis will have *no* sample size because it will ignore pre-smear positive events. Hopefully, the Judge sees Dewey's analysis for what it is, especially when he gets a full dose of Phillip Dewey."

"Bill, I talked with the Rapinoes and they don't think they can get a new loan as they exit bankruptcy. They put out some feelers to the lending community, and they just don't see it happening, so they feel we need to write the plan to restructure the Veridical debt as we discussed. They don't like the idea of staying in the lending bed with Veridical for a moment longer than they need to, but in the near term, they don't see any alternative."

"I can get on that. I already started to draft that type of plan," Pascale informed her. "After we talked, that seemed like the most likely scenario. I think we should be ready to go with the plan as soon as the injunction hearing is over."

"Agreed."

"Say, that was a nice dinner last night at The Hey Hay."

"It was," 3J agreed. "I'm a huge Clark Terry fan. His music always perks me up, and that's what I needed last night," 3J rose to return to her office. "But, as they say on T.V. 'And now, back to our regular show.'"

CHAPTER 36

Monday, December 11, 2023

"ALL RISE," THE CLERK of the Court commanded. "The United States Bankruptcy Court for the Western District of Missouri is now in session. The Honorable Daniel Robertson presiding."

"All right, counsel. This morning, we will consider the Debtors' request for a preliminary injunction to replace the existing Temporary Restraining Order I previously granted, but which is about to expire. Ms. Jones, if I grant the request today, when and how do you expect to address the request for me to issue a permanent injunction?"

3J approached the podium. "Thank you, Your Honor. It is our intention as a part of the BJB and Rapinoes joint Chapter 11 plan to seek a permanent injunction and damages against Veridical Lending and Mr. Dewey. So, assuming this is ok with Your Honor, we anticipate using the confirmation hearing to consider approval of the plan and to present to the Court any further evidence necessary to support the permanent injunction."

"Thank you. I note in your comments, Ms. Jones, you did not mention Edmond Richardsen."

"Correct, Your Honor. We are still scoping out our view on whether to proceed against him for anything other than an injunction barring further smear posts. Once we served him with the TRO papers, the posts ceased." As 3J spoke, she kept a watchful eye on the Judge's body language, as well as looking over to Jennifer Cuello. 3J noted that the Judge had jumped immediately to the procedure to be used for him to enter a permanent injunction. She viewed that as a good sign. *Always good when a judge starts off by asking what procedure to use when I win.*

The Judge took opening statements from both 3J and Toomey. Toomey spoke little about the Bankruptcy Code and instead focused on Covid-19 and how it had negatively affected BJB's business. "The Debtors suffered no harm, Your Honor. Therefore, the Court should award no remedy to the Debtors, whether in a continuation of the injunctive relief or, pray tell, monetary damages." As Toomey spoke, he looked down at his notes almost exclusively. 3J noted his lack of eye contact with Robertson. Since Toomey was an experienced litigator, she assumed his failure to look at the Judge was because of his discomfort with the Bankruptcy Code, the message he delivered, or both. *Why take a case in Bankruptcy Court if you aren't comfortable practicing here?*

What Toomey missed, as he looked down at his notes, was Judge Robertson's body language – the Judge frowned at the notion that there might be no harm and, therefore, no remedy. 3J and Pascale saw it; the frown was hard to miss, except for Toomey. He was representing a client who the Debtors had caught in a lie and could show wantonly violated the automatic stay. He was anything but a sympathetic character. Toomey knew the "no harm, no foul" strategy would be a hard sell, and he didn't need to see the look on Judge Robertson's face as he rejected what Toomey was peddling. As Toomey looked down, Pascale thought, *Always good to know your audience. Always bad to miss a frown of disagreement from the Judge because you've established no connection.*

The trial proceeded with 3J first calling Richardsen to the stand. Richardsen came to the witness stand from a middle of the seating area pew, rows behind where Toomey and Dewey sat at the attorney's table in the courtroom. He continued his newly minted custom of distancing himself from Dewey and his own lawyer.

His courtroom testimony mirrored the truthful portions of the testimony he gave at his deposition. Because he retold his story without once straying from the truth, 3J had decided not to delve into the lies Richardsen had initially spouted at the deposition.

In short order, he admitted to the posts, and implicated Dewey in masterminding the plan. Securing the admissions and the damning testimony against Dewey took less than fifteen minutes. When 3J completed her testimony, the Judge asked Toomey if he had any cross-examination. Without looking up from his pad, Toomey said, sounding unbothered – and, indeed, bored – by Richardsen's testimony, "No questions, Your Honor." Judge Robertson raised his eyebrows momentarily and then immediately furrowed his brow, clearly surprised by the strategy. Since he didn't look up, Toomey again missed the Judge's body language.

3J next called Adam Rapinoe to the stand. Adam gave the Judge a quick tour of the history of jazz in Kansas City, from the roaring Twenties all the way through the Hyatt Skywalk collapse and the resulting end of the Friday night tea dance party, leading up to their plan to bring live jazz back to Kansas City. To show the Rapinoes' level of passion for BJB's business, 3J asked, "Mr. Rapinoe, why did you and your wife leave a thriving, well-established real estate development business to pursue live jazz clubs in Kansas City?"

"Real estate gave us a way to make money and prosper. Music gives us the way to express ourselves and give back to the city. It helps us keep the rich history of the city alive," Adam explained.

As Adam testified, Dewey opened his eyes wide, and then ever-so-slightly rolled them in a non-verbal "Give me a break." In fact, it was a brief moment when Phillip went to his dark place, and Joshua surfaced to survey the situation. The eye roll was almost imperceptible to everyone in the courtroom – except Jennifer Cuello. She was scanning the courtroom as Adam testified and happened to look at Dewey at that very moment. She made a note to share her observation with the Judge at a break.

Adam did not testify about the damages. 3J, Pascale and the Rapinoes had decided to leave that issue completely in the expert hands of Ralph Kane. When Adam finished his testimony, the Judge again asked Toomey if he had any cross-examination, and Toomey again declined. "Not necessary, Judge."

Judge Robertson smiled at Toomey and said, "Mr. Toomey, it's unnecessary for you to share with me your thought process as to whether or not cross-exam is necessary. Simply advise me yes or no when I ask you if you want to cross-examine the witness."

"Understood, Your Honor," Toomey replied, delaying standing until he was midsentence.

3J next called Ralph Kane to the witness stand. Kane ably set out his damages analysis, and under questioning from 3J, supported all of his assumptions to arrive at a total damage calculation of $5 million caused by the negative effect of the posts on BJB's business. Both Judge Robertson and Jennifer were laser-focused on Kane's testimony. As 3J asked Kane each question, he looked directly at her, then turned to the Judge and gave him his answer confidently and clearly. When Kane completed his testimony, Toomey rose to cross-examine him.

"Mr. Kane, I represent Veridical Lending, Phillip Dewey and Edmond Richardsen. Tell me, sir, what áre the principal assumptions you've made to support your calculations of damages?"

"Mr. Toomey, there are several. First, to calculate what BJB's business would look like absent the posts, I took the years 2018 and 2019, assumed a modest increase in net revenues thereafter of 1.5% per year, and projected net revenues into the remainder of 2023 through 2028. So, five years of projections."

"So you ignored 2020–2022 in your analysis?"

"I wouldn't say ignored. I considered those years, but concluded that to include those years' performance in my projections, I would also have to work on the premise that the Covid-19 pandemic would continue beyond the spring of this year. Those pandemic years were so extraordinary that I rejected them as reliable predictors of the future. I would argue that it is not valid to include pandemic-depressed numbers in my calculations, since we are no longer *in* a pandemic."

"Do you have support for that methodology, Mr. Kane?"

"Yes. I believe all appraisers are making similar adjustments when valuing income generating property. I likewise believe that all finance experts are doing the same. Therefore, my methodology is the accepted one being commonly used post-pandemic. I also believe that as the country came out of the Great Depression in the 1930s, and farmers in bankruptcy needed to project future revenues for post-depression years, experts used this same method and thus declined to include the miserable revenues from depression-era farming. They turned to pre-1929 revenues to support post-1938 projections: the same methodology I am using. The courts back then accepted the methodology as sound, as I would hope the Court today will as well." As he responded, Kane turned his head to speak directly to Judge Robertson. The Judge had adopted his poker face, however, and while he listened carefully, he didn't reveal any reaction.

"Very well, sir. What other assumptions?"

"I don't know that my last step in the process was really an assumption. I have actual numbers for most of 2023 for BJB and therefore I could test if, post-pandemic and pre-smear, the business was returning to normal levels. It was. Therefore I have 2023 actuals that support my projections into the future. As to the post-smear performance, I don't need projections or assumptions to show what has happened to the BJB business. It is a cold, hard reality."

"Well, is that *really* true? Didn't you take what you call the 'cold hard reality' and predict what would happen into the future?"

"Yes, I did – it's my job to do so. And I might point out that my prediction of what will happen into the future because of the smears is remarkably similar to Mr. Dewey's projections on the effect of Covid-19 on BJB's business."

The back and forth continued for several additional minutes, with neither Toomey nor Kane giving any ground. As 3J and Pascale watched the cross-examination unfold, they both thought Kane did an admirable job in defending his projections, but that Toomey was skillful in pointing out the baked-in weaknesses of the analysis.

After Kane's testimony finished up, 3J called her last witness, Phillip Dewey, to the stand, holding his deposition transcript in her hand as ammunition if he changed any of the testimony he had already given. Dewey answered her questions the same as he did at his deposition. He admitted he was behind the BJB and Rapinoe posts, and asserted First Amendment rights, much to Toomey's chagrin, as he had implored Dewey to steer clear of things that would irritate Judge Robertson. Dewey admitted he conducted a prior smear campaign against other non-bankruptcy borrowers designed to get them to pay him off.

The Judge watched Dewey carefully as he spoke. He had hoped to garner some insight into the man's personality and his level of veracity by observing his body language. He had *not* expected Dewey simply to admit to everything that had occurred, so instead of making a conclusion about whether he was lying, he found himself fascinated, in a horrified way, by Dewey's demeanor. He found Dewey repulsive.

Before turning to Dewey's damages analysis and views, 3J asked, "Mr. Dewey, do you remember at the deposition that we discussed your views of Black female debtor's lawyers?"

Dewey closed his eyes and said, "I do indeed, Ms. Jones."

"Do you remember we discussed the topics because you referred to me as 'your kind?'"

With his eyes remaining closed, he said, "Indeed."

"You remember I asked you if 'your kind' referred to the fact that I am Black, a woman, or a lawyer, and you responded that it was a bit of all three?"

"Correct."

As 3J asked her questions, she was unconcerned with Dewey's demeanor. Rather, she looked directly at Judge Robertson with each question to emphasize how outrageous and inappropriate Dewey's conduct was. The implication hung heavily in the air that if the Judge accepted Dewey's damage analysis over Ralph Kane's, then he was aligning with a misogynist, racist, lender with no regard for the automatic stay. The Judge showed no signs that he sided with 3J, but allowed the eye contact between 3J and himself to remain unbroken throughout this line of questions.

Judge Robertson was not surprised that Dewey had made his deposition comments to 3J; he was quickly reaching the conclusion that nothing about the strange man should surprise him. As he watched Dewey's testimony unfold, he passed a note down to Jennifer that simply said, "Hard to watch this guy." She read the note, turned around to the Judge and nodded her head in agreement. In response, he shook his head only slightly from side to side in disbelief. They both returned to the task of observing Dewey.

3J then turned to Dewey's analysis of the damages.

"In your damages analysis, sir, you have assumed that post-Covid, there would be no recovery for the BJB business. Is that correct?"

Dewey opened his eyes and scanned the room and said, "Correct."

"You have assumed no return to live music bookings, correct?"

"Correct."

"You have assumed no increase in dining patronage, correct?"

"Correct."

"You have therefore opined that post-Covid, BJB will operate at the same levels as it did *during* the pandemic?"

"Correct."

"In making this assumption, you ignored the post-Covid increases in BJB's business – at least, until you began the smears campaign?"

"Too small a sample size, counselor, for consideration," Dewey said confidently.

"What is your support for the assumption that post-Covid, BJB would operate at the same levels as it did during the pandemic?"

Dewey smiled thinly and explained, "In order for BJB to survive Covid, the Rapinoes needed to use their not-insubstantial fortune to prop up the business, which they did for a period. Rather than continue to do so, however, they opted instead to file these Chapter 11 cases. From that decision, I have concluded, reasonably I might add, that they no longer had any interest in using their personal assets to keep BJB alive. Therefore, it is clear to me, and should be clear to anyone looking at this situation without an advocacy lens, that BJB would not – no, could not – survive into the Covid endemic phase."

"And you believe that, sir?"

Dewey nodded and said, "Indeed, I do. It is simple math and logic."

"If that were true, then why did you need to instigate the smear posts, rather than just let nature take its course?"

"My dear Ms. Jones," Dewey responded, smiling more broadly and shaking his head like a schoolteacher who had just fielded a silly question from a student. He again closed his eyes and tilted his chin upward, and sighed as he said with an air of fatigue, "You miss the point, counsel. I should not need to wait for a death spiral to play itself out. My act of posting was akin to euthanasia of a dying business. It was humane."

Toomey heard the word "humane" and imperceptibly grimaced. *He just won't stay on script*, he thought. *His own worst enemy.*

"'Humane,' you say, sir? Let me quote one post: 'The Rapinoes are deadbeats who relish not paying back legitimate debts they owe. Dear patrons – they are not worthy of your business. They are bad people.' You are telling the Judge here today that this post was *humane*?"

Dewey nodded and opened his eyes.

Judge Robertson said, "You must answer audibly."

Dewey turned to the Judge. "I am."

3J stood at the podium and let the answer ring in the Courtroom. She wanted Judge Robertson to hear the answer, "I am," over and over in his head. She wanted him to feel disquieted by Dewey's performance and cavalier attempt to justify his disregard for the automatic stay and the Bankruptcy Code. She wanted him to channel his discomfort into anger. She got all of that when she saw the Judge stare at Dewey and shake his head slowly in disbelief.

"No further questions of the witness, Your Honor."

Toomey stood to ask questions of his client. His questions were brief; he saw no upside in giving Dewey the opportunity to elaborate on his inappropriate comments.

When Toomey finished his abbreviated examination, 3J had no further questions and Dewey stepped down from the stand. The Judge, significantly, did not thank him for his testimony. 3J advised the Court that she had no further witnesses, and Toomey announced the same.

The Judge asked for oral argument, saying, "Ms. Jones, I fully understand the Debtors' position. And I know it is a little out of the ordinary, but I would like to first hear from Mr. Toomey. I have some questions I would like him to address and clarify. Mr. Toomey?"

Toomey approached the podium and before he had even reached the lectern, the Judge said, "I assume you've read the *Andrus* case, sir?"

"I have, Your Honor."

"On the issue of the violation of the automatic stay, why doesn't *Andrus* carry the day?"

"It's an Illinois case, Judge. It doesn't govern matters in Missouri."

"It would certainly govern matters in Missouri if I agree with it."

"I understand, Your Honor."

"So, Mr. Toomey. Tell me *why* I shouldn't agree with *Andrus?*"

Toomey could not offer a cogent defense of his assertion that the Judge should ignore *Andrus* and instead attempted to promote the theory that because there had been no harm, there should be no injunction.

Judge Robertson glared, and interrupted him. "I am not a great believer in the notion that creditors can violate the automatic stay, and then come into this Court and suggest that because the Debtor would have gone out of business anyway, there is no harm."

"Well, Judge, that's not *exactly* what we're saying —"

"Oh yes. I stand corrected. The argument is that your client performed a *public service*, by euthanizing the Debtor so it would suffer no further pain. Do I have that about right, Mr. Toomey?"

Toomey said nothing. There really was nothing he could say. For all his years of experience, he knew no lawyer could ever get quite used to getting lambasted by an angry judge like this one. And he knew he had no way to wiggle out of the impossible spot Dewey had placed him in by describing the posts as humane. Silence was Toomey's only argument.

Hearing nothing in response, the Judge said, "I think I have all I need. I'll be back in thirty minutes with my ruling. Thank you, counsel."

3J, Pascale, the Rapinoes, and Ralph Kane met in a small room adjacent to the courtroom while they awaited the return of the Judge.

"Well, that was certainly quite extraordinary," 3J said. "And, remind me – you found this Dewey guy in what sewer?"

"No kidding," Pascale added.

"Like we told you when we first met you – Dewey was the biggest mistake we've ever made in our lives," Bey said.

"Well, I think Judge Robertson got the message. We'll just have to see how he sorts it out. No predictions," 3J added.

"No predictions needed," Adam said. "During our many years in real estate, we learned that there was no real point in asking our lawyers what they guessed would happen. It's better to be patient and just wait for the official answer."

Dewey and Toomey went to the end of a deserted courthouse hallway to talk. Richardsen didn't accompany them, even though Toomey was still his lawyer, but stood alone near the courtroom door.

Toomey spoke first. "You just aren't very able or willing to follow advice, now are you?" he asked sarcastically.

"I am perfectly able to follow *good* advice, Mr. Toomey."

"*Good* advice, eh?" Toomey parroted. "Lucky for us then that you are so good at discerning good advice from all the other advice I might have given you," Toomey said, the sarcasm dripping.

"Your tone is not lost on me, sir."

"Good. I was hoping you wouldn't miss how I feel. I'm pleased you understand how *I* think it went in there without me needing to elaborate further," Toomey said, pointing back to the courtroom.

"And I suppose you are expecting me to thank you and then pay you with this attitude?"

"That's why I have the retainer. Oh, I'll get paid. If not from you, then from the $75,000 deposit. Count on it, Mr. Dewey. Not a concern in the world," Toomey explained as he turned and walked away from Dewey. He didn't need to have this kind of discussion as he awaited the Court's ruling ... or ever, for that matter. *Dewey will pay. Yes he will.*

Judge Robertson kept his black robe on as he entered his chambers from the Courtroom and sat down behind his desk. Jennifer took her customary place in the large chair facing the desk.

"I don't think we'll spend much time here in chambers on this one, Jennifer."

"I understand, Judge."

"Here's what I'm thinking. Please weigh in." She nodded her understanding. "First, I will announce that I adopt *Andrus* as the law in these parts. That should take care of this ridiculous First Amendment stuff. You're never *completely* free to say what you want; you can't yell 'fire' in a crowded theatre, as an example. There are always potential consequences, and here the consequences are a violation of the automatic stay. Second, I will rule that Dewey willfully, knowingly, intentionally, and indeed proudly violated the automatic stay when he instigated the campaign to take control of the Debtors' property and attempt to put BJB out of business. I wondered how Ms. Jones intended to prove that element – turns out, all she had to do was get this Dewey character on the stand and step back as he freely explained his twisted thought process. Third, I will rule that Dewey has convinced me he's capable of, and willing to, resume the posts. So, the TRO will convert to a preliminary injunction to bar Richardsen and Dewey from such posts. Richardsen won't be a problem, in my estimation, but he's still earned the continued imposition of the injunction."

Jennifer nodded. The Judge had obviously given his potential ruling a great deal of thought before the hearing and he knew exactly what he intended to say.

"Next, I will address the damages issue. At this point, I don't think I need to rule on damages. I just need to find that there was harm that is both measurable and quantifiable. I can let the finding of how much damage BJB suffered await the final trial, which I understand will occur in conjunction with the Chapter 11 plan confirmation process. Do you agree?"

"I do. The damages evidence you heard is pretty extensive, but all you have to find at this point is that there is a likelihood of success on the merits of the damages claim and then let that issue go until the final trial. There are some really interesting issues presented in the methodology used, and I found Kane's reference to the Great Depression to support his approach intriguing." Jennifer paused to gauge Judge Robertson's reaction. "But I don't think you need to resolve all of that today, Judge."

"Agreed. Good." Judge Robertson paused and said, "Anything else I'm missing?"

"I'm not sure if this is my place, but are you going to let Mr. Dewey off the hook here?"

"Not in a million years. I've been making some notes and I have some – let's call them observations – that I'll make when we go back in." He smiled at Jennifer. "I'll let you hear them live along with everyone else in the courtroom."

"Judge, one more thing. Did you catch Mr. Dewey's eye roll when Mr. Rapinoe testified?"

"I missed that." Silence as he thought about that revelation. "But I'm pretty sure I caught everything else. Or at least, I think I've got everything I could need from this gentleman." He shook his head in continuing disbelief as he replayed Dewey's comments in his mind. "Say, Jennifer, could you call down to the Marshals' office and tell them I am about to make a controversial ruling from the bench and see if they can send up a marshal to sit in the courtroom? You know, just in case."

"On it, Judge. That'll make everyone in the courtroom feel better … except maybe Mr. Dewey."

"All rise. Court is now in session," the Courtroom Deputy announced. "You may be seated."

"Alright, everyone. Thank you for waiting as I reviewed this matter and collected my thoughts."

As Judge Robertson scanned the courtroom before announcing his ruling, he saw Richardsen sitting as far away from Dewey and Toomey as he could; the marshal in the first row of the spectator pews; the Debtors' table full with clients, witnesses and attorneys; Dewey, without a pad or pen, with hands folded on the table; and Toomey, leaning back in his chair, seeming to put as much distance as he could between himself and the Judge while still remaining seated.

Jennifer sat at the law clerk's desk, eagerly awaiting her first courtroom ruling since coming on board. The Judge looked over to Jennifer, raised his eyebrows slightly and nodded. *Showtime.*

"In order to grant a request for a preliminary injunction, I must examine whether the Debtors are likely to succeed on the merits, whether the Debtors are likely to suffer irreparable harm without the injunction, whether the balance of equities and hardships are in the Debtors' favor, and whether an injunction is in the public interest. These factors are all in the Debtors' favor.

"Before I get to those elements, let me dispense with what I can only describe as Mr. Dewey's complete misunderstanding of the intersection of free speech and the automatic stay. Free speech is not absolute, and never has been. I can no sooner go into a crowded movie theatre and cause a stampede by yelling 'fire,' than Mr. Dewey can ignore the automatic stay and communicate online in a blatant attempt to put the Debtors out of business. That is the law not only in Illinois, from where the *Andrus* case hails, but it is the law here in Kansas City."

3J watched the Judge as he delivered his ruling. While he was in complete control of his emotions, she sensed he was struggling to stay calm, collected, and judicial as he made his comments. He looked at Dewey, who looked away and shrugged his shoulders like a child who reacted to a parental scolding with a dismissive, nonverbal "whatever" to their parent.

The Judge frowned at Dewey's petulant demeanor, then gathered himself, and continued, "The Debtors are not just likely to suffer irreparable harm without the injunction, they have *already* suffered significant harm at the hands of Mr. Dewey's master plan. And harm was, of course, the stated intent: to hasten the end of BJB.

"The balance of equities and hardships is an easy one in this case. There is no hardship in requiring a creditor to follow the letter of the Bankruptcy Code. And it is completely equitable for a bankruptcy debtor to have the benefit of one cornerstone of bankruptcy – the automatic stay, under which all actions to control a debtor's property must cease. Enforcement of the automatic stay is so obviously in the public interest that it hardly merits discussion.

"That leaves only the 'likelihood of success on the merits' element for me to address. When I read the Debtors' complaint two weeks ago, and granted the request for a Temporary Restraining Order, I wondered what the preliminary injunction hearing would be like. I did *not* expect to hear the kind of evidence I heard today. I would describe the testimony I heard today as like no other I have heard before. To Mr. Richardsen, I say that while your actions in doing Mr. Dewey's bidding were reprehensible, and your use of your powers and knowledge to harm the Debtors inexcusable, your decision to come clean both in your deposition and here today in open court provides me some measure of solace that you have now finally done the right thing. Based on your testimony, there is no question that the Debtors' will likely succeed on the merits."

Richardsen nodded his head in regretful acknowledgement and the Judge wondered whether he was acknowledging his role in causing harm to the Debtors or that he had now done the right thing.

Judge Robertson paused, and turned his attention to Dewey, adopting a stern look on his face. "Mr. Dewey. In all my years as a bankruptcy practitioner, and in my years on this bench, I must admit that never have I bumped into anyone who held the workings of the Bankruptcy Code in such low regard as you do. Your open disdain for the operation of this critical federal law is nothing short of stupefying. Your antipathy for what is right and decent is bewildering."

He nodded in Dewey's direction. Dewey ignored him and instead closed his eyes. When he reopened them, Phillip had gone to his dark place and Joshua appeared. He reached into his pocket to retrieve a metal nail file. The Judge continued, "But ... not to worry, sir. The Code gives me considerable power and discretion, so I may attempt to right the wrongs you have committed. Today's evidence shows that your violations of the stay are willful, intentional, in bad faith; the result of a detailed and orchestrated plot to harm the Debtors and BJB's business, and in your testimony, you made no attempt to hide your pride in the plan."

3J could see the Judge looking at Dewey, trying to get his attention. She followed the Judge's gaze over to Dewey, who was looking at his hands, but she couldn't see what he was doing. He seemed to fidget; then she saw the nail file, and thought, *My Lord. Is this guy trying to further piss off Judge Robertson? Does he have a courtroom death wish?*

Joshua made no eye contact with Judge Robertson. Joshua had never looked at Mother when she doled out a beating, and he employed the same strategy of not looking at Judge Robertson during the verbal lashing.

The Judge paused his ruling to watch Joshua, assuming he would look up to pay attention to the ruling. To his surprise, however, Dewey did not look up. Instead, Toomey leaned over and whispered in Joshua's ear, presumably asking him to pay attention. The courtroom proceedings confused Joshua, but he surfaced because he sensed danger for Phillip. He listened to part of the proceedings before surfacing, but he didn't understand, and didn't want to understand, the legal mumbo jumbo. Now Joshua looked around the courtroom through narrowed, distrusting, squinted eyes.

The Judge saw Joshua's confusion and wondered how this confident man, who had moments ago touted his euthanasia story, could so quickly become confused. The marshal rose, moved quietly over to Joshua, tapped him on the shoulder, and pointed to the bench in a silent directive for him to pay attention. Joshua pulled his shoulder away from the marshal and exclaimed, in a deep voice unlike Phillip's, "Hey! Don't touch me!"

Everyone in the courtroom turned their gaze on Joshua, who then looked at the Judge, and nodded his head as he closed his eyes as if to say, "Please continue." When his eyes opened again, Phillip was back, unaware of what had just transpired.

Judge Robertson decided to resume explaining his ruling without commenting on Dewey's strange behavior. "The only defense – if I can call it that – offered by Mr. Dewey, is that because of the devastating impact that the pandemic had on businesses such as BJB's, it would have gone out of business anyway and as a result, there was no harm in attempting to hasten its demise. The Court rejects that defense out of hand. Virtually every Chapter 11 debtor in this Court has had a brush with financial demise. Often, debtors wait too long before seeking bankruptcy assistance and they find themselves not just in financial straits, but at the doorstep of failure. In this country, we give debtors, even those at the brink of disaster, the opportunity to reorganize, and we afford them the benefits of the automatic stay. We give them a chance to stabilize their business and attempt to make a go of it. If I was to adopt Mr.

Dewey's working premise, then every creditor in every case could violate the stay with impunity, and when caught, could simply say to me, 'no harm, no foul.' Or, to use Mr. Dewey's words, 'they simply euthanized a dying business and performed a public service in doing so.'" The Judge paused for emphasis. "Mr. Dewey, please read my lips as I utter these words: I reject your premise, sir." He spoke directly to Dewey, saying each of the five words slowly, distinctly, and emphatically. "That type of defense has absolutely no place in my Court, or any bankruptcy court for that matter." As he watched Phillip's reaction to the ruling, he began to doubt whether the man understood what he was saying. He seemed to be distracted, distant; off somewhere in his thoughts, but not present in the courtroom.

The Judge continued, "I will need to quantify the extent of the damages suffered by BJB, but not today. For purposes of issuing a preliminary injunction, I need only find – as I do – that the Debtors suffered irreparable harm by Mr. Dewey's actions in his own right and on behalf of Veridical. We will determine the amount of damages, both actual and punitive, at the final injunction hearing, which we will hold in conjunction with plan confirmation." He flipped through his yellow pad quickly and reviewed his notes to make sure he'd covered all matters he planned to. "Mr. Dewey; Mr. Richardsen: a preliminary injunction is hereby issued against each of you, and against Veridical Lending. You three will do nothing to control the Debtors' property or hurt their business in any fashion. You will post about the Rapinoes and BJB no more. And Mr. Dewey. I caution you, sir. Any further actions will violate this Court's injunction order and you will be in contempt of this Court. I will not hesitate to punish you for any continued malicious activity.

"Last, I know that Veridical and BJB had struck a deal regarding the use of cash under which the Debtors would begin to make partial payments to Veridical shortly. *Sua sponte*, I hereby modify that agreement, and my order approving that agreement, to require the Debtors to make those payments, as they come due, into escrow and not directly to Veridical. The escrowed funds will protect Veridical, without the necessity for Veridical actually to receive the funds. At the confirmation hearing, I will decide if those funds are to be distributed to Veridical or returned to BJB."

This last ruling, made at the Judge's own behest, took both 3J and Pascale by surprise. It showed the beginnings of the evolution of the Court's thinking of how to punish Veridical for Dewey's scheme. Simultaneously, they concluded that Judge Robertson was fuming not too far under the surface of his measured, outward demeanor.

The Judge paused, and this time looked directly at James Toomey. Before Toomey could figure out why the Judge was looking at him, he gestured to the podium with one hand, and raised his eyebrows, and nodded without saying a word. Toomey rose, still confused, and trudged to the podium as silently directed. "Mr. Toomey, I have my doubts as to whether Mr. Dewey fully appreciates just how outrageous his conduct has been. I also have my doubts as to whether he fully appreciates the magnitude of my ruling today against him. Neither am I convinced Mr. Dewey understands just how significant his remaining problems with me are."

Toomey stood erect at the podium. All he could think to say was, "I understand your concerns, Your Honor."

"I am not entirely sure that you do. But so we are clear, I expect you to counsel Mr. Dewey when this hearing concludes and provide some assurances to the Court and the parties concerned that your client has the capacity to understand what has transpired as well as the capacity to understand what may transpire in the near future."

"Again, I believe I understand your concerns, Your Honor."

"Very well, then. Court will be adjourned," Judge Robertson announced, rose and, along with Jennifer, exited the courtroom.

"The Judge misunderstands me. He likewise misinterprets the law," Phillip calmly said to Toomey in a small room near the courtroom where they went to talk after the trial concluded. "Please lodge an immediate appeal of the Judge's rulings, James."

"Look, Phillip," Toomey said, using his client's first name in an attempt to use a conciliatory tone of familiarity for the message he was confident Dewey would reject. "I don't see how an appeal will help at all. You did all the things the Judge said you did, and, frankly, probably more. An appeal is not the answer. You need to be worried about what comes next in this Court, not what an appellate court might say months from now. Plus, it's not a final ruling. It's just preliminary and the courts would not likely permit an appeal at this point."

"Are you saying, James, that the matter ends here, today, with this ruling?"

"I *wish* that's what I'm saying. What I'm really saying is that if the Judge adopts Kane's damages analysis, Veridical's claim is going to be reduced by millions of dollars. And if he awards punitive damages, Veridical's claim is going to be reduced by millions more." Phillip blinked twice, looked blankly at Toomey, but said nothing and remained eerily still. Toomey continued, "Like the Judge, I too am concerned that you're not getting it, Phillip. When the dust settles on this one, you're not going to get paid back in full."

"Oh, I will – because I always get paid back."

"Oh, no. You won't. Not —"

As Toomey spoke, Phillip closed his eyes, and when he opened them, his demeanor changed. His irises darkened, seeming to turn to a brownish-red. Toomey had not noticed when this had happened before, and he stopped in mid-sentence. Before his eyes, Phillip appeared to morph from quiet control to outright menacing. When he spoke, his voice was not even-toned; it wasn't even a man's voice. It was a brash woman who spoke, a woman with a drawling Southern accent on full display. This new iteration of Dewey, named Harriet, said, "He fully understands, James. I'm the author of the plan to bring down the Rapinoes. I convinced Phillip of the plan. I'm the one who convinced him to hire Edmond. I'm the one who had Joshua rid Mother from the house once and for all. The Debtors will repay us. So, if you don't mind, James …" Harriet paused, her eyes widening, and then she screamed, "Fuck off!"

The outburst flabbergasted Toomey. What Dewey was saying made no sense to him; *how* he said it was terrifying. It didn't look like Dewey. It certainly didn't sound like Dewey. *Who the fuck are Joshua and Mother?* Toomey became flustered, even concerned for his safety; he looked at his watch, gathered his papers, put them in his briefcase and stuttered as he moved for the door, "We … We …We … We'll t-talk later."

Harriet closed her eyes, and moments later, when they re-opened, Phillip Dewey was back. Phillip gathered himself and his belongings, unaware that Harriet even existed and of anything she just said, unsure why Toomey had exited so abruptly. He left the courthouse, wondering whether Toomey would file an appeal for him or not.

Toomey got into his car, breathless from both the walk and the encounter. His trembling hands clenched the steering wheel. *Holy shit,* he thought. *How many Deweys are there? I'm not sure my trusty handbook on how to be a lawyer tells me what to do in this situation.*

"Something's off with this guy Dewey," Judge Robertson said to Jennifer back in his office as he removed and hung up his robe. "He just looked to me as if he wasn't really there in the courtroom as I explained my ruling."

"I've seen nothing quite like it, Judge. He almost seemed to nod off during the ruling. He certainly closed his eyes for more than a moment."

"We don't have competent-to-stand-trial rules in civil proceedings like for a criminal defendant. And he violated the stay, hands down. He can't plead insanity in a bankruptcy case," the Judge said as he shook his head in disbelief. "In bankruptcy, unlike criminal law, we also don't ask if folks like Dewey know right from wrong. I have my doubts that he does, but it doesn't matter in this Court." Silence as they were both lost in thought. "Well, I think we'll have to rely on the lawyers to sort this whole Dewey thing out. We're just lowly federal judiciary employees. Over our collective pay grade, I am afraid," he said to Jennifer, only partially kidding.

CHAPTER 37

Monday, December 11 to Monday, December 18, 2023

ONCE BACK HOME, THE entire court experience left Phillip tired and confused. Without Mother on the mantle, he had no one with whom he could consult. He considered Toomey's comments that Veridical would not receive payment in full from the Rapinoes and BJB. He looked in the dark place to see if Joshua could confer with him, but Joshua was nowhere to be found.

Weighed down with concern he could not manage, Phillip decided to leave his home and check into a small, run-down motel in an older part of the metropolitan area where no one could find him. Once at the motel, he kept the drapes drawn, and sat on the edge of the lumpy bed, in silence.

He worried about the trial. He worried about Veridical. And he worried about his alter. Phillip had grown out of always sleeping in the dark place when Joshua surfaced, but he worried that he may have lost consciousness at times during the injunction hearing and during the after-hearing meeting with Toomey. He had no recollection of who had taken over, but he assumed someone did. *Was it Joshua?* He tried to summon Joshua to explain himself, but there was no response. Phillip tried to summon anyone else in the Body, and asked them to reveal themselves, but no one did.

What he knew for sure was that if the Rapinoes and BJB failed to repay Veridical in full, Veridical lacked the liquid capital necessary to pay off its bank group, and would shortly default. Then the bank group could step into Veridical's shoes and deal directly with BJB. The bank group could receive all future payments, and even negotiate directly with BJB. Veridical would, in short order, be out of business, Phillip feared. He could feel himself getting more and more anxious as he considered Veridical's fate. Everything he had labored to build – his company, his life, his station in the community – was in jeopardy. As so often happened, Phillip's growing anxiety awakened Joshua, who finally peered out from the darkness and decided that he and Phillip would communicate, to Phillip's relief.

In response to Phillip saying that he wasn't entirely certain what was happening, Joshua said to him, "Have you not met Harriet?"

"Harriet, who?"

"Hey Harriet. Meet Phillip."

Phillip felt himself getting tired and his eyelids getting heavy, as if he would fall asleep immediately. But this time, he didn't sleep: while he closed his eyes, he remained conscious. In his state, he heard a refined, Tennessee-accented woman say, "Phillip, Veridical is done for. My entire plan has failed. It's time for we three to move out, and move on."

Phillip was aware, but could not converse with Harriet. All he could do was listen.

Joshua said with eager anticipation, "You mean leave Kansas City?"

"Precisely," Harriet explained.

Joshua said eagerly, "I'm good with moving on. I never liked it here, and I hate it when Phillip takes me to Troost. Where'll we go, Harriet?"

"Pretty much anywhere would be better than here," Harriet replied. "Don't you think?"

Joshua agreed and said, "This place is nowhere. And nowhere's no place for us to be. We alters need to be somewhere … somewhere new."

"What about Knoxville, Tennessee? I'd fit right in there," Harriet suggested.

"Never been, but anything new sounds fine to me," Joshua said.

Phillip wanted to raise his eyelids and object. But he could not. All he could do was summon his thoughts. *Move from Kansas City? Never. I am an established, well-respected businessman*, he reasoned. *Knoxville? Never. What would I do there?* He thought he should have a say, and certainly at the very least a vote. But the whole time that Harriet and Joshua talked and worked to undo everything Phillip had created for himself in Kansas City, he had no words he could vocalize. It was as if Harriet or Joshua had turned his speaking switch to the off position. He was helpless to object.

"I may just stay in charge from now on," Harriet suggested. "A new Primary. Give old Phillip a well-deserved rest."

"I'm in favor of that," Joshua said, "As long as we leave this hellhole. If you're gonna captain the Body, we're gonna need to get you some appropriate clothing and whatnot."

"Whatnot, indeed. I am partial to blue dresses," Harriet said as she considered the prospect of proper clothing for the first time in her life.

"Then off we go," Joshua said enthusiastically. "We can drive out tonight. It's probably at least seven hundred miles, so it'll take us all night and all day to get there."

Phillip again tried mightily to say something, but failed.

Joshua could sense Phillip stirring and said, "Go to sleep, Phillip. Don't fight it, man."

"We'll let you know if we need your help," Harriet drawled like a confederate general commanding their troops, and Phillip drifted immediately into a state of hibernation.

For a week after the trial, Toomey tried to communicate with Dewey. He drove by the Hallbrook house. He called. He texted. He emailed. In return, all he got was radio silence. He went to Veridical's offices, only to learn that no one there had seen or heard from Dewey. As a last resort, he took a trip to Paxico to see if his client had again fled there. He found no Dewey in Paxico.

On the drive back from Paxico, he contacted Richardsen and asked if he had heard from Dewey. Richardsen said he had not, and never wanted to again; if he wasn't in Hallbrook or Paxico, then Edmond didn't know – or care – where he was.

Toomey concluded Dewey had left. Left Kansas City, left the bankruptcy cases, left his place of business. Virtually overnight, vanished into the ether. To where, he had no idea. But he knew it was impossible to represent a noncommunicative client. The representation was over, and he used the retainer to pay himself for the services he had performed. Like the Body that Harriet, Joshua, and Phillip occupied, Toomey moved on.

CHAPTER 38

Thursday, December 21 to Friday, December 22, 2023

IN SHORT ORDER, JUST as Phillip had feared, Veridical defaulted on the payments it owed to its bank group. The bank group, of course, could not talk with Dewey, and quickly took steps to protect its position. As Harriet knew would happen, the bank group called its loan to Veridical, which after years of payments, now owed $7 million, and stepped into Veridical's shoes to deal with all of their borrowers, including the Rapinoes and BJB.

3J gathered her papers into her work backpack, slung it over one shoulder, and headed to her car and the Friday trip to O'Brien's. As she approached her car, she multitasked between walking and reading emails on her iPhone. As she drove, she had Siri read the new texts to her. Clients, counsel, the courts, the trustee's office, partners, associates, department managers, law firm staff. She knew she could just drive and let the music engulf her and allow her mind to drift, but she also knew she wouldn't do that. There was just no turning off the barrage of incoming communications. Write it and send it and know they will receive it instantly. No office hours; no office doors to lock at quitting time. The instant access of 24/7 electronic communications from smartphone to smartphone was like an electronic opioid that no lawyer – no person, for that matter – could resist. An entire world, hooked. *Steve Jobs must be smiling from the great beyond.*

She arrived on Westport Road, pocketed her phone in the silent mode, and as she entered the bar, she waved at Ronnie Steele behind the bar, bent over a sink cleaning glasses, who grinned and waved back. She quickly made her way to the booth she liked to call her home away from home and took her seat across from Pascale, already nursing a wheat beer. Steele arrived shortly with a double whiskey for 3J.

"No waitress? The royal treatment tonight, eh Ronnie?" 3J asked, smiling.

"Barb called in sick. So we're shorthanded, and I'm happy to be of service," Ronnie replied as he turned and hustled back to the bar to tend to the growing Friday night crowd.

3J watched Ronnie disappear behind the bar, and Pascale, noting her gaze following Steele, said as he beamed, "You ought to ask him out on a date, 3J."

"Thanks, Dad," 3J said sarcastically, and then added in a more serious tone, "Thinkin' about it, Bill. Between the pandemic and, of course, work, it's been so long since I had a date, I'm not sure I remember how to," she said with a grin.

"I'm told it's like ridin' a bike, 3J, but I'm certainly not one who'll be able to offer you a tutorial," he replied. "It's been decades since I had a date."

They each drank their liquor of choice, and 3J then said, "New topic, ok?"

"Of course."

"Got a call just before I headed out from a bankruptcy lawyer in Denver. Barry Hamilton. Ever had a case with him?"

"Can't say that I remember him in any case of mine," Pascale replied, shaking his head at the same time.

"Well, he represents a group of banks that lent money to Veridical."

"No shit," Pascale said slowly. "I bet I know where this is heading."

"Exactly. Veridical just defaulted. The banks can't find Dewey. They called the loan and stepped into Veridical's shoes. Meet our new secured lender: a small bank group led by Denver Bank & Trust."

"Was Hamilton a yeller and a screamer?" Pascale asked.

"Nope. Sounded very reasonable on the call. Even laid-back. Thankfully, he didn't add any stress to the end of my work week," 3J said.

"How up to speed was he on the Rapinoes' cases?" Pascale asked.

"Not completely. Didn't know about the damages issue still to be resolved."

"Ahha," Pascale said, "that could change him from reasonable to rabid, I suppose."

"Didn't sound like the rabid type," 3J offered. "Seemed measured, but we'll see. I sent him papers to help him get up to speed so he's got a lot of reading on his plate and he'll be absorbing a good amount of Mr. Dewey as he gets into it." 3J sipped the whiskey and continued, "On the way over, I starting thinking about the numbers. An interesting piece of this development is that BJB owes $17 million, but Veridical owes the bank group $7 million out of the $8 million it originally borrowed. If the bank group accepted Kane's damage analysis, the plan would pay the banks $10.75 million, and they'd make $3.75 million more than they're actually owed on their Veridical loan. More than 40% bonus over and above what they lent to Veridical."

"Indeed," Pascale agreed. "And … the rich just get richer." He thought about the implications of the banks taking over the Veridical claim. "That *is* quite a development. As you were talking, I thought that perhaps, just maybe, this new bank group could be the take-out lender that the Rapinoes need to get out from under Veridical and Dewey. Maybe, after all the bad things in these cases, something really good just fell right into their laps."

"Given that we still don't have a good sense of Judge Robertson's view of Kane's damages analysis, it seems like an opportunity to settle up with the banks somewhere between the debt owed by BJB and that $7 million figure and resolve this whole mess once and for all," 3J mused.

"Agreed," Pascale said. They drank in silence as they both contemplated a quick end to the bankruptcy cases.

"Anything exciting on tap for the weekend, 3J?" Pascale asked, trying to move the conversation away from the inevitable shop talk.

"I'm going over to The Belfrey on Saturday night. I'll sit at the bar and drink house-made, private label Bourbon with Celina and let her cook for me."

"Sounds like a plan. She's the best."

"And you?"

"I'm feeling kinda free and easy; at least, freer and easier than I can remember in recent history. So no wandering park walk, no going through the motions at church on Sunday, and no obligatory work this weekend," Pascale said, watching 3J for her reaction. She clasped her hands and rested her chin on the hand hammock she formed. "Instead, I'm going all wild and crazy."

"And what's a wild and crazy Pascale going to do?"

"On Sunday, I'm gonna go watch a close friend's high school kid play soccer. She's in the goal. She's my goddaughter."

"Ooooh – I do like that. I like that a lot."

"I'm not like you – I'm not a soccer afficionado – but I'm looking forward to it a great deal. Just standing on the side-lines, cupping my hands to my mouth, and shouting. Haven't shouted in quite a while. Might be a little hoarse come Monday morning."

"Well, I'll look forward to you whispering at work on Monday. That'll tell me you had a good time."

She thought he'd finished explaining, but he hadn't. "And on Saturday … On Saturday night, me and my Fender are going to play a gig with some bandmates."

3J sat up, startled. "Bandmates? When did this happen? I mean, it's wonderful, but I'm surprised."

"I've been hanging around with them for the past three months or so."

"Anyone I know?"

"Nope. No lawyers in the crew except me," he explained.

"Well, I know more than just lawyers, y' know," 3J admonished him.

Laughing, Pascale said, "Well, true enough. I don't think you know any of these folks, though. We're not great or anything but we're having fun with it."

"You guys have a name?" 3J asked.

"Not really. I guess we need one pretty quick before the gig, eh? They'll need to call us something."

"Where will this take place, if I might ask?" 3J inquired.

"So … that's just the thing. I don't want anyone there who I know. At least, not just yet. I'm trying this on for size and when I know if it fits, then I'll let you know the next where and when."

"Fair enough. Fair enough, my friend. But, on Monday, in your hoarse voice, I do want to hear all about the concert."

"A concert it will *not* be. We'll do two or three songs on an open-mic night and see what happens."

"Got it, Pascale. Still want to hear all about it if I'm not permitted to see it live."

"Ok. Pretty humble beginnings, but it's a start – if I don't pass out from nerves."

3J went back to her hand hammock where she rested her chin and said, "Just remember, the Beatles were pretty bad in the earliest days when they first went to Hamburg, and look how that turned out."

"Indeed."

They finished their drinks, settled up with Ronnie, who smiled for an extra long moment at 3J, and headed for the O'Brien's door and the weekend beyond. 3J started her car, and she thought, *Bill on stage. I wonder if he can sing? Maybe I'll find out someday.*

CHAPTER 39

Joshua Parsons Recalls Friday, December 22, 2023

AFTER WE GOT HARRIET some proper clothes, we drove throughout the night, me and Harriet. She had no last name, so I offered her mine. She accepted, saying it was as good as any. Harriet Parsons. She was in charge: the Primary running the Body. She liked that job. I didn't much like having to make decisions, so I was fine with her taking charge. I could go back to what I did best – protection. Safety. Those were my things. I mostly protected Phillip, but he was safe now, so I figured my new job was protecting Harriet.

I thought about Phillip. He and I were close, at least until I'd gotten rid of Mother way back when we were teens. After that, I didn't have as much to do, but I didn't mind kicking back. Let Phillip have complete control, I'd thought. And Phillip did. Seemed to enjoy his life, at least for a while. He worked for a living. He tried to be normal. I knew little about that lending company of Phillip's. Not me. He seemed to work awful hard. Now it was his turn to rest. I suppose he earned it. Poor bastard.

I didn't know if Harriet had ever worked for a living, but she seemed to know much more about the company than me. She said we would need money, and that Phillip had a good chunk of change. She said she'd take care of getting the money. She figured she could sell the Hallbrook house and the Paxico place. Good she was in charge, 'cause no one would want me to be responsible for getting the money thing right. I mean, I did want to know if we would have enough money for the rest of our lives. After all, it had to account for three people – I mean alters – at least three that I knew of. She told me not to worry. If it ran out, we'd just have to cross over and find a convenience store to share its money with us. She said if it came to that, she had a plan. She said it wouldn't be the first time a convenience store shored up her finances. I wasn't a criminal, at least except for the Mother thing. So her suggestion bothered me. I wouldn't do well in jail; *we* wouldn't do well. And I didn't want to be a part of that kind of a plan. When I told her that, she said, "If you want to have the light, you have to light the flame." I didn't like the sound of that at all. But maybe I didn't understand what she was getting at.

I decided I'd leave it to her to figure out the details. I'd just have to hope her details were to my liking. *Yup. Harriet certainly seemed like she had things all figured out*, I thought as she drove. But I didn't know that much about Harriet's life. Neither did Phillip. I guess I'd have to from now on.

And she drove and drove. Columbia, St. Louis, Paducah, Nashville, Cookeville, and finally Knoxville. In the dead of night, it seemed like it'd be fine. Didn't really matter to me. All that mattered was the one thing I was sure of: it ain't Kansas City, so … perfect, as far as I was concerned.

Only once during the trip did Phillip wake up when we were gassing up at a service station. Harriet closed her eyes as she held the gas pump and Phillip appeared. Phillip told me he had nothing to live for. He said he had nothing to look forward to. He said he was going to his dark place for an extended period and maybe he would just rot away. He closed his eyes, and Harriet reappeared. She probably never heard Phillip. If she did, she probably wouldn't have cared.

Life with Phillip mostly sleeping would be very different for me. Y'know, Phillip was ok to me, but as I watched him, he was kind of an asshole to others – the non-alters. But he was a clever one. He was one of those assholes that pretended to be nice. But he wasn't. I knew that, and some of the non-alters came to know that shortly after Phillip entered their lives.

I once asked Phillip why he treated the non-alters the way he did. He narrowed his eyes and responded with a question and an answer. "Why must I chase the cat? I suppose it's a little bit of the dog in me." I still don't know what he meant, but he could be like that sometimes. If he was a dog, maybe Mother gave him that.

I wondered what would happen to Veridical? Billy Milligan eventually filed a bankruptcy case to deal with Ohio's quest to get its hands on his book royalties. Would Veridical have to file? Would Phillip have to as well? How would that affect Harriet and me? Made my head hurt even to consider the possibilities. Before Phillip took his nap, I think he finally realized that his time as a successful Kansas City businessman was fleeting. The fate of an alter I suppose. Nothing lasts. Nothing can.

While she drove, I asked Harriet where we would stay in Knoxville. She said she had that all figured. We finally drove up to an old motel Harriet had picked out, and she checked us into a room. Reminded me a little of Mother's place off of Troost. Seemed like it would be sufficient for the three of us. I don't need nothing fancy.

Phillip had wondered from time to time if it was normal to have so many different people inside the head. I know little about normal. Once we settled into the room, I asked Harriet if she thought it was normal. At first, she just shrugged her shoulders and said nothing. A few minutes later, she smiled that sneering smile of hers and said that normal was for regular folks, but not us. She said us alters didn't have to worry too much about normal.

CHAPTER 40

Saturday, December 23, 2023 to Saturday, January 6, 2024

Over the next two weeks, Pascale finished and filed the plan and disclosure statement. In the plan, the Debtors proposed that the total damages from the smear were $5 million based on Kane's analysis, plus punitive damages of $1.25 million, and therefore, the resulting bank group claim, as successor to Veridical, was $10.75 million, to be paid with 4.5% interest in a twenty-five-year amortization, and a balloon payment on the eighth year anniversary. The banks' expert opined that the damages were only $2 million with a resulting claim of $15 million. The banks' lawyer and 3J each deposed the other side's experts, and both were credible – a standoff.

Back in conference room 27B several days after the expert depositions sat the Rapinoes, Kane, 3J, and Pascale. 3J spoke first. "Hard to predict how the Judge sorts this out, folks. Both experts are credible; both have defensible methodologies; both present well on the stand. And they aren't testifying to fact. They're offering their educated guesses."

Pascale jumped in, "Yeah. The Judge can't call it a tie. At trial, someone has to win. When it was Dewey as our opponent, I think we could use a baseball rule and say that a tie would go to the runner – here for the Debtors. Dewey was so bizarre and hideous that he would garner no sympathy from Judge Robertson. But the banks have done nothing wrong, unlike Dewey, so the sympathy vote may not be as strong."

3J added, "The Judge will know that the banks can't get around the consequences of Dewey's conduct. He won't forget that. But the bank group's expert is a real upgrade to Dewey's presentation on the damages issue."

"What about the fact that the banks aren't really owed $17 million; they're in for only the $7 million left owing on their loan to Veridical?" Adam asked.

3J responded, "That's an important emotional issue potentially, but legally, the banks' claim is the full $17 million against the Debtors."

Pascale elaborated, "This issue used to arise in the 1980s during the savings and loan crisis. An S&L went under and the Resolution Trust Corporation stepped in and might sell a failed S&L's defaulted loan to a solvent bank who then held the paper. Maybe that successor bank paid only thirty cents on the dollar for the loan. The successor bank then sued the defaulting borrower, who defended by saying that the amount owing was only thirty percent because that's all the successor paid. The courts pretty well rejected the argument out of hand time and time again. The rulings were simple – the borrower owes whatever the loan documents say the borrower owes, no matter whether it's the original creditor or a successor."

"We understand," Bey acknowledged. "Just seems like we were about to win against Dewey, and now we're not so sure what's gonna happen next."

"Would you consider trying again to resolve this through settlement discussions?" 3J asked.

"Would we make the first offer or the banks?" Bey asked.

"I would say our offer is in the plan already, and it's the banks who would have the next move," 3J said. "But I think it would be appropriate to reach out to Hamilton and see if the banks want to engage."

"Yes. Then let's do that and then report back any bank counteroffers. For that matter, let us know Hamilton's reaction, even if there isn't a counter," Adam directed.

"Of course. Will do."

The meeting broke up, and 3J headed to her desk.

CHAPTER 41

Tuesday, February 6 to Tuesday, February 27, 2024

DESPITE BEST EFFORTS, 3J had been unable to settle the remaining issue with the banks. How much they would be paid under the plan would have to be tried with expert witnesses of equal veracity and then somehow, Judge Robertson would have to break the expert witness tie. At around 11 p.m., the night before the plan confirmation trial, 3J and Pascale each headed home; the glamorous life of Chapter 11 lawyers in middle America.

And now, February 7: Plan confirmation day.

With little sleep, 3J arrived back at her desk before the sun began to rise, and she listened to a voicemail on her desk phone from the banks' lawyer, Barry Hamilton. "Ms. Jones, if you are able, could we plan to meet at the courthouse, maybe an hour before the hearing commences? There may be some movement, finally, on my side toward a negotiated resolution. Thanks."

3J forwarded the message to Pascale for him to hear when he arrived.

The Court had scheduled the trial for 10 a.m., so Hamilton was suggesting they meet at 9 a.m. at the courthouse. 3J was fine with meeting, though she typically hated the last-minute settlement attempts on the courthouse steps. She often wondered why clients waited so long to have settlement discussions. Did they think the other side would be more pliable as they entered the courthouse to do battle? Were they really incapable of facing the settlement issue themselves until they climbed the twenty-two steps from the corner of Ninth Street and Oak to the entryway doors? Was there something strategic in waiting until the last minute? Cynically, was it a lawyer thing and not a client problem? Did the lawyer need to bill every tenth of an hour possible before carrying out settlement instructions from the client?

She never knew the answer. She just knew that many waited until the last possible moment and she never found that strategy any more effective to achieve a negotiated settlement than resolving differences well before trial.

Oh well, she thought. *It takes all kinds.* And she was ready for trial, so it was no skin off her back if a trial was necessitated by a failure to settle. She had done the work; all she had to do now was try the case and let the good Judge Robertson then wrestle with how to break the tie between the two experts.

Hamilton and 3J met on the sixth floor of the courthouse, just down the hallway from Judge Robertson's courtroom, in an austere, no décor, interior room set aside for attorneys. Hamilton came right to the point.

"Finally heard from my clients yesterday, late in the day. I think they finally recognize that we each have credible experts with good points to make. I think they've finally accepted my view that this expert horse race is too close to call. A toss-up."

3J listened. She hoped Hamilton would get right to the point. *If there isn't a settlement right here and right now,* she thought, *then this is a big waste of time and an unwanted distraction.* "Barry, we're both on the short end of the timeline here, and I know I certainly have things I should do to make my final prep for the trial. I'm sure you have a similar list. So, without intending to sound abrasive, could we cut to the chase?"

"Not abrasive at all. Just thought you should know that the delay was the clients' doing and not mine."

3J nodded. "Understood."

"So, here's the offer. Your side is in at $5 million of actual damages. My side is in at $2 million. We should split the difference as to actual damages – $3.5 million."

"And what of the punitive damages?"

"That's a harder lift for us."

"Maybe so," 3J said, "but you also have less of a chance of winning that argument. You read the transcript. Your clients are stuck with the Phillip Dewey stink. He violated the stay. He was proud of it. He pissed off Judge Robertson. You have no witness for the punis. I think the Judge will grant us all the punis."

As 3J spoke, Hamilton listened respectfully. He nodded. He looked thoughtful. When 3J finished, Hamilton said, "It looked to me that the punis you want amounted to 25% of the actual damages. Correct?"

"Correct," 3J agreed.

"If I use your formula, and we agreed to $3.5 million of damages, then punis would be $875,000."

"Is that the offer?" 3J asked. "I note you said 'if I use your formula,' and not 'if my clients use your formula.'"

"My clients will go for $875,000 of punis. Total damages for settlement would then be $4,375,000," Hamilton said as both he and 3J each hurriedly sketched out the math on their yellow legal pads.

"Got it. Give me ten minutes to find my clients and get you an answer."

Hamilton stepped out of the meeting room. 3J called Pascale, who was just about to leave for the courthouse, explained the situation, and asked him to conference in the Rapinoes. They were in their car on the way to the courthouse. 3J explained the offer and the rationale. She didn't say it was a "take-it-or-leave-it" offer, and they didn't ask for a recommendation from the lawyers. Rather, Bey said, "We were up late last night talking about the parameters of a settlement offer we'd accept. We concluded that a discount of $4 million was where we were willing to land. This is a greater discount than our bottom line. I'm looking over at Adam as he's driving, and he's nodding his head in agreement. So, yes, take the offer and we'll see you shortly."

3J leaned out of the meeting room and signaled Hamilton to return. She told him that the Rapinoes would take the offer and, as a result, the new amount owing to the banks under the plan would be $12,625,000; down from $17 million.

Hamilton agreed.

"What is Judge Robertson's practice when there's a courthouse steps settlement like this one, 3J?"

"He'll want us to let his law clerk know we have a deal, and then put it on the record when the hearing starts."

"That works fine," Hamilton said.

"I don't think we can confirm the plan today because we'll need to file a quick modification to reflect the new debt to the banks. But it should be smooth sailing from here out," 3J said.

"All rise," the Courtroom Deputy commanded.

"Be seated," Judge Robertson said. "Ms. Jones. I understand we have a settlement here today?"

"That is correct, Your Honor," 3J said as she walked from her table to the podium, in her medium blue suit, light gray shirt, and her black Gucci slingback pumps. "In short form, Your Honor, the banks and the Debtors have agreed that the actual damages suffered by the Debtors because of Mr. Dewey's conduct is $3.5 million, and the parties agree to punitive damages in the amount of $875,000. Those amounts will offset against the banks' claim of $17 million inherited from Veridical, and the resulting claim to be paid to the banks under the plan is $12,625,000."

"Thank you, Ms. Jones," Judge Robertson said nodding his head. "Mr. Hamilton, on behalf of the bank group, do you concur?"

Hamilton had already walked to the podium as Judge Robertson requested his concurrence. Standing next to 3J at the podium, he said simply, "The banks agree, Your Honor."

"Thank you, Mr. Hamilton. Other than the dispute as to the net amount owing, am I correct that the banks lodged no other objection to the plan as filed?"

Hamilton replied, "That is correct, Your Honor. To be precise, when the Debtors amend the plan to provide for payment of $12,625,000 with a twenty-five-year amortization, 4.5% interest, and a balloon payment due on the eighth anniversary, the banks will vote to accept the plan."

"Very well, Mr. Hamilton, thank you. Ms. Jones, how should we now proceed?"

3J smiled at Hamilton and then addressed Judge Robertson. "Your Honor. I can amend the plan to reflect the new debt owed to the banks and send it out for approval. We can then have a new confirmation hearing thereafter."

"Thank you, Ms. Jones. I wonder if that's necessary? We have everyone here today that matters. As I understand it, the banks filed the only objection to confirmation. Let's do this:

put on your evidence for confirmation today. Then modify the plan and send out a notice that says that unless anyone objects within twenty-days of the notice, I will confirm the modified plan without further hearing."

3J nodded her approval of the suggested procedure and said, "That'll work, Judge," smiling at his helpful suggestion. "Your Honor, Mr. Pascale and I divided duties on this one. I was handling the damages issues, and he was handling the plan confirmation issues. So, with the Court's permission, he will take over now and put on the necessary confirmation evidence."

"Sounds like a plan … no pun intended," Judge Robertson offered, smiling.

In short order, Pascale put on the evidence to justify confirmation of the plan with two witnesses – Ralph Kane as to the projections and feasibility, and Adam Rapinoe as to all other issues. There was no cross-examination and Pascale rested the Debtors' cases.

"Very well, counsel," the Judge said to Pascale. "Mr. Hamilton, I assume the banks have no evidence."

"None, Your Honor," Hamilton replied.

"Ok then. The Court confirms the plan subject to the modification of the amount owing to the banks, as previously discussed. The plan satisfies each required section of the Bankruptcy Code and I am convinced that the plan is feasible." He then turned his gaze to Bey and Adam Rapinoe and said, "First, I would like to wish both of you the best of luck under the plan and with your jazz clubs. Second, I want to make sure you appreciate how sorry the Court is that you had to endure the wanton and repeated violations of the automatic stay in these cases. I feel like that occurred under my watch and for that, I am deeply sorry. I want to commend the Greene Madison team for getting to the bottom of the posts and putting an end to them." He paused and looked at 3J and Pascale and smiled. "Anything else, counsel?"

"Nothing from the Debtors, Your Honor."

"Anything else from the bank group, counsel?"

"Nothing, Your Honor. Thank you."

"Very well. The Court will be in recess," and Judge Robertson and Jennifer exited the courtroom.

3J and Pascale stood, walked to Barry Hamilton, and the three lawyers shook hands. Hamilton said, "Nicely done, folks. See you at the next rodeo," smiling broadly.

"Indeed," 3J said.

On the walk back to their office, Pascale said, "Hamilton seems like an ok chap."

"My thoughts exactly. I think he had to drag his clients kicking and screaming to the settlement finish line and for that, I'm grateful. But he seems to've done a nice job of it, and now, I think the Rapinoes have their new lenders. And no one named Dewey!"

No creditor objected to the plan revisions and twenty-five days later, Judge Robertson signed the order approving the plan and the new arrangement with the banks. *The Kansas City Star* carried an article titled "Jazz Survives Bankruptcy." Harriet found the article online and read it aloud so, if he was listening, Phillip could hear the outcome of the bankruptcy case. She thought he was entitled to know the end of that chapter.

Shortly after reading the piece, Harriet closed her eyes and Phillip reappeared. As he took control, he cracked to Harriet and Joshua, "I am back. Absence makes the heart grow fonder, doesn't it?" Phillip then smiled. "I have decided to seek out a therapist with the goal to fuse you both into me. I am the Primary and I should be in control of the Body," he proudly stated. As he said "control," his eyes fluttered shut and Harriet reappeared.

Both Harriet and Joshua felt threatened by the notion of therapy and integration of the alters. Harriet told Joshua she wasn't Linda Blair in *The Exorcist* and had no interest in an exorcism disguised as therapy. To both Phillip and Joshua, she said, "Whether the planned therapy is tomorrow or next week, Phillip, listen to me: it's not going to happen, because for you, tomorrow's not gonna come. Never. Back to your dark place, now." Harriet had no plans to yield her new function as Primary.

3J sat on her couch looking north along Walnut Street to the river beyond. *Crazy case. And Pascale moving on. Such big changes on the horizon. Change, but maybe not progress. Only time would tell.* Just like Walnut Street. No more iconic streetcars sharing the road with bumper to bumper Model T autos driven by Kansas City up-and-comers. No more cafes, hotels, jazz clubs, and copiously available drinking despite the Eighteenth Amendment and resulting prohibition – just not in Kansas City, whose officials turned a blind eye to the city's not-so-well-kept secret tradition of thinking of prohibition as a suggestion, and not, well, not a prohibition. No more scarlet houses, and concert saloons, and gambling clubs, some with extra heavy steel doors to protect against raids, and each fed their liquor by the T.J. Pendergast Wholesale Liquor Company, Inc. No sin to lure the partiers. No more department stores. 3J remembered an older partner at Greene Madison had once told her that one of the fabled Walnut Street department stores was home to the law firm's predecessor. He joked that when a patron got into the elevator, the operator would announce loudly and proudly, "first floor, women's suits; second floor, men's suits; third floor, lawsuits."

Walnut Street's transformation from a dirt trail with one structure on a bluff overlooking the Missouri River in the 1800s, to Kansas City's center of commerce in the 1900s, to nothing more than a place for office workers to gather in the twenty-first century might not be progress at all, just like she wondered if her Pascale-less career at the firm would be an advance or not. *Time will tell.*

EPILOGUE

3J, Pascale, the Rapinoes, and Ronnie Steele gathered in 3J's condominium for a post-confirmation Saturday evening of wine, food, views, conversation, and celebration of the plan confirmation. 3J had begged her friend Celina Tio to cook for them, and Celina was more than willing to produce a master-piece. On the Sonos, 3J had teed up a queue of jazz guitarist Jim Hall albums. The first in the queue was The Jim Hall Trio's *These Rooms*, the perfect Post-Bop sophisticated, refined, and elegant music to celebrate the reorganization of BJB's jazz clubs in modern-day Kansas City. 3J shuffled the playlist.

As they all marveled at 3J's dusk skyline view, Steele took Pascale aside and whispered, "Still planning on packing in the law biz, friend?"

"Yep. I'm rounding third and heading for home," using a baseball metaphor for the two former players.

"Hey, Coach used to tell me that you were never that fast, so just be careful you don't get thrown out at the plate," Ronnie warned.

Pascale nodded and smiled. "I got it, Ronnie. Or at least I think I got it."

The two headed back to the group. As they reintegrated, 3J raised her glass and offered, "A toast to the Rapinoes. May the road always rise up to meet your feet, may the wind always be at your back, and may you always have the music in you for all of us to enjoy."

As Tio finished expertly preparing scratch-made ravioli with homemade ricotta cheese filling and braised veal shank with blue cheese gratin, agra dolce mushrooms and pesto, along with brown butter green beans, everyone made their way to the dinner table and eagerly awaited plating by the evening's star, Chef Tio. 3J circled the table and refilled everyone's wineglass as the intimate celebration dinner moved into the total culinary satisfaction phase. 3J cut the fresh-baked bread from nearby Ibis Bakery, Tio took her seat at the table as well, and the small dinner party began the shock and awe of a James Beard chef home-cooked meal.

As they ate, Bey looked at 3J and Pascale and said, "Y'know, Duke Ellington once said that the most important thing he looks for in a musician is whether he knows how to listen. I don't have the words to thank both of you for listening to Adam and me and finding a way to keep jazz alive in this great music town. We're forever indebted."

Pascale and 3J both beamed. 3J said, "Our pleasure, folks."

Just as Jim Hall and the band began to play their signature tune, "Where or When" – dedicated by Hall to long-time Count Basie guitarist, Freddie Green – the friends finished their main course, and up next was Tio's signature Chocolate Ganache with Boulevard Beer's Dark Truth Stout caramel.

Steele said, "I've seen all kinds of crazy in my day, but I gotta say I've never seen crazy quite like Phillip Dewey. And, truthfully, a little of 'like-client-like-lawyer' as well on this one."

Pascale responded, "Yeah. We're on a bit of a roll. We've had some crazy bank lender cases the last few years. Usually, the banks are quite staid and predictable. I'm sure 3J is hoping to get back to staid and predictable. Right?"

"Absolutely," 3J agreed.

An hour-and-a-half later, the Rapinoes departed. 3J told Tio to leave the kitchen for her to clean, and Tio reluctantly agreed and departed with the Rapinoes.

Steele grabbed his coat and started for the door, thanking 3J for the evening. 3J said, "Let me walk you to the door, Ronnie."

At the door, 3J said softly, "I'm glad you could come. Fun evening. First time I think I've enjoyed an evening like this in quite a while."

"Me too. Chef's food was out of this world."

3J looked into Ronnie's eyes and asked, "Say, Ronnie – just wondering. How would you feel about catching a bite to eat with me next weekend?"

Steele smiled, blinked twice, and said, "Why, Ms. Jones, you mean like a date between Josephina Jillian Jones and Ronald Ellison Steele?"

"Why, Mr. Steele," laughed 3J. "Yes. I mean, if old folks like us are permitted to date in the modern era."

"I believe I'd enjoy that. Yes, I would. A great deal."

"Good. Then details to follow. Drive carefully, Ronnie."

As he bent to reach for the door handle, she kissed him and as she straightened back up, Ronnie said, "Right here in front of Dad?" nodding back to where Pascale was still sitting in the living room.

"Oh, he won't mind," 3J said, smiling.

Ronnie departed, smiling broadly, and 3J returned to the living room.

She refilled her wineglass and asked Pascale if he wanted a refill. He held up a hand and said, "Thanks, but maybe just a half.

"Everything ok with Ronnie?" Pascale asked, smiling knowingly.

"Everything A-ok," 3J said. She sipped her wine in silence, hoping Pascale would not probe further. He didn't, and she felt relieved. "How was open-mic night?"

"We had a blast. Three songs. The last one was my own."

Surprised, 3J exclaimed, "Really? I didn't know you wrote."

"Oh, every once in a while the moment arrives, and I put it down on paper."

"Song title?"

"Tonite."

"Genre? Blues?"

"Nah. More jazz than anything. Maybe eclectic if that's a genre."

"Theme?"

"Just live in the moment."

"That's a good one for sure. So happy for you, Bill."

They watched the skyline for a few moments and 3J asked, "So, you're really outta here, Bill?"

"Here? Meaning Greene Madison?"

"Yes. And the practice of law?"

"I am. Don't want to wake up one day nothing more than a lonely old man." Silence. 3J was deep in thought. Pascale said, "When I told Swanson my decision was final, he looked perplexed. Then I said that I had gone from mature to vintage in the practice of law and it was time. He actually seemed to get it."

3J smiled; this time, a smile of understanding and acknowledgment. "There's a phrase in New Orleans – *Prends ton temps*. Meaning, take your time. When you move on, take your time in your next season. You earned it."

Pascale nodded.

3J asked, "When does all of this happen?"

"Not entirely sure, but my guess is that I'll try to remove my last boxes from my office late this year or maybe early next."

"Got it."

"Might've been sooner, but you've seen my office," Pascale said playfully, chiding himself for his lack of office organization.

"I certainly have. Do *not* ask me to help you," 3J said, joking but emphatic.

"Pretty sure you couldn't, even if I asked. No, that's a one-man job. Can't wait to see what I find hidden in the piles," he said, smiling. "It'll be good practice for the next stage as I uncover what life has to offer me going forward."

Silence as they both watched the skyline twinkle.

"Not sure how I'm gonna do this without you at the firm, Bill."

"You will do more than fine. You will do great."

"Maybe. When I first joined the firm, I felt pretty invisible in a sea of white lawyers. I felt like I had limited possibilities because I wasn't part of the prevailing tribe. I had a sense of purpose. The law gives you that. But not trust and belonging. I needed you and you were there. With you, I was able to find trust and a sense of belonging. It's a better place now. Not perfect, but slowly, it's gotten better. I'm not sure what it'll be like without you there."

"Like I said, you're in line for great things at Greene Madison. Soon you'll be on the firm's board, is my guess."

"Maybe," 3J said softly, as she turned to watch the lights of the city.

Evening in New York City. Moses Aaronson gently stroked Emily's silky ears as he sipped a dry martini and read the latest Michael Connelly police thriller. Another Saturday evening in the city that never sleeps. He loved it and wouldn't change a thing.

Evening in North Kansas City, just north of the river. Jennifer Cuello sat on her couch as she surveyed her first Chapter 11 confirmation process. She wondered if they were all as crazy as the Rapinoe cases. She didn't care. She was on her way to a life as a bankruptcy lawyer and pretty happy with the path she saw in front of her. Maybe, when her clerkship ended, she would even find a job in Kansas City and would get to appear in front of Judge Robertson. She decided that was a little too much forward thinking. One day at a time.

Rome awakened as Sunday's first London light of day streamed into her apartment window. She had fallen asleep with her laptop open. Another day in the Swinging City. *Maybe a trip to Chelsea Market*, she thought.

Midnight in the City of Marble, Knoxville, Tennessee. Another unhappy evening as Phillip found himself trapped in his dark place with Harriet well in control. Nearby, Joshua lounged. Also trapped by Harriet, but happy for the respite. He told Phillip to chill out. Instead, Phillip spent his time in his dark place plotting a path back to control as the Primary. Phillip believed Joshua had become emotionally unavailable to him. He felt all alone.

The bank group's private investigator had found the three of them in Knoxville and served Harriet with a lawsuit. While the bank group did well on the BJB loan, it lost money when it stepped into Veridical's shoes on other loans. The group was now after Phillip to pay back the shortfalls. Harriet's plan was to ignore the bank group. At first, Phillip had thought that might be a good way to go. But now he knew the bank group's concerns had to be addressed. He didn't know how, but he knew he was just the person to do so; the only alter who could. He could save Veridical. He had to. He just needed to figure out how. But first, he would have to figure out a way to make Harriet relent and convince Joshua of the soundness of his plan. Perhaps he could rekindle their closeness and Joshua's need to protect Phillip – this time from Harriet.

AFTERNOTE

MY STRUGGLES WITH HARRIET continued, but I was able to surface more frequently. I think her energy had ebbed. I could be relentless. At some point, while I was Primary for several hours, I wrote and mailed a brief letter to Ms. Jones.

> Ms. Jones:
> I write to explain a few things. While it is a rare emotion for me, I feel regret for sharing my feelings about you during my deposition. You should know that those were not necessarily my feelings, *per se*. I am still sorting that part out.
>
> I simply wanted you to know that sometimes I am Phillip; sometimes I am Harriet, and sometimes I am Joshua. And always I am all three, if that makes sense to you. There may be others in the Body. So sometimes, I may be them as well. We refer to each of us as an alter. Sometimes one of us does something bad of which the others are unaware. We come and go. While in Kansas City, I was the Primary. The alters came out from time to time, but not often, at least not until things got out of hand.
>
> Harriet says that the smear campaign was her idea. I can't be certain. She can be difficult to dissuade

once she gets an idea in her head and, at times, I think she may be right.

The others say I am weak, and perhaps I am. But perhaps, weakness is our strength. If so, I am the one with it and I am the one who should be the Primary.

I hope to return to Kansas City and eventually straighten things out with my bank group. I also hope to seek out therapy that will integrate us in the Body. That seems appropriate. The reason we became three, or at least three I know of, no longer exists. But there is resistance from the other two. Integration scares them.

For now, I can't tell you precisely where I am but I can assure you I am working on making sure the Body is sound.

If you have gotten this far in the letter, that is good, and that is all I have to tell you for now.

Have a good day.
Phillip.

I thought the letter might start to bring me closure, but I was wrong. I found myself still in Knoxville, in my dark place, and still working out a plan. Knoxville continued to be no place for Phillip Dewey. I just needed a plan. Eventually, I knew I would have one. I always do.

3J received two deliveries on the same day. The first: a dozen salmon-colored roses from Bey with a card that simply said: "*All That Jazz* roses from Adam and Bey Rapinoe. With great affection." The second: the letter from Phillip Dewey, days after he'd mailed it. The envelope had no return address, but from the postmark, she knew it came from Knoxville, Tennessee. She read it several times. It was a lot to unpack. She knew what Dissociative Identity Disorder was, formerly known as multiple personality disorder. She had loaded up on psychology classes at her undergraduate alma mater when she thought she might pursue a career as a psychologist. The DID assignments were a popular read among the students; just like in Hollywood, always sensationalized.

She knew it typically developed when the person suffered an extreme trauma, often as a child, and usually physical abuse. She wondered if that was Phillip Dewey.

She had never met a multi. Now, apparently, she may have – she wasn't sure. In college, she had learned that while it was an accepted diagnosis, it also may've been over-diagnosed. A diagnosis of convenience for some of the shadier therapists. When Pascale came by her office to read the letter all he said in response was, "Too convenient. Not buying it. Just Dewey refusing to take responsibility." Not an uncommon reaction, even among therapists. 3J wasn't able to be as certain as Pascale; she knew just enough to wonder. She knew that the presence of alters meant the Primary might eschew responsibility and point a finger at an alter and claim the alter was responsible for a bad act, just as Dewey's letter seemed to do. But she knew DID was real. And she knew she was a bankruptcy lawyer, not a therapist, and all the twists presented by Dewey's DID revelation were well beyond her capacity to verify and validate.

As Pascale left her office, he turned and said, "Oh, and beautiful bouquet."

She brought the letter to the courthouse and let Jennifer Cuello copy it. Jennifer read and shared it with Judge Robertson. In the solitude of his office, after the Judge read it, he stood and walked over to his office window, stared out, put his hands deep into his pockets, shook his head in confusion and disbelief, and exhaled slowly. Like so many, he had seen movies about other famous multis – Eve, Sybil, and Billy Milligan. Compelling drama on the silver screen, but a drama he could do without in his bankruptcy courtroom.

The violation of the automatic stay by a multiple personality lender claiming a right of free speech, he thought. He knew that alone made the BJB and Rapinoes cases unique. *Oh, that and Dewey's stated belief that Debtor-euthanasia was an exception to the automatic stay.* As he watched the Missouri River from the quiet of his office, he hoped the inevitability of the water rolling eastward to the Mississippi would do what it usually did for him: help him gather his thoughts and sort out and make sense of conundrums.

Not this time. The river was not helping him decide what to make of the Phillip Dewey encounter. But the river could be like that. Majestic in one moment and a beast the next as it flooded and took out swathes of Kansas City. A constant and predictable, until it wasn't. Judge Robertson had gone from thinking that nothing about Dewey excited pity or sympathy, to now maybe everything about him should. He wondered if Phillip had violated the automatic stay or whether it had been one of the alters. Shaking his head again, he thought, *Well, that probably doesn't matter in my Court. I'm a judge, not a clinician, and the only thing I know is there are no mental health exceptions in the Bankruptcy Code.* As he moved back to his desk, he concluded, *Every once in a while, something is way over my paygrade.*

That night, when he arrived home, he hugged his wife for a longer than usual period of time, and she asked, "What's up, Daniel?" After a moment, Judge Daniel Robertson replied, "Not a thing. Just another one of those days at the bankruptcy shop."

ACKNOWLEDGEMENTS

Thursday, January 13, 2022

My sincerest thanks to the following, who helped me create *Automatic Stay.*

Athelene Gosnell, who patiently tried to teach me tech for all of those many years – at times a losing battle – and for being my tech sleuth to find Anne Beahm who found Jack Rhysider. Not quite a *Crowded!* process, but close.

Jack Rhysider, host of the amazing podcast, *Darknet Diaries.* Thanks for taking my cold call and for spending time to answer my hacking and Dark Net questions. I hope the questions weren't too off the wall.

Zac Shaiken, who always is willing to talk with me and give me leads about the Dark Net, crowd sleuthing, Bellingcat, and for keeping me technologically honest, or at least as honest as a baby boomer can be when it comes to tech.

Craig Buckley, who helped with historical research about Walnut Street in downtown Kansas City. Thanks, bud.

Donna Gonzalez, who wears the most amazing shoes, and who is the inspiration for 3J's shoes and attire. I think you would enjoy meeting 3J someday. Or maybe you already have and just didn't realize it?

Cindi Woolery, to whom I owe a huge thank you for being my original and always automatic stay compadre for all these years. Thanks, as well for your willingness to count the W.D.Mo. courthouse steps, one of those typically unusual Shaiken undertakings.

John Aisenbrey, one of the lawyers who worked on the Hyatt skywalk litigation, for all of your knowledge about the cause of the 1981 tragedy and your willingness to share it with me.

Dr. Graham Cody, for the discussion and insights about DID.

James Kane, for teaching me about tribes and the importance of purpose, trust, and belonging.

Celina Tio, chef extraordinaire at the real Belfrey in Kansas City, for always feeding me when I needed it, pouring me your bourbon, teaching me some of your cooking secrets, and for letting me include you in *Automatic Stay*.

Loren Shaiken, for putting up with me as I make notes to myself at all hours of the day and night, and when I zone out of a conversation because I have just thought of something I need to add, delete, modify, or amplify. And, of course, for being there.

Emily Shaiken, our sweet sixteen-pound rescue pup, for providing the inspiration for Emily Aaronson.

For my research, thanks to Karla Deel and her wonderful book *Storied & Scandalous Kansas City – A history of Corruption Mischief and a Whole Lot of Booze*; Frank Driggs and Chuck Haddix for their book *Kansas City Jazz – From Ragtime to Bebop – a History*. Both books provide the inspiration for many of the references to all things historic in *Automatic Stay*.

Paul Edelman, for helping me with my Strat and my blues, whenever I ask and for helping always know that music is life and the world needs more of it.

The Browns – Rebecca and Andrew Brown of Design For Writers, for their wonderful and creative work on *Automatic Stay*'s cover design, and the formatting, and editing of *Automatic Stay*. Our third book together, guys!

To Tom and Cree Bol for the photos of me and for our years of friendship: www.tombolphoto.com

And, to all the bankruptcy lawyers who came before me and taught me about the automatic stay, and all the bankruptcy lawyers who I worked for, with, against, and alongside, and the judges I appeared in front of. I have the greatest admiration and respect for each and every one of you. I think you know who you are.

Amazon Review

YOU WOULD MAKE AN author very happy if you would please consider leaving a short, Amazon review of *Automatic Stay*.

UNFAIR DISCRIMINATION
A 3J BANKRUPTCY THRILLER

Watch for the release of my next bankruptcy thriller, *Unfair Discrimination*, starring Josephina Jillian Jones, with her supporting cast, and a host of others.

Enjoy my other books –

And … Just Like That:
Essays on a life before, during and after the law.
http://aws.org/HNT9GF

Fresh Start.
https://tinyurl.com/49dkfs7w

Automatic Stay Litigation in Bankruptcy,
co-authored with Cindi Woolery.
https://tinyurl.com/9hh9bdz3

Join my mailing list to stay up to date at
http://markshaikenauthor.com.

Connect with me and let me know what you think at
markshaiken@fastmail.com.

Made in the USA
Las Vegas, NV
01 September 2022

54508653R00236